PRAISE FOR P.J. PARRISH

DEAD OF WINTER

Edgar Award Finalist

"A wild ride with a really fine writer." —John Sandford

"Moves along briskly, pulling the reader along for an invigorating ride." —*Baltimore Sun*

"Brisk, fast-paced, well-conceived yarn." —*Chicago Tribune*

AN UNQUIET GRAVE

Michigan Notable Book
International Thriller Award Winner
Shamus Award Winner

"A standout thriller. With fresh characters and plot, a suspense novel of the highest order." —*Chicago Sun-Times*

"Gripping and atmospheric . . . a quality read that will remind many of Dennis Lehane." —*Publishers Weekly*

"A wonderfully tense and atmospheric novel. Keeps the reader guessing until the end." —*Miami Herald*

A KILLING RAIN

Shamus Award finalist 2006
Anthony Award finalist

"Opens like a hurricane and blows you away through the final page. It's a major league thriller that is hard to stop reading."
—Robert B. Parker

"Not many authors today so successfully combine an examination of the characters' psychological lives with hardcore action and unrelenting suspense the way that Parrish can . . . This combination of suspense and thoughtfulness makes for truly compelling reading."
—Oline Cogdill, *South Florida Sun-Sentinel*

"If you haven't discovered the fast-paced action, terrifying suspense and hair-pin plot twists of rising star P.J. Parrish yet, now's the time."
—Mystery Guild

"From the startling opening to the stunning finale, a masterpiece of shock and surprise, a gritty Florida tale told with relentless skill. P.J. Parrish's best book yet." —Ed Gorman, *Mystery Scene*

A THOUSAND BONES

"Crime fiction at its finest. Beautifully written, beautifully imagined and packed with raw power, like an iron fist in a velvet glove."
—Lee Child

"High class suspense . . . stunningly crafted page after page, on the way to a thrilling climax." —Linda Fairstein

"A riveting page-turner, I was kept up half the night reading because I just had to know what happened next." —*Spinetingler Magazine*

HEART OF ICE

Shamus Award Winner

"Louis Kincaid is one of my favorite protagonists in all of crime fiction. P.J. Parrish is one of the best in the business and this book is clearly their best yet." —Steve Hamilton, Edgar Award author of *Die a Stranger*

"Easily one of the best books of the year." —Ray Walsh, *Lansing State Journal*

"Tense, thrilling. You're going to bite your nails!" —Lee Child

ISLAND OF BONES

"The tension builds to a near palpable level . . . secrets as dark and warped as the primal landscape. Parrish's second Kincaid mystery, *Dead of Winter*, earned a nomination for an Edgar, and this book merits another." —*Publishers Weekly* (starred review)

"A killer ending will have you looking forward to the next entry in the series." —*Orlando Sentinel*

"A stunner of a book. Amazingly skilled at creating a sense of place, P.J. Parrish stays true to her characters." —*Romantic Times*

SHE'S
NOT THERE

OTHER TITLES BY P.J. PARRISH

Dark Of The Moon

Dead Of Winter

Paint It Black

Thicker Than Water

Island Of Bones

A Killing Rain

The Unquiet Grave

A Thousand Bones

South Of Hell

The Little Death

The Killing Song

Claw Back (A Louis Kincaid Novella)

Heart of Ice

SHE'S NOT THERE

P.J. PARRISH

THOMAS & MERCER

Text copyright © 2015 P.J. Parrish
All rights reserved.

Published by Thomas & Mercer, Seattle

www.apub.com

Amazon, the Amazon logo, and Thomas & Mercer are trademarks of Amazon.com, Inc., or its affiliates.

ISBN-13: 9781503945043
ISBN-10: 1503945049

Cover design by David Drummond

Printed in the United States of America

To our midwives Neil, Sharon, Christine, and Miriam

Why I come here: need for a bottom, something to refer to;
where all things visible and invisible commence to swarm.

—C.D. Wright, "Lake Return"

CHAPTER ONE

She was floating inside a blue-green bubble. It felt cool and peaceful and she could taste salt on her lips and feel the sting of it in her eyes. Then, suddenly, there was a hard tug on her hair and she was yanked out of the bubble, gasping and crying.

Her eyes flew open. It was dark and cold. And her hands . . . When she tried to bring her hands up to her face, she couldn't move them.

The voices were back. She had heard them whispering before, but now they sounded sharper and closer. And now she could understand what they were saying.

She's awake.

You better page Haskins.

A light came on, making her squint. She blinked hard, and a woman's face came into focus, hovering above her. She could feel the gentle press of something warm on her forehead, and it took her a moment to realize it was the woman's hand. She tried to talk but it came out in a strangled moan. The woman was stroking her hair now and making shushing sounds.

"It's all right. You're going to be okay."

She closed her eyes.

She had dreamt it, she realized, the floating in the blue-green bubble. But she knew it was a real memory from long ago, one that she had forgotten until now. She was six years old and had walked out into a lake and the sand beneath her feet had given away. Her mother told her later that she would have drowned if someone hadn't pulled her out by her hair.

Mother . . .

She realized suddenly she couldn't remember what her mother looked like. She couldn't even remember her mother's name.

The cold swirled around her and she began to shiver violently. She couldn't remember her own name.

"Get her another blanket."

The salt taste was on her lips again and she licked away a tear.

◆ ◆ ◆

Who are you?

The voice was back again. She opened her eyes and the blur of pink slowly formed into a woman's face. But not the same woman as before. This woman was wearing a white coat and glasses.

"I'm Doctor Haskins. You're in the hospital. You have a very serious concussion. Can you tell me your name?"

She tried to open her mouth but couldn't. Her jaw hurt but she wasn't able move her hands to touch it.

"You had no purse or ID when you got here," the doctor said. "Can you tell me who you are?"

She felt a hard knotty pressure deep inside her breast, and when she tried to take a deep breath, she couldn't.

"Can you tell me your name?"

"I . . . don't . . ."

"Do you know what day it is?"

She stared at the doctor.

"Do you know what year it is? Do you know who the president is?"

What year? President? Why was this woman asking such stupid questions? But then she realized she didn't know the answers. She swallowed hard, and the pain shot through her chest. She tried to move her hands but again she couldn't. When she looked down at them, she saw that her wrists were tied to the sides of the bed.

"I think we can get rid of these now," the doctor said. She began to untie the gauze. "We had to do it because you kept trying to pull out your IV."

When her wrists were free, she tried to massage them but the pull of the IV line made her arm ache so she gave up and just lay still. She ran her tongue over her lips. They were cracked and dry and the lower one felt fat and tender.

"The light hurts my eyes," she whispered.

The doctor got up and went to the window, closing the blinds. "That's normal," she said, coming back to the bed. "Do you have a headache?"

She nodded.

"How bad is it?"

How bad? It felt like her brain was sloshing loose in her skull.

"On a scale of one to ten."

"Ten."

"Well, we'll give you something to help, but first I need you to stay awake for a little while longer and try to answer some questions, okay?"

She nodded.

"You suffered a hard blow to your head, some bleeding in your skull, and you have a brain bruise," the doctor said. "You're going to have headaches and dizziness for a while and some amnesia, likely retrograde and possible anterograde."

The doctor kept talking, her words tumbling out, and she had to watch the woman's lips move to try to make sense of them. It was the harsh B-words she grasped: Blow to the head. Brain bruise. Bleeding. What had happened to her? Why couldn't she remember anything? Why couldn't she even remember her own name?

Amnesia. The doctor had said amnesia.

She tried to concentrate, tried to conjure up something from her memory. Faces, names, images . . . but nothing was coming. It was like being back in that blue-green bubble. She was just floating, with no strength to swim up to the surface.

"How did I get here?" she whispered.

"Someone dropped you off here in the emergency room."

"Dropped me?"

"Yes, a man brought you into the waiting room."

A man . . . she was trying to see a face, any face, but nothing was coming. "Who?"

The doctor let out a slow breath. "We don't know who he was. He sat you down in a chair and left. The admitting nurse found you, and you were brought up here to the ICU. We only know this much because he was caught on the security camera."

She stared at the doctor. "What happened to me?" she asked.

Again, the doctor was slow to answer. "We don't know. I suspect, given your injuries, you were in a car accident. In addition to the concussion, you have a large bruise across your chest and two broken ribs. You might have hit the steering wheel."

She struggled to remember, but there was nothing in her head but a black swirl, like a dark sheet of hard rain advancing toward her. Then came a wave of nausea, and she had to swallow hard to fight it back.

"How long have I been here?" she asked.

"About forty-eight hours," the doctor said. "We called the police, but no one with your description has been reported missing."

Missing . . . no one was missing her?

She reached up to touch her throbbing lip, but the doctor gently pushed her hand back down to the bed.

"Your lip has a bad split, but it will heal." The doctor paused. "You have a very bad cut on your chin, and you have some stitches there. You might have a small scar."

"Can I see a mirror?" she asked.

"Maybe tomorrow, okay?"

She shut her eyes. Red flashes exploded on the screen of her eyelids, and for a second she could glimpse a man's blurry face and dark hair but then he vanished.

When she opened her eyes she blinked hard to keep from crying. She realized there was a television mounted on the wall. The sound was muted and all she could make out on the screen was a blur of moving colors.

A scraping sound made her look back to the doctor. She had pulled a chair near the bed and was typing something on a black tablet. The doctor was so close she could see every detail on the woman's face, right down to the mole near her upper lip.

Why could she see this but not the TV?

Something clicked in her mind. "I wear contacts," she said.

"Yes, that's right," the doctor said. "We had to take them out."

The doctor began to tap on the tablet again and the *click-click* of her nails sounded very loud.

"We need to figure out who you are so we can call your family," the doctor said.

Why was no one missing her?

"Maybe if I tell you what else we know about you it will help you remember something."

She nodded slowly.

"You're five nine and weigh one twenty-six. I'd say that's on the thin side for your height but you have excellent muscle tone. We did some X-rays, and you have two bone breaks in your left foot but they're old breaks. Your feet are quite callused and you have some blackened toe-nails. Are you an athlete, a marathon runner maybe?"

"I don't know."

More tapping. "You were wearing a black cocktail dress when you came in." She looked up. "Chanel."

"Chanel? That's French." Why could she remember that when she couldn't remember her own name?

"Yes, your dress is in the closet," the doctor said. "But you didn't have any shoes on when you came in."

"What else do you know about me?"

"You've had a recent manicure. You've got hair extensions and you're blonde, but it's not natural. You probably go to a tanning salon. Does any of this trigger anything?"

She let out a tired sigh and shook her head. The tapping sound resumed.

"Oh, this says you were wearing a wedding ring."

She slowly brought up her left hand. It was bare, except for a faint white tan line on her ring finger.

"Where's the ring?" she asked.

"It's in a safe at the nurses' station."

"I want to see it."

"I don't think—"

"Let me see it, please."

The doctor hesitated and then nodded. "Okay, maybe it will help trigger your memory. I'll see if I can get it for you." She rose, holding the tablet against her white coat.

"You're going to be all right," the doctor said.

She didn't want to cry, but she couldn't help it. The tears fell, pool-ing hot on her neck. The doctor held out a tissue, and she took it with a shaking hand.

"I know this is very frightening," the doctor said. "But you're going to be all right."

The doctor's voice was soothing, but the voice inside her head was screaming: *You don't understand! I am afraid! And I can't remember why!*

The doctor smiled and held up her black tablet. "Your brain is like this computer," she said. "It's like your memory board has been temporarily erased."

"Temporary? When will it come back?"

"Well, I can't tell you exactly. It will be gradual, as you heal. Little things will trigger other things, like smells or songs. But it will come back, I promise."

She shut her eyes.

There was a murmur of voices, the doctor talking to someone, her voice brisk and business-doctor now. Then the voices were gone and there was just a soft mix of sounds—a beeping from somewhere above her head, a phone ringing somewhere far away.

She felt herself drifting into sleep, but suddenly the dark-haired man was there again. The man who had brought her here? Or someone else? And if he had helped her, why did she feel an awful tightening in her chest when she thought of him? What was she afraid of?

Maybe it wasn't about not knowing who he was. Maybe it was about not knowing who *she* was. What if the doctor was wrong and her memory never returned? That happened to people, didn't it? What if her life was gone forever? What if she was gone forever? What if the awful emptiness inside her never went away and the only thing she had was that faceless man?

Make pretty.

What?

No ugly. Make ugly go away. You try make pretty.

Who was talking to her? It was a man and the accent was foreign, maybe Russian.

Make ugly go away. She pushed the dark-haired man from her mind and tried to fill the black void with something else.

Her head was pounding, and she shut her eyes tighter against the pain. Then, very slowly, images began to form. Just blurs of color at first—blues, whites, and greens—that began to move. Clouds drifting against a blue sky and stabs of green that she realized were the swaying tips of palm trees.

Next came the feel of sun hot on her face and body, and a sharp medicinal smell like . . .

Chlorine. A swimming pool.

Something cool and hard under her feet, and in her mind she looked down and saw her bare feet against white marble and the edge of a black-and-white rug, like a zebra skin. Clothes hanging in a big closet, and a red chair. The feel of fur on her skin . . .

"Brody," she whispered.

"Is that your last name?"

She opened her eyes. The doctor was back.

"Did I say something?"

"Yes, you said 'Brody.' Is that your last name?"

She closed her eyes in exhaustion. "I don't know."

The doctor was holding a small manila envelope. "I have your ring," she said. "Normally, you'd have to sign a form for this, but that can wait until you remember your name." The doctor shook the ring into her palm and held it out.

She took the ring. It was a large square-cut diamond. She had been expecting a wedding band and looked up at the doctor. "You're sure this is mine?"

"You don't recognize it?" The doctor sounded disappointed.

"No." She put it on her finger. It fit perfectly.

A nurse interrupted them. "Dr. Haskins, they're still waiting for you down in neurology."

"All right, I'm on my way." The doctor turned back to the bed. "I'll put in the order for something for your headache. And something to help you sleep."

She looked up at the doctor. "I don't want to sleep."

"Why not?"

What could she tell her? That she was afraid that if she slept the man's face would be there in her dreams?

She brought up her hand to look at the ring again, and that was when she noticed the white hospital band around her wrist. She turned it so she could read the writing. Some numbers, one set that looked like a date, and above that, JANE DOE.

From somewhere deep in her head, she heard a violin playing. Vivaldi, it was Vivaldi's "Winter." How did she know that? Then she could feel someone's hand holding hers, feel the hand slipping the ring on her finger and she could hear the words . . .

I take thee, Amelia.

Her eyes flew up to the doctor.

"Amelia," she said. "My name is Amelia."

CHAPTER TWO

He came to an abrupt stop just inside the doorway and stared at the woman in the bed. She was covered in a white sheet and was lying so still that for a moment he thought she was dead. But then he saw the steady blip of her pulse on the monitor. His eyes took it all in, even as he could feel his mind racing to make sense of what he was seeing. Her swollen face, turned slightly toward him, a gauze square on her chin standing out stark white against the ugly splash of purple and yellow bruises on her cheeks. Her hair like wet rope against the pillow. Her lips, fat and tender looking. One nostril crusted with dried dark blood.

He brought up a shaky hand and ran it over his face. Was it her? She looked so shattered, so different, he wasn't even sure.

As he moved closer to the bed, his eyes locked on the tubes snaking down from the plastic bags above, down to her thin bruised left arm, then to her hand and the diamond ring.

He carefully picked up her hand. It was warm. He pressed it between his own and closed his eyes.

"Sir?"

He turned. A nurse was standing there, holding a plastic bag of clear liquid.

"No one is supposed to be in here," she said.

"I'm Alex Tobias. She's my wife."

The nurse's face softened.

"I just got a call from the police. They said she was in some kind of accident. Is she . . . in a coma?"

"Coma? Oh, no, she's just asleep. I just gave her a pill."

"Do you know what happened to her?"

"No, I just came on duty. I'm sorry, sir, but you'll have to move aside. I have to change her IV."

Alex set his wife's hand on the sheet and stepped back to the corner, focusing on the smiling cat faces on the nurse's bright blue scrubs, watching her pink hands flutter like fish over his wife's body. His head was pounding, and there was a hard nub of something he imagined as gray stone forming in his chest.

"Are you all right?"

He looked into the nurse's chubby face.

"What?"

"Do you need to sit down, sir?"

"No, no. I need . . . where is the doctor? I need to talk to a doctor."

"Dr. Haskins is on her rounds right now. I'm sure she—"

"Can you call her? I need to talk to someone."

"She'll be back up here soon, Mr. Tobias."

The nurse was checking a chart, and when he started to move back toward the bed she stopped him with a firm hand on his arm. "She needs to rest. Let's go outside."

Alex followed the nurse back into the hallway. He saw flashes of green as people in scrubs moved quickly by him. Carts rattled down the hallway. Telephones trilled. Everything felt sharper, louder. He couldn't think.

"The police wouldn't tell me anything over the phone," he said. "What happened? How did she get here?"

"As I already said, sir, I don't really know. But Dr. Haskins will be back in about a half hour. I'm sure she'll explain everything."

He glanced around and ran a hand through his hair. "God, I can't believe this. Is there—Jesus, look at me, I'm shaking—is there someplace I can sit down?"

"There's a cafeteria just down the hall. Why don't you go down there and get some coffee? As I said, Dr. Haskins will—"

"I want to stay close by. I have to be here when she wakes up."

"There's really nothing you can do right now," the nurse said. "I gave your wife a sedative. Please, Mr. Tobias, go wait in the cafeteria. As soon as Dr. Haskins gets back I'll tell her you're here."

She gave him a gentle nudge and he moved away, following the signs on the walls that directed him toward the cafeteria. It was a large room, with a lunch counter, vending machines, and orange plastic tables and chairs. Alex got a coffee from the machine and slipped into a chair near a window.

He wiped his eyes with the back of his hand and raised the plastic cup to take a sip of coffee.

His hand was still shaking.

Jesus . . . he had to pull himself together. He couldn't let Mel see him like this when she woke up.

When he took a drink, the acrid coffee burned down the back of his throat and settled into his stomach, mixing uneasily with the vodka. When had he last eaten? He couldn't remember. But the churn in his gut right now came from something other than hunger.

Alex looked out the window, trying to clear his brain, trying to focus on something, anything that would help him calm down. He stared down at the street. He had driven here so fast he didn't even know where he was exactly.

Andrews . . . that was Andrews Avenue below, he slowly realized, the road that he often used as a shortcut from his office to the airport. It was an ugly street that had been bypassed by the wave of gentrification that had produced the glass-tower condos and boutiques of downtown Fort Lauderdale. The street was home to bail bondsmen, chiropractors, dive bars, and pizza joints.

His eyes settled on the sign on a peeling pink stucco office.

DAVIES & CORMER. SE HABLA ESPANOL. IMMIGRATION. PERSONAL INJURY. WE CAN HELP! SOMEONE SHOULD PAY!

Someone should pay . . .

Oh yeah, someone always paid, didn't they?

The ring of his cell—Bach's Prélude from the movie *Master and Commander*—jerked him back. He grabbed the cell from his jacket pocket and checked the caller ID. It was Owen.

He hit "End Call," but he knew he should have answered it. There was only one reason his partner would be trying to reach him on a Sunday. It meant that the Swanson-Leggett merger had hit a snag, the investors probably finding out that Swanson was being invested by the SEC for securities fraud. It was a bogus charge, but when people were asked to put up millions, they tended not to trust a CEO whose future might include a stint in federal prison.

His phone chirped with a text message:

Swanson out. New money in.

Deal done. Opening Cristal.

Where R U?

He heard the rasp of the door again and looked up. A woman in a white coat and glasses had stopped just inside and was scanning the room. She spotted him and came to the table.

"Mr. Tobias? I'm Dr. Haskins."

He started to get up, but she motioned for him to sit back down with a nod to the chair. She took the chair opposite.

His words rushed out in a torrent. "What happened to Mel? The nurse said she had a concussion but no one will tell me anything else and I need to know if—"

"Take a breath, Mr. Tobias," Dr. Haskins said.

Alex realized he was still clutching his cell. He set it facedown on the table and pulled in two jagged breaths.

"First, your wife is going to be all right."

Alex stared at the doctor for a second, and then tears formed in his eyes. He looked away.

"She suffered a cerebral contusion and an intracranial hematoma that—"

He came back to her. "I'm sorry, what does that mean?"

"She has a pretty bad concussion and there was some cranial bleeding, but we've got it under control. However, her brain was bruised and this has manifested itself in amnesia."

"Amnesia? She's lost her memory?"

"I don't know how bad it is yet," Dr. Haskins said. "Your wife regained consciousness only about an hour ago so I haven't had much time to assess her condition. I'll know more when we do cognitive tests. Right now, I'd say the amnesia appears to be retrograde, meaning she remembers nothing that happened to her before she was injured."

"Nothing? Does she remember me?"

Dr. Haskins hesitated. "At first, she could only tell me her name was Amelia. But when she remembered her last name, the police ran her driver's license, and that's how they found you."

Alex stood up abruptly. "I need to see her."

"Please, Mr. Tobias, not now. We've got to do more scans and tests. We'll know more tomorrow. But right now, the thing she needs most is quiet."

Alex sank back down on the hard chair, putting his head between his hands.

"Amnesia from head trauma is quite common—car accidents, sports injuries," the doctor said. "My nephew got a concussion playing high school football and made a full recovery. The only thing he can't remember is getting hit in the game."

Alex said nothing, didn't move. The doctor kept talking, her voice dissolving to a painful buzzing in his head. She was saying again that Mel would get better, that her memories of her life, friends, and family would come back, that any image, sound, or even smell might trigger things. But that it would take days or weeks for the whole picture to form again.

Mel . . . my Mel . . . what happened?

"The police couldn't tell me anything," he said. "Do you know anything about what happened?"

"Not really," Dr. Haskins said. "She was dropped off here."

"Dropped off? What do you mean dropped off?"

"The admitting nurse found your wife in the emergency waiting room. She had fainted in the chair and—" Dr. Haskins paused, pursing her lips. "Well, to be honest, no one noticed she was there for at least an hour."

"What? How the fuck did you—"

"Calm down, Mr. Tobias. This happened late Friday night. Do you know what a county hospital emergency room is like on a Friday night?"

Alex stared at the doctor. *Friday night? Mel had been gone for two days?* He shut his eyes.

"I'm sorry," he said. "Go on, please."

"It was only later, after she was taken to the ICU, that we started to put things together."

"What do you mean?"

"We checked the security tapes. The cameras in the emergency entrance and waiting room showed a man bringing your wife into the room and then leaving. He drove away in a truck. That's all we know. The police have the tapes and are looking for him."

"Do they think he . . . this man, do the police think he did this to Mel?"

"I don't know. You'll have to talk to the police. There was an officer here earlier. He said he was coming back." The doctor paused. "Look, I know I shouldn't speculate about anything but your wife has a bruise across her chest that is consistent with hitting a steering wheel. I think she was in a car accident and this man found her and brought her here."

"Car accident? Why didn't he just call an ambulance?"

Dr. Haskins shook her head. "I can't answer that."

The doctor looked up suddenly, toward a speaker in the ceiling. Alex heard it, too, a page for Dr. Haskins.

"I have to go," she said, rising and starting away.

"Wait."

The doctor stopped.

"Your nephew," Alex said. "You said he couldn't remember getting hit?"

"Pardon me?"

"You said that after he got hit, he couldn't remember it."

The doctor gave an odd smile. "He couldn't even remember the game. Three years later, he still can't."

Dr. Haskins turned and left. Alex slumped down in the chair and closed his eyes. His cell chirped and he turned it over. It was another text from Owen.

CALL ME NOW

It took all Alex's energy to sit up and dial. Owen answered on the second ring.

"Where the hell are you?"

"Broward General. Mel's been in an accident."

"Accident? What kind of accident?"

"I don't know exactly. All I know is some guy found her and brought her in. She has a concussion."

16

"Jesus . . ."

"Look, Owen, I can't talk now. I have to—"

"Is she okay?"

"No, she's not okay. She doesn't even . . ." He was on the verge of crying. He couldn't let Owen hear him bawling like a girl. "Owen, I'll call you when I know more."

Alex hung up.

He sank back in the hard chair. Soft sounds swirled around him— the door opening, the intercom belching out a page, the swoosh of something in his ears that he finally recognized as his own pulse. There was another sound, and at first he thought it was Muzak, but he realized it was coming from somewhere deep inside his head.

A memory pushed forward. It was music, but he couldn't tell what it was. Then he heard the violins and remembered the name "Vivaldi" and how Mel had told him the music was perfect because they were getting married in December.

The music was suddenly gone.

He had to see her now.

He jumped to his feet and went quickly back down the hall to the nurses' station. The nurse in the blue cat scrubs was coming toward him and blocked his way.

"Mr. Tobias, did Dr. Haskins find you?"

"Yes. I want to see my wife now."

"I told you, Mr. Tobias, I gave her a sleeping pill—"

"I just want to see her."

The nurse touched Alex's shoulder. "Okay, you can go in for a few minutes, but please don't try to wake her up."

He nodded. The nurse disappeared around a corner and Alex stood for a moment, one hand on the desk to steady himself. Then he went slowly down the hall to the last room on the left.

When he went in, it took several seconds for what he was seeing to register—the bed was empty.

He moved closer and looked down at the end of the IV tube lying in the tangle of sheets. A small stain of blood stood out dark red against the white.

He spun and went outside, scanning the hallway. The nurse in the blue cat scrubs was coming toward him.

"Mr. Tobias, are you all right?"

"Mel, my wife," he said. "She's not there."

CHAPTER THREE

The doors closed behind her with a gentle *whoosh*.

Out! She was outside.

When she pulled in a deep breath to calm herself, the thick humid air came as a sudden hard press in her lungs after the icy air she had felt moments ago inside the hospital.

She took a quick look around to try to figure out where she was. There was an ambulance parked nearby and beyond that, if she squinted hard, she could just make out the large red EMERGENCY sign.

The sound of the door opening made her spin around. Two men emerged, one pushing an empty gurney. They gave her a long look. She heard them talking and wanted to run, but she forced herself to turn and walk calmly toward the red EMERGENCY sign.

Out to the street, down the sidewalk . . . keep going . . . don't look back.

The sun was hot, and her head was pounding. She couldn't read the street signs, but she could make out a bench just ahead. If she rested for a second, maybe the nausea would ease. At the bench, she sat down and looked back toward the emergency entrance.

No one was following her. But they would, as soon as they realized she was gone.

Her right hand was throbbing, and she could feel something in her clasped fist. She opened her hand.

A yellow pill.

She concentrated, trying to replay in her head what had happened.

The nurse had given her the pill with a cup of water, telling her it would help her to sleep. But she didn't want to sleep so she had faked swallowing the pill and hidden it in her hand.

She stared at the pill for a moment and then threw it into the grass. Sleep . . . she had been so afraid to go to sleep, believing that if she did, the man would be there. But now she knew that he wasn't someone she had imagined.

Back in the room, she had heard his voice. And when she opened her eyes for that one second she had seen him, or just a blur of him, a tall dark-haired man, standing by the door.

I'm Alex Tobias.

The name had meant nothing to her but she knew his voice.

I'm Alex Tobias. That's my wife.

Wife?

Yes. She knew that now. He was her husband. And he had hurt her.

The terrible crushing pressure in her chest was back, and she could feel the panic rising up again. She tried to pull in a deep breath, but it made her feel like her ribs were on fire.

Why had she run from the room? Why was she afraid of him? Had he thrown her from a car? Had she jumped? There was nothing in her memory to explain it, but the only thing she knew was that she had to get away from him.

But he's my husband.

She looked down at the diamond ring on her left hand.

Blood . . . she was bleeding. The top of her hand was bleeding. She clasped her right hand over it and shut her eyes.

More memories tumbling around in her head, coming back now in a quick flashback. The sting as she pulled the IV needle from her hand. The spinning of the room as she swung her feet over the bed. Finding the black dress hanging in the closet and putting it on. No shoes . . . the doctor had told her she'd had no shoes when she came to the hospital so she had found a pair of white slippers in the nightstand and put them on. There was also a comb, a toothbrush, and a tiny tube of toothpaste in the drawer. She put them in a plastic bag and left the room. Blurred figures far down the hall. And in the opposite direction, just a few feet away, the red exit sign.

Then . . .

Flap-flap-flap. The sound of her slippers hitting the floor had seemed so loud to her ears. She pushed through the exit door and into a stairwell. Down two flights and through another door. In the empty hallway, she looked down at the colored lines on the floor and chose the red one. It led her through a maze of narrow hallways filled with steel food carts and empty gurneys. She passed a few people, keeping her head down, and then she was out, out into the ambulance bay.

She opened her eyes now and looked down at her hand.

The bleeding had stopped. And her head felt a little clearer. She had to get moving.

But where?

Away from the hospital. Away from him.

Clutching the plastic bag, she pushed up from the bench. There was a traffic light ahead and she made her way to it, ending up on a busy four-lane street. Across the street, she could make out a cluster of four buildings, one with a peaked roof that made her think it was a church. She crossed the street.

Yes, it was a church. Maybe they would help her?

She went up the steps and tugged on the doors. Locked. She turned back toward the street. The low slant of the sun told her it was maybe four or five. It would be dark soon. She had to make a plan.

The building next to the church had a sign in the window: ST. ANNE'S THRIFT SHOP. Shoes . . . she could buy shoes there, and other clothes. But not without money. She would need money to get away.

There was a vacant building next to the thrift shop and she trudged past it. Then she stopped, looking up at the neon sign on the last building.

NATIONAL PAWN.

She looked down at the ring on her left hand and pushed open the door.

The inside of the pawnshop registered in her head as a blur of color and shapes. Shelves crammed with silver coffee sets, bronze horses, porcelain dolls, suitcases, knives, gold clocks, and guitars hanging from the ceiling. And a long glass counter that ran the length of the narrow room, filled with jewelry and coins. There was music playing, something so very familiar, something about a woman named Eleanor who kept her face in a jar. But she couldn't pull the name of the group from her memory.

The large bald man behind the counter watched her as she approached.

She shut her eyes, fighting back another wave of nausea.

"You okay, lady?"

She opened her eyes and nodded. She twisted the ring off her hand and held it out. "What can you give me for this?"

"Pawn or sell?"

"Sell."

He took the ring, gave her another long look, then reached below the counter and pulled out a small metal gadget, using it to peer at the ring. He looked up at her.

"I need to take this in the back and test it, okay?"

What choice did she have? She had to trust him. She nodded and he left. The music filled the emptiness and she realized it was the Beatles. It made her feel better somehow.

Then, suddenly, she saw herself. At first the image in the mirror behind the counter didn't even register, but with a brush of her hand through her hair she realized she was looking at herself.

Her reflection was in soft focus, but she could see lank blonde hair, and a sleeveless black dress encasing a tall, slender body. She leaned over the counter, trying to see her face more clearly.

"This is a ten-carat diamond."

She took a step back from the counter at the sound of the voice. The big bald man was coming out from the back room, holding up the ring between two meaty fingers. A woman came out after him, a tiny leather-skinned thing with frizzed red hair, wearing jeans and a pink halter top.

"What can you give me for it?" she asked.

The man set the ring on the counter. "I'm guessing this is worth about two hundred thousand."

She was stunned into silence.

"Our normal rate is fifteen percent of that."

She couldn't do the math. She had a sudden weird stab of memory that whispered she had never been good at math.

"I can give you thirty grand for it," the man said.

She had been staring at the ring, and now her eyes shot to the bald man. He wasn't smiling.

"All right," she said.

Now he smiled. "Okay, just give me your driver's license and we'll do the paperwork."

"License?"

He had been digging for something beneath the counter but now he stopped and looked up at her.

"I don't have a license," she said.

His face went to stone. "Then we don't have a deal."

She could feel the redheaded woman's eyes on her but didn't look back.

"I'll take less," she said.

"Lady, this ring could be hot—"

"Twenty. I'll take twenty thousand," she said.

The bald man shook his head slowly.

"Please," she said.

"No can do."

She felt tears threaten but for some reason she didn't want to let this man see her cry.

"Give her the money, Frank."

The redheaded woman had pushed forward.

"Tracy, you know I can't—"

"I said give her the money."

"You want me to lose my fucking license?"

"Go get the goddamn money, Frank. And none of this lowball bullshit. Give her forty grand."

The bald man swore under his breath and trudged off. The redheaded woman watched him go, then reached below the counter and came up with a clipboard and pen.

"What's your name?" she asked.

She hesitated. "Amelia."

The redheaded woman looked up, her small green eyes scrutinizing Amelia's face, hair, and the black dress. "Look, I can make up a license number and address for you, but I need a last name to put on here."

I'm Alex Tobias. That's my wife.

"Brody," she said.

The redhead scribbled some more on the form, flipped open an ink pad, and turned it toward Amelia. "I need your right thumbprint here," she said, pointing to the form.

Amelia hesitated and pressed her thumb onto the pad, then onto the form.

"Sign here."

She took the pen and signed the form. The bald man returned, a big stack of bills in his hand. He slapped the money on the counter with a glare, and then disappeared again into the back room.

The redhead watched him go and turned back to face Amelia. "You got something to put this in?" she asked.

"This is all I have."

The redhead eyed the plastic hospital bag and then turned to the shelves behind her. She pulled a brown leather duffel down and brought it back to the counter. "Here, take this."

As Amelia stared at the bag, something clicked in her head—a sudden vision of Louis Vuitton luggage stacked on an airport cart. And the trill of a foreign language. Italian?

"I don't need something this expensive. Do you have something else?" she asked.

"Take it. It's a fake, so it's no good to me," the redhead said.

Amelia unzipped the duffel and put the plastic hospital bag and the money inside. When she looked up, the redheaded woman was slumped back against the shelves, arms folded, staring at her again.

"Thank you," Amelia said softly.

The redheaded woman nodded. "Can I give you some advice?"

Amelia waited.

"Don't let no man ever knock you around again."

Amelia nodded slowly, picked up the duffel, and started toward the door.

"Hey, wait a sec."

She stopped and looked back.

The redheaded woman was holding out a pair of scissors. "You'd better get rid of that," she said, nodding toward Amelia's wrist.

She looked down at the white hospital band and went back to the counter. The redheaded woman cut off the band and stared at the name "Jane Doe" on it. When she looked up, her mouth was set in a hard line but her eyes were soft.

"Good luck, Amelia Brody," she said.

CHAPTER FOUR

The smell was pungent—mothballs, dust, dime-store perfume, and a faint trace of body odor—and it was so familiar that Amelia was certain she had surely been inside a thrift store before. But she couldn't remember, and she was a woman who wore Chanel dresses, wasn't she?

She ignored the stare of the woman behind the counter and headed straight for the racks of women's clothing.

Jeans . . . she needed some jeans. What size did she wear? She didn't know. So she pulled out different pairs of blue jeans and held them up against her hips. Every pair she tried was too short until she decided to try the men's racks where she found a pair of Levi's. As she headed to the dressing room, she grabbed a faded blue oxford shirt and a floppy canvas hat.

In the hot cramped dressing room, she peeled off the black dress. When she turned to the mirror, she froze.

Back in the pawnshop she had seen only a soft-focus image of her face. But now, standing close to the full-length mirror, she saw herself clearly for the first time.

Naked. All angles and sharpness. Thin. Long legs, narrow hips. Small high breasts below a sharp shelf of collarbone. There were long, raw scrapes on both her arms and ugly purple bruises crossing her chest.

Dr. Haskins's words came back to her. *You're a little on the thin side.*

And then other words, but she didn't have the faintest idea who had said them to her—*I need to see your bones*—words that had made her cry.

She leaned closer and stared at her face.

It was a mosaic of yellow and blue bruises framed by long hanks of oily blonde hair. A large piece of gauze was taped to her chin. She reached up to touch her swollen lip.

An image came suddenly into her head. A painting hanging on a white wall—*was it Picasso?*—a woman's face chopped into shards of color.

"Hello?"

She jumped at the sound of the voice outside the dressing room curtain.

"Are you almost done in there? We're getting ready to close now."

"Yes . . . yes! I'll be out in a minute," she called. She turned away from the mirror and pulled on the jeans and shirt. The black dress was crumpled on the floor and as she picked it up, she saw the back was streaked with dried mud.

Rain . . . it had been raining, she remembered suddenly. But where had she been and what had happened?

No time to think about it now. She had to get out of there.

Outside the dressing room, she paused to stuff her hair up into the canvas hat. After a stop in the shoe racks to find a pair of black flats, she went up to the counter.

The woman looked at her over the top of her glasses but said nothing as she rang up the clothes, shoes, and hat.

"That's twenty-two fifty," she said.

Amelia started to pull two twenties from the Vuitton duffel and then paused. "Wait, do you sell glasses?"

"No," the woman said. "But folks donate their old ones. They're over there."

The wire basket at the end of the counter held a tangle of frames. Amelia tried on ten pairs before she finally found the big purple plastic frames that allowed her to read the small print on the NO RETURNS sign behind the counter.

"Can you throw this away for me, please?" Amelia asked her, holding out the balled-up black dress.

The woman shook out the dress, pausing when she saw the label. "Is this real or a knockoff?"

Amelia had been rolling up the sleeves of the oxford shirt, and it took her a moment to come back to the woman. "What?"

"Is this real Chanel?"

"Yes, it's real."

"I'll take it in trade for your clothes."

Amelia's head was starting to pound again. She managed a nod and headed to the door. She heard the woman lock it behind her, and then the lights in the thrift shop went out. The sun was gone now, and a stiff breeze was moving in, bringing the biting zing of a coming rain. A whining sound made her look up, and she watched a commercial jet circle and make its descent, disappearing into the darkness somewhere nearby. She looked across the street at the huge beige hospital. Silhouettes moved against the yellow windows on the upper floors.

For a moment she wanted nothing more than to go back inside the hospital and crawl into her bed, to feel the cool gentle press of the nurse's hand on her forehead.

She was tired, so very very tired. And for the first time she could remember, she felt the scrape of hunger in her belly. But the voice in her head was clear, so clear this time it was almost like hearing her own voice.

Get away from here. Get away from him.

She looked to her left. A gas station's lights beckoned. She could at least get a candy bar or something there.

Inside the station she bought Aleve, a bottle of water, a chicken sandwich wrapped in plastic, and an apple. At the last moment she grabbed a newspaper from the rack near the counter. She was heading out the door, newspaper tucked under her arm, biting into the apple, when she saw the police car pull up.

The cop got out and came toward her. She froze, fumbling with the plastic bag. Surely they were looking for her by now, maybe called the police. But they would be looking for a blonde woman in a black cocktail dress. She pulled the canvas hat down harder on her head and held her hand over the gauze on her chin as she passed the cop.

"Ma'am?"

She turned.

"You drop this?" He was holding out a newspaper.

She went to him and took the paper. "Thank you," she said.

She could feel his eyes on her as she walked away. A horn blared, and she jumped. She was standing in the glare of headlights.

"Jesus, lady! Watch it!"

A man was leaning out from behind the wheel of a taxi.

She looked back at the gas station. The cop was standing at the door staring at her. She tossed the apple in the trash, jerked open the taxi's back door and got in, struggling with the duffel.

"Let's go," she said.

"I gotta gas up first," the driver said.

"Please. I need to go. Now."

He leaned over the seat to look at her. Then with a glance at the cop, he put the taxi in gear and pulled out into traffic. She turned in the seat, but when she saw the cop wasn't following, she sank back into the sticky plastic and closed her eyes.

The driver rolled up the windows and turned on the air. It flowed cold over her bare forearms, raising goose bumps. Maybe she should have bought a sweater back at the thrift shop, she thought.

"Where to?"

Amelia pushed the purple glasses up onto the bridge of her nose. "I . . . where are we now?"

"Andrews heading north."

Andrews? It meant nothing. No one had even told her what city she was in. The whine of the jet came back to her. The airport was somewhere near here. She could get a flight out. But that was impossible without ID. A train? Rent a car? No, there was no way to do any of that if you couldn't prove who you were.

She sat forward in the seat. "Is there a bus station here?"

"What kind of bus?"

An animal . . . a bus with a running dog on the side. She had been on a bus like that before, and she had a flash of memory of seeing cornfields flying by outside the window. "Greyhound," she said.

The taxi crossed a drawbridge and entered a downtown area, and Amelia tried to find something that would strike a chord in her memory. A towering blue glass riverfront condo, an old Woolworth's converted into a nightclub, office buildings and banks, a big boxy library fronted by a small park filled with homeless men. The taxi turned left onto a busy street and the names flashed by—Starbucks, Subway, Whole Foods Market—signposts for everywhere and nowhere.

The newspaper . . .

She unfolded it. *The South Florida Sun-Sentinel.* Was she in Miami? Then she noticed the headline—"Robbers Stab Lauderdale Valet."

Fort Lauderdale. Was this place her home? Did she and Alex Tobias live here? She glanced at the date at the top of the front page: "Sunday November 16, 2014."

The date triggered nothing, but it made her feel better somehow. It was something tangible she could grab onto, something that anchored her in time at least.

The taxi pulled up to the Greyhound station, an old low-slung building in a rundown neighborhood. The lot reeked of exhaust fumes and urine. Inside the station, the only smell was of the disinfectant being used by a cleaning man mopping the tile floor. An old woman in rags, her arms looped with bulging plastic shopping bags, was banging on a candy machine, yelling profanities.

Clutching the fake Vuitton duffel, Amelia went to the window. The woman behind the glass didn't look up.

"Do I need ID to buy a ticket?" she asked.

"Not if you pay cash."

"Okay, one ticket, please," Amelia said.

"Where to?"

Amelia hesitated. She felt the press of someone behind her and looked back into the face of an old black man holding a little boy's hand. The man was wearing an old Army fatigue coat and he looked tired, yet he gave her a small smile. Amelia's eyes moved beyond the man to the bus parked outside the doors. She looked back at the woman behind the glass.

"Is that bus leaving soon?" she asked.

"Ten minutes."

"Where is it going?"

"Charlotte, North Carolina."

"One way to Charlotte, please."

"One fifty-six fifty."

Amelia dug in the duffel and handed over eight twenties. Pocketing her change, she moved away from the ticket window and took a seat on a hard metal bench. She unwrapped the chicken sandwich. It was dry and hard, but she ate it anyway, washing it down with the bottled water and three Aleves.

The clock on the terminal wall read seven thirty when the call came to board. Amelia found a seat in the back and leaned against the window. The old black man and the little boy took seats on the aisle across from her.

The bus pulled out, and Amelia watched the lights of the downtown high-rises disappear as they headed away. She caught sight of the street sign—**BROWARD BOULEVARD**—as the bus swung onto a busy street lined with check cashing stores, auto repair shops, Laundromats, and liquor stores. When the bus passed the sprawling complex of the Fort Lauderdale Police Department, she turned away from the window.

It had begun to rain by the time the bus turned onto the freeway, and then there was nothing to see but the blur of billboards and white headlights and red taillights.

She closed her eyes. Did she sleep? For how long? She wasn't sure. She wasn't even sure what made her open her eyes. But when she did, she turned her head and looked into the face of the old man.

He was holding a thermos and pouring something carefully into a small paper cup. He looked over at her, and then held out the cup to her across the aisle.

"Would you like a sip, miss?" he asked.

"What?" She was so tired she could barely speak.

"You look like you could use a little of this," he said.

In the dim beam of the overhead light she could barely make out his face. It was sad and deeply lined, like one of those old drama masks, the ones that represented tragedy and comedy.

What had made her think of that?

"What is it?" she asked.

"A little courage for the journey ahead," he said. The mask creased up into a smile. "Go ahead. I've got more cups."

She accepted the cup and took a sip.

It took a moment but then the taste registered on her tongue. Red wine. Sweet. The taste triggered something in her head, someone speaking a foreign language. And she could see a big open window with two oranges and a bottle of wine on the sill and a view of blue water beyond. She took another drink and let the wine flood down through her body. She finished the wine and passed the cup back to the man.

"Thank you," she said.

He screwed the top back on the thermos and set it under the seat. Then he tucked the Army fatigue jacket over the shoulders of the sleeping boy. He leaned his head back against the seat and slanted his eyes toward her.

"Where you headed, miss?" he asked.

"North Carolina," she said.

"Got family there?"

The feeling of floating in the blue-green bubble came back to her again, and she remembered that she had someone who had saved her from drowning and a mother who had told her about it. Was her mother still alive?

"Yes," she said softly. *I hope so.*

Her eyes went beyond the old man to the sleeping boy. With a start she realized she didn't even know if she had children. If she had a child, how could she possibly be running away like this? How could she leave a child?

She shut her eyes and desperately tried to summon up a child's face, a name, a smell, but there was nothing there, there was no one there. She felt that in her soul. She let out a long breath of relief.

"You all right, miss?"

She turned her head and gave the old man a nod. She looked again at the boy. "How old is your boy?" she asked softly.

"He's seven," the man said. "It's been a long day for him. We started out in Miami this morning, but the bus broke down twenty minutes out and we had to wait two hours for the other bus to come, which took us backward instead of forward. So then we finally got on this bus in Fort Lauderdale and here we are."

She nodded. It was getting hard to keep her eyes open. The rain had turned into heavy pelting drops that smacked against the window and turned the car lights beyond into red streaks in the black.

"Would you like a cookie, miss?"

When she turned back to the old man, he was holding out an open package of Fig Newtons. She started to reach across to take one but then drew her hand back. Another voice was there in her head.

You don't need that. Put that back, Jelly-Belly.

"Go ahead. We got plenty," the old man said.

She took a cookie but didn't eat it, instead looking back out the window. She saw a flash of a sign in the darkness, an exit to some place called "Stuart."

"My great-grandson loves his Fig Newtons," the old man said.

The sudden sadness in the man's voice made her turn back toward him.

"It was all there was in the kitchen—Fig Newtons," he said. "My granddaughter, she didn't know how to take care of him right. He was alone and living on cookies and water when I got there."

His voice had gone soft and distant. "The drugs destroyed her brain. It was like she wasn't even there anymore. So I had to go down there and take the boy and now we're just trying to disappear." He paused. "There was no choice, you see. I had to give him a new life. I just hope he don't remember much of the old one."

His eyes were liquid in the dim light. He carefully wrapped up the cookies and stowed them away. Then he reached up and turned out the overhead light.

"'Night, miss," he whispered.

Amelia settled down into the seat and leaned her head against the window. The glass felt cool on her cheek, and the whirring of the bus's tires was lulling. She closed her eyes, almost drifting off into sleep until she realized she was still holding the Fig Newton.

The cookie was soft and sticky in her hand. Slowly, she brought it to her lips and took a bite.

It started on her tongue, a rush of sensation—soft crumbling crust, molasses-sweet fruit, and the soft grit of the seeds—and it flooded through her whole body. And with it came a memory so sharp her heart ached.

A warm kitchen on a snowy day. Green wallpaper with weeping willows. A cat curling around her ankles. A plate of Fig Newtons and a glass of milk. The touch of a mother's hand on her hair. Her mother's hand . . .

She still couldn't see her mother's face. But she was filled with a rush of soft sadness that felt like it was coming from the very walls of the kitchen, from those willow trees.

I know this is very frightening for you, but you will get better. Your memory has been temporarily erased. But it will come back.

She wanted to believe that, wanted to believe what the doctor had told her. She took another bite of the cookie and waited for another memory.

CHAPTER FIVE

Alex jumped to his feet. The police were back, two officers in black uniforms coming toward him. He had been sitting here in the open area by the elevators, waiting for the cops to return, waiting for two hours while they looked for Mel.

There was a third man with them, a fat guy in a security guard uniform. The faces of the cops were neutral, but the security guard looked upset.

"Did you find her?" Alex asked.

"No, sir," the short cop said.

"No? What do you mean no?"

"I mean that there seems to be no sign of your wife, Mr. Tobias."

Alex's eyes flicked from the short cop to the tall one and finally to the security guard. The first thing the nurse had done when she realized Mel was missing was to call hospital security. It's common for patients to wander off, she had told Alex, and your wife couldn't have gotten very far.

But he had been in a big county hospital before. Ten years ago, he had spent a week in a Houston hospital waiting for his mother to die, and during those awful days he had paced the corridors for hours, so he knew that Broward General, spread over four city blocks, was a sprawling labyrinth of tunnels, twisting hallways, and dark rooms where a person could get lost.

"Have you looked everywhere?" he asked the guard.

"I've had four men looking ever since the call came in," the guard said.

"What about outside? Have you searched the neighborhood?"

The short cop turned to the security guard. "Mr. Bennett, could you give us a moment with Mr. Tobias here?"

"No problem. I've got to check in with my men." He started down the hallway, pulling a radio from his belt.

"Sit down, please, Mr. Tobias," the short cop said.

Alex looked at the cop's name tag—SPECK—and dropped down onto the chair. Speck perched on the edge of the other chair; the second officer stood over him, holding a small notebook and pen.

"What about the guy who brought her here?" Alex asked. "He might know something."

"We have a partial plate on his truck," Speck said. "Plus there's a bumper sticker shaped like a tomato that says *un centavo más*. It's a slogan of the migrant workers. We're thinking he was on his way up to Immokalee when he found your wife and brought her here. But he bolted because he's probably an illegal and didn't want to get busted."

"Any chance of finding him?" Alex asked.

"Not much."

"What are you doing then to find my wife?"

"We're canvassing the neighborhood around the hospital," Speck said. "We also put out an alert with your wife's description. But the nurse told me that your wife dressed herself, removed her IV and left her room.

We also have a videotape from the ambulance bay of her leaving the grounds. She didn't seem disoriented. If anything, she seemed scared."

He paused. "What would your wife be scared of, Mr. Tobias?"

"Scared?" Alex's eyes moved from one cop to the other. "She has fucking amnesia. Of course she's scared. Jesus, I can't believe this . . ."

"Calm down, sir."

"No! Don't tell me to calm down, goddamn it." Alex stopped, feeling the weight of the cop's eyes on him.

Stay cool. Don't lose it.

"I need to ask you some questions, Mr. Tobias."

"Yes, yes . . ."

"Where were you Friday afternoon and evening?"

"What does this—"

"Just answer the question, sir."

Alex drew a deep breath. "Friday afternoon I was in my office until about five and—"

"Where is that, sir?"

"What?"

"Your office."

"On Las Olas, in the New River Center Building."

"Where did you go after you left your office?"

"I went home, picked up my bag and drove to Palm Beach."

"Palm Beach? Why did you go there?"

"I had a golf date with a client. What does this have—"

"You said you picked up a bag?"

"Our tee time was seven Saturday morning so I went up the night before. I stayed at the Ritz-Carlton."

"What's your client's name?"

"Dan . . . Dan Nesbit."

"What about your wife?" Speck asked.

"What do you mean?"

"Was your wife at home when you left?"

Alex hesitated. "Yes, I think so."

"You think so?"

"I . . . I was in a bit of a hurry and didn't talk to her before I left."

"Why didn't your wife go with you to Palm Beach?"

"It was just a golf thing with a client. She doesn't play golf."

"Did she have any plans Friday evening?"

Alex hesitated again. "I don't know. She didn't mention anything."

The taller cop was scribbling away in his notebook.

"What time did you check in to your hotel?"

Alex looked back at Speck. When the cops had first arrived at the hospital, their attitude had been solicitous, respectful. Now it was different. It was as if the short cop had grown five inches in two hours. And he was looking down at Alex as if Alex were . . .

It hit him like a punch in the gut—they were treating him like a suspect. For *what*?

"Mr. Tobias? What time did you check in at the hotel?"

"Between seven and seven thirty."

A clap of thunder rattled the window. Speck's radio spat out some static and a message, but Alex couldn't make it out. Speck turned down the volume.

"Did you call your wife Friday night from Palm Beach?"

"No."

"Why not?"

"I . . . I was pretty tied up with the client. We had dinner and drinks." He paused. "Dan's a big drinker. It was a late night."

"When did you return to Fort Lauderdale?"

Alex had been looking at the window, and it took a moment for him to realize Speck had spoken again.

"I'm sorry, what?"

"When did you get home, sir?"

Alex felt his stomach churning again. Why the fuck had he drunk that second vodka earlier? Why the fuck hadn't he eaten anything?

"Ah . . . I got home around three."

"You mean yesterday, sir, Saturday?"

Alex nodded.

"So when you got home, at what point did you get concerned that your wife wasn't there?"

Alex hesitated.

"Mr. Tobias?"

"We were supposed to go to the Heat game that night," he said. "My law firm has a center court suite, and Mel always comes along, you know, to entertain the client's wife. So when she wasn't home by five, that's when I figured . . ."

"Figured what?" Speck prodded.

"I figured she had stayed with her friend."

"Friend? What friend?"

"Mel had mentioned that she might go visit a friend of hers. The friend, she just had a miscarriage, and Mel was worried about her."

Speck exchanged looks with the other cop who was still taking notes. "You said you didn't talk to your wife before you left on Friday. How did you know about this friend?"

Alex stared at Speck. "I forgot about it until just now."

"What's this friend's name?"

"I don't know."

Speck cocked his head to the side. "So you think your wife was planning to visit this friend. And when you got home Saturday afternoon and realized she wasn't there, you still didn't get worried, even though you had planned to go to the Heat game together?"

Alex stared at Speck. "Okay, I thought she was just pissed at me."

"About what, sir?"

"About having to go to the damn game. I thought maybe it was her way of sending me a message that she was tired of babysitting bored wives at basketball games."

"Did you call her?"

Alex nodded. "It kept going to voice mail."

"So you went to the Heat game alone?"

Alex nodded. His mind was spinning.

"And this morning?" Speck asked. "Your wife had been gone two nights and wasn't answering her phone. When did you intend to get concerned?"

Alex pushed out of the chair and went to the window. He stood staring out at the blur of lights below. A palm frond slapped against the glass.

"Mr. Tobias?"

The elevator pinged and Alex turned. He was surprised to see Owen McCall get out. Owen stopped abruptly when he spotted Alex and then came forward slowly, his eyes taking in the cops before settling back on Alex. His blue suit was spotted with rain and his mane of white hair was plastered to his head. Alex had the thought that in their twelve years together, he had never seen his partner look so upset.

The tall cop's cell rang and he turned away. A second later, he motioned for Speck to join him near the elevator. Owen came over to the window.

"Why are the police here?" he asked.

"Mel's missing," Alex said.

"Missing? What do you mean?"

"She walked out, Owen. She just walked out of here."

"Jesus, Alex. Did she . . . ?" Owen ran a hand over his wet face. "Did you talk to her? Did she say anything?"

Alex shook his head slowly. "She just left."

"Mr. Tobias?"

Speck was back. He gave Owen a quick once-over and then focused again on Alex. "We found your wife's car," he said.

"Where?"

"Out on County Road 29, about two miles off Alligator Alley."

It took Alex several seconds to pull up a mental map. Alligator Alley was the slang name for I-75, the interstate that cut across Florida from one coast to another. But 29 was just a two-lane blacktop road off the Alley that ran south through the wildest part of the Everglades. He had been on that road once, years ago, when a bunch of clients had gathered down at the Rod and Gun Club in Everglades City. Until you reached Everglades City, there was nothing on that road but scrubland and drainage canals.

"Do you know what your wife was doing out there, Mr. Tobias?"

Alex looked at Speck. "I . . . I don't know."

Owen pushed forward. "Are you accusing him of something?"

Speck looked up. "Not yet."

"Then this interview is over," Owen said.

"Who are you?" Speck asked.

Owen stared at him. "I'm his attorney."

CHAPTER SIX

The sunlight streaming through the window woke her up. Amelia blinked and slowly sat up, her body in knots from being curled into a ball on the bus seat all night. She pulled her purple plastic glasses out of the seatback pocket, put them on and looked across the aisle. The old man and the boy were gone. The bus was empty.

She looked out the window. The bus was parked in front of a small Greyhound station that looked like it might once have been a drive-in restaurant before it had been repainted red, white, and blue. Passengers were standing around smoking cigarettes and drinking from Styrofoam cups.

Picking up the duffel, she went out into the bright sunshine. The bus driver was coming toward the bus carrying a silver travel mug when she stopped him.

"Where are we?" she asked.

"Brunswick, Georgia, ma'am," he said. "You've got about twenty minutes for a breakfast break and then we're pulling out."

She touched his arm as he started to board. "There was an elderly black man traveling with a little boy," she said. "Do you know where they are?"

"They got off last night at Daytona," the driver said over his shoulder as he climbed on the bus.

Amelia looked around the narrow street lined with old live oak trees, the twisted branches netted with Spanish moss. It was warm, and the humid breeze had a pleasing briny tang to it, as if there were fishing boats nearby. Across the street was a small white brick building with a sign above the door that read RED BONE CAFÉ.

Clutching the duffel close, she walked toward the café. Inside, it was a sliver of a diner just wide enough for four red vinyl booths along the windows and a Formica counter with six old-fashioned round stools. It smelled of burnt coffee and bacon. She slid onto a stool next to an old man in overalls, eyed the apple pies in the glass case, and ordered a coffee and toast.

The coffee was strong and peppery, a taste she recognized as chicory, and she had to douse it with milk. But the toast, limp with butter, was delicious, and she wolfed it down.

God, she was so hungry.

And dirty. She needed a shower.

A blast of a horn made her look to the window. The passengers were filing back onto the bus. The waitress came over to refill her coffee and Amelia started to pull out some money but then paused. Even the smallest movement made her ribs ache, and she felt fragile, as if her body were made of glass. She knew she couldn't get back on that bus.

"Is there a hotel nearby?" she asked the waitress.

"Well, there's a Motel 6 near the mall. But that's way out by the interstate."

"Is there anything here in town?"

"Not really."

The waitress was staring at her in a way that reminded Amelia of the redheaded woman back in the pawnshop—intense curiosity coupled with an odd, almost protective tenderness. Amelia resisted the urge to touch the gauze covering her chin.

"Okay, I know one place you could stay, maybe," the waitress said. She leaned over the counter and pointed out the window. "That's Gloucester Street. Turn right there and head through downtown. Turn left on Union Street and look for an old yellow house with a big wrap-around porch. You can't miss it. The woman who lives there is a friend of mine. She takes in boarders sometimes. Her name is Hannah. Tell her Missy sent you."

The bus was just pulling away when Amelia emerged from the café. She watched it disappear and then started toward Gloucester. She passed through a small downtown of old red brick buildings that had been restored as cafés and shops. The lampposts were hung with American flags and baskets of geraniums. There was a sign in a real estate office window advertising tickets to a Christmas Eve mass, and a man on a ladder was stringing up Christmas lights.

Christmas? It didn't feel like Christmas here. But she wasn't sure what Christmas really felt like. She walked on, the sun warm on her face.

Was she an impulsive person? She didn't have any idea. But her decision to stay here in this strange town hadn't come from some sudden, irrational urge. Sometime in the night on the bus, as she was drifting down into sleep, she had realized that going all the way to Charlotte was not a good idea. It was a big city—that much she could remember—and a city was a place where she could disappear and be safe from the man who haunted her dreams. But she could also get lost there. What she needed now was a place with boundaries and fences, a place where the streets had names instead of numbers, a place where she could feel real again instead of anonymous. She needed a place where she could heal and try to remember what had happened to her.

She turned onto Union Street and walked down the block. The yellow house was there in front of her, a big shabby Victorian almost hidden by trees and vines. The front door was open, and as she climbed the steps, she could see beyond the screen door to a long narrow hallway and a staircase. There was no bell so she knocked on the screen door.

She heard barking and, a moment later, a small white poodle appeared behind the screen door, still barking but wagging its tail so hard it almost fell over.

"Angel, shut the hell up!"

A tiny woman came to the door, hair as white and tightly curled as the dog's, face lined and pale, and a mouth stained with bright red lipstick. She gently nudged the dog aside with her slipper and opened the screen.

"What can I do for you, hon?"

Amelia smiled. "I'm looking for Hannah."

"You found her."

"I was just at the Red Bone Café and the waitress said you had rooms for rent. I need a place—"

"I know. Missy just called and said you'd be coming. Well, come on in then. Don't mind the dog. She's half-blind and full crazy."

Amelia followed the old woman down the hallway toward the back of the house. The poodle trailed behind, its toenails tapping on the wood floor. Amelia glimpsed small, high-ceilinged rooms stuffed with old furniture. The cross breeze made the thin curtains sway like ghosts in the shadows.

In the kitchen, Hannah motioned for Amelia to sit at an oak pedestal table. The room was hot compared to the rest of the house, and Amelia caught the smell of cinnamon and baking apples. She saw three pies sitting near the window.

Hannah came over to the table carrying a spiral notebook with a Hello Kitty emblem on the front. She saw Amelia looking at the pies.

"I'd offer you a slice, but I make those for sale at the café," she said. "I got some Little Debbie donuts if you're hungry."

"No, I had breakfast, thank you."

Hannah sat down and flipped open the notebook. "So what's your name?" she asked, pencil poised.

"Amelia Brody."

"How long you staying?"

She hesitated. "I'm not sure. Can I rent by the week?"

Hannah's eyes dipped to the Vuitton duffel on the floor and then came back up to Amelia's face. "I used to take in a lot of boarders, mainly the shrimpers before that all dried up. Nowadays I've got to be careful who I rent to because I'm getting too old to worry about other people's problems, and everybody seems to have problems these days." She tapped the pencil on the pad. "I gotta ask you, hon. You got somebody after you?"

Amelia hadn't seen a mirror since the thrift shop. She could only imagine how disheveled she looked, how bad the bruises were by now.

"No, I was in a car accident," she said.

Hannah was staring hard at her, and Amelia resisted the urge to touch the gauze on her chin.

"My son Greg—he's living in Atlanta now—he keeps telling me I should get a computer so he can send me e-mails instead of birthday cards," Hannah said. "He says that if I had a computer I could check people out before I rent to them. You can find out anything about anybody with a computer, you know. I don't trust the damn things, though."

Amelia nodded, barely listening. Her head was starting to pound again, and she suddenly felt very tired. Something brushed her leg, and she looked down. The poodle had settled down on the linoleum, resting its snout on her feet.

"Angel seems to like you," Hannah said. She hesitated, then penciled Amelia's name in the notebook and closed it. "Okay, the room's ten dollars a night and since you're the only renter right now I'll throw in breakfast if you make it down to the kitchen by eight."

"Thank you," Amelia said.

Hannah rose and stuffed the notebook on a shelf between two cookbooks. "Follow me, hon," she said. "I'll show you where you can lay your head."

The room was above the kitchen and smelled of apple and cinnamon. It was large and bright with sunlight. There was a sagging bed with a paint-chipped white iron headboard, a fat carved bureau, and a round braided rug on the scuffed wood floor. The wallpaper was patterned with faded blue flowers and darker rectangles where pictures had once hung.

Amelia's eyes lingered on the bed. God, all she wanted to do was just crawl under that white chenille bedspread and never come out. She turned back to Hannah, who was standing in the door, holding the white dog.

"It's lovely," Amelia said.

"If you need to make any phone calls, there's a phone downstairs in the hallway," Hannah said.

"I won't need the phone," Amelia said.

"Yeah, no one does anymore because everyone has a phone in their pocket. I got no use for the damn things, myself. Cell phones give you brain cancer, you know."

Cell phone.

Amelia had a sudden stab of memory—standing somewhere in the dark rain, holding a cell phone and listening to it ring. She could remember the feeling of her heart beating too fast and even what she had been thinking at that moment—*Please, please answer the phone.*

Who had she called? Had anyone answered?

"You sure you're okay, hon?"

She looked at Hannah and nodded. "I'm just a little tired."

Hannah smiled. "Well, the bed's old but comfy. Don't worry about locking your door. Nobody here does. The bath is down the hall, and there's towels and shampoo in there. I'll be down in the kitchen if you need anything else."

She left, leaving the door ajar.

Amelia set the duffel on the bed and unzipped it. She stared down at the wad of money, debating whether to try to hide it, but then decided to leave it in the bag. She pulled out the bottle of Aleve, shook two pills into her hand, and went down the hall to the bathroom. She downed the pills with a handful of water and then looked in the mirror.

The gauze had come loose, so she carefully peeled it off her chin. The sight of the black stitches made her wince. She would have to get Band-Aids, a nightgown, some fresh clothes.

But not now.

Her eyes drifted to the claw-foot bathtub. Right now, a long soak in the tub was the only thing she needed.

She ran the water, stripped, and got in the tub. The hot water embraced her, and as she washed herself, she saw two large bruises on her left leg and a bad scrape on one elbow that she hadn't noticed before. Several of her fingernails were ragged, and the palms of both her hands were raw and red, like she had fallen and slid across concrete.

She eased farther down into the warm water, resting her head back on the tub's edge. The tub was too small for her long legs so she had to prop her feet on the faucet. She lay there for a long time before she finally looked down at her feet. She sat forward and focused on them—on the gnarled toes, bulging blue veins, crusted callouses and bunions, and blackened nails. Ugly feet. Deformed feet. How had they gotten that way?

A new question pushed its way forward in her head.

Who was I? What was I?

She settled back against the tub and closed her eyes. The electric current of fear that had been with her since waking up in the hospital was subsiding a little, almost as if the warm bathwater was leaching it away. But she knew it would not go away completely, that she would never feel safe or at peace, until she found out what had made her run.

She couldn't go back to Florida. Did she have a friend she could contact? Who had she called that night in the rain? Did she have family somewhere? The dream of floating in the blue-green bubble came back to her, and though she still couldn't remember her mother's name or even what she looked like, she had a strong feeling that her mother was alive.

A plan . . . she needed a plan. She had to find out more about herself and her past. If she found out who she was, she could figure out what she needed to do. Tomorrow she would start over.

The water was turning cold. She used the tiny bottle of hotel shampoo to wash her hair, then pulled the stopper and got out, wrapping the scratchy white towel around her.

The sun was streaming in full force through the windows when she got back to her room. She found the plastic bag she had taken from the hospital and pulled out the comb. After ten minutes of tugging it through her tangled hair, she gave up. Extensions, the doctor had said; she had hair extensions.

She felt a sudden small surge of anger. Why did she need them? What was wrong with her real hair?

She set the comb down and looked at the bed. There were two indentations in the sagging mattress with a slight hump in the middle, as if the old bed still carried the memories of the two people who had slept there, side by side, for a very long time.

Another flare of memory.

Alex.

She could feel him, the press of his body, hard and sweat-slick against hers, his face a grimace above her and his breath hot against her neck as he whispered her name over and over.

Mel . . . Mel . . . my Mel.

She shut her eyes, and his face was gone.

She dropped the towel, pulled back the chenille bedspread and got into the bed. She found a comfortable spot in one of the hollows and closed her eyes.

Sleep wouldn't come. There was an awful noise of voices in her head, like a radio that couldn't get a signal, and she struggled to sort them out, to figure out who was talking to her, who was yelling at her, and why. Sleep was inches away when she felt something brush her arm, soft as a caress. She opened her eyes.

Black eyes. A blur of white. It was the little white dog. It sniffed her face and then moved away, scratching at the chenille bedspread. The dog made a tight circle, four, five times, then with a deep sigh settled into the crook of her knees.

She reached down and pulled the dog closer.

CHAPTER SEVEN

When Amelia opened her eyes, she was surrounded by a soft blue blur and for a second, she thought she was back in the bubble dream. She reached for her glasses on the nightstand and put them on. The flowers on the blue wallpaper came into focus. She looked down at the bedspread. The white dog was gone.

When she swung her legs over the side of the bed, she winced. The pain was still there in her body and she still had a headache but at least she felt rested. The smell of strong coffee drifted up from downstairs. Her stomach rumbled.

After a quick trip to the bathroom, she dressed in her jeans and blue shirt and went downstairs to the kitchen. There was a clock on the wall near the sink, a black plastic cat whose cartoon eyes and pendulum tail swung slowly back and forth. It was eight thirty.

Jesus, she had slept more than twenty hours straight.

There was no sign of Hannah, but there was a half-full Mr. Coffee on the counter, an empty mug, and an open cartoon of chocolate donuts. Amelia filled the mug and took a donut. She stood at the window over the sink, looking out as she ate. It had turned colder overnight, leaving a morning fog hugging the ground and making the trees in the backyard look like they were levitating. She heard the click of the dog's toenails and turned.

The poodle came quickly to her, wagging its tail. But Hannah, trailing behind with a leash, drew up short just inside the door.

"Good lord, hon, what happened to your hair?"

Amelia realized that yesterday her hair had been hidden beneath the canvas hat. "Bad perm," she said with a smile.

Hannah shook her head and went to the coffeemaker. "You going to want more coffee?"

"No, I'm good." Amelia sipped her coffee, watching Hannah pour out the carafe and wipe down the already spotless counter. "Hannah, I need to buy some toiletries and some clothes. Is there someplace downtown?"

"Downtown? Nah, not unless you wanna pay five hundred dollars for a sweater in one of those tourist places." She stooped to get the dog's bowl and refilled it with water. "I'm heading out to my doctor's appointment and I could drop you off at the mall if you like."

Amelia reached down and gathered the dog into her arms. "If it's not too much trouble."

"No trouble at all, hon," Hannah said. "You'd better buy a jacket while you're there. We got a cold spell coming."

◆ ◆ ◆

The mall was just opening when Amelia walked in. A yawning girl was rolling open the metal grating at Aéropostale, and the smell of baking pretzels from the Auntie Anne's kiosk mixed with the scent of lemons oozing out of the Bath & Body Works shop. All down the long wide aisle, lights were going on in the shops. The smells, signs, window displays, colors—it all came at Amelia in a rush of sensation, and for several seconds, she had to just stand still, letting her brain absorb it all and scan for connections.

Of course she had been in a mall before. But when and where? Nothing . . . nothing was coming.

But then she heard music and she recognized it immediately as a Christmas carol, though she couldn't recall which song it was. Amelia felt a stab of sadness that she had forgotten something so simple, that she couldn't remember the last Christmas she had celebrated or any Christmas in her entire life for that matter.

She squared her shoulders.

No. No more sadness.

Anger was what she needed right now. Not the anger of frustration, but the kind of cold anger that would help her form a plan for going forward, that would force her brain to be calm and calculating enough to let her deal with whatever shit was thrown at her.

Shit?

She didn't even know if she was the kind of woman who used words like "shit." No matter, she decided. She was now.

She found a mall directory and decided to head to JCPenney. But halfway there, a light went on above an imposing wall of glass. She stopped and looked up.

It was a white apple. No name, just a giant glowing apple.

The lights inside the store flickered on, revealing rows of sleek white tables and walls of blue screens. There were four people milling around inside, all wearing jeans and bright blue T-shirts with large square pendants hanging around their necks. She had the crazy thought that it all looked like some strange alien spaceship.

But then she looked up again at the white apple and it clicked in her head. Apple. She once had something with that emblem on it.

Was it a computer? Computers could tell you anything about anybody, Hannah had said.

Amelia went inside and walked slowly down the aisle of computers that were lined up like artwork on the white consoles. She stopped, staring at the image on one screen. It was moving, a swirling nebula of green and blue, like her bubble dream.

"Can I help you?"

Amelia turned and looked down into the round face of a young woman, who smiled at her from beneath her fringe of heavy black bangs. The pendant hanging on her chest was a name tag with the name MARIA, and below that were two flags, an American flag and a red, white, and green one Amelia didn't recognize.

"Yes, I need some help. I need a computer."

"Well, this is the MacBook Pro," the clerk said. She tapped a key, and the nebula disappeared, replaced by a bright blue screen. "It comes with eight gigs but you can always add more RAM. What do you need it for mainly? Watching movies? Are you a gamer?"

"No, I just need to look things up."

"O-kay." Maria pursed her lips. "The Pro's got a nice touch. Go ahead, try it out."

Amelia positioned her hands above the middle row of keys and for a moment it felt like her fingers knew what to do, where to move. Did she know how to type? Had she been a secretary once? She knew what computers were but there were gaps, as if she couldn't remember the terminology or exactly how to do things. .

"Show me how to search for something," Amelia asked.

Maria stabbed at some keys and looked up. "What do you want to search for?"

"Myself," Amelia asked.

Maria's smile hardened as her eyes took in Amelia's matted hair, baggy jeans, and rumpled blue shirt. "Listen, maybe you should go to the public library. They can—"

"No," Amelia said. "I just need a little help here, and if you can't be bothered then I will go buy a computer someplace else."

Maria blinked several times. "Okay, what's your name?"

"Amelia Tobias."

Maria tapped some keys and then looked up. "Wow, you're in a magazine."

"Magazine?"

Maria stepped aside so Amelia could see. It was a page from *Florida Design*. There was a color photograph of a blonde woman in a red halter dress standing near a pool. A large pink house with palm trees and a white yacht was visible behind the woman. The type below the picture read "Mrs. Alex Tobias in front of her Fort Lauderdale Isles home: 'When we remodeled Casa Rosa, we were careful to preserve the past.'"

Preserve the past . . .

Voices in her head again, and this time one of them was her own.

This is the house I wanted you to see.

She could see herself. She was standing in front of the pink house, but it looked nothing like the house in the magazine. It had boarded-up windows, a jungle of vines and trees, a dry fountain, and there was a red sign near the door—**FORECLOSURE. PRICE REDUCED!**

She could hear screeching sounds from above and see a flurry of acid green wings against a blue sky. The screeching mutated into a man's voice.

Mel, this is a teardown. I want something new and clean.

But I like this place, Alex. This place feels right.

And then . . .

The feel of arms enfolding her, his arms, and his lips pressed on hers, and the rustle of palm fronds and dying screams of the wild parrots as they flew away.

"Is that really you?"

Maria's voice brought her back. When Amelia turned to look at her, she knew the young clerk was trying to reconcile the bruised, disheveled woman in front of her with the sleek creature on the computer screen.

She couldn't answer. Her headache had returned, and when she looked up at the ceiling, the lights were haloed.

"I need . . ." Amelia closed her eyes for a second and then opened them. "I need to buy a computer," she said. She hoisted up the Vuitton duffel. "I need something small and light that I can carry in this."

There was new respect in the young woman's eyes. "I've got just what you need—a tablet. Compact, light, and fast, but it comes with sixteen gigs." Maria smiled. "You can never have enough memory, right?"

◆ ◆ ◆

It was just a sliver of black glass and aluminum that weighed only a pound. Five hundred dollars had seemed like too much to pay for the tablet, but the clerk had assured Amelia that she could search for anything with it, that the whole world was hers at the brush of her fingertips.

She left the store exhausted, her head pounding after the lesson the clerk had given her on how to use the tablet and how to connect to the Internet with the prepaid wireless SIM card she had been able to purchase with cash.

The mall was warm and crowded now, the people pushing around her in a fast current. The piped-in Christmas carols were like a broken-fluorescent-light buzz in her head.

See the blazing Yule before us.

Fa la la la la, la la la la . . .

The image from the magazine of that blonde woman standing in front of the pool was burned in her brain. Had that really been her? What else was the tablet going to be able to tell her about herself? And what was she going to be able to find out about Alex?

Fast away the old year passes! Fa la la la la, la la la la!

A sudden wave of nausea overtook her, and red and green sparks shot across her vision. Amelia stopped and shut her eyes, clutching the plastic bag from the Apple store to her chest.

Someone was laughing, a cruel shrieking laugh.

Fa la la la la! Ha la la la la!

"Hey, are you okay?"

She opened her eyes. A young man with spiky platinum blond hair was standing in front of her. He had a tiny silver ring in his nostril, and she focused hard on it, trying to stop the spinning.

"I just need to sit down," Amelia said.

His hands were gentle but firm as he led her into a store. He sat her down in a chair and she bowed her head, closing her eyes. Slowly the dizziness began to pass.

"Here, drink this."

She opened her eyes to see the young man holding out a glass of water. When she didn't take it, he added, "I've got some wine in the back. Do you want that instead?"

She shook her head and looked around. It was a beauty salon, but all the other chairs were empty. The whole place was empty except for a sleepy girl with pink hair manning the desk by the entrance.

Amelia looked in the mirror, catching the eye of the young man standing behind her. "I had a concussion and get dizzy sometimes," she said. "Thanks for helping me. I'm okay now."

He was studying her, with one palm cupping his chin. "Are you sure? I mean, are you sure there's not something else I can do for you?"

Her hair, she realized—he was staring at her hair. It looked even worse than it had this morning when she got up, matted lank ropes hanging to her shoulders.

"What happened?" he whispered.

She let out a long sigh. "Can you fix it?"

"Girl, I can fix anything," he said, smiling. He drew a pink cape over her and picked up a brush but then paused. "You have extensions," he said, feeling her scalp. "I don't think I can save them. They're put in with glue, you know."

"Then cut them out."

"I'd have to cut you pretty short. You sure?"

Amelia nodded.

"What about the color? I can touch you up. Same shade of blonde?"

Amelia took off the purple plastic glasses. "No, change it back to my natural color."

"What is it?"

She couldn't tell him that she wasn't sure. "Why don't you just decide what will look good."

He gave her a huge smile. "God, I wish all my clients were like you."

The next hour went by like a sensual dream. The warm scented water of the shampoo, and the stylist's hands—his name was Martin, and he was working at Supercuts only until he could get to New Orleans—were ever so gentle as he cut out the extensions. The pink-haired girl went next door to Sbarro and brought Amelia pizza, which she ate with slow and deliberate pleasure.

As she was finishing a second pizza slice, she had the odd thought that pizza was not something she was allowed to eat.

Allowed?

That Russian voice was there in her head again and she heard the words more clearly now than she had back in the thrift store.

I need to see your bones.

The Russian man's face came slowly into focus—a thin hooked nose and sparse white hair—and he was poking her in the ribs, telling her she was too fat, while the girls around her giggled. And a different man was telling her to put the cookie down and calling her Jelly-Belly.

She swallowed the last bite of pizza, and along with it the anger over the old man who had made her cry and the other man who had called her that name. What kind of a person had she been that she had given these men such power over her?

Finally, Martin stepped away from the chair and Amelia put her glasses back on. In the few times she had seen her reflection since waking up in the hospital, she hadn't recognized the woman staring back at her. She still didn't.

The woman in the mirror had dark brown hair cut close and boyish with spiky bangs. The haircut made her face look round and her neck very long.

"Is it okay?"

She looked up at Martin. He looked worried.

"It's sort of just how I pictured you for some reason," he said. "Sort of Leslie Caron circa *An American in Paris*."

Amelia stared at her reflection and then smiled. "I like it. Thank you, Martin."

He let out a long breath. "Well, one thing's for sure. No one's going to recognize you."

♦ ♦ ♦

It was near one by the time she made her way to JCPenney. Hannah was due to pick her up outside at two, so she didn't linger as she bought underwear, socks, a nightgown, and a light robe. She picked up a pair of short flat boots and, on impulse, a pair of turquoise Converse sneakers. In the women's department, she filled her arms with jeans, khaki pants, a heavy nubby gray sweater coat, and five black long-sleeved T-shirts. She quickly tried on the jeans in the dressing room, and was gathering them up to leave when she froze.

Music . . . sweet-sounding, tinkling music. More Christmas music, but not carols this time. Something else, something so very familiar that it was almost like it was coming from deep inside her head instead of from the speaker up on the ceiling.

Nuts? Nut . . . *Nutcracker*. She let out a sigh of relief. That was the name of the music, *The Nutcracker*.

And then, floating on the edges of the music, she could hear words, foreign words, like the ones that had come to her before, but this time she was certain it wasn't Italian. It was French that she was hearing.

Piqué, piqué, arabesque allongé. Pas de chat, pas de chat, pas de bourrée.

It was the same voice, the Russian man who had said, "Make ugly go away. You try make pretty."

Suddenly, she could feel something shift in her body, something buried deep inside her. Without realizing it, she extended her left leg, pointed her toe, and raised her arms over her head.

She stared at herself in the triple mirror. But she was seeing herself reflected back in many, many other mirrors, walls of mirrors, mirrors with railings, mirrors clouded with the steam of condensation in rooms filled with music, the smell of coffee, and wood floors marked with resin. And the Russian was there. He had been her teacher.

Make pretty.

Her mind had forgotten but her muscles had not.

I am a dancer.

I am a dancer!

CHAPTER EIGHT

When he arrived at the restaurant, there was nowhere to sit. At least no place that suited his needs. There was one spot open at the bar, but it would have required him to sit with his back to the door and that was never going to happen in a million years.

So Clay Buchanan waited, standing near the door, savoring the last drags on his Dunhill, and when a seat opened up on the patio facing the street, he snuffed out his cigarette and slid into the rattan chair.

YOLO. It was a dumb name for a restaurant, he thought. But when he glanced at the matches he had snagged from the hostess, he saw that it stood for *You Only Live Once.*

He ordered a Pappy Van Winkle bourbon. Sixty-five bucks a shot, but he wasn't paying. He took a sip, closing his eyes in pleasure at the caramel taste.

Carpe diem, baby.

The restaurant was starting to fill up as the nearby glass office buildings disgorged their inhabitants for happy hour. For the next half hour he sat nursing the bourbon and watching the young women *click-clack* in on their sky-high heels, long hair and short hemlines swinging, their eyes honing in on the male prospects.

God, the women were beautiful here.

Silicone-pumped and pouty-lipped beautiful. Not his taste really—he liked his women with real curves on their bodies and more lines on their faces—but these women were exotic compared to the ones back home in Nashville and, like rare birds, interesting to watch.

And watching was what he was really good at.

He had found that out when he was just twelve—that morning out in the duck blind on Old Hick Lake with his dad—found out that he could spot the green heads even before the dogs could hear them. It took him ten more years of sitting in blinds before he realized he didn't like shooting the ducks. He just liked watching them. He liked watching any creature that flew. He liked the fact that he could tell a Ruddy from a Merganser on the wing with his bare eyes. Liked the fact that he could check off another line in his journal after a sighting. Liked that he had a Wings Over Tennessee certificate on his wall that said he had recorded five hundred sightings. And he really liked the fact that nobody who came into his office had ever had the balls to ask him why a guy like him liked to watch little birdies.

Buchanan took another sip of bourbon, his eyes flitting over the bar crowd.

When he was in a place like this, or any place where humans gathered, he saw himself as a big bird of prey—a peregrine falcon maybe—soaring high above and looking down at the world below from all the angles. He could see things that others, so intent on their little grounded lives, could not. He could see the big picture.

Funny how things turned out. There had been some bad detours in his life and a soul-killing job as an insurance fraud investigator. Yeah, it was funny, that all those mornings freezing his ass off in a duck blind had led to this, doing something that he was really good at.

He finished the bourbon and thought about ordering another but he was tired from the job he had just finished up in New York and the plane ride in from Kennedy, and he needed to stay alert. He asked the bartender for a glass of water instead and glanced at his watch.

Almost six . . . a half hour late. So where was this guy Alex Tobias?

Then he saw him, getting out of the white Mercedes G-Class SUV about twenty feet away.

The man looked just like his Google images—an easy six six and reedy thin, like he ran marathons or, more likely, power-biked up computer-screen mountains. He had thick black hair and was wearing a gray suit, white dress shirt, and light blue tie.

Buchanan honed in on the details: The suit was a two-button tight fit, probably John Varvatos. The shoes were sleek and black, maybe Tod's. The effect was stylish but restrained, like Tobias wanted to be the hippest guy in the room but pulled back from the edge just enough to keep the old guys from feeling too old.

Buchanan wished he'd had more time to check out Tobias. He didn't like taking on a case without knowing as much as he could ahead of time.

Back at Kennedy, there had been just enough time for him to fire up his Acer in the airport and do a quick search on the man. Plenty of sites popped up that gave him the basics: that Tobias was thirty-eight, had graduated from Florida State law school but was now a partner in McCall and Tobias. It was one of the Southeast's best law firms, complete with sleek mahogany and glass offices in a high-rise, a staff of eighty, and a client list peppered with the names of basketball stars, banks, and cruise-line titans. The firm even had a motto: "We're In This Together."

Tobias was a hotshot in social circles, donating major bucks to Big Brothers, American Cancer Society, Humane Society, the Dan Marino

Foundation. Just three months ago, according to the *South Florida Sun-Sentinel* business pages, he had paid $800,000 for a vintage gullwing Mercedes at the Auctions America classic car auction. His house was featured in *Florida Design*, and Tobias himself had been a cover boy in *Lawyer Monthly*.

A visit to the Broward County property appraiser's site told Buchanan that Tobias lived on Castilla Isle in a house he bought in 2007 for $1.2 million. Five keystrokes later, Buchanan found the Tobias home on Trulia with a current value of $4.8 mil. A nice tidy increase in just seven years.

Buchanan wondered if the guy came from money or if he'd had to work his way into it. Maybe he started out with a strip mall office in Tallahassee and one Men's Wearhouse suit in his closet. He had that sort of trying-too-hard look about him. But then, most of the people Buchanan had seen here did. He decided he'd do a deep dive search on Tobias later.

For now, he just watched as Tobias handed the keys to the valet, yanked off his tie, and tossed it in the SUV. Tobias came toward the bar, pausing at the edge of the patio. He took off his sunglasses, hung them on the pocket of his shirt and scanned the crowd.

Picking up his Dunhills, Buchanan shook out a cigarette and lit it, deciding to let the bastard twist for a few seconds, letting him worry that maybe he had popped for that first-class ticket from Kennedy for nothing.

Buchanan watched Tobias, watched him searching the crowd, watched him getting pissed that he didn't know the face of the man he was meeting. This was a guy, he decided, who wasn't used to being fucked with.

Enough. It was time to get on with business.

Buchanan met the man's eyes across the crowd and nodded. The guy practically pushed his way over.

"Are you Clay Buchanan?"

"That would be me. Sit down, Mr. Tobias."

Alex Tobias slid into the chair and signaled the blonde server with a wave. When she ignored him, he swung his gaze back to Buchanan.

"Thank you for coming on such short notice, Mr. Buchanan," Tobias said.

"A five-thousand-dollar consult fee showing up in my QuickPay account has a way of clearing my calendar rather quickly."

Tobias forced a smile. "I should tell you, this wasn't my idea."

"What wasn't?"

"Hiring you, Mr. Buchanan."

"Whose idea was it?"

"My law partner, Owen McCall. He said you're the best at this sort of thing."

When Buchanan's cell had chirped back in the bar at JFK, he hadn't recognized the name McCall-Tobias. But experience had taught him not to ignore calls from law offices. Still, he had been surprised when a secretary told him that the firm wanted to "engage his services" to find a missing woman, the wife of one of the partners, Alex Tobias.

The secretary didn't hesitate when Buchanan told her his fee. Buchanan didn't ask any details. The ticket to Fort Lauderdale was waiting for him at the Delta counter, and his money was in his bank account by the time he landed. This was just a consult. If things didn't smell right, he could always walk away and keep the five grand. It went like that sometimes.

Tobias took his sunglasses off his pocket, started to put them on, then carefully set them down on the table.

"Owen said he read a book you wrote—*Nowhere to Hide*, or something. He told me about this Mexican millionaire's son who was abducted and how you traced him—"

"I know the ending," Buchanan interrupted. He didn't want to rehash his resume with this man. The book had just been a quickie thing he published himself to make some extra money. It had sold maybe twenty copies, but Tobias didn't need to know that.

"Owen said you're not like any normal private eye."

"I'm not like *any* private eye, Mr. Tobias. I'm a skip tracer."

"A what?"

"Skip tracer. I do one thing and one thing only. I find people who don't want to be found."

Tobias frowned. "I don't understand the difference."

"You will. If I take your case."

Tobias nodded slowly and then his eyes slid toward the bar, looking for the server again. When he turned back, Buchanan got his first good look into the man's eyes. They were the color of the Cumberland River on a cloudy day—a muddy blue-green but shot through with tiny red veins. The guy had been drinking.

"So if hiring me wasn't your idea, what changed your mind?" Buchanan asked.

"I don't know how else to find my wife," Tobias said. "The police won't do anything. They say that since she walked away on her own, she's not technically missing."

"She walked away on her own? From where?"

"Broward General Hospital." He frowned. "No one told you any of this yet?"

"Someone from your office called me four hours ago, Mr. Tobias, and hired me to come down here for a consultation about finding a missing woman. That is all I know. Maybe you better fill me in."

Tobias sighed, seemingly frustrated he had to tell his story again. Buchanan figured he'd already been grilled by the doctors at the hospital and the cops. He'd cut him a break and get him a drink. Loosen him up a little. Buchanan caught the blonde server's eye and she came over quickly.

"Another bourbon?" she asked him with a smile.

"Club soda for me." He looked to Alex. "What are you drinking?"

"Armadale on the rocks," Tobias said.

The server left and Buchanan leaned back in his chair. Armadale vodka. Just like the man himself—corporate-clean and a little too polished.

Buchanan had always been good at reading people. It was just like watching birds, really. He could identify almost any bird just by being patient and looking for the details—its shape, size, voice, coloration, or flying style. Birders called it *jizz*, that special vibe you got when you watched a bird that helped you figure out its species even if it was hiding in the trees. The word was supposedly an acronym used by WWII pilots—"General Impression of Size and Shape" of an aircraft. Now it was a porno term, but birders didn't care. *Jizz* was theirs. And it was never to be ignored.

Right now, Alex Tobias was putting out some weird *jizz*—confusion, anxiety, worry, fear, and a musky bass note of desperation to keep things under control.

The drinks arrived. Tobias took a long swig of his.

"What exactly happened to your wife?" Buchanan asked.

Tobias set the glass down. "Four days ago, Mel was in a car accident. She was alone when it happened, but some guy in a truck found her and left her in the emergency room."

"Police find the guy?"

"No. They have his truck on the security camera but no plate number. They think he was an illegal immigrant and was afraid of getting busted, so he left Mel and ran."

"Why'd your wife leave the hospital?" Buchanan asked.

"I don't know. No one seems to know anything." He took a big drink of vodka. "She has a brain injury, a concussion. She has amnesia."

"Amnesia?"

Tobias nodded. "Yesterday, she finally remembered her name and they called me. When I saw her, she was asleep and they made me leave. But when I came back twenty minutes later, she was gone."

"Has she called you?"

"No."

"You've tried to call her, of course."

"I haven't stopped. But it just keeps going to voice mail."

"Does it ring?"

"What?"

"When you call her phone, does it ring before it goes to voice mail?"

Tobias shook his head. "The police told me the phone was turned off. They said that's why they couldn't use the GPS to find it."

"They can trace the phone's last location. Have they told you anything?"

"Yes. They said the last known location of the phone was about two miles from where her car was found. But they never found the phone or her purse."

"What about the car's GPS?"

"It doesn't have one."

"And you don't know where your wife was going?"

Tobias shook his head slowly. He picked up his glass, stared down into it for a long time, and then finally took a drink.

"What do you know about the accident?"

"Not much. They said the car spun off the road in the rain and went into a ditch. It happened out on some road in the Everglades."

"Everglades? What was your wife doing driving alone in the Everglades?"

Tobias stared at him for a long time, as if he were trying to figure something out. Then he shook his head. "I don't know."

What the fuck did this guy know?

"I'll need to see the accident report," Buchanan said.

"Why?"

When Buchanan gave him a hard stare, Tobias held up a hand. "I'll get it to you."

"Where's the car now?"

"My insurance agent said it was towed back here last night. It's in the police impound."

Since the police did not consider Amelia Tobias to be a missing person, Buchanan knew their initial search of the wrecked car had probably been cursory. He knew, too, that even the smallest clue could lead to something big. With no GPS, Amelia Tobias could have scribbled directions on a piece of paper. And if he could figure out where she had been going, maybe he could find out where she went. He would need to check out the car.

"You said the police looked for your wife?" Buchanan asked.

"Yeah, they searched the hospital and the neighborhood, but there was no sign of her," Tobias said. "She has a brain injury, but they aren't even looking for her now. My wife is missing and the fucking police won't do a thing. Does that make any fucking *sense* to you?"

The two women at the next table turned to stare. Tobias glanced at them and then picked up his glass and drained it.

"Actually it makes perfect sense," Buchanan said. "The way the police see it, if your wife was healthy enough to walk out of the hospital then she must be in good enough shape to make her own decisions, concussion or no concussion. And since she's an adult, if she's decided she wants to disappear, she has a right to do that."

Tobias's blue-green eyes were fixed on him.

"Does your wife have good reason to want to disappear, Mr. Tobias?"

Tobias rose. "I don't have to put up with this shit. We're finished here."

"Sit down, Mr. Tobias."

Tobias glared at him.

"Sit down. Please."

Tobias hesitated and then dropped back into the chair. He ran a hand over his sweating brow.

"You want another drink?" Buchanan asked.

Tobias shook his head slowly as he stared vacantly out over the patio. There was a faint roll of thunder, and Buchanan looked up to see storm clouds. The temperature was dropping, and the patio was emptying fast. In the small parking plaza fronting the bar, there was a fifty-foot fake Christmas tree. Its white lights blinked on, the reflection falling like glitter on the Bimmers, Audis, and Bentleys arranged like presents under the tree.

"Let me tell you something about how I work," Buchanan said.

Tobias looked up.

"I track down people who will do almost anything not to be found. I am very good at this because I am willing to do whatever it takes and go as far as necessary. I am a liar for hire. But I don't bring back women who have a good reason to want to get away from their husbands."

"I would never hurt my wife," Tobias said.

Buchanan waited. It was always better to say nothing and let the silence slice away at the other person's comfort level. Human nature abhorred a vacuum.

"I need you to find her," Tobias said.

Again, Buchanan waited.

"Mel *wants* to be found."

It came out almost in a whisper with a small break in the voice. Alex Tobias was a man with a hole somewhere deep inside him, that much was as easy to discern as the grassy perfume of the women at the next table. But there was something else there, something Buchanan's senses were not quite picking up.

"Okay," Buchanan said. "I'll take your case. I'll find your wife."

Tobias met his eyes.

"But this is how it works. All I do is find her and tell you where she is. The rest is up to you—and her."

Tobias nodded. "Thank you. That's all I want." He collapsed back in the chair, as if he had no air left in his lungs. "What's the next step?" he asked.

"You tell me everything you know about your wife," Buchanan said.

"Then what?"

"Then we wait for her to make a mistake."

CHAPTER NINE

The headlights swept across the chain link fence, illuminating the big green sign—**FORT LAUDERDALE POLICE VEHICLE IMPOUND.**

Buchanan leaned forward in the taxi's seat and pushed a wad of bills through the plastic. "This is good," he said. "Keep the change."

Buchanan eased out of the taxi and it sped away, leaving him in the dark drizzle. Beyond the ten-foot chain link fence, he could see the misty glow of security lights falling on the rows of cars and SUVs like moonlight on tombstones. A small warmer yellow light deeper in the lot pulsed brighter for a second as a door opened and then closed.

Buchanan heard the man's footsteps before he saw him. A flashlight shined in Buchanan's eyes and he blinked.

"You Buchanan?"

"One and the same."

Buchanan heard the *jingle-clank-creak* of the fence unlocking and opening. As he went through, he caught a glimpse of a fat man in a dirty Dolphins cap and orange plastic rain poncho. After leaving Tobias at the restaurant, Buchanan had called his contact at the Fort Lauderdale PD, who had told him the impound guard was good, that he'd let him in for fifty bucks. Buchanan was having trouble remembering the impound guy's name.

Quirk . . . that was it.

"Listen, Mr. Quirk—"

"Quark. The name is Quark, like the subatomic particle."

"Okay, Mr. Quark. I'm here to see a car."

"Yeah, Larry told me. The Mercedes SL that came in yesterday. So where's my Christmas present?"

Buchanan pulled an envelope from his pocket and handed it over to Quark. The man peeked in the envelope and then slid it into his pants pocket.

"Follow me."

Quark clicked on his flashlight again, and Buchanan followed him along the line of cars. The first few rows were all in good shape: Toyotas towed from parking lots, Escalades seized in drug raids, and Lexuses lost to loan default. But the farther they went into the lot the worse the cars looked until they deteriorated into crumbled masses of metal.

Quark stopped and pointed the flashlight beam. "There she is."

The car was wedged between two other wrecks—a Kia and an accordioned Ford Fiesta. It was small, about the size of a Miata, and though the grill was damaged, the distinctive Mercedes emblem was still visible.

Something was itching at Buchanan's memory, something from his Google of Alex Tobias. "Can I have your flashlight?" he asked Quark.

Quark handed it over, and Buchanan trained it on the car's side. He couldn't see the doors, but he knew what he was looking at—a Mercedes 300SL gullwing.

That's what Buchanan had been trying to remember. His Google of Alex Tobias had revealed that Tobias had paid $800,000 for the gullwing at an auto auction. It was the kind of collectible car you didn't even drive on city streets. What was Amelia Tobias doing driving it out in the Everglades?

It started to rain.

"You about done here?"

Buchanan looked back at Quark, turtled down into his poncho.

"No, I'm going to be a while."

"Well, I'm going back to my office. Make sure you drop the flashlight off before you leave."

Quark left and Buchanan looked back at the Mercedes. The passenger side appeared intact. The driver's side had taken the brunt of the damage, and its front fender was smashed, the headlight broken. The Mercedes was wedged smack up against the wrecked Ford so there was no way to see inside. Buchanan climbed on top of the Kia. He had to lie down on the hood to angle the flashlight beam into the car's interior.

The light picked up the glitter of glass from the broken driver's-side window. There were brown smears on the tan bucket seat and on the dashboard—dried blood, Buchanan guessed. When he moved the flashlight beam, he saw the spider crack in the windshield over the steering wheel.

Buchanan started to get up but then stopped. Suddenly he was seeing what wasn't there.

Seat belts.

The gullwing was a classic car, but that didn't mean it couldn't be retrofitted with seat belts, even though any such alteration would diminish the car's value. With no seat belt to stop anything, Amelia Tobias's head had smashed into the windshield.

Again, the question: What was she doing driving a car like this? Most rich women surrounded themselves with as much metal and airbags as bulky sedans or SUVs could provide. He made a mental note to find out if she had another car.

Buchanan jumped off the Kia down to the mud. The rain had turned into a downpour, beating an ear-splitting tattoo on the hoods of the dead cars.

Something was still bothering him, something about the car's gull-wing doors, but he couldn't figure out what it was. And then there was the big question: Where the hell was Amelia Tobias going that night?

His experience and his instincts were telling him she had been on her way to meet a lover. But who wore a Chanel cocktail dress to a tryst in the swamp?

He clicked off the flashlight and trudged off through the rain.

♦ ♦ ♦

Amelia Tobias's life was spread out before him on the bed.

Buchanan's eyes swept over the scattering of papers and photographs. For two hours now he had been working the phones, scouring the Internet, and printing out the results of his search, working to put together a clear picture of the woman. Normally, after even this limited amount of time and research, he had a good bead on what kind of runner he was chasing.

All he had to do was sift through the mundane data of their daily lives—phone records, Facebook postings, credit card bills, what books they bought on Amazon, what movies they rented from Netflix—and the runners always revealed themselves.

It was, he always thought, like watching one of those old Polaroid pictures come into focus. And once he got a clear picture of what the person had been, he could always figure out where they had gone.

But this one . . .

There was a strange *lack* of information on Amelia Tobias.

There had been plenty of stuff on Alex Tobias: articles about his law firm's cases, his successes, and his business holdings. Amelia— "the lovely Mrs. Tobias"—was mentioned in his big profile in *Lawyer*

Monthly. But the only things Buchanan had found on Amelia herself came from the society pages.

He sat down on the edge of the bed and picked up a printout.

It was a home décor piece from *Florida Design*. It showed the Tobias home, a big pink Spanish-style place. To his eye, it looked like some place Zorro would live if he had no taste. But apparently, Amelia had rescued what was an important "Mizner-style manse" from the wrecking ball. There were quotes from her about how she had devoted three years to overseeing the renovation, accompanied by lots of pictures of the big white rooms. There was a photo of Amelia standing in front of the pool in a red dress.

The only other pictures of her that he had found were in *Gold Coast Magazine*'s "Scene and Heard" section and in *City and Shore Magazine*'s "Out & About." The names of the events changed—Diamond Ball for Cancer Research, Pawpurrazzi Party for the Humane Society, Opera Guild Disco Night—but the pictures were always the same. Alex Tobias in a tux, clutching a champagne glass and showing a lot of teeth. And there at his side was Amelia, beautiful for sure, but always with one of those smiles that said *I'm here but I'm really not here.*

It was like she lived in a bubble. The woman didn't even have her own Facebook page.

The rich are different from you and me, Bucky, and it's not just the money.

He knew that. He had worked cases for a couple people who could buy Alex Tobias ten times over. But he had never gotten used to the world they lived in. He tossed the printout to the bed, and his eyes drifted around the hotel room. He had to admit, though, that when the case paid well enough, it was nice to hover around the gilded edges.

After leaving the impound lot, he had retreated to a nearby bar and fired up the laptop to find a hotel on Expedia. He had chosen the W Hotel on the beach, deciding he deserved to stay in a place *Condé Nast Traveler* called "the perfect balance of style and soul." Tobias was paying the freight—three ninety a night—for what was called "A Cool Corner Room."

It was almost nine hundred square feet, bigger than his apartment back in Nashville, the king-sized bed flanked by two walls of floor-to-ceiling windows that opened onto a wraparound balcony. Even the crapper had an ocean view.

Buchanan rose, grabbed the last wedge of a club sandwich off the room-service table, and went to the desk. He punched a key on his Acer, and the notes he had transcribed from his meeting with Alex Tobias flashed up on the screen.

It had taken two hours and two more Armadale vodkas to get Tobias really talking.

Tell me everything you know about your wife's past.

Why?

Because there's a good chance she's still here in town and she might go where she feels safe.

He hadn't mentioned that might be a lover's bed.

Tobias's recall of his wife's early years was sketchy, but Buchanan knew he could fill in the gaps himself later.

Amelia Tobias had been born in Morning Sun, Iowa, thirty-three years ago. Daughter of Barbara and George Bloodworth. Mother a housewife, father a salesman for John Deere, strict Baptist home. Father died in a car accident when Amelia was twenty; mother died five years ago from cancer. Older brother Ben killed in action in Afghanistan three years ago. Amelia met Alex Tobias in 2004 at a gala party for the Miami City Ballet. Amelia was a ballet dancer, first with the New York City Ballet, but then she had moved to Miami to take a position with the ballet company there. She left the Miami City Ballet in 2006 and married Tobias soon after.

Tobias had paused at that point to stare down into his empty glass.

After she stopped dancing, she dedicated herself to building our life. I was nothing before I met Mel.

Well into the third vodka, Tobias had gotten pretty puffed up talking about how he had been hired by one of Florida's most prominent lawyers—Owen McCall. They had partnered up to start a new firm, luring away the biggest clients from McCall's old firm down in Miami. Success had come fast. Or as Tobias had poetically put it, "it was like we were white-water rafting in a lava flow of gold."

Tobias filled his garage with cars and his wine cellar with old Burgundies. The couple honeymooned in Provence, rented villas in St. Barts, and skied in the Italian Alps, often with Owen McCall and his wife Joanna. Tobias talked about how Joanna had taken Amelia under her wing and gotten her involved in charity work and social circles. The law firm thrived; money rolled in.

Mel was happy. We were happy.

But then Tobias had gone morose as he stared down into his vodka.

Buchanan paused at a note he had made. *No kids. Diagnosed fallopian tube blockage. Tobias seems upset talking about this.* But Buchanan knew it couldn't be as simple as that. It never was.

He rose and went back to the bed, picking up the *Florida Design* article again. He stared hard at the photograph of the blonde woman in the red dress but he was remembering something his dad had told him one morning in the duck blind.

See that crested grebe, Clay? Well, it's all bright and red now in summer. But come winter, it'll change itself to gray. It won't look like the same bird because it needs to blend in and hide.

Buchanan went back to his laptop and pulled up his e-mail. It took only a second for the photograph to download. It came up on his screen large and bright, and in lovely clear 500-pixel resolution.

Back at the restaurant, Buchanan had asked Alex Tobias if he had a good picture of his wife. Tobias had quickly e-mailed him one from his iPhone. At the time, Buchanan had thought it was strange he didn't have a photo of his wife in his wallet. But Alex Tobias was thirty-eight, ten years younger than he himself was. Some young guys didn't even carry wallets anymore.

Buchanan stared into Amelia Tobias's eyes.

Blue . . . Windex blue.

Tobias had told him that Amelia wore contacts, which she had left at the hospital. The contacts were tinted blue, and her eyes were really brown.

Buchanan leaned back in the chair.

So now Amelia Tobias had brown eyes. And maybe tomorrow she would have red, black, brown, or purple hair. In a couple days, he might be looking for a woman who looked nothing like this one. Because if she really was a runner, her primitive brain would kick in and she would do three instinctively animal things—find a place to hide, cover her tracks, and change her spots.

Disguises.

He had seen all manner of them, seen the weird lengths people would go to when they were desperate to disappear. Men shaving themselves bald, women resorting to bad wigs that made them look like the mother from *The Brady Bunch*. And then there was the tax evader he had chased for three years before he finally found him living in Costa Rica. The man was black but had bleached his skin with Fair & Lovely whitening cream and sewn up his nose, like a cook trussing a chicken, to make it look smaller.

How desperate was Amelia Tobias? And where the hell had she gone?

The voice came again, softer this time: *This one's special, Bucky.*

Buchanan glanced at his watch. It was almost ten, which meant Amelia had been officially missing for thirty-five hours. How far could a woman with a concussion—and no phone, money or ID—get in such a short time?

Buchanan had instructed Alex not to cancel his wife's credit cards, just on the chance she might try to call and get replacements. But there had been no activity on either her Visa or Amex accounts since last week, when Amelia charged a visit to a Pilates studio. Even if she did somehow get her hands on some money, without an ID there was no way she could rent a car or buy a plane ticket. She couldn't even apply for a replacement license because the Florida DMV wouldn't take cash to pay for the fee, and they required you to show a photo ID.

ID . . . that was what usually tripped runners up. Since 9/11, the world had gotten more complex, but his job had gotten easier because of it. There was no way to get along in the real world without an ID. The only way she could travel without ID was by bus. But even the Greyhound folks needed money. And so far, there was no indication Amelia had spent a dime.

There was a knock on the door. Buchanan went and opened it to see a young man wearing a W blazer and holding out a large white mailer.

"This just arrived for you, Mr. Buchanan," he said.

"Thanks," Buchanan said, taking the envelope. It was emblazoned with a gold and black logo—MCCALL AND TOBIAS ATTORNEYS AT LAW, and under that the firm's motto: "We're In This Together."

He stuck his hand in his pocket, groping for his wallet.

"That's not necessary, sir," the young man said, and started back down the hall.

"Wait," Buchanan called. "Can you ask them to send me up some bourbon?"

"Of course, sir. What kind?"

"I changed my mind. A bottle of Jack Daniels will do."

"Yes, sir. Right away, sir."

The young man left, and Buchanan took the envelope to the desk.

Back at the restaurant, he had told Tobias he needed access to his wife's computer and e-mails. Tobias had told him Amelia didn't have a computer and hated anything "techy."

The police had probably run her phone LUDs—local usage detail. But as long as they were looking at Tobias as a suspect in her accident, they weren't going to share those. And while it was easy enough to bribe an impound guy, Buchanan had no contacts in Lauderdale PD high enough to get a copy of the police report.

Normally, Buchanan would be able to access Amelia's iPhone contact list through her iCloud account. But unlike her fastidious husband, she had never bothered to back up her phone list.

Instead, she kept track of phone numbers in a Day Runner book. The only gadget she used, her husband said, was her Kindle, which she took to bed with her every night.

Buchanan tore open the mailer. Inside was a red leather Day Runner and the Kindle. He opened the Day Runner to the week that Amelia disappeared.

Nothing exceptional. Amelia had written in the Pilates appointment, a dinner at YOLO with Joanna, notations for "guild meet," "hair," and "Greta facial." Her last entry for Friday morning was "Fantasia Spa 9 a.m." The only other entry was a scribble in the box for tomorrow: "J's birthday!" Had to be Joanna McCall.

Buchanan flipped to the address section. Amelia had recorded names, addresses, and phone numbers in her neat straight handwriting. At first glance, the entries appeared to be all doctors and personal stuff like trainers and manicurists.

According to Tobias, Joanna McCall was Amelia's only close friend in Fort Lauderdale. Tobias had told him Amelia's only other friend was a woman named Carol Fairfield. Carol had been a dancer with the New York City Ballet but retired ten years ago and was now living in Minneapolis. Tobias said his wife flew up there every August to see Carol because their birthdays fell within days of each other. Tobias told him he never went on the visits, that it was Amelia's annual "chick trip" and Carol never came to Fort Lauderdale.

Buchanan had done a quick Google and PeopleFinders search for Carol Fairfield. It turned up nothing, but that meant she was probably using a married name now. His call to the New York City Ballet got him a promise from a clerk to check their records and get back to him.

Buchanan flipped the Day Runner's pages to *F*. No listing for Carol Fairfield. Odd, but then an old friend's address and phone were often just stored in a person's memory.

Problem was, Amelia didn't have a memory right now, according to her husband.

He tossed the Day Runner down and picked up the Kindle. The books and magazines runners downloaded left virtual breadcrumb trails. He had once traced an embezzler to Manila because the dumb fuck had downloaded *Lonely Planet Guide to the Philippines*.

He popped open the bright pink cover and fired up the e-reader. He got a screen that read ENTER PASSWORD.

Password? Who the hell password-protected their books?

He began to type in various combinations of Amelia's name, maiden name Bloodworth, and her date of birth, because he knew most people relied on the most obvious shit for their passwords.

Nothing.

He stared at the blinking cursor, but in his mind he was hearing Alex Tobias's petulant voice.

She takes the thing to bed with her every night.

Buchanan turned the reader over in his hands. It was a Kindle Fire, which meant it had Internet capability. He had a sudden vision of Amelia Tobias lying next to her husband with her Kindle, not reading her books or magazines, but reading her e-mails.

Carol Fairfield's e-mail was probably hidden in Amelia's Kindle. And maybe others that Amelia didn't want anyone to find, like that of a lover?

He switched off the Kindle and set it aside. He leaned his head back and closed his eyes as the long day finally began to settle into his muscles and brain with a throbbing ache.

There was a rumble of thunder, and he looked to the sliding glass doors in time to see a zigzag of lightning. He pushed himself from the chair, went to the doors, and slid them open. The heavy night air rushed in, smacking up against the artic air-conditioning. He stepped out onto the balcony.

Ten floors below, through the wind-whipped palm fronds, he could see the lights of the cars creeping along A1A. He couldn't see the beach because the streetlights were off. Knocked out by the coming storm, maybe?

There was a soft rap on the door. He went to answer it and found a woman in a black W uniform holding a tray. It held a bottle of Jack, a glass, and a bucket of ice.

"Your order, sir."

"Yeah, good. Just set it on the desk there, please."

The woman set it down and held out the room-service bill for Buchanan to sign. A rumble of thunder and a gust of wind came from the open sliding glass doors.

"Shall I shut that for you, sir?" the woman asked. "There's a bad storm coming."

"I guess so. It's already knocked out the streetlights."

"Streetlights?" The woman looked to the open doors. "Oh no, the city shuts them off on purpose."

"Why?"

"For the turtles."

"What?"

"The sea turtles, sir. It's turtle season. They lay their eggs in the sand and when the babies hatch, they use the moonlight to guide them to the ocean. But if the streetlights are on, they lose their way and follow the bright lights up to the highway."

Buchanan nodded. "Where they die."

"Yes, sir, I'm afraid so."

She started toward the sliding glass doors.

"No, leave them open, please," Buchanan said.

She nodded, gave him a smile, and left. The room was quiet for a moment and then came another rumble of thunder. Buchanan went to the tray, dropped some ice cubes into a glass and opened the bottle of Jack Daniels. He filled the glass halfway and drank it quickly.

Bucky?

The voice was there in his head again, not his dad this time but the other one, the gentle voice that came like a ghostly whisper, echoing in his hollow insides. The only one who ever called him by that nickname.

No more, Bucky, please.

And then she was gone.

He drained the glass, wincing at the scorching in his throat, waiting for the numbness to come. When it didn't, he poured another glass and took it out onto the balcony.

Below, it was nothing but blackness. He could smell the rain and hear the rumble, but there was nothing else there. Then, suddenly, there was a break in the black clouds and the moon emerged. Moonlight, soft and silvery, slid over the sand, lighting the way, and then it was gone.

CHAPTER TEN

Buchanan got only twenty feet into the lobby of the Lauderdale Yacht Club before he was stopped.

"Are you a member, sir?"

The man who had stepped in front of him was wearing a hard smile and a blue blazer with a little flag emblem on the breast pocket.

"No, I am not," Buchanan said. "I'm a guest of Joanna McCall's."

"Ah. Yes. She's waiting in the bar, sir. Just beyond the trophy case."

Buchanan eyed the silver cups and model boats in the case as he passed, and then paused at the entrance to the bar. It was well past lunchtime, but the place was still full of big dogs in Maas Brothers sherbet slacks and polo shirts, with a few Brooks Brothers types thrown in. There were only a few women, most of them old tsarinas and a few sleek young SWANKS—second wives and no kids.

He scanned the crowd for Joanna McCall, looking for a woman who matched the ones he had seen in the society rag *City & Shore*. He was looking for someone who was all teeth, tan, and gold jewelry. King Tut's trophy wife.

A blonde in the corner was waving to him. He went over to the table.

"Mr. Buchanan?" She offered him a smile and her hand. "I'm Joanna. Please, won't you sit down?"

He shook her soft warm hand and sat down across from her.

"Thanks for meeting me on such short notice," Buchanan said.

Her smile faded. "I want to do whatever I can to help find Mel."

Joanna McCall wasn't young, probably past fifty, and she had worked hard and paid a lot of money to turn back time. But with her good skin and thick blonde hair cut in a long bob, there was a softness to the woman that was undeniably attractive. Her green eyes were liquid and slightly reddened, and he knew it wasn't from the untouched Bloody Mary in front of her. The woman had been crying.

There was a scattering of pastel paint chips on the table, and she began to gather them up. "I'm sorry," she said. "We're building a new house up on Hillsboro Mile, and I was trying to pick out paint colors." She set them aside, shaking her head. "I can't decide anything right now."

Her voice carried just a hint of Southern drawl, but from where, he couldn't pinpoint.

"Would you like something to drink?" she asked.

She motioned to a waiter, and he was at the table in two quick strides. Buchanan ordered coffee. The half a bottle of Jack from the night before was still sloshing around in his gut.

Buchanan watched the waiter disappear, and when he looked back at Joanna McCall he knew she was studying him, almost like he was a biology specimen or an alien life-form. He was used to it. The people his clients employed—the gardeners, maids, and au pairs—were just shadows moving along the peripheries of their lives. But he was different, and Joanna McCall knew it. He was one rung up, like a dentist, someone who you didn't need until you were in pain.

"I'm sorry I was so abrupt when you called this morning," Joanna said.

"Suspicion is not a bad thing these days."

"It wasn't suspicion." She picked up the Bloody Mary and started to take a drink but then set it down. "It's just, this whole thing with Mel, it's just so unbelievable. Outside of getting a ticket once, I've never had to deal with the police. But Owen says you can be trusted and that you are very good at what you do."

"I get results," Buchanan said.

She nodded slowly. Buchanan wondered how much her husband had told her about how he worked. He decided she was probably like many of his clients who didn't want to know the dirty stuff.

The waiter brought his coffee. He poured in some cream and stirred in two sugars.

"Mrs. McCall," he began.

"Call me Joanna, please."

He took a sip of the coffee, considering his approach. Might as well go right for the jugular because she wouldn't be expecting it.

"Do you know where Amelia is?"

Her green eyes locked on his. "No. Why would you ask that?"

"Has she contacted you?"

"No. I would have told Alex if she had."

"Not if she wanted to get away from him."

Joanna's eyes were steady on his for a moment and then she looked away, taking a drink.

"You're her friend," Buchanan said. "Her only one here in Fort Lauderdale, from what I can tell. Do you know where she is?"

When Joanna looked back at him, her eyes were brimming. "No," she said softly. "I wish to God I did."

If she was lying, she was good at it, Buchanan thought. But her *jizz* was telling him that she was telling the truth.

Buchanan knew people were staring at them, probably wondering who was this guy who was making Owen McCall's wife cry. With his rumpled khakis and blue blazer he wasn't fooling anybody into thinking he belonged there.

"Mom? You okay?"

Buchanan looked up. A young woman had come to the table. She was wearing a short white tennis dress and carrying a racket. Her blonde hair was pulled back in a ponytail with little wet tendrils around her neck.

"Oh, hello, honey," Joanna said, smiling quickly.

"What's wrong?" the young woman asked.

"Nothing's wrong. I just have some business to talk about here."

The young woman's gaze moved to Buchanan. Her lips were pink pillows, and her wide-set eyes were a compelling hazel green flecked with gold. She was, Buchanan imagined, what Joanna McCall had looked like thirty years ago.

Joanna touched the woman's arm. "Are you and Elaine done with your game?"

"She had to leave early, and I don't have my car. Can Jack drive me home?"

"Not right now. I won't be finished here for a while. Why don't you go get showered and changed and—"

"I'll wait here with you."

Before Joanna could object, the young woman sat down. Joanna's eyes carried a hint of apology as she glanced at Buchanan. "Megan, this is Clay Buchanan," she said softly. "He's a private investigator looking into Amelia's disappearance."

Joanna reached up to gently push a strand of hair from the young woman's face but Megan eased away from her touch.

"This is my daughter, Megan, Mr. Buchanan," Joanna said.

"My pleasure," Buchanan said.

The young woman's eyes frosted over. She held Buchanan's stare for a moment and then turned back to her mother. As she did, he caught a slight movement of her chair as she scooted it farther away from him.

"Do you have to meet him here?" Megan asked softly, leaning close to Joanna.

Buchanan wanted to say something—like he didn't have a disease she could catch across a linen tablecloth—but he kept his mouth shut. He needed to keep Joanna relaxed, and insulting her daughter probably wasn't the best move.

"Yes, I do," Joanna said. "You don't have to stay."

Megan gave a small sigh and settled back in her chair. She crossed her legs and laid the tennis racket across her knees. "So they haven't found her yet?" she asked.

"You know about Mrs. Tobias?" Buchanan asked.

"Of course," Megan said.

Joanna's eyes were steady on Buchanan's. "Alex is trying to keep this quiet, as you can imagine. But Megan knew something was bothering me. I had to tell her." She shook her head slowly. "I still can't believe this is happening. I keep thinking about Amelia wandering around out there somewhere, alone and hurting."

She took a sip of the Bloody Mary.

"Mrs. McCall—"

"Joanna."

"Joanna . . . In my experience I've found that people who go missing always end up making contact. So if she contacts you, I need to know, okay? You won't be betraying her. You'll be helping her."

Joanna nodded slowly. "So that's all I can do? Just sit back and hope she calls?"

"No, of course not. For now, I need you to tell me anything you can think of about Amelia that might be useful to me."

"Like what?"

"Tell me about her and Alex."

Joanna glanced at Megan. The young woman was playing with something on her wrist, a red plastic stretch band with a locker-room key attached, but Buchanan knew she was listening intently to every word.

"I think it's best if you excuse us now, dear," Joanna said.

Megan let out a sigh. "Fine," she said. She rose but made no move to leave. "But if you ask me, this whole situation is just ridiculous."

"How do you mean?" Buchanan asked.

"Megan, please."

"Amelia ran away," Megan said, ignoring her mother. "Wives do that all the time, don't they? I don't understand why everyone's so bent out of shape about it."

"Megan, that's enough," Joanna said.

The young woman didn't look at her mother. Her eyes stayed steady on Buchanan's, as if daring him to ask her more, but finally she picked up her tennis racket. "I'm going to shower," she said. "I'll find someone to take me home."

Megan sauntered off toward the door. Buchanan watched her and then looked back at Joanna.

"I must apologize for my daughter," she said. "She can be a little immature sometimes."

"So tell me about Alex," Buchanan said.

Joanna kept her eyes lowered, and Buchanan had the feeling she was remembering something she wasn't going to share.

Let them fill the silence.

Joanna finally exhaled a deep sigh and looked up. "Alex . . . Where do I start?"

"How did they meet?"

"It was at a ballet gala."

"Yes, I know. But details are important and Amelia's husband isn't very good at details."

Joanna gave him a sad smile. "No, he's not." She took another sip of her drink before she went on. "Owen and I have been Miami City Ballet patrons for years now. One night, just after Owen and Alex started their own firm, Owen wanted Alex to come along, to get him to meet the right people. It was Christmas and it was *The Nutcracker*, of course."

"Of course."

"Well, Alex was bored, and at intermission, he wanted to leave. He's like a hummingbird, can't sit in one spot very long." Joanna paused, her expression turning distant, almost dreamy.

"But then, Amelia came onstage," she said. "She was Coffee."

"Coffee?"

"It's a solo. Amelia is very tall, and they always give the Coffee solo to the tall girls. She was wearing a harem costume, and the music is very slow and sensual, the movements very seductive." Joanna paused, smiling slightly. "You can imagine what it was like. The men in the audience— well, the straight men at least—they always sit up a little when Coffee comes on."

"Did Alex?"

She nodded. "The solo ends with the dancer doing a split and then sort of slithering across the stage toward the audience. Alex was spellbound. When Amelia crawled across that stage, it was like she was crawling to him."

Buchanan made a mental note to find the ballet on YouTube when he got back to his room.

Joanna sat back in her chair. "After the ballet, we went to the gala. There was a fundraiser thing where you could buy the pointe shoes of the dancers. Alex bid five hundred dollars for one of Amelia's old shoes."

Buchanan almost laughed. He picked up his coffee and took a long drink instead.

"Alex asked her out that same night," Joanna said. "He was relentless once he decided he wanted her. He wanted to get married right away but Amelia had just been promoted to soloist. It was two years before she finally said yes. It happened very quickly, just time for a little ceremony at the Church by the Sea before they were off to France on the honeymoon. Alex didn't even get her a real diamond until later."

"Was Amelia a good dancer?" he asked.

"Oh yes. She got a scholarship to study in New York and then was hired into the corps of the New York City Ballet when she was just a teenager. And in Miami, Mel had wonderful reviews."

Reviews? They would have popped up in a simple Google search. Why hadn't he found them? Then he knew.

"Did Amelia use a stage name?"

Joanna nodded. "Yes, there was a soloist in the New York City Ballet with a very similar name, so to avoid confusion they told Amelia she had to come up with a stage name. She was Melia Worth."

Amelia Bloodworth.

Melia Worth.

Mel Tobias.

"How did she end up down here?" Buchanan asked.

Joanna gave him a long stare. "The Miami City Ballet is a world-class company."

Okay, he had offended her somehow, maybe because she had forked over a lot of money to the ballet. But to his mind, Miami was Vegas South, a place people went when someone was chasing them or their options had dried up. Or when they wanted to reinvent themselves.

"I only meant that New York is a bigger arena," he said. "Why do you think she came down here?"

"I don't really know. Mel never told me anything about her years in New York. I know she got the scholarship when she was only sixteen and had to go live in New York. They have dorms for the younger dancers and people to watch over them. But it couldn't have been easy. And the New York City Ballet . . . well, it's huge and terribly competitive. It's not uncommon for dancers to leave there if they feel they can get better roles at a smaller company."

"You said she had great reviews in Miami. Why did she quit?" Buchanan asked.

"She got injured," Joanna said. "She took a really bad fall during a performance and broke her hip. It was bad enough that she couldn't dance anymore."

Buchanan wondered why Tobias had neglected to mention the injury. He remembered that the guy had turned pretty morose for a while during their interview, and Buchanan had assumed it was because they hadn't been able to have children. But there were obviously more currents flowing under the surface of this marriage. There always were.

And it explained why Amelia had finally given in to Alex. Dancers didn't make much money, and Alex Tobias had to have looked like a pretty good exit ramp after she got injured.

"Did Amelia ever mention a friend she had named Carol Fairfield?" he asked.

Joanna nodded. "Yes, they were in the corps together in New York. Amelia used to visit her every summer. I think Carol lived in Chicago."

"Minneapolis."

"Yes, that's it. I never met her. But Amelia used to really look forward to seeing her."

"What about other friends, maybe someone from her childhood?"

Joanna shook her head slowly. "I can't remember her ever mentioning anyone. Her family is all gone now, you know."

"Did she talk about her childhood to you?" he asked.

Joanna smiled slightly. "She was from Morning Sun, Iowa. I think they have like eight hundred people living there or something. I always had the feeling Amelia was a little, well, embarrassed about where she came from. The only thing she really talked to me about was her ballet classes there. She told me her mother used to drive her down to Burlington three times a week. I don't know anything about her father. Amelia never talked about him."

"Did you know she had an older brother?" he asked.

Joanna nodded. "Yes. I never met him, but I got the feeling they were close. His death hit her really hard. She was quite depressed for a while after that, as you can imagine."

"Would you say that you and Amelia are close?" Buchanan asked.

"Well, Amelia's a very private person. But yes, I'd say we're close."

"Alex told me that when they first got married you took Amelia under your wing."

Joanna nodded and smiled. "You have to understand. Amelia grew up wearing clothes from Sears and eating Swiss steak on Sundays."

Buchanan wondered if those details came from Amelia herself or just Joanna's imagination.

"She had to leave high school when she got her dance scholarship, and it took her a couple years to get her GED up there," Joanna went on. "She didn't go to college, so marrying a man like Alex and moving into his world, she was a little . . ." Joanna gestured toward the room at large.

Buchanan took it all in with one sweeping glance. The glossy women, the tanned men, the tall bank of east windows that looked out on a huge sapphire pool, backdropped by sleek white yachts.

"Intimidated?" Buchanan said.

"I was going to say lost," Joanna said.

The waiter reappeared, asking Joanna if she wanted another drink. She declined, but Buchanan got a refill on his coffee. He needed to take a piss, but he had the feeling that if he took a break now, Joanna McCall's trip down memory lane might hit a dead end. The woman suddenly looked really beat.

Joanna was looking around the room again, but finally her eyes came back. "After she quit dancing, Amelia was sort of adrift. So I thought if she got involved in social things, it would help. I made sure she met all my friends, and I helped her fit in. She tried very hard. I mean, she had no real education, but she was really quick to pick things up."

"What do you mean?"

"Well, after she stopped dancing, she seemed determined to remake herself. She changed her hair color and hired a personal shopper at Neiman's to pick out her clothes. She threw herself into redoing that old house, agonizing over every detail. She took gourmet cooking classes and got those Rosetta Stone tapes to learn Italian and French. One summer we all rented a villa in Lucca and by the first week, Amelia was speaking Italian to the maid. Every time I saw her she had a book in her hand."

"Or a Kindle?"

Joanna gave him an odd look.

Buchanan reached into his canvas bag and pulled out the pink Kindle, laying it on the table.

"Oh, you mean that reader thing," Joanna said. "Yes, she always seemed to have that with her. But it was more than books. It was like there was always so much more to Amelia than what you saw on the surface." Her eyes brimmed again. "And now this brain injury . . ."

She picked up a cocktail napkin and dabbed at her eyes. "I'm sorry," she said softly. "I'm just really tired. I haven't slept well since this all started. Are we finished?"

"Just one more thing. How's their marriage?"

"Alex adores her."

"Does she adore him?"

Joanna leveled her eyes at him. "She never talks to me about her marriage. She's very private that way."

"You saw them together all the time. What do you think?"

"I think she loves him very much."

But she had taken an extra beat before answering. If she knew anything about what went on below the surface of the couple's marriage, she wasn't going to tell him. Women were no different than men. They protected their own.

Joanna McCall was staring at her glass.

"I have to ask you one more personal thing," Buchanan said.

She looked up.

"Was Amelia seeing someone else?"

Joanna was silent, just staring at him. Then she let out a long sigh. "I don't think so," she said softly.

"Think hard. Did you ever see her with someone? Did she ever mention a name? If there was another man, she might have gone to him."

"I was her best friend. I would have known." She shook her head slowly. "No, there was no one else in her life. I'm sure of it."

Buchanan sat back in his chair. He realized the background murmur had died. The room was empty except for the waiter hovering by the bar. And a man in a black suit standing stiffly by the door watching them.

Joanna looked toward the man and gave a discreet nod. He started toward their table.

"If you don't mind, I'd like to end this now," Joanna said, looking back at Buchanan. "If you need to speak with me again, you can reach me at home."

She didn't make any move to get up, and Buchanan realized she probably expected him to rise first in respect. He did, and that's when he saw the glint of metal on the chair next to hers. Two metal crutches, which had been hidden beneath the white linen tablecloth.

The man in the black suit was at the table. "Are you ready to leave, ma'am?" he asked.

"Yes, Jack, I am, thank you," she said.

The man helped her out of her chair. Joanna slipped on the crutches and they started slowly away.

"Mrs. McCall?" Buchanan called after her.

She turned and smiled. "Joanna."

Buchanan smiled back. "I just wanted to wish you a happy birthday, Joanna."

Her smiled faded. "Birthday? Today's not my birthday. Whatever gave you that idea?"

"Sorry, my mistake."

She turned and continued on to the door, her driver's hand protective on her shoulder. Buchanan watched until she was gone and then sat down at the table. He reached into his bag and pulled out Amelia's Day Runner, flipping it open to the current week.

No, he had remembered it correctly. Amelia had inked in "J's Birthday!" for today. If it wasn't Joanna McCall, who the hell was it?

She ran away. Wives do it all the time, don't they?

Buchanan had the feeling that Megan McCall had unknowingly given voice to his own suspicion—that Amelia had a lover somewhere.

He looked out the windows at the gleaming pool and the yachts beyond. Past the yachts, across the Intracoastal Waterway, he could see a row of pastel mansions. He closed the Day Runner and rose.

It was time to poke around inside the Tobias home.

CHAPTER ELEVEN

The Tobiases' maid, a small woman in a white uniform and severe black bun, gave Buchanan the same weird greeting as the guy back at the yacht club: a smile on her mouth but suspicion in her eyes.

Buchanan had called Alex Tobias, asking if he could look around the home for clues about Amelia, and Tobias, tied up in Miami inking the papers of some important merger, told him he would call Esperanza and let her know Buchanan was coming.

Esperanza looked like she hadn't gotten the call. But when Buchanan showed her his driver's license, she stepped aside, holding the massive carved wood door to let him into the foyer.

It was freezing, like walking into a meat locker.

A nicely decorated meat locker, though—shiny white Carrera marble, white wainscoted walls, and a staircase that wound like a helix, drawing his eye upward two stories to a chandelier that floated from the ceiling like a giant crystal sea hydra. There was a sleek white pedestal table in the middle of the foyer with a huge arrangement of white orchids and thin curls of branches. Tucked off in one corner was a white baby grand piano.

It was, Buchanan noted, one of those Disklavier models with a compact disc player stuck below the keyboard that you could program to play anything from Rachmaninoff to Jerry Lee Lewis. The rich man's player piano, except you didn't have to sit there and pump the thing with your feet, just hit "Play" on the remote.

"Mr. Tobias said I need to show you his house."

Buchanan turned back to the maid. She looked perturbed, though whether it was because a stranger was in her lair or because she was expected to babysit him, he couldn't tell.

"That's not necessary, Miss . . . ?" He paused respectfully.

"Mrs. Diaz," she said.

He smiled. "I can look around by myself, Mrs. Diaz. I'm sure Mr. Tobias wouldn't want you wasting your valuable time with me."

Her eyebrows knitted into one black caterpillar. But then she turned and walked away, her shoes squeaking on the marble.

Buchanan looked around at the rooms and hallways radiating off the foyer.

Where to start? The bedrooms were always the richest depositories of clues, but he decided to make a quick tour of the first floor to give Esperanza enough time to lose track of him.

Two white marble pillars guarded the entry to what Buchanan supposed was a living room, though he was sure not much living went on inside.

It was the size of a basketball court, more white marble topped with two zebra rugs. Two curved black silk sofas set off a coral-rock fireplace like quotation marks. A pair of modern white leather chairs sat in lonely isolation by a bank of long windows. The details were just as stark: crystal lamps with silver lacquer shades, crystal amoeba ashtrays, and lots of mirrors.

He moved on through more white rooms, stopping in what he guessed was Alex's study. It was all white lacquer built-ins, the chrome-and-glass desk topped only with a white Apple laptop. The only thing on the wall was a framed diploma from the Florida State School of Law.

Buchanan headed down a long white hallway lined with large framed black-and-white photographs. They were landscapes, beautiful stark images of swamps, egrets, and twisty trees swagged with Spanish moss. He caught the signature in the corner of one—Clyde Butcher—and filed the name away in his memory.

He poked his head in an open door. It was large room, dark as a cave. There was a dimmer switch just inside the door, and as he eased it upward, the room came to life—soft ceiling spots illuminating gray suede sofas and ottomans facing a ten-foot projection screen built into a wall of black cabinets.

Buchanan lingered just outside the door, thinking about his dusty forty-two-inch Samsung with its ugly tangle of cable cords. He turned off the dimmer and moved on.

In the white dining room, he paused. Three walls of mirrors and one of floor-to-ceiling windows that faced west offering a view of a flagstone patio, white loungers, and a glistening aqua pool. Squinting in the sunlight, he could glimpse the bow of a white yacht. He turned away from the blinding sun, but the outdoors was still there all around him in the mirrors, reflected back as if to infinity.

For a second, he felt disoriented, like when he was seven and his dad had taken him to the funhouse at Buckroe Beach Park. He shut his eyes, trying to tamp down the beginnings of a headache.

What kind of people lived in a place like this? A place where everything was bleached out and bone bare, where the only color came from outside and was glimpsed through mirrors?

He left the dining room, passing through a gleaming butler's pantry and into the kitchen. More French doors, white countertops, two giant Sub-Zero fridges, a hulking black stove. Black and silver pots and pans hung like art from a ceiling rack. There were some arrangements of ruffle-edged dishes and some rustic-looking baskets stuck here and there for a humble effect. The one spot of color was a white ceramic bowl filled with acid-green apples.

A Palm Beach designer's wet dream of Provence.

Buchanan was tempted to open one of the Sub-Zeros to see if there was any food. He grabbed the refrigerator handle and gave it a jerk but then heard the squeak of rubber soles on marble and turned.

Esperanza was standing there, holding a dustpan and tiny broom, staring at him. He figured this was as good a time as any to pump her for whatever she could offer. But first, he had to defrost her a little.

He shut the refrigerator and gave her his best smile. "I was looking for some water."

She moved to a cabinet and took out a tumbler. She filled it from the tap and held it out.

Buchanan took the glass. "Thank you."

She seemed to be waiting for something, so he drained the water and handed the glass back to her. She rinsed it thoroughly and then stuck it in the dishwasher. With a glance back at him, she set about wiping down the spotless counter.

"This is a beautiful house," Buchanan said. "I don't think I've ever seen anything like it. It must be a lot of work for you, keeping things so . . . white."

She kept wiping.

"It's not easy," Buchanan went on, "keeping people's houses up just the way they like them to be, I mean. I know how hard it is. My mother was a housekeeper."

It wasn't a lie, exactly. His mother had changed the sheets and scoured the bathrooms at the Hilton off Interstate 38 for ten years. She came home at night smelling of Pine-Sol with her pockets filled with pilfered tubes of Crabtree & Evelyn hand lotion.

The wiping slowed, but Esperanza still didn't look at him.

"Would you mind answering a few questions, Mrs. Diaz?" Buchanan asked.

She turned. "What kind questions?"

Start easy. "How long have you worked for Mr. and Mrs. Tobias?"

"Two months, almost."

Shit. Not much time for her to get a good bead on the domestic dramas here. "Did Mrs. Tobias hire you?" he asked.

"No, Mr. Tobias. He hire all the maids."

"All? There are others working here?"

She hesitated, but her dark eyes were steady on his. "No, only me. I mean he hire all the ones who have come here." She paused. "My boss, he say Mr. Tobias not seem to be happy with anyone."

"So Mr. Tobias is . . . hard to please?"

Again she hesitated. "Better I not talk. He write my checks. I need this job bad."

Buchanan nodded. "What about Mrs. Tobias? Is she hard to work for?"

Esperanza shook her head. "No, she nice lady."

She turned away, stowing the towel she had been using under the sink. Her eyes roamed around the gleaming kitchen, as if looking for something she had missed. Buchanan had the feeling that even though she had worked in this house only two months, she didn't miss much.

"Mrs. Diaz, do you live here in the house?" he asked.

She shook her head. "No, I come every morning. Except Monday. That is my day off."

"So you were here Friday?"

She nodded.

"What time do you start work here?"

"I get here at nine. But last Friday I come at eight because my husband go to work early that day and he drop me off early."

"And Mrs. Tobias was here that morning?"

Another nod.

"You're sure? You saw her?"

"Yes, I saw her, right here in kitchen." Esperanza glanced toward a door in the corner. "I always come in that door, and Mrs. Tobias was here in kitchen. She was cleaning the sink."

"Cleaning? You're sure?"

"Yes. She wear my yellow gloves and she clean sink. I think I surprise her and that she . . ." She frowned. "She get all red and I think she . . ."

"Was embarrassed?" Buchanan finished.

Esperanza nodded. "I think sometimes she clean house before I get here but I did not know before then. When she see me she was . . . embarrassed, yes, that is the word."

Buchanan looked beyond the maid out the French doors. A young man in shorts and a T-shirt was scooping leaves from the pool, his brown body swaying to whatever was piped in from his earbuds.

"That Friday," Buchanan went on, looking back at Esperanza, "did you notice anything strange about Mrs. Tobias?"

"Strange?"

"Did she act strange? Say anything strange? Did she seem normal?"

Esperanza was quiet, thinking. "She quiet. She stay in her bedroom most the day."

"Did anyone come over?"

She shook her head.

"Phone calls?"

"We not have phone here. Just the cell phones."

Buchanan let out a sigh.

"There was one thing strange," Esperanza said. "Every day, she has glass of red wine at four o'clock. Friday I take it to her bedroom, and she wasn't there. I set it on bed table and I start to leave but I hear her crying. I go to bathroom door because I worry she not well, and I see her sitting on edge of tub crying."

"Why was that strange?" Buchanan said.

"She was reading."

"Reading?"

"Yes. She cry while she read."

Buchanan felt a click in his brain, the click that always came when something was falling into place. "She was reading her Kindle," he said.

Esperanza frowned. "Kindle?"

"It's a small computer that stores books. Was she reading that?"

Esperanza nodded briskly. "Yes, that pink thing that she keep by her bed."

"What happened after that?" Buchanan prodded.

"I sneak out so she not get . . . embarrassed. About an hour later, she come downstairs and tell me she is going out."

"Was she wearing a black dress? Like a fancy party dress?"

Esperanza nodded.

"Did she tell you where she was going?"

"No. She seemed in hurry."

"And she left in her own car?"

Another nod. "It was raining, so she used the door over there to go straight into the garage."

"No one was with her?"

"No."

"Did she take anything with her?"

"Just a purse, I think."

"No suitcase?"

"Suitcase? Wait, yes, she had suitcase. But she bring it in not out."

"Bring it in? What do you mean exactly?"

"I remember good now. She left, went to garage and I hear the car go out. But then she come back in front door. I was going up the stairs when she came back in. She had suitcase. She see me and tell me to take suitcase back to garage."

"Garage? Are you sure she said to take it into the garage?"

"Yes. That where I put it. Then she drive away."

Buchanan shook his head. None of it made any sense. Why would Amelia tell the maid to take a suitcase to the garage?

"Did you move the suitcase after that?" he asked.

"No, it still in garage."

"Can you show it to me?"

She nodded, and Buchanan followed her through a door, down a narrow hall, and through another door. The four-car garage was huge and almost bare, except for some stainless metal shelving holding large plastic storage bins, two sleek bikes suspended on racks, and a shiny red BMW motorcycle with tires so clean Buchanan doubted it had ever seen pavement. Except for one tiny oil stain, the place was as clean as an operating room.

"Mrs. Diaz, how many cars do the Tobiases have?" he asked.

She paused. "Three. Mr. Tobias drive that big white truck thing and Mrs. Tobias drive a white car that has a silver cat on front of hood."

"A Jaguar?"

"I don't know. Very nice car. Very new."

"What about a small dark blue car? Did you ever see that here?"

She nodded and pointed. "Yes. It is always there. I not know where it is now."

"Where is Mrs. Tobias's white car?"

"I think it is out being tuned. Yes, Mr. Tobias said something about the car need tuning."

"Where did you put the suitcase?"

She pointed again to a shelf. Buchanan went to it and pulled down the suitcase. It was maybe three by four, and covered in soft tan leather. It looked old, like something out of one of those British colonial movies. He undid the straps and opened it. Empty.

"You're sure Mrs. Tobias brought this into the house that day?" Buchanan said, turning to Esperanza.

She nodded, but she was frowning, as if she was upset with herself. It made him think, not for the first time, that sometimes the people whose lives were straightforward—people like maids, waitresses, and security guards—liked getting involved in his investigations, liked being brushed by the cold fingers of mystery. And Esperanza was thinking that she had somehow disappointed him.

Buchanan closed the suitcase and put it back on the shelf. "You've been a great help to me, Mrs. Diaz," he told her.

She gave him a cautious smile. "Mrs. Tobias nice lady. I hope she come home."

"I'd like to look around some more if it's okay with you?"

"Yes. I will be in kitchen if you need me."

Buchanan followed her back into the house and then retraced his steps to the foyer. He climbed the helix to the second floor, looking in three rooms that appeared to be guest suites. There was a set of double white doors at the end of a long hallway so he headed toward them. The doors opened with a sigh onto a master suite dominated by an oversized bed decked out in a quilted white silk bedspread and a litter of throw pillows. It faced a white fireplace surrounded by more built-ins like those downstairs. It was only after Buchanan ventured farther into the room and turned around that he saw it—an exploding nova of color on the far wall.

A painting of a face. A woman's face? He went closer.

Yeah, it was a woman because now he could see the harsh brush strokes that formed her long eyelashes, and a string of pearls around the elongated neck. It was modern in style with the carved-up perspective of Picasso crossed with the Crayola crassness of Leroy Neiman. He didn't know much about art, just what he had absorbed from hanging around the homes of clients. So he wasn't sure exactly what he was looking at.

But he knew who he was looking at.

It was Amelia. Bright primary yellow streaks for the hair, pool-blue for the eyes, a magenta slash for a mouth. And just like in her photographs, that strange feeling of emptiness behind it all.

He turned to the fireplace, topped with a big plasma TV, and flanked by shelves of books. The books were, Buchanan thought, the first evidence that normal human beings, with likes and dislikes, interests and pastimes, dwelled here.

He did a quick scan of the left side. The titles were variations on a theme: *The Story of My Life* by Clarence Darrow. *In the Shadow of the Law* by Kermit Roosevelt. *Emotional Intelligence: Why It Can Matter More Than IQ* by Daniel Goleman. *The Legal Analyst: A Toolkit for Thinking about the Law* by Ward Farnsworth. *One L* by Scott Turow.

He turned to the right shelf. It held hardcover fiction bestsellers, stuff by Jodi Picoult, Wally Lamb, Mitch Albom, Nicholas Sparks. Another shelf held travel books, mainly slick coffee-table editions about Tuscany, Paris, the Greek isles. On the bottom shelf was a collection on fitness: *French Women Don't Get Fat. Perfection Through Pilates. The Happy Book: 30 Fun-Filled Exercises for Greater Joy.*

It was all pap. Nothing that was evidence of the kind of mind that Joanna McCall described as "so much more than what you saw on the surface." And, oddly, no books about dance.

Buchanan turned, looking for something, anything, in the vast white bedroom that could tell him what kind of woman he was looking for.

There was a frosted glass door across the room that he suspected to be a closet. He didn't know much about art, but he was up to speed on clothes and labels because what people chose to hang on their bodies or put on their feet spoke volumes about their personalities. Plumage . . . it was all part of the *jizz.*

He opened the door. It was Alex's closet. Walls of white lacquer and glass cabinets and long shelves. Racks of dark suits on wood hangers at perfectly spaced intervals. Rows of gleaming shoes, drawers filled with folded dress shirts still bearing their paper laundry bands, pullout metal racks filled with a rainbow of silk ties. And behind one glass panel, pastel cashmere sweaters stacked like mints in a candy box.

He left the closet and turned to a second frosted glass door. It opened onto a closet even larger than the first one. The same walls of white cabinets and long shelves but transformed into a mini-Versailles of gilt, chandeliers, and mirrors. And in the middle of it all, sitting like the Queen of Hearts' throne, was a tufted blood-red satin chair and a small matching ottoman.

Alex's closet had given off a faint smell of newly polished shoes. But Amelia's was heavy with perfume.

The scent was oddly familiar, and Buchanan closed his eyes, trying to place it. He was certain he had smelled it before, somewhere and sometime deep in his past.

Finally he opened his eyes and began to explore the closet. Behind one door was a pyramid of matched Vuitton luggage, ranging in size from a trunk on the bottom up to a large purse on top. So where had that odd suitcase down in the garage come from? He tried one of the cases but it was locked. He turned over a white airline tag on one of the suitcase handles—MSP, FLIGHT 86, 8-23-14.

He recognized the airport code: Minneapolis–St. Paul. He made a mental note to call the New York City Ballet office again about Carol Fairfield.

Buchanan turned his attention to the racks of clothes. Amelia's taste ran to classic styles and neutrals, lots of gray Armani, beige Burberry, and black and white Chanel. Her taste in accessories was just as bland—low-heeled Chanel slingbacks and Prada pumps, black Fendi clutches and tan Gucci totes. There was a drawer of beige and black sweaters, and another drawer holding scarves and shawls, Hermès mainly, in muted colors. He opened a third drawer but stopped halfway when he saw the neatly folded lingerie in white, beige, and black. Expensive, sure, but nothing to stir any man's juices. When he tried to close the drawer, it stuck on something in the back.

He pulled out a small shopping bag. The writing on the front said "La Perla, Bal Harbour." When he opened it, he saw a tangle of color, and he pulled out a delicate web of lace—a turquoise bra. The bag also held a sheer red camisole and a tiny triangle of panties the color of a ripe peach.

He had a hunch these weren't for old Alex. A sudden snippet of music floated into Buchanan's head, some old disco song about a guy named Tommy who "lost his lady two months ago, maybe he'll find her, maybe he won't."

"Cherchez La Femme." That was the name of it.

Buchanan put the lingerie back in the bag and the bag back in its hiding place. Then he stood, hands on hips, and exhaled a deep breath of frustration. This was nuts. On the surface, Amelia Tobias was a cipher. But experience had taught him that no one really was, at heart. Especially a woman who kept peach-colored panties hidden in her closet.

And that damn perfume, *her* perfume, was there, swirling about him.

What was he missing?

His eyes traveled over the cabinets. In the far corner, one cabinet door stood ajar, and he spotted the corner of a box on the floor inside. Not a nice box that matched the white cabinets either; this was plain old cardboard. He went to the closet and pulled it out.

The old box, big enough to hold a microwave oven, was crushed down to half its original size. Someone had written Amelia's name and address in Magic Marker on one flap. And in smaller type, a return address in Morning Sun, Iowa.

Buchanan slipped a finger under the yellowed packing tape and opened the box.

On top was a pilled purple cardigan sweater, a stuffed bear missing one ear, a pair of beat-up pink ballet shoes, and a small faded blue T-shirt with lettering on the front: UNIVERSITY OF OKOBOJI.

Buchanan dragged the box across the carpet and sat down in the red silk chair. He set the top items aside, revealing a layer of books. A "Tiger" yearbook from Crusade High School, Childcraft volume five

Life in Many Lands. A stained yellow cloth book called *Dance for a Diamond Star* by Rosemary Sprague. A children's book by Neil Gaiman called *The Graveyard Book.* And a worn picture book by Eleanor Estes called *The Hundred Dresses.*

Buchanan turned the book over and read the back copy.

Wanda Petronsky wore the same faded-blue dress to school every day. It was always clean but it looked as though it had never been ironed properly. One day when a classmate showed up wearing a bright new dress that was much admired, Wanda said, "I have a hundred dresses at home." That had started the teasing . . .

Buchanan set the books on the little red ottoman and returned to the cardboard box. More old clothes, a small blue plastic jewelry box, a plastic flamingo, and some letters bound in ribbon, the top one with a return address of a military base in Kandahar, Afghanistan. He set those aside, along with a red Capezio ballet slipper box filled with snapshots. One thing left in the box. He pulled out a large green scrapbook.

From the first page, he knew what he was looking at: Amelia's history as a dancer. It was all there, from the faded program of Amelia Bloodworth's first ballet recital at age seven at Graham's Dance Center in Burlington, Iowa, right through to her last review as Melia Worth with the Miami City Ballet. Page after yellowed page of her touchstone moments: a letter of acceptance from the School of American Ballet in New York; her first review in *Dance Magazine* from a student concert; a copy of her corps member contract with the New York City Ballet.

Outside of the one student concert review, there were no others from Amelia's time in New York, and Buchanan knew it was because as a corps member, her only job was to blend in. But the reviews from the Miami years, when she was a soloist, were glowing, all mentioning Melia Worth's "intelligence," "sensuality," and "joy in movement."

And the photographs . . .

Heart-shaped face and big dark eyes, framed by the severe ballerina-bun hairstyle in a dark shade. And always a dazzling smile of pure joy, whether it was a candid moment caught in performance or a formal portrait headshot. Melia Worth was lit from within.

He thought of the blank face of Amelia Tobias in the society rags. It was like he was looking at two different women.

Buchanan slumped back in the red silk chair. The sweet perfume was heavy in his nostrils, teasing his brain.

Magnolias . . . it was magnolias.

I'm here, Bucky.

Buchanan shut his eyes. The smell was all around him and suddenly, so was she. Coming in from the backyard in their little house in Berry Hill carrying the flowers just cut from the tree. Arranging them in a blue vase, pouring in Sprite to make them last because magnolias never lasted long enough.

When you coming back?

Around eight maybe.

It's going to rain. The tires are bad on your car. You should take my truck.

I'll be fine. I'll be back before you can miss me, Bucky.

Buchanan opened his eyes. The perfume was still there, but she was gone.

He sat there for a long time, his hands light on the scrapbook open in his lap. Enough . . . he had to get his mind back to the task. He had to find something to unlock Amelia Tobias's life because he knew from experience that the longer a runner was missing, the harder it was to find her.

He looked down at the things he had set on the ottoman. Maybe it was there in her brother's letters or in the box of old photos. He'd have to take it all back to the hotel and go through it carefully. He set the scrapbook back in the box and repacked all the other things. As he closed the flaps, his eyes caught the return address in Morning Sun.

Amelia's family were all dead, and his instincts were telling him that if her memory returned she might go to Carol Fairfield—or maybe a lover. Still, he'd have to check out the Morning Sun connection to be sure.

He rose and picked up the box. He started to walk away but then stopped, staring at the ottoman.

There was something lodged in the side of the cushion. He bent down and pulled it out. It was a tiny rubber bone.

Damn. It wasn't an ottoman. And that Vuitton purse . . .

He went back to the first closet of luggage and pulled down the purse. It had mesh on both ends. It was a dog carrier. He looked at the airline tag. Someone had inked in: "Brody Tobias."

But where was the dog? He hadn't seen any other evidence of an animal, not even a water dish in the kitchen.

He put the dog carrier back in its place, and hoisting up the box of memories, he retraced his steps to the foyer. He left the cardboard box there and went to the kitchen. Esperanza was just coming in from the French door leading out to the patio.

"You are finished now?" she asked.

"Yeah, I'm just leaving," Buchanan said. His eyes did a quick sweep of the kitchen. No sign of the dog. Maybe it had died. But that airline tag had been for a trip to Minneapolis just three months ago.

"Mrs. Diaz, does Mrs. Tobias have a dog?" he asked.

She smiled. "Yes. Brody the dog."

"Where is he?"

"At dog place."

"What, the vet?"

"No, place where they clean him. Mrs. Tobias take Brody there the day she left. But then she didn't come home and things go crazy around here." She said something else in Spanish, shaking her head.

Buchanan was trying to remember what was in Amelia's Day Runner. The Friday of the car accident there had been a notation about an appointment at a place called Fancy . . . no, Fantasia Spa. He had assumed it was her own spa.

"I better call Mr. Tobias," Esperanza said. "He go get Brody at dog place."

"No, you're very busy," Buchanan said quickly. "I'll tell Mr. Tobias about the dog."

Esperanza gave him a small smile and thanked him. Buchanan said a quick good-bye, grabbed the cardboard box from the foyer, and left. He had no intention of telling Alex Tobias about the dog. Because there was a good chance that Amelia might remember the dog and go back to get it. If she hadn't already.

He pulled out his cell as he walked toward his rental car. He summoned Siri and asked for Fantasia Dog Spa. Her nasal voice came back immediately with the number and dialed it for him.

"Hi. You've reached Fantasia Dog Spa. We're closed for the day and your fur baby is tucked in for the night. But if you'd like to leave a message . . ."

Damn it. He clicked off and looked back at the Tobias mansion, glowing deep pink in the waning sunlight. He'd call again first thing in the morning.

But for now, there was nothing to do but go back to the hotel. There was a minibar stocked with good scotch and a Kindle that might be unlocked with a dog's name.

CHAPTER TWELVE

When Amelia woke, the room was cold. It took a few disorienting moments for her to remember she was in the boardinghouse in Brunswick, Georgia. She heard a flapping sound and looked to the window. The shade, pulled down against the wan morning light, was moving in the stiff breeze.

She started to pull the chenille bedspread up over her but then remembered the small white dog that had nestled in the crook of her knees. She was gone. Yet in her mind, she was still there, as real and as warm as . . .

"Brody," she said.

She bolted upright. Brody was a dog. *Her* dog. She could see him and feel him as clearly as if he was there in the room with her—a tiny terrier-Chihuahua mutt.

She could suddenly remember everything about him. He was black, one of his ears was broken, and the tip of his tail looked like a paint-brush dipped in white. A kid had found him under a freeway bridge, tied to a chain-link fence, probably abandoned by a homeless person. He was sick with pneumonia, infested with fleas, and starving. The kid had the good sense to drop the dog off at Animal Control nearby. It was there that Amelia had found him, curled up in a cat cage because the dog cages were all filled with howling pit bulls. He was twenty-four hours away from being put down.

Why had she been at Animal Control that day? She couldn't remember. All she could remember was that she knew she had to have that dog. And she knew she had to have him here with her now.

She sat still in bed as a flood of emotion washed through her chest like warm water. It was relief. Relief that things were coming back, just like the doctor had said they would.

Another memory pushed forward. Alex. And what his face had looked like when she walked in the door cradling the sick dog.

What the hell is that?

I found him at Animal Control.

Animal Control? I don't want a dog in the house, Mel.

Why not? I want—

They're dirty. And who's going to take care of it?

I will.

Mel . . .

I'm keeping him, Alex.

Amelia swung her legs over the side of the bed. She had to find out if Brody was okay because she couldn't be sure that Alex wouldn't get rid of him.

Pulling the spread off the bed, she wrapped it around her and went downstairs to the black rotary phone on the hall table.

Details were starting to come into focus fast now, and she could see herself handing Brody across a counter to a smiling plump-faced woman and she could hear muted barking in the background just discernible below the murmur of Muzak.

We'll take good care of him, Mrs. Tobias.

She had left Brody somewhere. The vet?

You can pick him up tomorrow after nine.

He hadn't been sick, she remembered. She had taken him in for a teeth cleaning and grooming and they had to keep him overnight. But where? What was the name of the place? She shut her eyes, trying to summon a name, but all she could see in her mind were hippos dancing in tutus. Like that old Walt Disney movie . . .

Fantasia.

Her eyes shot open and she grabbed the receiver. She dialed information and they connected her.

"Good morning, Fantasia Dog Spa."

"Yes, hello, this is Mrs. Tobias and—"

"Oh, hi, Mrs. Tobias. This is Kristin."

Kristin. The young groomer with the lizard tattoo. "Yes, yes, hello Kristin," she said. "I'm calling to check on Brody."

"Well, we just opened like five minutes ago and I haven't had time to check in on him yet."

"But he's still there?"

"Oh yeah. I saw him last night. He was fine, just a little mopey because he wants to go home. Weren't you supposed to pick him up yesterday?"

Yesterday? She had dropped Brody off and then gone home. She remembered that later she had showered and put on the Chanel dress. Everything after that was still a black blur.

"Mrs. Tobias?"

"Yes, I'm here," Amelia said. "I've . . . I've had a change in plans and had to go out of town suddenly. Something has come up, a family emergency, and I have to be away from home for a couple weeks."

"No problem. I'll call Mr. Tobias so he can come get—"

"No! No, don't call my husband."

Silence on the other end. Amelia took a deep calming breath. "I'd like to arrange for Brody to be sent to me."

"Sent? Sent where?"

"Georgia," Amelia said.

"Geez, Mrs. Tobias, I don't know if we could send Brody—"

"Of course you can. We can arrange it all with the airline and you could have him flown up here. You can just charge it to my account, right?"

"Wouldn't it be easier if I just called Mr. Tobias and—"

"No, don't do that." Amelia interrupted. "My husband is out of town on business for the next two weeks. I need you to send Brody to me."

"Well, geez, Mrs. Tobias. I need to talk to Mrs. Chapinski, and she won't get here 'til like nine."

Mrs. Chapinski . . . she was the spa owner. Amelia knew the woman would be able to arrange for Brody's transport.

"Okay, call me back when you find out what we can do," Amelia said. "I really don't want to leave Brody there any longer than I have to."

"Will do, Mrs. Tobias."

Amelia started to hang up but then stopped. "Wait! Kristin?"

"Yeah?"

"I don't have my cell. Call me at this number, okay?" Amelia picked up the old rotary phone, squinting to read the number scribbled in the middle of the dial. She gave Kristin the number and hung up.

The creak of the stairs made Amelia look up. Hannah was coming down, hands holding her robe closed. Angel came bouncing down after her.

"I thought I heard you down here. You okay, hon?"

Amelia reached down and scooped up the dog. "Yes," she said, with a smile.

♦ ♦ ♦

Buchanan threw the Kindle down on the bed in disgust. He was smarter than this. Why couldn't he figure this out?

He had spent half the night trying to break the Kindle's password, using every variation on "Brody" he could come up with. People often used their pet's name as a password so he had combined the name with every number and fact he knew about Amelia Tobias. But the damn Kindle stayed locked.

He glanced at his watch. Nine ten. Time to call about the dog. A woman answered on the second ring.

"Fantasia Dog Spa. Can I help you?"

"Yes, I'm calling about Brody."

"Oh, hi there, Mr. Tobias."

It never ceased to amaze him how much people assumed on the phone. Now he just had to play his cards right and make nice. It was a little harder with women—they were always more suspicious than men—but this one sounded young, and they were usually more trusting.

"Yes, hello. Ah, forgive me, but I've forgotten your name." He had to work a little to hide his Southern accent. He hadn't had to do it in a while.

"This is Kristin."

"Kristin! Well, listen, Kristin, I won't keep you—"

"That's okay. We just opened and I'm not busy."

"I just wanted to make sure everything went okay with Brody."

"Oh yeah, he's cool. Like I just told your wife, he's just a little—"

"My wife? She called?"

"Yeah, about a half hour ago."

Sometimes you just get lucky.

"Well, you know how my wife is about Brody, Kristin. She can't stand being away from him, even for a day."

Patience . . . don't press her.

"Yeah, she did seem sort of upset."

Keep her talking. Get whatever you can.

"Yes, she is upset," he said. "Her mother is in the hospital, you see, and Mrs. Tobias had to go . . . home to take care of her."

"Yeah, she mentioned she had an emergency. That's terrible about her mom. But I talked to Mrs. Chapinski and it looks like we'll be able to ship Brody to her after all."

It was just like he had told Alex Tobias. All he had to do was sit back and wait for her to make a mistake.

"Well, that's good news, Kristin. Did she give you the address?"

"No, not yet. I have to call the airline and see when they can take Brody. I was going to call Mrs. Tobias back and update her."

"Don't bother, Kristin. I'll call her. Damn, I can't find her mother's phone number. I know I have it here somewhere. My desk is a mess . . ."

"I got it right here, Mr. Tobias."

Kristin rattled off the number. Buchanan thanked her and hung up. The area code was 912, not Florida. He grabbed his laptop, called up his PeopleFinders account, and typed in the phone number. The result came up immediately:

Owner Name: Hannah Lowrey
Full Address: 1877 Union Street, Brunswick, Ga.
Phone Type: Landline

Was this a relative? The name had not turned up in any of his research, so he doubted it. Well, at least it was a landline, which was a helluva lot easier to find than a person toting a cell phone.

He pulled up the Delta Airlines website. There was a flight from Fort Lauderdale to Brunswick Golden Isles Airport, via Atlanta, leaving in two hours. He booked the ticket.

Why the hell would Amelia Tobias go to Georgia? It didn't matter. The only thing that mattered was that he find her, report back to the husband, collect the rest of his fee, and go home. What happened between Alex and Amelia Tobias was none of his concern.

He closed the laptop and began to pack his bag.

◆ ◆ ◆

It was near six by the time Buchanan turned onto Union Street. He slowed the rental car to a crawl, trying to read the numbers on the houses. Between the three-hour delay in Atlanta and the flight to Brunswick, it had taken longer than he had expected.

There it was—number 1877. He pulled to the curb in front of the big yellow house and rolled down his window. There were lights on down-stairs and an old Chevy parked in the driveway. If Amelia Tobias was inside, all he had to do was confirm she was here and call the husband.

A man was coming down the street. He gave Buchanan a look as he passed but continued on. Buchanan watched him go, realizing he was too easily spotted sitting here at the curb. Amelia wasn't expecting anyone to trail her here but experience had taught him to be cautious in small towns.

The wind was picking up, filling the car with the smell of brine. He glanced left and saw the dark outlines of a church. No lights on, and fronted with a dark parking lot. He put the car in gear, headlights off, and swung into the lot, parking behind a hedge that gave him a good view of the house but enough cover to be hidden.

He killed the engine and slumped down in the seat, considering his next move. He could wait here, hoping Amelia would come out. It was only six thirty, but it was already dark and the temperature was dropping fast. That left one other option—sneaking up to the house and looking in the windows.

He pulled out his Dunhills and lit a cigarette, his eyes locked on the yellow house.

He had been reduced to this sad state once before, when he was just starting out. Crouching in the snow outside the window of an Econo Lodge in Anchorage, peeping at a female embezzler, like some cut-rate Norman Bates.

And even the good money hasn't made it any better, has it, Bucky?

Her voice was coming often now. Too often. And there was nothing he could do to silence it. Except drink, and he couldn't risk that right now. Later, after this damn case was finished, he could go home, crawl back in his hole, and let the screech of scotch drown out her voice and the past.

The porch light went on.

Buchanan tossed the cigarette out the window.

A moment later, an elderly woman came out onto the porch. She wrapped herself in a big sweater, went to the porch swing and sat down.

Then a second woman emerged from the house, carrying a tray and trailed by a small white dog.

Buchanan sat up straighter in the seat, trying to get a better look. The woman was tall, but she had what looked like a quilt draped over her shoulders so it was hard to see her body. She wore glasses and had short dark hair. She sat down in a chair next to the old woman and handed her a mug from the tray. She took off her glasses and rubbed her eyes.

Buchanan reached over to his bag on the passenger seat and pulled out his Armasight binoculars. He had bought them years ago for a night birding trip to Assateague Island to spot great horned owls. But the goggles were perfect for situations like this.

He trained the binoculars on the porch. The little white dog was pawing at the shins of the young woman. She bent down to pick it up and held it high like a baby, tipping her face up to the porch light.

The woman's face glowed bright and clear in the hard green light of the binocular lenses. It was the face of the young ballerina in Amelia's scrapbook.

Buchanan set the binoculars aside, picked up his cell and punched in a number. Alex Tobias answered on the third ring.

"I've found your wife," Buchanan said.

CHAPTER THIRTEEN

Amelia wasn't sure what made her do it. Maybe it was the soft weight of the accumulated kindnesses of the last two days. The redheaded woman at the pawnshop who had handed over the money, the old black man on the bus who had shared his wine, the waitress at the Red Bone Café who had brought her toast, and Martin the hairdresser whose gentle hands had given her a new way to look at herself.

Maybe it was just because Hannah rekindled a shadow of a memory of someone in her past who had once been good to her. Whatever it was, Amelia, sitting on the porch wrapped in the old quilt with the little dog in her lap, felt safe enough to tell Hannah what had happened.

When she was done, Amelia was glad Hannah couldn't see her face clearly in the shadows cast by the porch light. It was a long time before Hannah finally spoke.

"You really got no memory?" Hannah asked.

"It's coming back, slowly," Amelia said. "But I can't tell sometimes which ones are real and which aren't."

The porch swing creaked as Hannah sat back. "My first husband gave me a diamond necklace," she said. "It was as bright as one of those Fourth of July sparklers. I found out it was just glass, as phony as he was."

Amelia looked over at Hannah, waiting.

"Maybe memories are like that," Hannah went on. "The fake ones can look the most real."

"I can't remember anything about the night I got hurt," Amelia said. "Only a man with dark hair and a feeling that he was trying to kill me."

"You really think it was your husband?" Hannah asked.

"I don't know," Amelia said softly. "I just know I have to get away from him."

The creaking of the porch swing stopped. Hannah had gone silent and still. From somewhere close by came a church bell, tolling the hour—seven o'clock.

Amelia looked over at Hannah. The old woman was just sitting there, staring out at the dark street. Had she imagined it, that note of disbelief in Hannah's voice? It seemed like such a crazy story now that her head was clear enough to really consider it. But that gnawing fear wasn't crazy. It was real. So was this new fear, that maybe she had made a mistake in confiding in the old woman. God, would she ever be able to trust anyone again?

"It's getting cold," Amelia said softly.

Hannah nodded and folded her sweater tighter over her chest.

"Would you like some more tea?" Amelia asked. "I can go in and heat up the water."

"No, I'm fine," Hannah said. "I'm a little tired, though. I think I'll go tuck in early tonight." She rose slowly and started to pick up the tray.

"Leave it. I'll take it in," Amelia said.

Hannah gave her a long look and then nodded. She opened the screen door, waiting. Angel jumped from Amelia's lap and followed Hannah inside.

Amelia pulled the quilt up around her shoulders. She stayed outside for another ten minutes, but finally the cold started to seep into her bones. She rose, picked up the tray, and went into the house, pushing the front door closed with her hip.

In the kitchen, she washed the cups and set them to drain on a towel. Her ribs, still bruised from the car accident, ached, and she knew sleep would come hard tonight. Maybe a long soak in the tub would help.

The phone rang out in the foyer.

Amelia hurried to pick it up, hoping it was the dog spa calling back about Brody's arrangements. Mrs. Chapinski had called about three that afternoon and promised Amelia she would call back when she had everything finalized.

"Hello?"

"Mrs. Tobias? This is Kristin, from Fantasia."

"Oh, yes, good! Were you able to arrange to get Brody to me?"

"Well, almost. We're closed now, but Mrs. Chapinski wanted me to call you before I left so you wouldn't worry. We need Brody's vet to sign a health certificate first or Delta won't take him. So I'm going over to your vet tomorrow to get his papers. The first day the airline can ship him is the day after tomorrow."

Amelia leaned back against the wall and closed her eyes. "Thank you, Kristin."

"I'll call you back tomorrow when we get everything nailed down, okay?"

"I appreciate this, Kristin."

"Oh, by the way, I hope your mom is okay, Mrs. Tobias."

Amelia opened her eyes. "My mom?"

"Mr. Tobias said she's in the hospital."

Amelia straightened from the wall. "You talked to my husband?"

"Yeah, this morning. He called to see how Brody was doing. Right after I talked to you."

"Kristin, did you tell him where I was?"

There was a long pause on the other end.

"Kristin, did you tell my husband where I was?"

"No, I just gave him your mom's phone number. Geez, Mrs. Tobias, is there—"

Amelia hung up. Her heart was hammering.

What the hell was going on? She knew Alex never would have called to ask about Brody. Maybe it was someone else? She struggled to retrieve a face from her memory, the face of the dark-haired man in the car. Maybe it hadn't been Alex. But who else would want to kill her?

A noise outside, like a pounding. She hurried into the front room and turned off the lamp. She crawled onto the sofa under the window and peered out the gap in the curtains. Nothing . . . just a car rolling slowly away down the street, the deep *thump-thump* of its music echoing in the dark. She watched until the sound faded and the red taillights were gone.

"Hon, what it is?"

Amelia spun.

Hannah was standing in the doorway. "What are you doing down here in the dark?" She started to the table, reaching for the lamp.

"No, leave it off!"

Hannah stared at her for a moment and then came slowly forward. Amelia looked back out at the street. She could see nothing moving, except the branches of oak trees dancing in the wind.

"What is it?" Hannah asked.

Amelia turned to her. "He knows I'm here, Hannah."

"But how?"

"He called my dog's groomer, and they gave him your phone number." Amelia slid off the sofa. "I have to go."

"Hon, wait a minute. Amelia, wait—"

But Amelia was already up the stairs. She ran to her room and pulled the Vuitton duffel from under the bed. She changed into jeans and a T-shirt and packed the rest of her clothes. She headed to the bathroom and emptied her toiletries from the plastic hospital bag into the cosmetics bag she had bought at the mall.

When she got back to the bedroom Hannah was there, sitting on the edge of the bed, holding the white dog.

"Listen, maybe you should just go to the police," Hannah said.

"No. They won't believe me. Until I can remember what happened, I can't prove anything."

Amelia threw the cosmetics bag into the duffel along with her new iPad. She tugged on her boots and slid into her sweater coat. She turned in a quick tight circle, looking around the room to see if she had left anything. When she looked back at Hannah, the old woman was standing up.

She was holding a gun.

Amelia's eyes went from the gun up to Hannah's face.

"Take this," Hannah said, coming to her. "My daddy gave it to me for protection after my second divorce."

Amelia shook her head. "Hannah, I can't—"

"Yes, you can."

"I don't need this."

"Yes, you do."

Amelia tried to take a step back, but Hannah grabbed her hand and set the gun in her palm.

It was cold and heavy. "How does it . . . ?" Amelia asked.

"It's just a plain old .38 revolver. You just take the safety off, point it, and shoot."

Amelia's eyes went from the gun in her hand up to Hannah's face.

"You hold it like you do a man, hon," Hannah said. "You're in charge of when it goes off."

Amelia stared at Hannah, then she laughed. It came out as a hard, nervous bark.

Hannah gave a grunt and a small smile. Amelia slid the gun into the duffel and zipped it up. When she looked back, Hannah was at the window, peering around the downed shade.

P.J. Parrish

"I didn't want to say anything earlier because I didn't want to scare you." She looked back at Amelia. "I thought I saw something, across the street in the church parking lot, a light that came and went, like someone smoking a cigarette inside a car."

She let the shade fall. "I might be wrong, but you best go out the back just in case."

Amelia picked up the duffel from the bed. The white dog was curled up on the chenille bedspread. She stroked the dog's head and then turned to Hannah.

"Where are you going?" Hannah asked.

"I don't know," Amelia said.

"Will you at least find a way to let me know you're all right?"

Amelia nodded, then she gathered the old woman into a tight embrace.

"Go," Hannah whispered.

Amelia broke free and hurried from the room. She didn't look back until she was out the back door and into the alley. The lights inside the house dissolved into a yellow blur. She wiped the tears roughly away, hoisted up the duffel, and disappeared into the dark.

127

CHAPTER FOURTEEN

In the cold moonless night, a night that was slowly shrouding itself in a fog, she couldn't be sure which direction she was heading. But the smell of the river was growing fainter behind her, and she had the sense that she was heading back toward downtown. And once she found her way there, she could make it back to the Greyhound station.

Amelia stopped abruptly.

No . . . she couldn't go to the bus station. It would be the first place Alex would go. He had been smart enough to get Hannah's phone number from Kristin and he would be smart enough to figure out that she had taken a bus to get here. She couldn't risk it.

Where could she go?

Straight ahead, she could see the faint glow of Christmas lights, strings of them draped from the streetlamps downtown. She looked right, but saw only small houses, their windows lit with the blue throb of televisions. A car was coming slowly down the street, heading her way. She ducked behind a hedge and waited until it disappeared.

She turned to her left. Far off, maybe a hundred yards or so, she could make out a steady stream of fast-moving headlights. It was a highway, the road Hannah had taken the day she drove her to the mall. And the mall was out by an interstate, she remembered.

Martin the hair stylist was there in her head, and what he had said when she saw her short, dark hair for the first time.

No one's going to recognize you.

It wasn't enough, she knew now. It wasn't enough to just change how she looked. She had to change everything she did, even the way she thought. She had to become a woman, inside and out, who Alex would never recognize.

Amelia Tobias would never do what I am about to do. But Amelia Brody will do whatever it takes.

With a quick look around to make sure no one was following, she headed toward the highway.

It took her about an hour to get to the mall, a cold, tiring walk in the glare of headlights and in the wake of car exhaust. The mall lot was almost deserted and she knew it had to be past nine by now, maybe even later. She saw a road sign for I-95 North and kept going.

Then, there it was, just as she remembered. The towering yellow Waffle House sign, a Motel 6, a Shell truck stop, and beyond that the entrance ramp to the interstate. She trudged across the high wet grass of the median and headed toward the gas pumps.

If you ever get stranded, Mellie, hitch a ride with a truck driver. You can trust them.

Who had told her that? And Mellie? Who had called her Mellie? Her head hurt from the effort of confronting these frayed bits of memories that came at her out of nowhere without warning, like strangers emerging from the mist.

She paused at the first bank of gas pumps to adjust the duffel strap on her shoulder and looked around the sprawling station, gauging her chances of getting a ride. Three huge 18-wheelers sat silent and dark on the edge of the Motel 6 lot. Another one was just pulling out, grinding slowly up the ramp toward I-95. There was one rig left, idling at the diesel station. Amelia walked slowly to it.

The cab was empty. Amelia let out a long tired breath, lowered herself down onto the driver's-side step, and took off her glasses. She rubbed the bridge of her nose and shut her eyes.

"You scratch that paint job and I'm gonna have to kick your ass."

Amelia opened her eyes. The figure standing in front of her was in soft focus, no face in the harsh backlight of the station lights, just a squat body in black clothes. A woman?

"Sorry," Amelia said, standing and hoisting the duffel onto her shoulder.

"You look skinny and strung out, kiddo. You a tweaker?"

"A what?"

"Tweaker. Meth head."

Drugs. The woman was talking about drugs.

"No, I had to leave my house and I'm—"

The woman took her chin and turned Amelia's face to the light. Amelia pulled away, her hand going up to cover the stiches on her chin.

"I guess you got other problems then," the trucker said.

"Yes. But right now I need a ride."

The woman eyed her hard. "I'd like to help you out but we got new rules because of the insurance. No freeloaders."

Amelia scanned the parking lot. It was empty except for a dark sedan with a man inside. Who was that? Was that the same car she had seen earlier?

She looked back at the woman. "I can pay you."

"It's not the money, it's the rules."

Amelia studied the woman. Her hair was spike-cut and two-toned, yellow and black. She had a tattoo of a parrot down her neck and a tiny sapphire piercing in her lower lip.

She couldn't let this woman get away. "You don't look like a woman who always obeys the rules," Amelia said.

The woman stared hard at her. "What happened to your face?"

"I ran into something."

"Yeah, some fucker's fist, right?"

Amelia started to explain, but suddenly she was too tired. And too desperate. "Yeah, that's what happened. Please help me."

The woman glanced around the parking lot and then back at Amelia. "Where are you going?"

"Anywhere."

"I'm heading northwest through Memphis and then straight west."

"That's fine. I just need to get out of here."

The woman motioned for Amelia to follow and walked her around to the passenger side of the massive truck. She opened the cab door.

"Climb on up and toss your duffel in the rear."

Amelia climbed into the cab, taking note of the bed tucked into the space behind the seats. The other door opened and the woman climbed inside. She set her thermos in a holder between the seats and hit a button on the dash. With a roar, the truck's engine sprang to life.

"My name's Dolly," she said, as she pulled the seat belt across her chest.

"Amelia Brody. And thank you."

The truck started to move, first like a train, then more like a monorail, smooth and heavy and not as rumbling as Amelia thought it would be. She could see the truck was new, with clean windows and a leather dashboard lit up like an airplane cockpit. A photograph was wedged into the edge of the clock but the cab was too dark for her to see it clearly.

"You look like a zombie," Dolly said. "If you want to crawl back there and sleep, that's cool."

Amelia glanced back toward the bed. She was exhausted but still keyed up, like she could almost feel the sting of adrenaline running through her veins. She leaned her head against the side window, and as she watched the lights of the gas station recede in the side mirror, she thought about the man in the car Hannah had seen.

Was she being paranoid? Was someone really after her or was this strange fear just a result of the concussion? It wasn't like the headaches that came and went. The fear was always there in her gut.

"You mind some music?" Dolly asked.

"No, go right ahead," Amelia said.

Dolly plugged in an iPod. "I sleep by day and drive by night because there's fewer weirdos on the road. Usually, I just roll the windows down and listen to the whine of my turbo and my heartbeat. But when it's cold like this, I need my rock and roll to keep me going. I'm working my way through the decades, and I'm up to the seventies now."

The cab filled up with the sounds of a guitar and a man's buttery voice. Amelia closed her eyes and leaned her head back.

"You sure you don't want to go catch forty?" Dolly asked.

Amelia opened her eyes and glanced back at the blanket and pillows. "Yeah, I think I will," she said softly.

Dolly turned the music down to a murmur. "I'll wake you for breakfast."

CHAPTER FIFTEEN

"Turn off the lights."

Alex turned to face his partner Owen McCall. "What? Why?"

"That's what Buchanan said to do," McCall said.

Alex switched off the headlights and steered the rental car into the dark parking lot. He pulled to a stop and leaned forward, peering out the windshield.

"Where is he?" he asked.

When McCall sat forward in the passenger seat, the streetlight turned his face into a chalky mask. He was silent, his eyes scanning the lot. Alex waited, knowing not to say anything. They had barely spoken on the flight up here, McCall sitting rigid in his seat, drinking club soda. Alex had finally gotten tired of his silence and retreated to the back of the firm's private jet. By the time the Learjet touched down at the Brunswick airport, he was two vodkas deep into his brew of hope and despair. Hope that they would find Mel. Despair that she wouldn't come home with him. But why would he even consider the second possibility? She loved him, she trusted him. She didn't know what he had done, and it wasn't too late for him to make everything right again.

"That's his rental car over there," McCall said.

Alex looked to his left just in time to see the glow of a cigarette lighter inside a darkened car.

"Let's go," Alex said, opening the car door.

McCall grabbed his sleeve. "Wait. Close the damn door."

Alex shut the door and the overhead light went out.

"I want you to listen to me, Alex. Let me handle this."

"She's my wife, Owen, goddamn it. She's not thinking straight and—"

"And neither are you right now. I need you to stay calm. We need Amelia to stay calm. We don't want to scare her. You want her to come home, right?"

Alex ran a hand over his face. "Okay," he said softly. "Okay, I just want to talk to her."

They got out and walked quickly through the cold wind to the other car. Alex started toward the passenger side, but McCall was there first, yanking open the door and getting in. Alex slipped in the back.

The car's engine was off, and Buchanan had his window rolled halfway down. The cold night air, stinking of fish, poured in, and Alex pulled up the collar of his sports coat. It had been seventy-five degrees when they left Fort Lauderdale. It was so cold here, he could see his breath pluming in the air.

He realized he was breathing too fast. He took three deep breaths to calm himself and sat forward between the front seats, staring hard at the house across the street. In the glare from the streetlight, he could see the house clearly, see the peeling yellow paint, the picket fence with its missing slats, the overgrown bushes, and the sagging porch. What the hell was Mel doing in a place like this?

"Is she in there?" he asked.

Buchanan didn't turn around, his eyes fixed on the house. "It was 6:15 when I called you," he said. "She stayed out on the porch with an old woman until 7:10 then they both went in." Buchanan looked at his watch. "I haven't moved from this spot in the last three hours and no one has come out since they went inside."

"How do you know for sure that it's Amelia?" Alex asked.

"I told you when I called you. She made a phone call from this house and I was able to trace it." He held out a piece of paper. "Plus I was able to ID her with this."

Alex took the paper. It was a five-by-seven black-and-white photograph. He stared at it for a long time. "This is Amelia when she was dancing. She doesn't look like this anymore."

"She does now."

"Where did you get this?"

"From her closet."

Alex stared at the back of Buchanan's head, a spasm of disgust moving through him, like the time that rapist had reached through the bars of the Tallahassee jail and grabbed his arm, grinning and saying he had never touched that little girl. Alex had gotten the man off. Two months later, he quit his public defender job and signed on with a small Orlando firm specializing in corporate law. It wasn't only for the money. He just wanted to feel clean.

He wanted to feel clean again. He wanted this man Buchanan out of his life. He wanted Mel back. He wanted everything to go back to the way it used to be. He started to put the picture in his coat pocket.

"I need that back," Buchanan said.

"Why?" Alex demanded.

"In case I have to show it around."

"But you said she was in—"

"Give it back to him, Alex."

Alex hesitated and then handed it over the seat. His eyes went to the house. "I'm going up there."

"No," Buchanan said.

"Why not? I know if I can just talk to her—"

"You don't know shit about her," Buchanan said. "At least not the woman she is right now."

"Now look, you asshole—"

"Shut up," McCall said sharply. "Just shut up for a second and hear him out."

Buchanan tossed out his cigarette and rolled up the window. "Your wife was scared enough to run from a hospital. I don't care why. But something changed her. Maybe it was her head injury, maybe it was something else. But she's different. Look at that house over there. It's not like that pink palace of yours back home, is it?"

Buchanan held up the photograph. "And look at this woman. She's not your pretty blonde Armani Barbie."

"What are you saying?" Alex asked.

"She's a different woman. And you're going to have to be a different man to get her back."

Alex shook his head. "This is bullshit."

McCall held up a hand. "What do you suggest we do?"

"You have no legal right to go into that house or make her do anything," Buchanan said.

"So we wait for her to come out?" McCall asked.

Buchanan nodded. "You wait until she's out in the open. You wait for the right moment when she doesn't feel threatened." He paused. "Maybe I should talk to her first."

The car was quiet.

"Fuck this," Alex said.

He jerked open the door, almost falling out of the car. He heard McCall yell something, but he kept going.

Wrong . . . they were both wrong. He knew Mel. He knew that if she could just see him, everything would be clear. She loved him, and somewhere inside her she had to remember that.

He started across the parking lot, breaking into a near run by the time he got to the fence. He hurried up the steps, yanked open the screen door, and pounded on the front door.

A dog barked from somewhere deep inside the house. But no one came to the door. His eyes caught movement at the nearest window—a curtain and a shadowy face. He pounded on the door again, harder.

The porch light went on, and another light inside. A moment later the door opened a crack. An old woman with white hair stared out at him. He could hear the dog barking but couldn't see it.

"Who are you?" the woman demanded.

Alex looked around her, trying to see inside. For one second, he thought of brushing past the woman.

Calm . . . stay calm.

"My name is Alex Tobias," he said.

"What do you want?" the woman asked.

"I want to see my wife, please."

"Wife? What the hell are you talking about?"

"My wife, Amelia. She's here and—"

"Nobody's here but me and my dog."

She started to shut the door, but Alex thrust out a hand, stopping her. The old woman stared hard at him. The barking grew louder and frenzied.

"You best take your hand out of there, mister, if you don't want it smashed up," the old woman said.

Alex dropped his hand and took one step back. "I'm sorry. Look, I know my wife is here. I know she made a phone call from this house."

The old woman's eyes drifted, as if she were glancing at something or someone off to her left.

"Please," Alex said. "My wife is not well. Please let me talk to her. I just want to take her home."

In the glow of the porch light, he saw something shift in the woman's face. Was she smiling?

"She's gone," the woman said.

"What?"

"You heard me. Your wife was here. But she's not now."

"I don't believe it."

The woman held the door open. "You want to come in and look?"

Alex felt a hand clamp down on his shoulder, and he spun around.

"Let's go," McCall said.

"No," Alex said. "I'm going in there!"

McCall stepped in front of him, his hand tightening on his shoulder. "Go back to the car, Alex. Now."

Alex stared at McCall's face, harsh yellow in the porch light. He had seen this expression only once before, eighteen months ago when he had stood next to McCall in the moonlight on the edge of that black-water drainage canal. He had wanted to fight McCall then, but he couldn't. Just like he couldn't now.

He spun out of McCall's grip and stumbled down the steps. He heard McCall say something to the woman but he kept going, heading back to the car.

CHAPTER SIXTEEN

Buchanan sat slumped in the seat, disgusted. Mostly with himself but with Alex Tobias as well. The man was in the backseat, wringing his hands and crying. What a fucking jackass.

What had spooked Amelia Tobias, he didn't know. No way would she have noticed his nondescript car sitting in a parking lot in the dark. This woman had no experience at running. She would not be that observant.

"We need to find her," Alex said. "We should be doing something."

Buchanan glanced in his rearview mirror. The man looked like a drunk after a three-day bender. Owen McCall was slumped in the passenger seat, staring at the house. Buchanan was still wondering why the hell the partner was even there, but this wasn't the moment to bring it up.

"We're lucky the old lady didn't call the police on you for pushing her," Buchanan said.

"Maybe we should get out of here before she changes her mind," McCall said.

Alex's head popped between the front seats, into the dim glow of the streetlights. His face was tear-streaked but his eyes held a sheen of rage.

"Maybe *we* should call the police," he said. "They can get in there and—"

"No police," McCall said.

Alex sank back into the shadows. McCall looked back at the house and then turned to Buchanan. "So now what?" he asked.

"I go after her. Again."

"How do you think she got this far?"

Again, Buchanan wondered why McCall cared so much, but given Tobias's mood, maybe it was good the older guy was here.

"Bus, most likely. You don't need an ID if you pay cash."

"How did she pay for her ticket?" McCall asked. "She didn't have a purse in the hospital. There have been no withdrawals or a request for a new debit card. Alex checked."

"Maybe she had a stash somewhere, a secret account. Wives often do."

Alex's voice came from the backseat. "No. All the accounts were in my name."

Buchanan glanced again to the rearview mirror. Alex caught the look and leaned forward again.

"She *wanted* it that way," he said. "She never wanted anything to do with money. She shopped, and I paid the credit cards."

"Maybe she socked something away."

"No way. I always knew to the penny what she spent."

"What about jewelry?" McCall said. "What about her ring, that rock you gave her?"

"How big a rock?" Buchanan asked.

"Ten carats," Alex said.

Buchanan's eyes shot back to the rearview mirror. Alex was staring at him but Buchanan looked away, out at the house.

"They would have removed her jewelry at the hospital and secured it," Buchanan said. "Did they give you any of her personal effects?"

"I haven't been back to the hospital. And no one has called me."

"Check it out," Buchanan said. "Talk to security and the nurses at the hospital. I need to know what she has with her."

"Yeah, okay, whatever," Alex said. "But what about right now? If she took a bus to get here, she might take a bus away from here. Why aren't we—"

Buchanan reached back over the seat. "Give me your phone."

"What?"

"Give me your phone."

Alex slapped his iPhone into Buchanan's palm. Buchanan asked Siri for the bus station in Brunswick, Georgia. When the Google map came up, the station marked with a red pin, Buchanan tossed the phone over his shoulder.

"There's your damn bus station," he said. "Go look if you want. But she won't be there. She might not know how we found her, but she's smart enough to know she has to come up with some new moves."

"She's not as smart as you think," Alex said, pushing open the car door. "She's running because she's brain-damaged and mixed up. Maybe you're the one who should find some new moves."

Alex slammed the door behind him. Buchanan watched him walk back to the rental car he and McCall had arrived in. With a roar of the engine, Alex disappeared into the darkness.

For a few moments, Buchanan and McCall sat in the car, silent.

"He blew this," Buchanan said.

"I know," McCall said.

Buchanan sighed, his disgust with Tobias growing.

"So what's your next move?" McCall asked.

"I'll spend tomorrow here in town, show her picture around. I need to put a tap on the old woman's phone."

"Why?" McCall asked.

"Amelia seemed sort of . . ." Buchanan paused. "Sort of affectionate with the old woman. She might try to contact her again. But if I don't get a lead here, I need to go back to Florida. I need some more background on her."

He thought about telling McCall about Carol Fairfield and his suspicion that Amelia had a lover, but decided to stay silent. McCall had been the one who had hired him, but there was something odd about his intense interest in Amelia Tobias's welfare and until he figured out what was going on, he wasn't going to volunteer any more than he had to.

McCall loosened his tie, and just sat there, staring straight ahead. "You'll need more money."

"You bet."

"How much more?"

"Five grand for another week."

McCall drew a long slow breath. Still, he didn't look at Buchanan. "What could you do for a million?" he asked.

"Pardon me?"

"What could you do for a million dollars?"

Buchanan sat back against the door, studying Owen McCall. The man sat straight as a statue, his face like clay in the slant of the streetlight.

"What are you asking me to do?" Buchanan said.

"Amelia wants to disappear," McCall said. "I want you to make sure that happens."

"You want her dead?" Buchanan asked.

Now McCall looked at him, his eyes hard as glass. "I didn't say that. I said I wanted her to disappear. How you make that happen is up to you."

Buchanan had heard some pretty bizarre propositions in his line of work, mainly runners who had tried to buy him off after they had been caught. But he had never been asked to carry out a hit on someone. This explained why McCall was here, but what the hell had this woman done to make her husband's law partner want her dead? Did McCall have anything to do with Amelia's car going off the road in the Everglades?

"Why do you want her dead?" Buchanan asked.

"That's not your concern."

"Does Tobias know about this?"

"Of course he does."

Buchanan shook his head. Enough of this shit. He had his five grand retainer. He was about to shove McCall from the car when McCall gave a small chuckle.

"Don't pretend you're above this."

"What do you mean?" Buchanan asked.

McCall reached into his jacket pocket, withdrew a folded paper, and handed it to Buchanan.

Buchanan paused and then began to unfold it, slowly because he knew what it was, and he didn't want to see it. It was a copy of an article from the Nashville *Tennessean*, dated September 12, 2009. The headline was black and ugly.

HUSBAND SUSPECTED

IN DISAPPEARANCE OF

WIFE AND INFANT SON

Buchanan was not surprised that McCall had done his own homework. But what did he think it would get him?

He tossed the paper back at McCall. "I was never charged."

"It's likely you were never charged because the police never found the bodies, Mr. Buchanan."

A slow burn started to creep up the back of Buchanan's neck.

McCall picked up the paper and carefully folded it into a square as he spoke. "You said during the investigation that you would do everything humanly possible to find whoever abducted your wife and son."

Buchanan glared at McCall, tempted to smash the man's head through the passenger window. But his curiosity about where this was going was stronger, so he stayed quiet.

"But you've done nothing, really," McCall went on. "You're charging me outrageous fees, but you haven't really been all that successful in your work. Your personal bank account has less than two thousand dollars in it."

"I have other accounts," Buchanan said. "One is for my daughter—"

"Who you lost custody of to your in-laws. Who by all accounts hates you because she thinks you killed her mother and baby brother."

Buchanan looked away. He knew he should throw this man out into the street and head to Nashville without looking back. But something was stopping him.

"Mr. Buchanan," McCall said. "I really don't care if you killed anyone or not. I'll make it two million. Use the money to clear your name, use it to get your daughter back, or just put it in a trust for her and go drink yourself into oblivion."

"Look, you bastard—"

McCall's hand shot up. "Like I said, I don't care what you did. I don't care what you do. But it's yours, right now—two million in cash that no one can trace—if you're willing to do what I asked."

"We're done," Buchanan said. "This is over. Get out of my car."

But McCall didn't move. "Mr. Buchanan, I have many friends, friends who tell me things they think I might need to know. One of them is the district attorney in Nashville. He's preparing an indictment against you."

Buchanan was so stunned he could only stare at McCall. It was quiet in the car, then he began to hear a strange rushing sound. It took him a moment to realize it was the sound of blood pulsing in his ears.

Jesus, was this never going to end? Five years and they had never found anyone else to go after? And what the hell did they have now that they could indict him on?

"Let me make this easier for you," McCall said.

Buchanan looked away.

"I will get you the best defense money can buy. No matter what they come up with, I can promise you won't see one day in prison."

Buchanan shook his head slowly.

"All right, I'll sweeten the deal," McCall said. "I will also make sure you get back custody of your daughter."

Buchanan closed his eyes. Against the flood of memories, against the feelings of pain and impotence. Against the voice, her voice, that he knew now he couldn't silence.

No, Bucky, not this way.

Buchanan opened his eyes. For a few seconds, they simply sat in the darkness. Then suddenly, all the lights in the old lady's house went out.

"It's a deal," Buchanan said.

CHAPTER SEVENTEEN

Amelia awoke to a screech of air brakes and nearly fell from the bunk. The truck came to stop, and she could hear Dolly muttering to herself. Amelia rustled her hair, slathered her mouth with a fingertip of toothpaste from her duffel, and climbed back to the cab.

There was a cottony gray light coming through the windshield, and the cold air, slithering in from Dolly's cracked window, had a sharp smell, like copper kettles and wet wool. Winter . . . it was the smell of almost-winter, Amelia realized. She looked out the side window at the bare black trees and the rolling hills covered with frosted grass. A roadside sign told her they were in a place called Jasper, slowed by a traffic jam.

"How long did I sleep?" Amelia asked.

"Over six hours," Dolly said. "We're coming to Tupelo soon. From there, we head to Memphis to pick up I-40 West then it's balls to the wall until we hit Kingman, Arizona."

Arizona. No, she couldn't go there. It didn't feel right. She didn't know where she wanted to go but she knew she didn't belong there. She needed to go . . . where? She needed . . . *what?*

She shut her eyes, struggling to summon up something of comfort from her past, but all she could muster was that strange sensation she had felt the day she had awoken in the hospital, that feeling of floating inside a blue-green bubble.

They crept along, Dolly cursing and shifting the rig through its gears. Then suddenly, the pulsating lights of a police car came into view ahead. Amelia's heart kicked up and didn't slow until they had passed the trooper standing on the side of the road, directing traffic around a car that had gone into the ditch. Dolly was quick to get the truck back to cruising speed.

"I got you a coffee when I stopped a few miles back," Dolly said, nodding to a Styrofoam cup in the holder. "And there's an Egg McMuffin for you in that bag there."

Amelia picked up the cup and lifted off the top. The coffee was lukewarm but good and strong. As she reached into the greasy bag, again she heard the Russian man's voice: *I want to see bones.*

Screw you, whoever you are. I want to eat.

A few minutes later, her stomach had stopped rumbling and the coffee was gone. Dolly had turned up her iPod and it was blasting out a song Amelia didn't recognize. But that was the norm now, hearing songs that sounded familiar but whose titles were lost to her.

Amelia's eyes drifted down to the photo on the dashboard. "May I?" she asked, pointing at the photo.

"Sure."

Amelia picked up the photo. It was a woman in baggy pants and a tank top, her sinewy arms cradling a rifle.

"Your sister?" Amelia asked.

"My hersband, Nikki," Dolly said.

The word didn't register, and Dolly laughed. "Partner, you know. My significant other. You don't have a problem with that, do you?"

Amelia smiled. "No, I don't." She slipped the photograph back into its place on the dash.

"Is Nikki in the army?" she asked.

Dolly smiled. "Hell, no. She's First Battalion Eighth Marines, Regimental Combat Team II. She's in Musa Qala, Afghanistan." Her smile faded. "She's as tough as woodpecker lips and I love her."

Amelia was still looking at the photograph when the images came, flooding her with such power she felt her body go slack.

Two skyscrapers crumbling to dust. Tanks rolling over sand. Men in camouflage but tan not green. Then she could hear a man's voice, the same voice that had told her about hitching with truckers.

It's my duty, Mellie. I want to defend my country.

The face formed slowly in her head, like someone moving toward her out of a fog—brown eyes, hay-colored hair an inch or two too long, a spray of freckles across his nose.

I'll come home safe. I promise.

The face stayed with her, moving through her head and settling deep in her heart. And finally, after a long moment, came a name.

Ben.

Amelia looked to Dolly, unable to stop herself from blurting out this new memory. "I have a brother," she said.

Dolly glanced at her as if to say "so?"

"He's a soldier, too."

"Still serving over there?"

Amelia had no idea, but she didn't want Dolly to know about her amnesia. She didn't want to have to explain anything, so she lied.

"No, he's home now."

But maybe it wasn't a lie. Ben—Benjamin Ross Bloodworth—was there in her head, as real as Dolly sitting next to her, and it brought her a comfort she hadn't felt in days. She had someone. She had family. But where were they?

The song changed from something high-pitched and girly to the steady strumming of a guitar followed by a man's voice that sounded as it were filtered through a shredder, imploring someone named Maggie to wake up.

Elton John? Billy Joel? Where were these names coming from? "Who's singing that?" Amelia asked.

Dolly smiled. "It's my man, Rod Stewart."

The morning sun when it's in your face really shows your age.

Amelia's heart jumped. Why? It was the words, the words to the song.

"Can you play that back?" Amelia asked.

"What?"

"Those last couple of lines. Please, can you stop it and start it over?"

Dolly hit a button and the song started over. Amelia leaned closer to the speaker.

The morning sun when it's in your face . . .

The morning sun.

She turned and crawled back to the bed, grabbing her iPad from her duffel. It booted right up and found a signal, just as the Apple clerk had said it would. In seconds, she had the search window up. She typed in the words "Morning Sun." Up came links for a newspaper in Michigan, some publication about China, and a small book publisher.

She added the word "Town."

Her first link was "Morning Sun, Iowa, Chamber of Commerce."

She clicked on "Images," and there it was. Narrow asphalt streets, white frame houses with wraparound porches, a tiny grocery, a tavern called The Sunspot, and trees, lots and lots of green trees.

And every bit of it felt real.

This was her home. This was where Ben was. Maybe where her family was.

She was so excited she could barely type, so excited that she knew Dolly was talking to her, but she couldn't listen. She quickly brought up a map and punched in directions from Tupelo to Morning Sun. Morning Sun was on the east side of Iowa, over five hundred miles north from where Dolly would have to break due west, at the Mississippi River.

"I need you to let me off when we get past Memphis," Amelia said. "Somewhere I can catch a bus north."

"Where are you going?"

Amelia looked down at the map, her eyes fixed on the small yellow dot of Morning Sun.

"I'm going home," she said.

CHAPTER EIGHTEEN

Was there anything more pathetic than staring at yourself in a bar mirror? But maybe that's what he needed right now, a good long hard look at himself. Confront the man in the mirror, stare deep into his soul. Find a bright shining moment of moral clarity.

Buchanan picked up his glass. What was that Michael Jackson song? "The Man in the Mirror"? How did it go? Something about making a change?

He finished his second scotch and set the empty glass down in the trough of the bar. On the plane ride back from Georgia, he hadn't had anything to drink. He had needed his head clear to think. Think about what might happen if he had to stand trial for Rayna's murder. Think about the deal he had struck. Think about what he could do with two million dollars. Think about what he was going to have to do to get it.

Owen McCall's face came back to him in that moment, how it had looked in the car, stone cold gray in the slant of the streetlight, how there was nothing coming from those hard blue eyes, like all the man's energy was directed inward. Maybe that's what it took. Maybe you had to filter everything and everyone out and laser-focus everything you had back into yourself to become a man like that—a man who was successful enough to buy anything on earth. Including a woman's life.

Could he do that? Could he be the kind of man who would do whatever it took to get what he wanted?

But what do you want, Bucky?

Buchanan shut his eyes.

Tell me, Bucky. What do you want?

"I just want you to be quiet," he said.

"Excuse me?"

Buchanan opened his eyes to see the bartender staring at him. He blinked her into focus.

"All I asked you was if you wanted a refill," she said. "If you're gonna get ugly, there's the door."

He held up his hands. "Sorry, I'm sorry. Yeah, bring me another, please."

The bartender moved away, and he looked back across the bottles of booze at his reflection, thinking again about McCall. Had he intended from the start to kill Amelia Tobias? Had McCall known that when he had hired him? Was this all some elaborate setup? McCall's last words to him in Georgia, just before he got out of the car, came back to him.

This is how it will work. When you get back to Fort Lauderdale, there will be a package waiting for you at the hotel. In it will be five thousand dollars, a cell phone, and a key. The five grand is for your expenses. The cell is how I will stay in contact with you. The key is to a locker where I will put two million in cash. When you finish the job to my satisfaction, you get the location of the locker. This is the last time we will see each other, do you understand?

Buchanan pulled out the cell phone. It was a cheap disposable Samsung with a prepaid plan that couldn't be traced. It was called a burner, used by drug dealers mostly. Buchanan had used more than his share in his line of work.

He focused now on the key. It was small, brass, with the number 328 etched on it. It could fit anything from a bus locker at Port Authority to a safe deposit box in Sao Paulo. Buchanan pulled out his wallet, stuck the key behind the photograph of his daughter, and put the wallet away.

The bartender brought his fresh scotch. Buchanan took a drink and then finally, sick of staring at his reflection, he swung the stool around and looked around the bar. He had found Kim's Alley by accident. After cabbing in from the airport, he had gone up to his room and started sorting through the box of mementoes from Amelia's closet, looking for something that would lead him to Carol Fairfield or Amelia's nameless lover. But after an hour of looking at faded snapshots and reading a couple letters Amelia's brother had written from Afghanistan, Buchanan gave up. He knew he needed to keep digging into Amelia Tobias's life, but since accepting McCall's deal, it was almost like he didn't want to know anything more about the woman. If she remained just a face in a magazine or a line in a dance review, he didn't have to think about her as a real person.

Finally, he had thrown everything back into the cardboard box and retreated to the hotel bar, expecting a quiet dark corner where he could think. But after fifteen minutes sitting on a gold silk banquette listening to bad jazz, he left. He wandered down A1A, his head hunched into the turned-up collar of his sport coat. The beach was deserted, the afternoon sky and the ocean below it roiling and gray. He walked far, turning away from the beach and finally into a strip mall. That's where he had found this place.

Kim's Alley was dark, smelled like beer and body odor, and except for the soft *thick-thock* of Ping-Pong balls, it was blissfully quiet.

He watched two guys finish their Ping-Pong game. The roar in his head had quieted. Even her voice was gone, for the moment at least. He knew this was dangerous, letting his mind go empty, because that's when the memories slid in. And they were coming now, not like they usually did, like he was seeing them through a soapy shower curtain, but with a sharp, stabbing, awful clarity.

It had been hot that September day, with tornado warnings crawling across the bottom of the TV screen as he watched the Titans game. The baby was crying in the kitchen, making that awful wheezing sound he made when his asthma was bad, and Gillian had made a mess on the rug with her Shrinky Dinks. Rayna had come into the living room and grabbed the remote, muting the TV.

Bucky, didn't you hear the phone?

No. Did it ring?

He hadn't even looked at her. The AC was on the fritz, he was hot and miserable, thinking that this was his first day off in two weeks and all he wanted was to be out in the woods with his binoculars and birds. He was thinking about the late mortgage payment and the baby's unpaid medical bills, thinking about his peckerwood boss and how much he hated working as an insurance fraud investigator. Thinking that if Rayna hadn't gotten pregnant again, the money they had saved might have been enough for him to go back to night school and finish his psychology degree.

When he finally looked up at his wife, he saw something there in her clear blue eyes he didn't want to see—himself, made small and mean, because this was never what he had envisioned for himself, and it was too late to go back and fix it.

Rayna, you and the kids are the only good things in my life, and I love you, but whatever is choking me from inside won't let the words come out.

That's what he wanted to say.

Instead . . .

You still going to your mom's?

Yeah, I have to get going. I'll take the baby so he won't bother you. Keep an eye on Gillie-Girl there.

When you coming back?

Around eight maybe.

It's going to rain. The tires are bad on your car. You should take my truck.

I'll be fine. I'll be back before you can miss me, Bucky.

And then she was gone.

He watched the rest of the game, helped Gillian clean up her sticky things, and even got the six-year-old to take her bath, eat some SpaghettiOs, and get into her Garanimals. His daughter was fast asleep in her room and the Sunday night game was half over when he saw the car headlights sweep across the curtains.

The murmur of police radios out on the porch and then a sharp knocking. He opened the door to see two Nashville cops standing there, heavy and pulled in, like birds get when they sense a storm coming and the air is too thick to fly, and he knew, he knew, he just knew . . .

We found your wife's car, Mr. Buchanan, in a wooded area north of town.

The driver's door was open, and there was blood on the seat.

There was a baby seat in the back. It was empty. Do you have a child, sir? I mean, besides the little girl over there?

Gillian had come out of her room and was standing there staring at the cops, twirling a strand of her blonde hair. After that, the cops followed him next door while he got Mrs. Prescott to watch Gillian. He was allowed to drive his own truck down to the station and they took him into a small hot room.

Were you at home all evening, Mr. Buchanan?

Can anyone verify that?

How was your marriage?

Are you having an affair?
Are you in any financial trouble?
How much insurance do you have on your wife?

As the questions went on and on, he got the feeling they were never going to let him leave. But they did, finally. Maybe it would have been easier if they had just kept him there, locked him up. Because in the days that followed, the house, emptied of Rayna and baby Corey, felt too huge and too filled with a deafening quiet.

In the first week, the TV trucks camped at his curb, and every time he answered the phone it was another reporter. The cops kept coming back with *just one more question, Mr. Buchanan.* Everyone wanted a piece of him; everyone wanted his confession on tape, because it was easier to believe "that nice man next door" could kill his wife and baby than it was to imagine a faceless monster out in the dark, and that it was just random good luck that the monster hadn't picked them instead.

In the second week, when Gillian left, wheeling her pink suitcase out behind Rayna's parents to their car, his last barrier to oblivion was gone. For a while, he hid the empty scotch bottles in the garage, not wanting the neighbors to see them in the trash by the curb. But finally he just didn't care.

Two months after Rayna and Corey disappeared, his boss called him in. He had been expecting it because how often could you drag in at noon smelling of booze before you were told that maybe you needed some time off to think? When he was fired, it was almost a relief.

Not long after that, the notice came in the mail. His in-laws were contesting custody of Gillian. He hired a lawyer and sat in the stuffy courtroom, watching the sleet pelt the windows, listening as they called him unfit to take care of himself, let alone a six-year-old girl, and all he could think was that it was true. Then his mother-in-law got up there and said he'd told Rayna that he had never wanted another kid.

Guilty, guilty as charged. Until I held my son for the first time.

After he lost Gillian, after his bank account was drained, he sold the house in Berry Hill, taking a loss in the lousy market. He found a furnished apartment in downtown Nashville and enough construction work to keep going. He was down to his last fifty bucks when his lawyer called him—out of pity, Buchanan guessed—saying he needed to track down a missing witness and was Buchanan interested in some freelance investigative work?

That was how it started. One desperate gig where he went looking for a loser and ended up finding himself.

He didn't even know then that it was called skip tracing. He just did the job and did it so well that within six months he had had enough money to buy a good camera and some business cards. He loved the work because it was nothing like the drudgery of insurance fraud. It let him move in shadows and silence, watching people the way he watched birds. It let him crawl inside other people's minds and emotions, mining their mysteries without giving back anything of himself.

He loved the fact he was finally able to send some money to help Gillian. He loved that it kept the memories of Rayna and Corey at bay. Or at least it had until now.

The district attorney in Nashville is preparing an indictment against you.

It had been five years, but he knew that charges could come anytime, even a decade after a murder, even with minimal evidence, even without a body. But he had hoped the truth would somehow keep him out of a courtroom again.

He had to know if what McCall had told him was true.

He pulled out his cell and scrolled to the Nashville name listed in his contacts—Gary Pitts. He had retained Pitts in the custody battle for Gillian, but he hadn't talked to him in years. Buchanan wondered if the lawyer would even take his call.

He did.

"You're lucky I'm talking to you," Pitts said. "You still owe me five grand, Clay."

"I know, and you'll be getting it soon," Buchanan said. "But right now I need something important."

Pitts was silent.

"I heard a rumor the prosecutor was taking the case to a grand jury, looking for an indictment," Buchanan said. "Is it true?"

He heard Pitts let out a slow breath. "I was going to call you once the grand jury went into session, but yeah, it's true."

Buchanan lowered his head, speaking softly so the bartender wouldn't hear him.

"What do they have now that they didn't have five years ago?"

"Your daughter."

"I don't understand."

"I don't have the statement in front of me yet but I heard Gillian's psychiatrist—she's been seeing one, you know."

"No, I didn't know."

"Well, I heard that the psychiatrist is claiming she's recovered repressed memories of the night Rayna disappeared. She's saying she heard her mother come home, heard an argument between the two of you, then heard a door slam."

"That's a lie."

"Maybe, but it's the meat of their argument."

"My in-laws have brainwashed her."

"Maybe that's true, too, but the grand jury will believe her, Clay," Pitts said. "She's a sweet, credible witness and juries, by their nature, look for someone to blame so they can feel like they did their job. I think you're in trouble."

Buchanan took a slow drink and then stared into the empty glass. "How much will it cost me to retain you for the trial?"

"I'm not a criminal lawyer."

"I want you," Buchanan said.

"No, you don't. I'd be in over my head. I'll come up with a few referrals for you, but I can't promise anything."

McCall's voice was in his ears again. *I can promise you won't see one day in prison.*

"I'll get back to you, Gary," Buchanan said. He hung up and dropped his phone to the bar. His eyes drifted back to the man in the mirror.

What is it you want, Bucky?

He wanted his daughter back.

And he would do whatever it took to make that happen.

♦ ♦ ♦

Back at the hotel, he stopped off at the desk to see if McCall had left anything for him. The clerk handed him a plain manila envelope. "And that young lady over there has been asking for you," he said, pointing his pen.

Buchanan turned. It took him a moment to spot the woman sitting in the corner. She was wearing a tan trench coat, her head bowed over her phone and her face hidden by a curtain of long blonde hair. When she tucked her hair behind one ear, he recognized her—Joanna McCall's daughter.

She looked up from her iPhone as he approached, her eyes sliding over his soaked jacket, down to his muddy boots, and back up to his face. She didn't smile as she stood up.

"Miss McCall." He couldn't remember her first name, and he had the feeling she wouldn't like him using it anyway.

"I've been waiting here an hour to see you, Mr. Buchanan," she said.

"You should have called. Your mother has my number. No need to make a special trip on such an ugly night."

"I didn't call because I don't want my mother to know about this. Let's get that clear right from the start." She dropped her phone into her big red feedbag of a purse. "Buy me a drink. My father's paying for it, right?"

He followed her to the same bar he had abandoned earlier that day and into a corner banquette set in an alcove with midnight blue walls and pinprick spotlights in the ceiling like a Milky Way sky. She ordered a glass of Sancerre; he opted for club soda. She shrugged off the tan trench, revealing black leggings and a white silky blouse. She had pulled out her iPhone, and her thumb was working furiously as she scrolled through her messages. He suppressed a sigh, waiting.

"So what's this all about, Miss McCall?" he asked finally.

Her eyes came up to meet his. She hesitated and then set the phone on the low table.

"There is something you need to know about Amelia," she said. "Something my mother didn't tell you."

"Such as?"

The waitress appeared, setting their drinks on the table. When Joanne McCall's daughter reached for her glass, her diamond bracelet sparked in the light. Her name came back to Buchanan in that moment—Megan.

"So why are we here, Megan?" he asked.

She took a drink of her wine before she decided to answer.

"Amelia was badly hurt," she said.

"No doubt. Her head made a good-sized crack in the windshield." He picked up his club soda.

"No," Megan said. "You don't get it. He hit her. Alex hit her."

Buchanan set his glass down.

"How do you know this?" he asked.

"I just know."

Buchanan shook his head slowly.

"You don't believe me."

"Not without some evidence. Did you ever see him do it?"

She shook her head.

"Did you ever see bruises or anything on Amelia?"

Again, she shook her head, but her eyes remained steady on Buchanan's. "You don't know Alex," she said finally. "You don't know what he can be like."

"Why don't you tell me?"

"Alex can be very charming, but he's a very jealous man."

"Amelia Tobias is beautiful. Husbands of beautiful women get jealous. It's normal."

Megan gave him a hard stare. "This wasn't normal. How Alex treated her wasn't normal."

She looked away, out over the bar. When he picked up his club soda, he angled his wrist so he could see his watch. Almost eight. He needed some food, and then his plan was to get upstairs to finish going through the stuff in that cardboard box more carefully. He still had to track down Carol Fairfield.

"Amelia told me," Megan said.

"Told you what?"

"That he hit her."

Buchanan shook his head. "Why would she confide in you about something like that?"

Megan lowered her head, and the curtain of blonde hair hid her face. When she looked up again, her face was flushed but her eyes were steady on his.

"I was raped," she said. "Seven years ago, when I was a senior at FSU. It was my boyfriend. I reported it to the campus police, but it never went anywhere because my mother convinced me I had to let it go. But she told Amelia about it and—"

"Why?"

Megan stared at him. "Why what?"

"Why would your mother tell Amelia something that personal about you?"

Megan didn't blink. "My mother tells her everything."

But Amelia, according to everything Buchanan had found out about her, told no one anything. "Why would Amelia tell you about Alex?" he asked.

"I guess she thought I'd understand."

"Does your mother know about Alex?"

"No."

"Your mother is her best friend."

Megan was silent for a long moment. "Friend isn't the word. My mother calls Amelia her older daughter."

There was touch of bitterness in the woman's voice.

"Amelia has a thing about never wanting to disappoint people," she said. "And my mother has this blind spot when it comes to Amelia." She let out a long breath. "My mother is very . . . invested in Amelia."

That much was true, at least. Joanna considered Amelia her very own Eliza Doolittle, and Amelia played that part to perfection. As for confiding in Megan, on a basic level it made sense. Joanna was at least twenty years older than Amelia, but Megan was only five years younger. If you needed to unload a secret on someone, wouldn't you talk to a woman your own age?

He studied Megan McCall in the dim light, trying to get a read on her. Her pain about her own rape seemed real, but why was she telling him this? What was in it for her?

"When I met you at the yacht club the other day, I got the feeling you don't really like Amelia," he said.

"I don't, especially."

"So why are you telling me this?"

Again her eyes were steady on his. "No woman deserves to be a punching bag."

"Did Amelia ever confide in you about other things?"

"Like what?"

"Like being involved with another man?"

Megan seemed mildly surprised by the question. "No. But like I said, Alex is really possessive of her, so maybe there was another guy, I don't know. More likely, I think she just had enough and decided to get away from Alex the easiest way she could."

"I wouldn't call wrecking your car in the Everglades an easy way to get away."

"She just wanted to leave. Why can't you let her do that?"

"I have a job to do, Miss McCall," he said.

"A job," she said slowly. "Alex didn't hire you, did he? My father was the one who hired you."

Buchanan said nothing.

"My father is very good at getting people to do things for him, even if they don't want to."

"What do you mean?" Buchanan asked.

She gave him another hard stare. "Do you like to gamble, Mr. Buchanan?"

Buchanan shook his head. "I don't like giving my money away."

"I love to gamble," she said. "It's not about the money, it's about winning. My father gambled on Alex. He took him from some little law office up in Orlando and turned him into a real lawyer, a very rich lawyer. Alex owes him big time, and you can bet my father will call in his marker someday."

Megan picked up her phone from the table and rose, draping her trench across her arm. "You don't owe my father anything," she said. "You should get out of this before you do."

Buchanan watched her disappear through the door and then signaled the waitress and ordered a scotch.

Did Megan McCall know about the hit on Amelia? But it made no sense for McCall to tell his daughter something that could expose her legally if this all blew up. But she had some kind of agenda, and he didn't think it was about Amelia.

Was it about Alex? Was Megan protecting him from something?

He picked up the scotch and took a long drink. Alex Tobias's voice was there in his head now, coming in that awful pleading tone.

Mel. Mel. My Mel . . .

Buchanan realized he couldn't remember Tobias ever saying his wife's name without attaching the possessive pronoun to it. And he was thinking about his first impression of the guy that day back at the restaurant. Hadn't this been in the back of his brain from the start?

It was always the husband, wasn't it? The husband was always the first suspect. The husband was always the monster.

CHAPTER NINETEEN

The first thing Alex did when he got home was go through the ground floor and turn out the lights. It had become part of his ritual since Amelia left. Coming back to the house each night and being confronted with all the whiteness and mirrors and glass made him feel exposed, like some *thing* that had washed up on a beach without its shell, like those deflated blue man o' war things he used to find on Destin Beach after storms.

The second part of the ritual was to get a glass and a bottle of vodka from the bar and go straight to his study. He never bothered to change out of his suit, just shucked off the jacket and tie and dropped into his chair.

The first drink went down as fast as he could stomach. After that, he tried to pace himself because even in the fog of his despair, he knew he was drinking too much, forgetting to eat and do most normal things a person did.

Alex ran his hand over his jaw. Had he shaved that morning? He couldn't even remember. He couldn't remember anything he had done today once he had closed the door of his office back at the firm. His secretary had left him alone. Even Owen had stopped bothering him.

Alex folded his arms on the desk and laid his head down.

"Mr. Tobias?"

He raised his head and squinted toward the door. Someone had turned on the hall light but the person standing there was just a small silhouette.

"Are you okay, Mr. Tobias?"

He recognized Esperanza's voice but didn't respond.

"It's six thirty. I leave for the night now, okay?" she said.

He nodded.

"You want I bring you something? A sandwich, maybe?"

He shook his head.

She hesitated and then came into the office. She set a stack of mail on the desk and reached for the light switch over the credenza behind him.

"Leave them off. Please."

She backed away from the desk. When she got to the door, she stopped and turned. "I sorry but I forget something."

"What?" he whispered.

"The dog spa call again today. They want to know when you come get Brody."

The dog. The damn dog. He couldn't even think about this right now.

"Tell them to keep him there," Alex said.

"But Mr. Tobias, they say—"

"I can't have the dog here right now. There's no one to take care of it."

"Okay, Mr. Tobias. I call them in the morning."

She left, leaving the door ajar to allow a shaft of hallway light to cut the darkness. For a long time, Alex just sat there, staring into the shadows. He was thinking about that picture Buchanan had showed him when they were sitting outside the house in Georgia, the picture of Mel when she had still been dancing. He was thinking about Buchanan's big ugly hands holding her picture, thinking about how he had wanted to do something in that moment—hit the fucker or break his fingers, because he was touching her.

But he hadn't. He had sat there in the backseat, his feeling of impotence rising in his throat and almost choking him.

The picture of Mel . . .

He stared hard at the cabinet across the room, and then he rose slowly and went to it. He opened the top drawer. It was there, just as he remembered.

He pulled out the red scrapbook, took it back to his desk and sat down. When he turned on the small halogen desk lamp, the lettering Amelia had printed in black marker on the front of the scrapbook jumped out at him.

The Story of Us

Years ago, when she had told him she was going to put their pictures in a scrapbook, he had kidded her about being sentimental and old-fashioned. Who bothered to paste things in a book anymore? Every photograph they had ever taken he had carefully stored in Dropbox. But Mel hated computers, hated the idea of their life "floating around in the Cloud," so she had prints made and created the scrapbook. When she showed it to him, it had bothered him at first, seeing his life laid out on paper. But in his deepest place, in the best part of his heart, he had loved her for it: loved the stupid banality of a scrapbook, loved the idea that she loved him so much that she had taken the trouble to put it there on these pages, in a big red book, for all to see even after she—they—were gone.

When he opened the cover, the binding made a small cracking sound.

He stared down at their wedding photo.

A beautiful eight-by-ten color portrait taken on their wedding day. Amelia in a white gown and him in a black suit, posed at the altar. From the first night he had seen her dance, to the moment captured in this photo, two years had passed.

He had wanted her from the beginning. After one performance, Joanna had had invited some of the ballet company's dancers to a party at their home on Mercedes Drive. Amelia was as mesmerizing on that crowded patio as she had been on stage, draped in a white silk dress, her hair sparkling with tiny green stones. They began dating the next week, and two months later, he proposed. She turned him down.

It's too soon, Alex. I just got promoted to soloist. I love you but . . .

He stopped asking, and they continued to see each other when they could. Lead roles came in quick succession for her, physically demanding ballets that left her exhausted and plagued with small injuries. She was always at rehearsal, taking class, or in physical therapy. On the nights she did come to stay at his home, she never got there before eleven. And the next morning, in the bathroom trash can, he would find the bloodied Band-Aids from her feet.

Then it all changed.

The company was on its last night of a five-week tour. He had gotten the call on his cell just as he was heading home from a long night at the office. Mel had taken a horrific fall during a performance.

The chartered jet got him to Tampa just as she was coming out of surgery. He was there holding her hand when the orthopedic surgeon told her she had undiagnosed early-onset osteoporosis and showed them an X-ray of her pelvic bone that didn't even look like solid bone at all but like white lace.

She cried when the surgeon told her she wouldn't dance again. He wanted to cry because nothing he said or did seemed to help. But the tears never surfaced because there was an ugly little whisper echoing in his head, repeating over and over, *my Mel is coming back to me, my Mel is coming back to me.*

And she did. Only six months after her fall, she accepted his proposal.

He was so afraid she would change her mind that he insisted on a quick wedding. There wasn't even time to buy her a good ring.

He turned the page of the scrapbook. First came all the photographs from the wedding ceremony and the small poolside reception at the yacht club. Then came the photographs from their honeymoon. Alex slowed as he turned these pages, the memories pouring back. They had picked up the rental car in Aix-en-Provence and driven without reservations or a set route, wending through the hills and stopping in whatever village caught their eye.

God, the photographs . . .

He had bought Amelia a new Nikon digital camera, and she had taken beautiful pictures. The Roman ruins in La Turbie, the ochre cliffs in Roussillon, the lavender fields in Saignon. And the view from the window of their hotel in Menton of a half-finished bottle of wine and two oranges on the sill with fishing boats beyond.

It was in Menton, the village near the Italian border, where he had found the ring. They were in an antique shop and he saw a slender silver band. It was carved to show two interlocked hands. The shopkeeper told them it was an old *fede* ring and that *fede* meant "faith." Alex bought the *fede* ring, and he slipped it on her finger right there in the shop.

She wore it until he insisted on buying her the ten-carat diamond, then she taped the little ring in the scrapbook, next to the picture of the view from their room in Menton.

He ran his fingers lightly over the picture, as if mere touch could bring it all back. And for a moment, it did. The silky taste of the Meursault wine, the sound of the rain, the feel of Mel's hair brushing his chest as she moved above him.

I never want to leave this place, Alex.
Then we won't.

But they did come home, back to the place where Mel's career had been fractured. Soon, she was on anti-depressants, still facing months of physical therapy. He and Owen were expanding the firm so quickly, sometimes he didn't even make it home at night. Joanna McCall took Mel in hand, distracting her with shopping and travel, and got her involved in charity work and her friends at the yacht club.

One night Alex came home to discover Mel had dyed her hair blonde and was wearing blue contacts. She surprised him again when she told him she wanted to buy a run-down mansion on Castilla Isle. And although he didn't want to own an old house, he was glad the long renovation kept her occupied, and he was proud when *Florida Design* did a cover story on the house and his wife.

Two years after she fell, Mel returned to the Miami City Ballet's production of *The Nutcracker*, this time to sit by his side in the audience. He didn't know how she felt about not being up there in the spotlight, and he sensed it was best not to ask. But he hoped that she was finally coming to terms with her career ending.

Alex flipped the pages back to the wedding portrait.

It had been an illusion, he knew now. It had been an elaborate act, like what happened on stage in the ballet. It was makeup, fake moonlight, and papier-mâché mansions. And Mel? Had she been playing a role, just like when she danced? And what about him?

Alex closed the scrapbook.

What had caused the next break between them? Was it when the doctor told Mel she had a blocked fallopian tube and could never get pregnant? Was it when, after sitting by her mother's bedside for weeks in Iowa, she'd had to watch her die? Was it when that man in uniform came to the door to tell them about Ben?

Joanna was the one who told him that Mel was drowning. He had been so consumed with getting the firm's new financial and tax planning department launched that he had missed all the signs. Joanna convinced him to send her away to some place in Boca Raton that specialized in depression treatment. But even when Mel came home, he knew nothing had changed.

She kept drifting away, withdrawing from him emotionally, bringing that damn dog and that Kindle to bed with her every night, pulling away whenever he reached for her.

Finally, he drifted away, too. Out of their bed and into the guest room down the hall. Back into eighty-hour workweeks where he at least had the satisfaction of watching the firm thrive. Back into the numbing solace of drink and the enfolding, welcoming warmth of . . .

"Alex?"

He looked up. Another woman was silhouetted in the hallway light, leaning against the door frame. He stared at her for a long time and then turned the scrapbook facedown on the desk.

"What are you doing here, Megan?" he asked softly.

As she came into the room, he caught the faint smell of her perfume mixed with rain.

"Why haven't you called?" she asked.

He shook his head slowly. He didn't look up at her as she came closer, pausing at the side of the desk. When she reached across the desk to pick up the bottle of vodka, he focused on her sleeve, on the beads of water glistening on the tan trench coat like the diamond bracelet on her wrist.

"How much have you had to drink tonight?" she asked.

He didn't answer. She picked up the glass, filled it from the bottle and took a drink. When she sat down on the edge of the desk, he finally looked up.

"How did you get in?" he asked.

"You gave me a key."

He did? He couldn't remember. In all their times together, they had never met in his home. "You shouldn't be here," he said.

"Well, where do you want me to be, Alex? How about the Ritz-Carlton? Would that make it easier? Do you want me to go back there and wait for you like a good little girl?"

He shut his eyes, thinking back to Friday night. The night of Mel's accident, the night he used the cover of a golf meeting with a client in

Palm Beach so he could be with Megan. He had lied to Owen about being delayed in getting to the Leggett merger celebration over on Marcos Island. Owen hadn't known where he really was that night.

Just like Owen doesn't know I've been sleeping with his daughter for six months.

"Are you going to answer me?"

It took every ounce of his energy to look up at Megan, and in that moment he understood that his crushing fatigue didn't come from not sleeping or eating. He realized, with a sudden stabbing clarity, that it came from the effort of living a life of lies. Not even the large lies, but years and years of little lies that built up on him like ice until he couldn't bear the weight anymore.

"Megan," he said. He looked away, down at his hands still resting on the scrapbook.

"Don't talk," she said.

He looked up. "What?"

"Don't say anything right now. You're not thinking straight. When was the last time you got any sleep?"

"I don't . . ." He shut his eyes and slumped back into the chair.

"What do you want?" she whispered.

He wanted . . .

"What do you need, baby?"

He heard the rustle of her trench coat and sensed her moving off the desk. When the halogen light went off, he still didn't open his eyes. Then her hands were on his knees, gently pushing his legs apart. Her smell swirled closer in the dark as her fingers worked on his belt buckle, and when she unzipped his pants he groaned.

The tickle of her hair on his forearm and then the wet warmth of her mouth as she took him in. He shut his eyes tighter as he reached for her head, pulling her closer.

What do I need? Who do I need?

"Megan . . ."

Her fingers moved up his thighs.

What do I want? I want to feel like I did ten years ago. I want to feel good and clean. I want to feel something, anything again. I want Mel.

"Megan, stop."

But she didn't.

He grabbed her head and moved her away. But she clutched his thighs and lowered her head again to his penis.

"Stop it!"

He gave her a hard push and she spun back against the desk, then slumped to the floor. She lay there for a moment, blinking hard. He reached for her, but she jerked away.

"What the fuck is the matter with you?" she said.

"I'm sorry. Jesus, Megan, I'm sorry."

Again he reached for her, but she scrambled to her knees, wiping her mouth. She got up slowly, putting out a hand to steady herself against the desk.

He stared at her. "This isn't going to work. It never really worked."

"You made promises to me, Alex."

He shook his head as he zipped his pants. "I know. I did a lot of things."

In a flash, he could see himself again standing by a canal with Owen in the darkness, looking down at the black water.

"I did a lot of things," he said. "But no more. It's over."

Tears welled in Megan's eyes, but unlike all the other times she had cried for him, he felt no sympathy. He just wanted her gone.

"I'm sorry," he said. "I'm really sorry."

She brushed her hair from her face. "That's the problem with you, Alex. You're always sorry."

She grabbed her trench coat and purse and left the office.

He stood there for a moment and then reached for the vodka bottle to refill his glass. After slugging it down, he sat back in his chair and opened the scrapbook.

Mel had looked so different then, her hair the color of brown November leaves, her eyes the color of pale tea. He thought back again to that moment in the car in Georgia, how Buchanan's eyes had lingered on Mel's picture before he handed it back over the car seat.

Buchanan's words came back to him, too, what he had said about Mel.

She's a different woman. And you're going to have to be a different man to get her back.

The bastard was right. Things had to change. *He* had to change. Ending the affair with Megan was just the first step. He wasn't sure what else he needed to do but he did know one thing—that he would do whatever he needed to get Mel back.

CHAPTER TWENTY

As Buchanan swiped his room key against the lock, his thoughts were still on Megan McCall and how she'd sounded when they had talked in the bar. Could a daughter's voice have any more venom in it when she spoke about her father?

Since then, he had been trying hard not to think about his own daughter, but Owen McCall's words kept coming back to him, what the man had said in the darkness of the car back in Georgia.

A daughter who by all accounts hates you because she thinks you killed her mother and baby brother.

Buchanan set his canvas bag on the desk, then dropped down onto the bed, thinking now about Gillian.

She had been only six when it happened. But she was eleven now, old enough to feel the ache of a mother's absence, old enough to listen to the lies poured into her head by Rayna's parents, and old enough to believe that someone had to pay.

In the rational part of his brain, he knew the courts would probably be on his side. The idea of repressed memory, especially in children, had been dismissed repeatedly by the courts in the last ten years. The doctors even had a new name for it—false memory syndrome. A memory, especially if it was fed by outside forces, might be factually wrong.

But the person, especially a girl, could still believe that it was true and carry it in her scarred heart for the rest of her life.

His phone pinged with an incoming text. He was tempted to ignore it, but finally he rose slowly and grabbed the phone off the desk. It was from Pitts, his lawyer in Nashville.

indictment coming 15 days

Buchanan deleted the text. It took almost all that was left of his energy, but he pushed Gillian's face from his mind and let Amelia's take its place. There was no time for anything now but doing his job. He didn't have much time to find her. He had to get this over with.

Using his iPhone, he scrolled through his e-mails, looking for something about his payment from Owen McCall, but there was nothing. He was about to delete the e-mail from someone named HKarmon.nybc@gmail.com when he read the subject line: INQUIRY EX DANCER. He called it up:

Dear Mr. Buchanan,

Elise Cummings in our administrative office forwarded me your inquiry regarding Carol Fairfield. I researched our records going back as far as 20 years and found no such person ever listed as a dancer for the New York City Ballet. You might check with other companies in . . .

He threw the phone to the bed in frustration. His check of Amelia's Amex bills for the last five years revealed she bought a ticket to

Minneapolis every August. If she wasn't visiting Carol Fairfield, why had she lied to both her husband and Joanna McCall about it?

His eyes drifted to the cardboard box sitting in the corner. He went to it, hoisted it up, and emptied the contents onto the bed. Amelia's past tumbled out onto the bedspread—the kids books, the yearbook, clothing, the plastic flamingo, ballet shoes. Photographs fluttered out of the Capezio shoebox, clutter spilled from the plastic jewelry box, and the envelopes from Afghanistan slipped from their blue-ribbon binding down onto the carpet.

Buchanan stood staring at the mess for a long time, his anger and frustration building. He let it roll over him like a wave and when it finally receded, he sat down on the edge of the bed.

He scooped up a handful of photographs, but he had been through them already and found nothing helpful, just family snapshots of Amelia, her brother, and some of her mother.

He tossed the pictures to the bed and looked down at the floor. Ben's letters were scattered at his feet, and Buchanan felt a pang of guilt, like he had somehow desecrated a soldier's grave. He began to gather the envelopes together but paused when he noticed a single postcard. He picked it up, staring at the front. It was an old picture, like from the fifties, and showed people wading into a lake. There was a white diagonal band that read GREETINGS FROM ARNOLDS PARK.

He turned it over, recognizing the half-printed, half-cursive handwriting from Amelia's Day Runner.

Bennie: I found this old postcard in Mom's things and thought you'd get a kick out of it. Summer feels like a lifetime ago. Am going to see The Bird next month. Stay safe. Love, your Mellie.

It had no stamp on it. Why hadn't Amelia sent it? Then he noticed the date she had written—July 2011. He remembered that her brother had died that same month, so that was likely the reason the card was never mailed. He stared at the date. July . . . which meant Amelia was planning to visit "The Bird" in August. Did that have anything to do with her annual trips to Minneapolis? And what the hell was The Bird?

He flipped the card back to the front. Arnolds Park . . .

He went to his desk and fired up his Acer. It was the first entry that came up in Google.

HOME | ARNOLDS PARK AMUSEMENT PARK

www.arnoldspark.com/

Arnolds Park

On the shores of beautiful Lake Okoboji sits Arnolds

Park Amusement Park a unique destination for summer fun.

Shit . . .

He hurried back to the bed and dug until he found the old blue T-shirt. The writing on the front said UNIVERSITY OF OKOBOJI. Clutching the T-shirt, he went back to his laptop and Googled "University of Okoboji." It took him to a souvenir store called "Three Sons" in the town of Arnolds Park that sold the shirts for novelties. When he typed "Okoboji" into Google Maps, he found the lake was in northern Iowa, a five-hour drive north from Morning Sun. His brain was firing fast now, and he typed "Minneapolis" in the Google directions box. It was only a three-hour drive *south* from Minneapolis to the lake.

He sat back in the chair, staring at the Google map. Amelia flew to Minneapolis every August but it wasn't to see the non-existent Carol Fairfield. It was to go to this lake. But why?

He looked down at the other things on the bed. There had to be something here he was missing.

And then he saw it. The jewelry that had spilled from the plastic box lay in a tangle. It looked to be just the normal cheap junk a teenage girl might keep except . . .

There was an ornate gold brooch in the shape of a peacock, the tail set with colored gemstones. And a second pin, a big gaudy red and green parrot. He picked them both up. They were not the kind of things a teenage girl would wear. They were old-lady pins.

Am going to see The Bird next month.

The Bird wasn't a thing. It was a person. He had no clue who it might be and no way of knowing how much of Amelia's memory had returned. But if The Bird was someone she was compelled to visit every August, someone she needed to lie about, then the connection might be powerful enough to cut through the fog of amnesia and pull Amelia to go there now.

It was a long shot, but he had to trust his instincts. He slipped the bird pins in his pocket and began to put the rest of Amelia's past back into the cardboard box.

CHAPTER TWENTY-ONE

Dolly dropped her off in West Memphis, Arkansas, at a gas station near the exit ramp. The bus station was only a few blocks away, so Amelia grabbed a coffee and walked along a boulevard of small factories, convenience stores, and empty storefronts.

At the bus station, she almost wanted to cry when she discovered there were no buses to Morning Sun. The woman behind the counter suggested that Amelia rent a car from a Klinger's Klunkers, a place down the street owned by a man named Ed Klinger who offered use of his rust-bucket cars for a few dollars a day.

She knew she couldn't rent a car without a credit card, but as she stood outside the bus station in the wind, sipping her coffee, it occurred to her that maybe Ed Klinger would *sell* her one of his junkers for the right amount of cash.

And he did. A 1998 red Impala for five hundred dollars, the bill of sale and title paperwork made out to Amelia Brody without question. Another five hundred bucks persuaded Klinger to leave the license plate on the car.

"If you get stopped by the cops, just tell them I forgot to take the plate off," Klinger said, handing her the keys.

"I won't get stopped," she said.

He just nodded as he tugged his ball cap tighter down on his head. "The doors don't lock, and the trunk latch is broken," he told her.

"That's okay," she said as she got behind the wheel.

He leaned into the open window. "You plan on driving far?"

It was almost five hundred miles and seven hours to Morning Sun. "No," she lied.

"Good. The tires ain't so good either." Ed Klinger paused, giving her a stare that wasn't unkind. "You be careful, missy."

◆ ◆ ◆

It was snowing when Amelia turned off Highway 61 and began her last mile to Morning Sun. The flat land was littered with crushed cornstalks and the sun was a blurry white glow behind frosted-glass clouds. The landscape held only a vague sense of familiarity for her, something she found disheartening. She had hoped, when she crossed the state line, when she started seeing farms and barns and water towers, everything would come rushing back.

A sign came into view, and Amelia slowed the Impala to a crawl, squinting into the snow flurries to read it.

South Blair Street.

She turned right, into a neighborhood of big leafless trees and a long row of wood-frame homes. Her heart started racing. She knew this street.

The house on the corner—the one with the blue shutters—that had been where Mrs. Addison lived with her daughter Margie who had Down syndrome. And the next house . . . that was owned by an old man who had called the cops on her and Ben for stealing apples from his yard.

Then, as the trees parted, she saw an open field with goalposts and beyond that a big brick building. She hit the brakes, overwhelmed with memories: a band playing off-key, laughing faces around a bonfire, blue and gold streamers in a dimly lit gym, and her pink junior-.prom dress, the one she had found at Kohl's in Burlington. For a while, she couldn't move, but finally, as the swell of emotions waned, her eyes settled on the sign on the yellow lawn—Crusade High School.

I was here. I existed here. And I know now where I need to go.

She made a right turn, then a left onto Kearney Street. The vision of the house—*her house*—was crystal clear in her head even before she stopped the Impala on the side of the street. And it hadn't changed at all. A double-peaked A-frame home, painted burgundy with white shutters, surrounded by a large porch. Her gaze swung up to the second-floor windows, and she knew that her bedroom was the one to the left, the one with the green curtains. Her curtains had been . . . pink.

But who was here now? Her mother?

For a week, she'd been living with the feeling that her mother was alive, but suddenly the certainty of that was gone, replaced by an overpowering feeling of loss, like her brain was trying to prepare her for something.

Drawing a deep breath, she got out of the car and walked to the front door and knocked. When the door swung open, the heaviness inside her deepened. This woman was large, with black curly hair and small brown eyes that squinted hard at the stranger at her door.

"Hello," Amelia said softly.

"What can I do for you, miss?"

"This might sound silly, but can I ask you, I mean, could you tell me if . . ."

God, she didn't know her maiden name.

"I'm looking for a woman who used to live here," Amelia said.

"You mean Barbara Bloodworth?"

She had a name. She had a mother.

"Yes, that's her."

"Why you trying to find her?" the woman asked.

"She's my mother and I . . ." She faltered and cleared her throat. "We lost track of each other many years ago."

"Oh, well," the woman said, shifting her weight. "I hate to be the one to tell you this but Mrs. Bloodworth . . . your mother . . . she died about five years back."

Amelia put a hand to the doorjamb to steady herself.

"Are you okay?"

Amelia nodded slowly. "Did you . . . did you know my mother?"

The woman shook her head. "This house was empty for a long time. I bought the place last summer for a little more than the taxes that was due. I'm sorry."

Amelia stepped to the side, trying to see beyond the woman. But the living room was dark and it gave out a fusty closed-up smell. The woman started to close the door.

"Wait, please," Amelia said. "Do you know where her son might be? His name is Ben."

"I don't know anything about him, sorry."

Again, the woman tried to close the door.

"May I come in for a few minutes?" Amelia asked.

"In my house?"

"Yes, please."

The woman's eyes narrowed. "No, I'm sorry, miss. My husband's been real sick and I don't really think it would be a good idea. I'm sure you understand."

"Wait—"

The door closed with a soft click. Amelia stood there for a moment and then returned to her car. Tears burned in her eyes, but she angrily wiped at her face and started the engine. She would see her mother the only way she could—at the cemetery. And when she realized that she knew exactly where the cemetery was, a wave of hope returned. As hard as this trip had been, her past was re-forming. She was getting better.

Elmwood Cemetery was in the northwest corner of town, back-dropped by fallow snow-crusted cornfields that stretched to the horizon. She drove a short distance inside the gates, then got out of the car and looked around, pulling the collar of her sweater coat up against the cold wind.

Her head was filled with fragmented memories of a graveside service held under a cold white sun not so long ago. Had she been here for her mother's funeral? Yes, she remembered that now. She remembered, too, that she had stayed in the house on Kearney Street for weeks, tending to her mother before she died. And she remembered that they had been alone there.

Amelia stood still for a moment, unsure which direction to walk, then decided to trust her instincts.

The wind grew stronger, kicking up leaves that skittered around her feet. She tucked her cold hands inside her sweater pockets and kept walking, her eyes constantly moving across the gray rows of headstones. Then she saw the name—BLOODWORTH.

She moved slowly toward it. It was a plain square headstone, the granite weathered from the hard winters, but the letters were clear.

George Miller Bloodworth

1942–1994

A pit formed in Amelia's stomach as the first image of her father pushed forward in her brain. A tall skeletal man sitting alone in the shadows of the living room, his face a blue-gray mask in the reflected light of the television, his long gnarled fingers wrapped around a shot glass filled with Old Crow bourbon.

Don't bother your father, Amelia. He's in one of his moods.

Amelia wanted to look away from the name on the headstone, uncomfortable with the memories and sensations, but she knew she had to do this; she had to remember it all.

You're getting fat as the pigs. Going to have to start calling you Jelly-Belly.

A wash of humiliation warmed her face. Here she was, a grown woman, and those words—suddenly familiar words—still hurt. She closed her eyes, but her father's voice kept coming.

We can't afford them damn dance lessons, Barb. She'll have to quit.

And her mother's voice, quavering but with a strange ferocity. *She needs to keep going, George. She loves it and she's good at it.*

Amelia opened her eyes and let her gaze move to the next stone, new enough to still have a shine on its granite face.

Barbara Martin Bloodworth

1946–2009

More memories moved in, unclear but powerful. Her mother's light brown hair and sad hazel eyes. The sharp jut of her shoulder blades beneath a thin yellow dress as she hung white sheets on a clothesline. A single word came to Amelia as she thought of her mother . . . enduring. Enduring the starkness of a house where quarters were hoarded in Mason jars and small comforts were found in the shelves of the town library and the pews of the Baptist Church. Enduring an unaffectionate husband who spent his days dulling his misery with whiskey while he stared out at the walls of cornfields that edged their lives.

With the memories came a new heaviness. Was it guilt? She had been here during her mother's illness, but was that all? Had she done anything to make her mother's life better after her father was gone? Had she left this place and run away? Yes, she remembered that now. She had left to go to New York to study ballet. But what about after that? Had she ever come back here to visit? Had she ever brought her mother to that grand pink house in Fort Lauderdale?

Amelia touched the top of the cold headstone. The memories were re-forming but everything still felt disconnected and unsubstantial. There had to be more to her past here than this. She scanned the nearby headstones.

There was one nearby engraved with a single name—MARTIN.

She moved closer and spotted the first name below that—"John Willis 1921–1989." Martin was her mother's maiden name. Was this her grandfather? She had no memory of him at all. On the same stone was the name of his wife Avis Nadine. The name triggered nothing.

Amelia turned to start back to the car. But then out of the corner of her eye, she caught a headstone that spun her back.

BENJAMIN ROSS BLOODWORTH
Beloved Son and Brother
US Marine Corps
Killed in Action Afghanistan
2011

Something inside her broke, and she dropped to her knees, her mind whispering *no, no, no . . . no.*

The pain doubled her over, and she sat on the hard ground and cried. When it finally stopped, she felt nothing but a raw emptiness. What was she crying for?

That I came all this way and all I found were headstones? That I'm home but all I can feel is the need to get away again? That I still don't know who I really am?

With a hard draw of cold air into her lungs, she opened her eyes. Her glasses were fogged and everything was soft gray—the sky, the ground, the headstones. Her fury was gone and something new and strange had moved in, something she had felt once before. She had felt it the day she had left this place to go to New York—that she had a chance. Not just to break free but to fly.

She took off her glasses and wiped them with her sweater. She stood up, put the glasses back on, and blinked everything back into focus.

Her eyes returned to the headstone for Avis Nadine Martin. A new voice came to her, a woman's voice but not her mother's. This one was gravelly from cigarettes. Then her grandmother's face came into focus. It was Avis but it wasn't. Because she and Ben had always called her by her nickname, "The Bird."

A tiny little woman, with a cap of unruly white hair and darting green eyes. She wore a black Persian lamb coat that always had a gaudy pin on the lapel. She smelled of Tabu perfume.

Amelia stepped closer and peered at the name again.

AVIS NADINE MARTIN

1926–

There was no date of death. Was The Bird still alive? My God, she'd be almost ninety.

It started to snow again. It was so quiet in the cemetery Amelia could hear the hiss of the snow as it hit the ground. She tilted her face upward, feeling the touch of the flakes on her skin, cold and gentle.

She would find her. Somehow, she would find The Bird.

CHAPTER TWENTY-TWO

It was close to 11:00 p.m. by the time Amelia saw the glow of lights in the town ahead. A search on her iPad had brought her to this place in north Iowa. When she had typed in her grandmother's name, a website called PeopleFinders had told her there was an Avis Martin living in a town called West Lake Okoboji. The site wanted her to pay $39.99 to get the exact address but she couldn't access it without a credit card.

But she didn't really need it. As soon as she saw the name Lake Okoboji, she knew in her gut it was the right place. She wanted to believe that her instincts were somehow melding with her memories, providing her a strange kind of compass she could rely on until something more solid came back. But she knew she had been here before.

A welcome sign told her the town ahead was Arnolds Park. That name, too, registered as familiar, yet nothing she saw *looked* familiar.

The Impala's heater didn't work well, and she was half-frozen and light-headed with hunger. She spotted a motel, and there was a bar next door. She pulled the Impala into the bar's lot and hurried through the snow to the entrance.

The heat inside was like a warm embrace. The walls were ancient knotty pine varnished by years of smoke and frying grease, and a row of cracked red vinyl booths lined the wall opposite the long scarred bar. A string of twinkling lights sparkled against a flyspecked mirror behind the rows of booze, and a Christmas song—"Feliz Navidad"—floated above the swish of a dishwasher. The only other people in the bar were two old men playing cards in a far corner booth. The bartender, a heavy-set woman in a Hawkeyes sweatshirt, threw Amelia a curious look as she made her way to the bar.

Amelia settled on the old wooden stool, her duffel on her lap. The bartender tossed down a cocktail napkin.

"Hey there," she said. "I'm Kathy. What can I get you?"

"Can I get a sandwich?" she asked.

"Just chili left this time of night. But it's good."

"Okay. Chili and a . . ." Amelia's eyes drifted to a Miller beer sign behind the bar and she had no idea why but suddenly she wanted one. "A Miller, please. The kind in the clear bottle."

Kathy wandered down to a cooler. "Glass?" she hollered.

"No."

Amelia glanced around, struck by the idea that the woman in the red halter dress in the Fort Lauderdale magazine wouldn't be caught dead in this bar, drinking beer from a bottle.

Kathy returned with the beer, and a few minutes later, set a bowl of steaming cheese-topped chili in front of Amelia. It was delicious. So was the beer.

Kathy washed some glasses and wiped down the bar, then she returned to Amelia. "Where you from?"

It occurred to Amelia that this was the kind of town where strangers were immediately spotted. But it was also a town of people who had lived here their whole lives, people who might know her grandmother.

"I'm from Burlington," she said. "I'm trying to locate a relative. Her name is Avis Martin. Do you know her?"

Kathy, who was probably shy of thirty, shook her head. "Sorry, never heard of her. You try calling her?"

"I don't know her number."

"And directory assistance won't give you squat, right?"

Amelia had a thought. "Do you have a phone book?"

"Phone book? Wow, do they even make them anymore?" Then Kathy smiled. "Hold on a sec."

She came out from behind the bar, went to the pay phone in the corner, and unhooked a bound book from its chain. She brought it back and slapped it down on the bar, and then left to take a new round to the old guys in the back booth.

Amelia turned it around and opened it to the *M* listings. There it was—Avis Martin, 3611 Fairfield Street, West Lake Okoboji.

Fairfield. She *knew* a woman named Fairfield. Carol Fairfield, a friend from . . . where? Not here.

You going to Minneapolis this year, Mel?

Of course, Alex. I go see Carol every year. You know that.

How about I come along this time and meet this woman?

You'd be bored stiff. It's a chick trip.

Then she knew. Fairfield wasn't a friend, it was a place. *This* place, the road where her grandmother lived. She had flown to Minneapolis and come here many times, but why had she lied to her husband about seeing her grandmother?

Kathy had returned. "You find your relative?"

"Yes, I think so."

"You going to call her?"

Amelia had been staring at the name "Avis Martin" in the phone book and looked up quickly. No, she didn't want to call because she wasn't sure what she would say to a ninety-year-old woman she didn't fully remember. Her hope in coming here was to see The Bird face-to-face, because she was sure that when she did, all the missing memories would fall into place and words would not be a problem.

"I don't have a phone," Amelia said.

Kathy pulled a cell phone from her apron. "Here, use mine."

Amelia hesitated and then took the phone. She punched in the number, her heart pounding. She got a recording saying the phone had been disconnected, and hung up.

"It's been disconnected," she said, handing the phone back to Kathy. Relief set in, then disappointment. Was The Bird dead and buried somewhere up here, for some reason never making it back to the family plot in Morning Sun?

She looked at the cover of the phone book. It was from 2004, ten years ago. But the PeopleFinders site had shown that Avis Martin was still living in West Okoboji, and everything inside her was telling her The Bird was here. She could drive to the Fairfield Street address and see if anyone was there, but it was near midnight, and right now she couldn't bear knocking on another door and having another stranger tell her they didn't know where her family had gone.

Her eyes moved to the two old men sitting in the back booth. She pushed off her stool and walked over to them. Up close, they looked like twin characters from a cartoon or fairy tale but she couldn't place the names. Pudgy forearms, bulbous noses, big ears, and white hair.

"Excuse me," Amelia said.

Both men looked up from their card game.

"My name's Amelia, and I'm wondering if I could ask you something."

"Sure, missy."

"Have you gentlemen lived here a long time?" she asked.

"All our lives," one of the men said.

"Now, that ain't exactly accurate, Al," the other said. "We came here when we were six. And when we were ten we had to go live in St. Louis for a year when Ma got sick."

Smurfs, Amelia knew suddenly. That's what they looked like.

"She doesn't care about all that, Fred," Al said. "How can we help you, missy?"

"I'm looking for Avis Martin. She used to live here."

Al scratched his chin. "The name sounds familiar."

"Avis Martin," Fred said. "Wasn't she that piano teacher over in Wahpeton?"

"No, you're thinking of Marvis Boyd." Al was frowning; then suddenly he slapped the table. "I know who you mean! Birdie! Birdie Martin."

Fred smiled. "Yeah, they called her Birdie 'cause of her name. Avis and Martin, those are birds, you know."

"Yeah, she had that ol' house on Fairfield out by Atwell Point, with all them big lilac bushes outside."

Suddenly Amelia could see the bushes, a curtain of purple flowers swaying in the wind. And the smell, God, what a glorious smell, every summer.

"Yes, that's her," Amelia said. "Do you know where she is?"

Al drew a deep breath. "I heard she was in a home now."

"A home? A nursing home?" Amelia asked.

Al nodded. "I don't know for sure, but you could check easy enough 'cause we only got one here. It's called Edge of Heaven, 'round the west side of the lake."

"Thank you," Amelia said. "Thank you so much."

When she returned to her place at the bar, Kathy was clearing away her bowl and looked up. "Were they any help?"

"Yes, they were." Amelia pulled three tens from the duffel and laid them on the bar. "Here's for my dinner. Buy those gentlemen a round and keep the rest for yourself."

"Thanks. Will do."

Amelia gathered up the duffel and left the bar. She pulled her sweater coat tighter against the wind cutting across the lake. She was exhausted, and the cold was settling deep in her bones. The red **VACANCY** sign from the Lakeside Motel glowed like a beacon through the snow. She started toward it.

Tomorrow would be good, she knew. She knew, too, that for the first time in a week, she would sleep well. She had found The Bird.

◆　◆　◆

Her dreams were filled with strangeness. Not nightmares exactly, she realized upon awaking, but vivid hallucinatory images and meanderings. A screaming peacock whose tail fanned out into a rainbow. A giant wheel that spun off sparks that flew up and embedded in the night sky as stars. And an exhilarating dream of standing on a roof with Ben as someone yelled at them to jump off and fly away.

When she called The Edge of Heaven, the receptionist told her that Avis Martin was, indeed, living there but that visiting hours were delayed until two because today was set aside for the residents' monthly physicals. Amelia took a shower, and when she wiped the steam from the bathroom mirror, she was pleased to see that the bruises on her face were almost gone. She gently pulled the remnants of the dissolving stitches from her chin and combed her hair carefully. She wanted to look her best when she saw The Bird.

It was three more hours until she could go to the nursing home. She couldn't bear sitting in the motel waiting. She decided to go see the house on Fairfield Road.

As she steered the Impala slowly through the curvy roads of the lakeside neighborhood, she knew instinctively where to go. She was guided by something deep inside her, like an internal compass had clicked on, helping her find her way . . .

Home.

She stopped the car. It was a compact, two-story wood-frame house in a faded gray color, with a sloping front yard dotted with bare thick-trunked oak trees. There were some old aluminum beach chairs stacked near a weathered wood picnic table.

She peered out the window at the house for a long time. The two small windows flanking the screen door stared back at her like dark eyes, beckoning her. She killed the Impala's engine and got out.

Amelia sensed the house was empty. It had a lonely feel, like it was waiting for someone to come back and breathe life into it. She picked her way down the icy slope to one of the windows, wiped away the dirt with her sleeve and peered in.

It was a living room. White wainscoting and flowered wallpaper, mismatched Victorian furniture, odd fringed lamps. Amelia focused on an aluminum walker standing next to an upright piano. Suddenly, she could see herself sitting on the bench next to The Bird, who was playing and singing loudly, a song about a budgie.

No, no . . . *buddy.*

And then words were there in her head. *Nights are long since you went away, I think about you all through the day, my buddy, no buddy quite so true. Miss your voice, the touch of your hand. Just long to know that you understand. My buddy, your buddy misses you.*

It was the song The Bird sang to her all the time. The emotion swelled up from Amelia's chest and made her throat tight. She needed to see more.

She went to the other window. It was the kitchen. Old white wood cabinets with glass doors, red Formica counters, two checked dish towels still hanging by the sink. Burnt cookies . . . the smell was there in her nostrils. And the shrieking stream of profanity that poured from The Bird's lips as she pulled the smoking cookie sheet from the oven, and the sound of plates breaking against the wall.

And Ben. He was there, too, whispering to her to go upstairs and wait until the tornado blew over. Tornado? Had there been tornadoes here? A tightness began to build in Amelia's chest, crowding up against the good memories, and she swallowed hard against it.

She moved quickly around to the back of the house. There, far below, down a zigzag of wooden steps, lay the lake. It was gray-green and wind-whipped, but in her mind, Amelia was seeing it as it looked in summer—sun-flecked deep blue waters crisscrossed by the wakes of speedboats and water skiers—and she was hearing it, too—calliope music from the amusement park drifting on the warm wind.

Where was the park? She couldn't see it. The wind was making her eyes water. She pulled her sweater coat tighter and went up to the bank of windows, looking in.

It was a sun porch, filled with white wicker furniture, a battered desk, and an old table covered with a checkered cloth. She could make out the pieces of an unfinished jigsaw puzzle on the table.

What will this look like when we're done, Grandma?

I don't know, Mellie. Let's put it together and find out.

They had never finished the puzzle, Amelia remembered. Why? What had happened? She knew now that she and Ben had come to the lake house every summer; that it was their safe house, their refuge from the shadows and chill of the house in Morning Sun. When had she stopped coming?

The sun had disappeared behind a bank of bruised clouds hanging over the lake. It had to be near two by now. It was time to see The Bird.

CHAPTER TWENTY-THREE

Edge of Heaven was set on a gentle slope in a copse of silver pines over-looking Lake Okoboji. With its green shutters and fieldstone pathways, the small L-shaped home looked more like a summer retreat than an elder-care facility.

The lobby was warm, with wood floors covered with pink and green Oriental rugs and furnished with sofas and wing-backed chairs. There was a small Christmas tree set up in the corner. A woman in a nurse's uniform and a red cardigan sweater looked up from the reception desk as Amelia approached.

"Can I help you?" she asked.

"I'm here to see Avis Martin."

The woman stared at her hard, her expression turning from courte-ous to confused. Then she flashed a toothy grin. "Mrs. Tobias?"

The name hit Amelia like a punch to the chest. She looked at the woman's name tag, partially hidden by the sweater. Jill.

"Yes, hello, Jill."

"I didn't recognize you. I *love* your new hair," Jill said. "It's so chic, you know? So much more you."

Amelia forced a smile, but her mind was racing. How did this woman know her?

Jill still looked mildly confused. "We weren't expecting you. You always call and let us know when you're coming."

"It was a last-minute decision," Amelia said. "Can I see my grand-mother?"

Jill came around the desk and motioned toward a hallway. "Well, you've come on a not-so-good day. She didn't eat her lunch and she's having a blue day so far."

Amelia fell into step with Jill as she started down the hall. "How is she in general, Jill?"

"A little better than the last time you were here," Jill said.

I was here? When?

"I know that was an emotional visit for both of you," Jill went on, "but she's doing much better since the doctor switched her to the risperidone."

Nothing, none of it meant anything to Amelia. What was wrong with her grandmother? "Why did the doctor change her medicine?" she asked.

"She was having some nausea with the divalproex," Jill said. "As you know, it's very hard to find a workable treatment for bipolar disorder in the elderly."

Amelia stopped. *Bipolar?*

Jill turned back to her. "You okay, Mrs. Tobias? You look a little pale."

"I'm fine."

Jill waited for her to catch up and then went on talking. "Her demen-tia has progressed some, as well, I'm afraid. She's taken to obsessing over her house, you know, that one over on Fairfield? She doesn't understand why she can't go back there."

"But she still owns it, right?"

Jill gave her an odd look. "You're not going to sell it, are you?"

It's mine?

"No, of course not," Amelia said.

"That's good to hear," Jill said. "She lived there for so many years, you know. It's always hard when they have to leave their homes. We try to make them feel at home here, but it's never the same."

Amelia had a million questions. How long had The Bird been here? When had she been diagnosed as bipolar? But there was no way to ask anything without having to explain what had happened back in Florida.

Jill pushed open a door, and the scent of rose air freshener wafted toward them. A woman sat in a wheelchair, a hunched gray silhouette against the window. Amelia watched, frozen by the door, as Jill went to the woman.

"I have something for you, Avis," Jill said, pulling out a pack of Juicy Fruit gum.

"I don't need yellow," the old woman said. "I need blue. You got any Black Jack?"

"It's hard to find Black Jack, Avis."

The old woman grunted and looked away. Jill came back to Amelia at the door. "Do you want me to stay?" she asked softly.

"No, I'll be fine." Amelia's eyes were locked on the old woman.

After Jill left, Amelia drew a shallow breath and went toward the window. Her grandmother didn't look up. She was concentrating on a long colorful paper chain that lay coiled in her lap.

Amelia wanted desperately to see her grandmother's face, but the old woman ignored her, her head bent, her small hands weaving tiny pieces of pink paper into the end of the chain.

Dementia. Bipolar.

Go slow . . . don't force her.

Amelia waited, focusing on her grandmother's hands. They were liver-spotted and mapped with blue veins, the fingertips stained yellow from nicotine. But someone had painted her nails red. Red, the brighter the better . . . that had been The Bird's favorite color. But there had been so many other colors, Amelia remembered. And a closet stuffed with leopard coats, flowery summer dresses, and a gold lamé gown, all of it smelling of Tabu perfume. And a big wooden jewelry box, she could remember that, too. The Bird had let her go through it, a pirate chest brimming with pearl necklaces, jangling bangles, big gaudy rings, and pins shaped like birds.

"Hello," Amelia said.

Her grandmother looked up. Her mouth was stitched with wrinkles, but her eyes were a sea-foam green, like jewels pushed into a pincushion. Her hair was white and silky, and Amelia had a memory of an old Christmas tree topper shaped like an angel with a skirt made from white spun glass.

Amelia's heart gave. Her eyes teared.

"Who are you?" Avis asked.

Oh no, no, no. Please, God, no.

Amelia brushed at her eyes. "I'm Amelia. Your granddaughter." It was a struggle to keep her voice normal.

Something registered in the old woman's eyes, and for a moment, Amelia was sure The Bird knew her. But then it vanished.

"I'm not your grandmother, young lady."

Amelia slid into the chair opposite. A strong feeling of déjà vu began to settle in as her last visit here finally began to re-form in her head. It had been very hot, August maybe? It had been the first time The Bird had not recognized her.

Avis went back to her paper chain.

"Do you have a granddaughter?" Amelia asked.

"I have a granddaughter *and* a grandson," she said without looking up. "Mellie and Bennie, Bennie and Mellie."

Yes, that is what The Bird had called them, almost like they were twins. A sense of emptiness came over Amelia, the same as she had felt at the cemetery looking at Ben's headstone.

Amelia looked around the small room. There were three picture frames on the dresser. "May I look at your pictures?" she asked her grandmother.

Avis's eyes moved to the dresser and then back to her paper chain. "Sure. Just be careful."

Amelia rose, gathered the three frames and brought them back to her chair. The first was a sepia-toned wedding photograph, which Amelia now recalled seeing on the top of the piano at the lake house. Her grandfather looked solemn in his plain suit, but The Bird wore a sly smile and a slinky pale gown.

The second photograph was of her mother, Barbara, sitting near a Christmas tree, holding a baby. A little boy—Ben—sat at her knee. The third photograph was of Amelia and Ben, standing on the porch of the Morning Sun house. Ben about age fourteen, wearing a baseball jersey and baggy jeans. And her, all twig arms and long knobby legs, wearing a pink leotard and a blue tutu.

Amelia stared at the picture for a long time, struggling to make the memory come, and slowly it did. The photograph had been taken the day of one of her ballet recitals. She had fallen during her performance and almost left the stage in tears.

I'm so embarrassed. I want to quit, Grandma.

Baby colts fall down, Mellie, you've seen 'em do it. But they get up again and again and they learn to run. Some of them grow up to be thoroughbreds.

Amelia looked back at The Bird. Her hands had stopped working and she was staring out the window, squinting in the light. Amelia studied her profile, seeing herself in the severe angles and high cheekbones. A few more memories trickled back, split-second snapshots of her and Ben at the lake house. The feel of The Bird's hands as she gently braided her hair. Sitting on the porch with Ben, scraping cake batter from a big blue bowl.

"Would you tell me about your granddaughter?" Amelia asked.

Avis looked at her with suspicion. "Why?"

"I'd just like to know her better."

"You got a cigarette first?"

"No, I don't smoke. I'm sorry."

"They won't give me any. What, they think I'm gonna croak from lung cancer at my age? Gimme a break."

Amelia hid her smile. Oh yes, she remembered The Bird now.

Avis was staring hard at her and for a moment Amelia thought there was a flicker of recognition. Then she held up the paper chain. "I made this," she said. "I made it out of gum wrappers. Mellie taught me how."

I did? I don't remember that.

Her grandmother held up a gum wrapper. "I could use some help."

Amelia set the frames on the table and took the wrapper. It was Teaberry gum. Its odd taste came back to her, like Pepto-Bismol. "You'll have to show me what to do," Amelia said.

The Bird picked up a wrapper from the pile on the windowsill and began to neatly fold it into a narrow strip, then into a V-shape. Amelia copied her motions, and for a long time, the room was quiet as Amelia folded the wrappers and The Bird wove them into her chain.

"So, what do you want to know about Mellie?"

Amelia's head came up. The Bird wasn't looking at her, still intent on her chain, but there was a new softness in her voice.

"Whatever you can tell me about her," Amelia said.

Her grandmother looked up and smiled. "Well, she was a sweet little girl," she said. "Smart as a whip she was, and fearless. That girl wasn't afraid of anything."

Amelia stopped folding, her thoughts returning to her strange dream of standing on a roof with Ben. But suddenly she knew it wasn't a dream. It had really happened. One day The Bird had taken them up on her roof and told them they could jump and fly. And Amelia had almost done it—anything to please The Bird—but Ben had pulled her back. Ben had always been there to pull her back when The Bird had tried to push her too far.

A manic episode, Amelia thought sadly. Isn't that what they called it? Wasn't that what happened to bipolar people when their mood swung too wide? That day on the roof and the screaming fit over the burnt cookies—they were the negatives to all the positives.

Of course she had known about her grandmother's illness. But like so many details of her life, it had been erased and now it was coming back. The good and the bad, she had to reclaim it all.

"Mellie's father was a real son of a bitch."

Amelia looked up at her grandmother. Her voice had turned cold.

"I never understood what Barbara saw in that man," her grandmother went on. "He wasn't a good man. He wasn't a good father. Never saw nothing in those kids but mouths to feed. Ben, now I never worried much about him, but Mellie was too tender to understand that some men just can't love babies the way they should."

Amelia had a stab of memory, of being very small and trying to crawl up into her father's lap and him pushing her away. And later, being much older, and how he had called her Jelly-Belly and fought with her mother over the ballet lessons.

Where did the money come from, Barbara?

My mother sent it. And we're taking it, for Amelia's sake.

Amelia looked up at The Bird. "You paid for your granddaughter's ballet lessons, didn't you," she said.

"Damn right I did." The Bird pointed at the gum wrapper in Amelia's hand. "You done with that one?"

Amelia handed it over and picked up another Teaberry wrapper to fold. Again the room was quiet.

"Mellie is in New York City now," The Bird said suddenly. "She's a star ballerina, you know."

A star. Had she been a star? She had been a dancer but could remember almost nothing of it. Was all that part of her lost forever? Was there anyone who could help her find that again?

"Mellie never comes to visit anymore," The Bird said. "But that's to be expected. They fly away, get out in the world and they forget where they came from and who they were."

Amelia touched The Bird's hand. "I promise you, she hasn't forgotten you."

The Bird looked down at Amelia's hand. Then she grunted, set her paper down and looked toward the window.

Amelia was quiet, her heart swelling with affection for this woman. She wanted to put her arms around her and tell her she loved her, but she had no idea how The Bird would react.

Still, this feeling had been buried there inside her all week, even when she hadn't known her grandmother's name or been able to visualize her face. And if *she* could feel love for a woman she had not been able to remember, maybe The Bird could do the same.

Amelia leaned forward and wrapped her arms around her grandmother. At first, The Bird stiffened but then she melted into the embrace, her hands coming up to rest on Amelia's arms.

After a moment, The Bird drew back and straightened her shoulders. With trembling hands, she dug out a Kleenex from her sweater sleeve and dabbed at her eyes.

"I'm tired now," she said softly. "My brain is tired."

A scene flickered in Amelia's mind. She was sitting in the dark on a staircase, watching her mother and father in the living room below.

You shouldn't leave the kids with your mother, Barbara. She's crazy.
She's not crazy. She's just spirited.
She's getting worse. I don't want them going to the lake anymore.
She'd never do anything to hurt them. And they love her.

And then it was like the memories sped onward, a tape stuck in fast forward, and she saw herself not as a child but as a grown woman, sitting across the kitchen table from her mother, and there was a sense of emptiness in the house, like it was only the two of them left.

We're going to get married, Mama.

Have you told him about Grandma yet?

I need to find the right time.

Don't do it, Amelia. You don't want a man like Alex to find out you got craziness in your blood. You don't want him to change his mind. That almost happened with me and your father. You don't want to be alone in life, Amelia.

Amelia shut her eyes. My God, she remembered it all now. Remembered how she had made up the friend Carol Fairfield, how she would fly into Minneapolis every year and make the drive south to visit The Bird. She had kept it all secret, lying that her grandmother was dead and gone, just because she was afraid Alex would find out and leave her. Jesus, what kind of woman had she been?

"She died once."

Amelia opened her eyes. "I'm sorry, what did you say?"

The Bird had still been looking out the window and now her cloudy green eyes locked on Amelia.

"Mellie," The Bird said. "She almost drowned, when she was just six. Right out there in that lake."

Amelia looked to the window. She couldn't see the lake through the trees, but she knew it was there. And so was the memory of being back in the blue-green bubble, drifting, drifting, drifting downward toward the black.

"What happened to her?" Amelia asked softly.

"She waded out way too far. She was always going too far," The Bird said. "But Ben saw her hair in the water, floating there like seaweed, he said. He saw it and pulled her out. The man in the ambulance said Mellie had died, but Ben brought her back."

Amelia could remember none of that. She could remember the day on the roof when Ben had pulled her back, but nothing about almost drowning. Just the blue-green bubble and the slow swirl down toward the black.

"Mellie was a lucky girl."

Amelia was still staring out the window, and she looked back to see her grandmother smiling.

"Mellie got a second chance to live," The Bird said.

CHAPTER TWENTY-FOUR

She had to see it. She had to see the place where she had almost died. It wasn't anything rational or reasonable. It wasn't even something she wanted to do to bring yet another lost memory into focus. It came from a deeper need inside her.

Ever since Amelia had woken in the hospital bed, she had felt as if she were drifting slowly down to the blackness. But these last days, since leaving Hannah's home and now finding The Bird, had felt different, like she had found the strength to fight the downward pull.

But the need was there. The need to first find the bottom and feel it under her feet. She had to see the place at the lake where she had died and come back.

Back at the nursing home, Jill had told her where to find it. There was only one place folks went swimming, Jill said, and that was "Boji Beach" at Arnolds Amusement Park.

The map Jill had drawn was open on the passenger seat of the Impala, but after a mile or two down I-71, Amelia hadn't needed to look at it. There were strip malls and new condos, but she recognized the old marina, the abandoned Lake Lodges motel, and the iron and stone entrance of Okoboji Cemetery. Then there it was on her left—the huge white arch over the road with the sign—ARNOLDS PARK AN IOWA CLASSIC.

There was a large empty parking lot on her right, but she still couldn't be sure someone wasn't chasing her, so she didn't want to risk leaving the car out in the open. She drove down the long straight road, passing a shuttered pavilion. About halfway down the road, she pulled in and parked the Impala between two buildings. The car wouldn't lock and the trunk didn't close without the wire hanger to hold it, so she grabbed her duffel, buttoned her sweater, and started walking down the rest of the long straight road.

The first thing she noticed was the quiet—a silvery kind of silence where nothing moved. It was close to four now, and the sun was a pale pink glow in the western sky. The wind was slicing cold and hard off the water ahead.

The midway booths were all shuttered, most of the rides disman-tled. In the children's area, the small merry-go-round was sheathed in heavy plastic and tarps, and ahead of her, an old wooden roller coaster loomed against the gray sky like the humped skeleton of a dinosaur. She paused to take it in, her eyes locking on a small sign perched on the first hill: POINT OF NO RETURN.

Don't be scared, Mellie. I'll hold onto you.
I'm not scared, Ben.

Vivid memories were filling the holes in her head—riding the coaster, the Whip, the Dodgem cars. And at night, soaring upward on the giant Ferris wheel with Ben, the midway lights sparking up into the starry sky.

It started to snow lightly, but Amelia walked on, her duffel crushed to her chest. The lake finally came into view, gray green against the steel-gray sky. The ground suddenly shifted, and she looked down to see that the asphalt had changed to sand.

Don't go too far out, Mellie.

She walked down the gentle slope to the shoreline, the snow swirling around her like talcum powder.

Her chest grew tight, and she stopped. Her eyes moved over the lake, and then she closed them, drew a deep breath, and willed the memory to come.

In her mind, she kept walking, walking into the lake, the cool water rising up over her knees, then up to her chest. She kept going until . . .

Silence dropped over her, filling her ears, so quickly it took her breath away. The water eddied around her, pulling at her body, pulling her deeper and deeper downward, farther and farther from the sunlit green surface.

A fire in her lungs.

Lead in her feet as she struggled to find something solid to push against.

Then a light, like a bright fluorescent in the filmy green. And suddenly she was floating in the calming cocoon of the blue-green bubble, bodiless and without fear.

A hard yank on her hair and she was out of the bubble.

She's not breathing! Do something, Ben!

Pain. A hard pain, like someone pushing on her chest.

The warm press of a mouth against hers like a kiss but not a kiss.

Coughing. Coughing.

She's back. Thank God, she's back.

And she could see Ben's face above hers, dripping wet, scared but grinning.

Amelia opened her eyes.

She tried to hang on to it, but Ben's image faded, replaced by the endless roll of gray-green water and the misty horizon. She was back in the moment, back in this life. And for the first time in this awful week, she was sure of what she needed to do.

She needed to go backward.

She needed to go back to Fort Lauderdale to find out what had happened. She needed to find out what had happened that night in the Everglades, to find out why she feared the man she had married, what had happened to the woman she had once been. The Bird had said her Mellie wasn't afraid of anything. So she wouldn't be afraid now. She needed to go back to find out where she had gone.

CHAPTER TWENTY-FIVE

It hadn't been hard finding The Bird.

Buchanan's first step was to go through his notes from his first interview with Alex to retrieve the name of Amelia's grandmother. A quick search at PeopleFinders found Avis Martin was not dead at all but very much alive and living in an assisted-care facility called Edge of Heaven in Okoboji, Iowa.

Edge of Heaven.

Buchanan drew in a breath. Edge of hell was more like it.

He swung his Toyota into the parking lot of the nursing home. He had driven thirteen hours straight through from Nashville. Not because he had any hard evidence that Amelia would show up here. It was something else, something born of his experience chasing runners and what he knew people did when they were scared or needed to hide.

It was like birds. Or any animal, really. They would always seek out a secluded place if they felt sick or threatened. Woodpeckers climbed into tree holes, pigeons crawled into pipes, and ospreys returned to their old nests.

Avis Martin was all Amelia had. And right now, his hope that Amelia had come here was all *he* had.

Buchanan did a quick tour of the lot—only three cars, all with Iowa plates—and swung his car into a far corner. What was his next move? He had to know if she had been here, but he couldn't let anyone see him so they could identify him later. Things were different now. He was off the grid. He couldn't use his personal cell to talk to McCall, couldn't use his credit cards, or risk leaving any kind of trail for someone to follow. He wasn't a skip tracer any more. He was a hired killer.

He pulled out his burner phone and dialed the number on the sign out by the entrance.

"Edge of Heaven, this is Jill. How can I help you?"

"Yes, this is Delta Airlines. We're trying to reach Mrs. Amelia Tobias. We've located her lost bag."

"Oh, you just missed her. She left just a little while ago."

Sometimes you just get lucky. Fuck that, he was way past luck now.

"Well, this is the only local number she gave us and we'd like to deliver her bag to her tonight. Do you have any idea where she's staying?"

"No, she didn't say."

Buchanan rubbed his gritty eyes.

"But she did mention that she was going to stop off at Arnolds Park. There are two motels right near there."

Arnolds Park . . . the place on the old postcard.

Buchanan thanked her and hung up. He glanced at his watch. Four thirty and it was starting to snow lightly. He slapped open the map on the passenger seat. The park was only about a twenty-minute drive south on Highway 71. He shoved the car in gear and sped out of the lot.

♦ ♦ ♦

As Buchanan drove under the white arch, he glanced up at the lettering—ARNOLDS PARK AN IOWA CLASSIC. He was surprised the park wasn't gated or that the entrance wasn't at least chained off for the winter but then he saw a sign that said BOAT RAMP and realized maybe locals had access to the lake all year round.

He drove down a straight two-lane asphalt road. Far ahead, maybe the length of a football field, he could see where the road dead-ended at the shoreline of Lake Okoboji. He drove slowly, scanning for cops or guards but saw no one. To his left was a shuttered ticket house and a pavilion, and to his right was a vast empty parking lot. Up ahead, he could see an old wooden roller coaster and beyond that, other carnival rides covered with tarps. But the place was deserted—no people, no cars, no sign that anyone had been here since summer.

No sign that Amelia was here either. It was snowing, but the wind was so brisk that nothing was accumulating on the asphalt to leave tire tracks.

Buchanan stopped the car about halfway down the road and put it in park. He leaned back in the seat, fatigue washing over him. He turned up the heat and considered his next move.

Most likely, Amelia would get a room here in town for the night, maybe go back to see her grandmother again. He would stake out the nursing home tomorrow.

He let out a tired sigh. Shit, how in the hell had Amelia Tobias even gotten this far? He had checked all the bus lines and nothing came anywhere near this place. Had she found someone to drive her? Had she bought a car? Alex had found out that her diamond ring was missing from the hospital, so it was likely she had pawned it and was moving around on the cash she had gotten for it.

But money was never enough. He knew that from years of chasing runners all over the world. The best ones had that special kind of intelligence along with animal survival instincts. And they were all good liars. And Amelia had lied about a lot of things in her life.

Still, it was more than that. Despite what her husband thought, this woman was smart, animal-smart. She was as smart as . . .

A fucking crow.

His father had taught him all about crows. That they were second only to humans in intelligence, even smarter than apes, and could learn fast.

A half-forgotten memory came to Buchanan: lying on his stomach by the side of a road with his dad watching a crow try to crack open a hickory nut. It took the bird only five minutes to figure out that if he dropped the nut in the middle of the road, the cars would run over it and split it open. The damn crow even figured out that if he waited for the traffic light to turn red, he could walk right out there and pick up his nut.

Buchanan sat up in the seat and glanced at his watch. He had to find a motel, get some rest, and regroup.

The windshield was snowed over, and he switched on the wipers. He started to put the car in gear and then stopped.

A sliver of motion far down the road. He leaned forward, squinting into the dusk.

Someone was walking along the shoreline of the lake.

Then the person—just a gray blur in the flurries—disappeared.

Buchanan put the car into drive and eased slowly down the road. He was about twenty yards from the dead end when he spotted the rear end of a red car. It was parked off the main road between two buildings. He pulled in next to it and killed his engine.

He got out and walked a slow circle around the old Impala. He felt the hood—still warm. Arkansas license plate, trunk held closed with a coat hanger. Nothing inside that he could see except a crumpled bag from Wendy's and an empty Coke can. He looked up, toward the lake.

Whoever he had seen was gone now. But from his angle, he didn't have a clear view of the entire shoreline.

He pulled up the collar of his coat, put on his gloves and started down the road.

There was a line of trees that offered some cover, but he wasn't that worried about being spotted. If it was Amelia he had seen, it was unlikely that she suspected someone had followed her here, and she had no way of knowing who he was. This place was deserted; it was almost dark. He could leave her body in the lake, and it might look like she drowned, a victim of a random attacker, suicide maybe. It was the perfect place to . . .

He was sweating. It was freezing, and he was sweating and his heart was beating too hard and fast.

He rounded the corner of a building and froze.

She was about thirty feet away, standing at the edge of the water with her back to him so he couldn't see her face. He edged closer, his arms rigid at his sides, his gloved hands clenching and unclenching.

I need to see her face. I need to be sure. I need to see her face. I need . . .

She was just six feet away from him now.

"Amelia."

She turned at the sound of his voice.

Her eyes, dark and questioning behind big purple glasses. Her mouth, dropping open to form an *O*. Her body, a swath of gray in the gloom, bending away like a tree in the wind. She was clutching a brown leather bag to her chest, as if it offered some protection.

"What?" she said. "Who are you?"

Don't think. Just do it.

He lunged at her, and she spun away. He got a handful of her sweater, but she jerked out of his grasp and stumbled away from him, running down the snowy shoreline. He went after her, tackling her just before she reached a rock jetty. She dropped the brown duffel, and they rolled on the snowy sand and into the lake.

Buchanan gasped as he plunged into the searing cold water. He could feel Amelia kicking and flailing against him, and he tightened his grip on her arm.

They both emerged coughing and panting.

She was strong, but he was stronger. He got on top of her in the shallow water, straddling her waist and holding her neck. Her hands came up to grasp his wrists.

His fingers tightened around her neck. He thrust her down into the cold water. She fought hard, her fingers digging into his hands.

Gurgling, awful gurgling sounds.

Her face was there just below him. He could see it, even under the water. He could see . . . Her eyes staring up at him. Dark, dark, dark with terror.

Eyes that had been blue before.

Eyes that had been just a picture before.

Eyes that had not belonged to a real woman before.

Oh Bucky, you can't, you can't, you can't . . .

He let go.

He stumbled backward. A second of blackness. A thrashing of water that made him lose his balance and fall back into the icy lake. Then, when he stood and looked up, he heard her and he saw her.

Mel. Melia. *Amelia.*

She was screaming and scrambling away, up the shoreline, away from him. She was crawling onto the snowy sand, and she was grabbing the brown duffel. She was pulling something out and she was standing up and . . .

A hard *pop* sound and a searing burn in his shoulder that spun him around and down back into the water. A second *pop-zing* into the water near his ear.

Gun? She has a gun?

Instincts kicked in, and Buchanan tried to crawl away. But the water was too cold and the wound was too hot, and even as he tried to stand up, he couldn't do anything more than get to his knees in the shallow water.

He squinted hard into the blur of swirling snow, feeling his chest grow tight and cold because as he watched Amelia grow dimmer and dimmer he couldn't tell if she was moving away or if he was.

Bucky?

His eyes were heavy. He had to close them.

I'm here, Bucky.

Yes, but where am I? The edge of heaven or the edge of . . .

CHAPTER TWENTY-SIX

Was he dead?

She wiped a hand across her glasses and stared at him, breath held, frozen hands gripping the gun.

Amelia inched closer. The man lay face up, his legs in the shallow water from his knees down. His face was turned toward her on the snowy sand and his eyes were closed. She could see a stain of red on the snow under his left arm.

Run!

She looked around frantically in the gathering darkness and finally spotted her duffel. She snatched it up and started to run. The snowy sand grabbed at her feet and she stumbled, her eyes searching for the road she had driven in on. Everything went by in a dark blur.

You shot a man!

She ran down the road, her mind racing, her lungs burning. Where the hell had she parked?

Then she saw a flash of red sticking out from behind a building. She fumbled with the duffel, dropped the gun inside and groped for her keys, terrified she had lost them in the struggle. But then her fingers touched the cold ring of metal.

She skidded to a stop. Not far from her Impala sat a second car—gray and dusted with snow.

It must belong to the man. Don't worry about it. Get out of here.

She yanked open the door to the Impala and threw the duffel inside. But her eyes swung back to the other car, and hand on her door, she hesitated.

Wait. Check the car. Find out something about the man who just tried to kill you.

Her eyes shot back to the beach. She couldn't see the man, couldn't see if he was still lying there or had gotten up, couldn't see anyone in the whirl of snow and darkness.

She hurried to the gray car, trying to take in everything she could in one sweep of her eyes.

Tennessee plates.

What the hell?

Look inside. Get a name.

She pulled on the passenger door. It didn't open and at first she thought it was locked, then suddenly it gave way, almost knocking her over. The dome light felt as bright as a search beacon in the gloom, and she looked back toward the shore again, but there was no one coming.

Hands shaking, she ducked inside the car, opened the glove box, and pulled everything out. Sunglasses, a pint of whiskey, receipts, manuals, and maps scattered across the passenger seat. She frantically sifted through them, finally finding a black leather folder. She opened it, found the car registration, and stuffed it in her sweater pocket. She was backing out of the car holding the leather folder when she spotted something else—a black phone wedged between the seats.

She decided to take it, too, so he couldn't call anyone when he got back here. If he got back here. If he wasn't dead.

What if he's dead?

She looked back toward the lake. Get to a phone and call the police? They would help her. They would help him. But did she want him to be helped? He had tried to strangle her.

No, she couldn't call the police. She had to make herself safe first so she could think this through.

She grabbed the phone and ran back to the Impala. It took her three tries to get the keys in the ignition, but when she turned over the engine, the car gave a dying groan.

Come on!

She wiggled the key and tried again. The Impala engine roared, and she jammed the car into drive. With one last look toward the beach, she wheeled the car around and raced down the road, under the big white arch and onto the highway.

CHAPTER TWENTY-SEVEN

Black and ice. Nothing but deepest black and coldest ice. His body was so stiff he couldn't even move a finger. Was he dead? Was this what it felt like? Not warmth and light but this awful piercing cold and darkness?

But then he began to shiver, so hard that his teeth hurt, and he knew he was still alive. Water was lapping under his legs and he could taste something gritty on his lips, like sand, and then it all came back— the pop of the gun going off and the burn in his shoulder.

And his head . . . it was throbbing, hard and steady. Buchanan struggled up to his elbows and looked around. It was pitch black, not a star in the sky overhead, but he could make out pinpricks of lights across the lake. He sat up further, fighting a wave of nausea, and touched his left shoulder. He couldn't see it in the dark, but he could feel it and smell it—blood, sticky on his fingers and metallic in his nose.

He reached up and felt the back of his head. More blood in his hair and a large knotty bump.

With a groan, he slowly turned over onto his hands and knees. His stomach heaved, and he let it all come up, the bile almost choking him. He had to wait for the wave of nausea to subside before he could push himself to his feet. He wiped his mouth on his sleeve and squinted into the darkness of the shoreline but couldn't see anything.

Then the clouds parted, and a sliver of moon gave him just enough light to see the rippling of black water on the shore, the glint of snow, and beyond that the outlines of the amusement park rides and buildings.

He looked right to the rock jetty. It was coming back to him now in detail, Amelia raising the gun with two hands, the first shot hitting his left shoulder, the second missing his head by inches; then he had fallen backward against the jetty, hitting his head on the rocks.

He looked down at the rock jetty. Jesus, if he had fallen to the right instead of the left he would have landed in the water and drowned.

How long had he been out? And how badly hurt was he? He felt dizzy and sick, and he was freezing. And he could feel the wound in his shoulder pumping out fresh blood.

The snowy sand dragged at his feet as he trudged down the shoreline and back to the road. He staggered to the building where he had left his car. The Impala was gone. He stopped abruptly, staring at his car.

The passenger's side door was open, the dome light on.

Clutching his arm, he went to the car and peered in. He hadn't left anything of value inside, his duffel and laptop bag were locked in the trunk. But the glove box was hanging open. On the floor was the Toyota's manual, maps, a bottle. He slid into the seat and thrust a hand into the glove box.

It was gone—the folder where he kept his car repair receipts, insurance card, and registration—was gone.

She had his name.

He leaned back into the seat, letting out a long slow breath that caught like a dull knife in the back of his lungs. Slowly, he brought his wrist up to his face and peered at his watch. Almost seven.

She knew who he was, and she had a two-hour head start.

His fleece was hard with dried blood, and he gently pulled it down his arm. In the glow of the dome light he got his first look at his shoulder. His shirt was soaked through, dark and wet, and the wound was still bleeding. Everything from his left ear to his elbow was stiff. He couldn't tell if the damn bullet was still in his flesh or not.

He wasn't going anywhere tonight. Not even to an emergency room. Because there was a chance she had gone to the cops, and if she had, they were probably already looking for him.

He was shivering violently now. He had to get warm.

Gritting his teeth against the pain, he pulled his keys from his jeans pocket and started the car. He almost passed out when he had to strain across his bloody shoulder to pull the door closed with his right hand.

He switched the heat on high, but when he reached down to put the car in gear he froze. It was gone. He had left the Tele-Bug receiver in the cup holder and it was gone. She had taken it. Most likely, she wouldn't even guess what it was for. But still, now his link to Hannah Lowrey was gone.

He sat motionless in the seat, eyes closed, as the car heated up. When he finally stopped shivering, he eased the car into gear and started back down the asphalt road.

Passing under the arch, he stopped.

North or south? Did it matter? Right now, the only thing he needed to do was find a good place to hide and hope he didn't bleed to death.

CHAPTER TWENTY-EIGHT

He stayed on US 71 heading north as long as he dared and then veered off onto back roads, eyes alert for cops. Finally he picked up Highway 9 going west. He passed up a Super 8 and a Ramada Inn, heading out into the flat emptiness of the Iowa farmlands. The lights grew farther apart and the night sky more vast until after about forty minutes he finally spotted lights ahead. It was a four-pump gas station—Kum & Go—with a convenience store. Two cars in the lot and too many bright lights. He slowed to a crawl, and that's when he saw the sign about fifty yards beyond the gas station for the Wind Vane Inn.

It was one of those old mom-and-pop motels, a long line of rooms facing the highway. There was one truck in the lot and no lights on, except in the office. Buchanan pulled the Toyota into the darkest corner, got out and popped the trunk. His strength was waning, but he managed to get a clean hooded sweatshirt out of his bag. He peeled off the bloody fleece, tossed it into the trunk, and slipped on the sweatshirt. He wadded up a T-shirt and worked it gently under the sweatshirt against his shoulder. He locked up the car and went to the office.

A skinny kid with pimples looked up from his comic book as Buchanan came in.

"I need a room, please."

The kid stared hard at him. Buchanan realized he should have put a hat on, that the blood in his hair might be visible. Suddenly, he felt like he was going to pass out or puke, and he had to put a hand on the desk to steady himself.

"You okay?" the kid asked.

Buchanan looked up and forced a smile. "Yeah. I'm just drunk. I don't want to drive any farther and end up wrapped around a telephone pole. I need to sleep it off. Can I have a room, please?"

The kid slid a card across the desk. "Fill this out. The room's forty a night, free HBO."

Buchanan filled out the form with a false name and address. He handed over two twenties, and the kid gave him a key.

Nothing about the room registered in Buchanan's consciousness as he entered except the strong smell of Lysol hanging in the cold air. He dropped his bag on the bed and began to slowly peel off his sweatshirt.

Pain and exhaustion were advancing on him fast now, and for a moment, the knotty pine walls seemed to move, undulating in the dim light, like he was on some sort of bad acid trip. He fought it off and went into the bathroom, holding the T-shirt against his shoulder.

In the hard glare of the bathroom light, he examined the wound. It had stopped bleeding, but the hole was swollen and red. He turned to look at his back in the mirror. He let out a deep breath of relief when he saw the dark hole crusted with blood.

Exit wound. The bullet wasn't still in him. That meant he had a good chance. He went back to the bag on the bed and rummaged inside until he found the bottle of Crown Royal. Back in the bathroom, he stripped off his jeans, underwear, shoes and socks, and stood in the small tub, holding the bottle of booze.

He screwed off the top, took a long drink, and then poured the whiskey over his left shoulder. He let out a howl as it burned into the bullet hole, but there was no one there to hear him. And there was no one there to pick him up when he buckled to his knees in the tub.

When the pain had passed, he rose slowly, steadying himself against the wall, pressing his forehead against the cool tile. He reached out to turn on the water to take a shower, but his hand was shaking and he was too exhausted to stand up.

He got out of the tub, staggered to the outer room, and fell down on the bed. He managed to pull the bedspread up over his naked body and then everything went black, as black as the sky above the lake.

◆ ◆ ◆

Amelia sat on the bed in the dark motel room, arms wrapped around her duffel, head bent. Her chest hurt from the constant pounding of her heart.

She had driven due south on US 71, not slowing until she hit her first red light in some small town called Milford. But once out into the farmlands again, she pushed the Impala up to the 65 mph speed limit, heading into the blackness on a road as flat as a velvet ribbon. Her plan was simple—get as far away from Arnolds Park as she could.

It was two hours later that she spotted the sign for the Little Sioux Motel. Ten minutes and fifty-five dollars later, she was here—locked inside an icy room in the middle of nowhere.

Amelia drew a breath and finally looked at her surroundings. Cheap paneling, floral drapes, a blond dresser with a flecked oval mirror. On the nightstand was a beige rotary phone and a Bible.

She got up, turned on the heat, and stripped off her wet clothes. In the bathroom, she blinked hard when she switched on the light, and looked in the mirror. Her neck was already bruising. She could actually see the pattern his fingers had left on her skin.

After a quick hot shower, she changed into clean jeans and a T-shirt. While she was hanging the sodden sweater coat over the heater, she felt something in the pocket.

She pulled out a piece of paper. It was the car registration from the black leather folder she had found in the man's glove box. She stared at the name and address.

Clay Buchanan. Nashville, Tennessee.

Who was this man?

Why had he tried to kill her?

God, her damn heart wouldn't stop pounding, her hands wouldn't stop shaking, and her neck was pulsing. She sat down on the edge of the bed. She needed to talk to someone, needed to not feel so alone.

Hannah . . .

Amelia pulled the phone on the nightstand to her lap and dialed, hoping Hannah would still be awake. Just as it started to ring, she heard a beeping coming from her open duffel on the bed beside her.

She looked inside. The man's black phone was lit up, flashing something on the small display. She pulled out the phone. The display read INCOMING CALL followed by Hannah's number.

Amelia slammed down the rotary phone's receiver and looked back at the display on Buchanan's phone. It read CALL ENDED.

What the hell?

She sat there for a moment, and then redialed Hannah's number on the rotary phone. The other phone chirped again, with the same message about an incoming call. Again, she hung up and again the display read CALL ENDED.

This phone—this strange black gadget—was somehow connected to Hannah's phone. But how? Did this thing also record conversations?

Amelia dialed Hannah again. The black phone chirped an alert, but Amelia didn't hang up.

"Hello?"

The sound of Hannah's voice melted Amelia's heart, and she wanted to tell Hannah she was okay, but she couldn't.

"Yes, I'm calling from American Subscription Service. Can I interest you in our offer for a subscription to *House Beautiful*?" Amelia asked, taking care to alter her voice.

"What? Hell, no. My house is plenty beautiful already."

Hannah hung up.

Amelia turned back to Buchanan's phone. The display now read: ONE NEW RECORDING PRESS # TO LISTEN. Amelia pressed the # button. Her own voice came back, asking Hannah about the magazine. She turned the thing off, in case it had a GPS connection. For a long time she sat there in the shadows, her mind spinning with questions.

The only person who could know about Hannah was Alex. He could have made the connection through her phone call to the dog spa. Had he shown up in Georgia after she left? Was he the person Hannah said she saw sitting in a car across the street? Had he tapped Hannah's phone, hoping Amelia would call her and tell her where she was?

But something in her gut told her Alex wasn't the type of man who would tap a phone. He had money and connections. He would have hired someone—this Clay Buchanan—to tap the phone.

Which meant he had also hired Buchanan to kill her.

Had the car accident in the Everglades been his first attempt? Had Alex hired Buchanan for that as well? But Buchanan had light hair. He wasn't the dark-haired man from her visions. She had always felt that it had been Alex in the car.

Tears burned in her eyes, and she squeezed them shut.

What had she done to make her husband want her dead? And who was this man Buchanan who would agree to do such a horrible thing?

God, she wanted to just curl up and sleep, to drift into a darkness that would feel safe and warm. But she couldn't.

She picked up her iPad and tried to go to Safari. No signal. She moved around the room, holding the iPad near the window. Finally, the signal icon appeared, and the Safari screen popped up. She sat down at a table under the window and typed in Buchanan's name. The first link read:

BUCHANAN INVESTIGATIONS
www.claybuchanan.com
Skip Tracer. I can find anyone, anywhere.

There were other links to him. An article in Eye Spy magazine: "Skip Tracers: The 21st Century Bounty Hunters." A blog called Technewsworld.com with the heading "Following Digital Footprints." And a story in *PI World*: "Clay Buchanan: Hunter of Humans."

Amelia shut her eyes, feeling sick.

When she opened them again, the screen seemed to waver before her, and she was about to shut down the iPad when another link caught her attention.

NOWHERE TO HIDE—AMAZON.COM
www.amazon.com/ClayBuchanan
Skip tracer extraordinaire Clay Buchanan recounts his
decades of tracking down scoundrels, scofflaws, and anyone
with secrets to hide.

She clicked on it, which took her to a page offering a book for sale for $19.95. The cover showed a motel sign and the shadowy silhouette of a man watching the place.

Amelia leaned back in the chair. The bastard had written a book. Was that how Alex had found him?

She scrolled back up and clicked on the link to his personal website. His photograph popped up and her heart caught. The man on her screen was a little younger, his face a little thinner, hair a little lighter. But it was the same man who had put his hands around her neck and tried to kill her.

The blurb on his site boasted that he could find anyone anywhere and warned people who wanted to disappear that because of technology and people like him, there was nowhere left in this world to hide. Under that was an image of his book cover and a link to buy it. At the bottom of the page was a final link: E-mail Clay Buchanan.

She stared at the e-mail link for a long time, not sure what she was feeling. She was almost tempted to send him an e-mail to tell him that she knew who he was and now it was his turn to disappear. But she knew that if Buchanan was dead, they could find her through his website. Still, the thought of rubbing her survival in his face gave her an unexpected feeling of satisfaction and something else. And she realized what it was—anger.

What's the matter, Mellie?

I hit a girl at school, Grandma. Mama took away my bike.

Was the girl bothering you?

She's always bothering me. Mama said I should've just ignored her, that nice girls don't lose their tempers.

Your mama is wrong. Getting mad is a girl's right. Sometimes it's all you got.

The Bird was right. Her anger was justified, but it wasn't all she had. Not anymore.

Amelia set the iPad aside. Her whole body hurt, and her mind was shutting down. She knew she needed to get some sleep. In the morning, she would pull up some newspapers online to see if there was any information about a body being found at Arnolds Park. Then she would decide what to do.

And where to go next.

CHAPTER TWENTY-NINE

His eyes burned, like someone had poured kerosene on his lids, and when he finally opened them, all he saw was an orange fireball.

The sun . . . it was just the sun filtering through the orange drapes, turning the motel room into his own little version of hell.

But it was ice cold in the room. And slowly it came to him that beneath the thin stiff bedspread he was naked. Had he even tried to turn on the heat? Where was he? The whole of last night was gone, lost in the tornado of pain.

Buchanan squinted toward the drapes.

Or was it last night? How long had he been out? Just one night or longer? His head was throbbing, and he couldn't think straight, like someone had pushed a button in his brain and erased his memory.

Except . . .

It was coming back now, the hard ride into the Iowa night, the pimply kid with the comic book, the burn down to his bones as he poured whiskey over his wound, and the helpless feeling as his knees buckled in the bathtub.

"Fuck," he whispered.

He brought his wrist up and squinted at his watch. Eight ten. He squinted hard at the inset date display—SAT 12.

Okay . . . he had only been out about eleven hours. Good, that was good at least. But he had to see how bad the wound was, and that meant he had to move.

When he tried to turn over, the pain came, a hard throb in his left shoulder, radiating down the length of his body, coming in waves that made his toes curl.

He gritted his teeth and used his good right arm to push up to a sitting position, trying to ignore the bloodstains on the sheet. When he looked down at the entry wound, he was relieved to see it was puffy and red but not bleeding. He stood up, staggered into the bathroom, and slapped the wall switch on.

He let out a long breath as he turned to look at the exit wound. It was ragged and raw, bigger than the front wound, but it was crusted and seeping only a pale pink bit of blood.

Which meant he was probably going to make it. If the damn thing didn't get infected.

He turned the spigot on and waited until the water got hot and then splashed his face. When he looked up into the mirror, he almost didn't recognize the man who looked back—whiskered jaw as gray as the winter sky, hair like tamped-down dead cornstalks, and eyes as empty and flat as the road that had brought him to this place.

You tried to kill her, Bucky.

He shut his eyes.

You can't do it.

If I don't, I can't get you back.

But I'm gone.

I failed. I failed you. I didn't find you. I can't do anything good in my life. I can't even do anything bad.

No, you can't, Bucky.

He squeezed his eyes tighter. Her voice was gone, but her words were still in his head. He couldn't do this. He couldn't kill anyone. Not even to get his daughter back. Not even to save himself.

It was over. He was going back to Nashville.

He looked back at his reflection. What a fucking irony. He wouldn't go to jail for trying to kill Amelia Tobias. But he might go to prison for killing his wife.

♦ ♦ ♦

The sky was huge and blue, but the wind cut across the back of his neck as he made his way across the hotel parking lot and to the Kum & Go. His plan was simple. Get some food and supplies, gas up the Toyota, and head back east on Highway 9.

There was no one in the store except an old woman behind the register who gave him a glance before going back to reading the *National Enquirer* spread out on the counter.

Buchanan grabbed a breakfast burrito and, stomach rumbling, he unwrapped it and started to eat as he roamed the aisles. He was looking for first aid stuff to dress his wounds but there was nothing but tins of Band-Aids.

His eyes went left to the baby stuff. He grabbed a package of Pampers, detoured to the automotive shelf, and picked up a roll of duct tape. Adding some Tylenol and a bottle of hydrogen peroxide, a large black coffee, and two more burritos, he went up to the counter.

As the old lady started to ring up his stuff, Buchanan's eyes roamed over the display of cheap wine.

"Do you sell whiskey?" he asked.

"Nope. You gotta go to a liquor store," she said. "Nearest one is in Arnolds Park."

He let out a long breath.

"Or you can head north up 86 to Grovers Lake."

"Where's that?"

"Minnesota."

His burner phone chirped. He grabbed it from his pocket and looked at the screen. McCall again. He hit "Decline" and stowed the cell. After paying for his supplies, he headed back out into the cold sunshine. He was halfway to the motel when the cell rang again.

Shit!

He jerked the phone out of his pocket and hit the button to answer "What?" he demanded.

Several seconds of silence, then McCall's voice was in his ear, distant yet as close as a shadow. "Why haven't you answered my calls?"

"I've been busy," Buchanan said.

"Have you found her?"

"Yeah."

"When's it going to be over?"

"When it's over. You'll be the first to know."

More silence on McCall's end. "You having a problem with this?" he asked finally.

Buchanan stared out toward the highway.

"If you can't do the job, I'll find someone who can," McCall said.

A semi barreled by, spraying up snow and noise.

"You hear me?" McCall asked.

"Yeah, yeah," Buchanan said. "We're good. I'm good. I'm good."

He hung up.

As he slipped the cell back in his jeans, it caught on his wallet. He took out the wallet, paused, then opened it and pulled out the small brass key. McCall had couriered to him back in Fort Lauderdale. The key to a locker somewhere, a locker that supposedly held two million dollars in cash.

He held the key up, and it glittered in the hard sunlight.

Two million gone. His chance to get Gillian back gone. Maybe his own life gone. What was left?

He stared hard at the key, thinking about McCall, thinking about why Amelia Tobias was such a threat to him, thinking that if he went back to Nashville now Amelia would be dead within a week.

I can't do anything good in my life. I can't even do anything bad.

No, you can't, Bucky.

He put the key back in his wallet and squinted into the sun, so hard that his eyes began to water. He would find her. He would find Amelia and make sure she didn't disappear.

"I'm good," he said softly. "I'm good."

CHAPTER THIRTY

If Clay Buchanan was dead, no one seemed to know about it.

Amelia folded the *Sioux City Journal* and punched the "Refresh" button for the web page on her iPad. The Internet newsfeed for KTIV out of Sioux City popped up again, with the same headlines that had been there all morning. A couple of robberies, a traffic fatality on I-29, and a tax increase for the people of Woodbury county.

No dead man on an Iowa beach.

That meant one of three things. Either the news had not yet reached the papers, in print or online, or they hadn't found his body. Or Clay Buchanan had gotten up and walked away.

Amelia picked up a fork and cut her last sausage. As she popped it in her mouth, the door opened and a man in a brown and beige uniform walked in. The state trooper ordered a coffee from the hostess. Then, gloved hand on his holster, he looked around the diner.

Amelia averted her eyes, chewing her sausage and then taking a drink of her coffee. The trooper looked at her with mild interest, then his gaze returned to the hostess as she handed him a Styrofoam cup. With a jingle of the bell over the door, he was gone.

Amelia let out a breath.

No way could he miss her. Or the red Impala sitting out front. If there was any kind of alert out for her, she'd be in handcuffs by now.

Buchanan had not gone to the police. But of course, he couldn't, she thought. He was a hired killer. How would he explain what he had done to get himself shot?

But if *she* went to the police, how could she explain what she had done? And would they believe her? She was a woman with a head injury who had bolted from a hospital room for no reason at all. She had hocked her wedding ring and hitchhiked across the country to a place she barely remembered. Then she took a shot at a stranger on a beach who had tried to strangle her.

She wasn't sure she would believe herself.

It was moments like this when she most missed Ben. She had always been able to confide in him. He had been her compass. He had been the one who had told her to move away from Iowa.

Get out of Morning Sun, Mellie, don't stay in this empty place.

Then another memory hit her like a hard slap, something he had written in one of his letters years later.

Don't stay in an empty marriage, Mellie.

Her memories of Alex had been slowly re-forming over the last eight days, but some core thing was still missing and she knew what it was. Love. She had stopped loving Alex a long time ago. Or maybe she had never really loved him at all. But then, why had she married him? What had happened to make her give up the dancing she loved and marry a man she didn't truly love?

She pushed her plate aside and laid her iPad on the table. She had searched the Internet for herself several times since that first day in the Brunswick Mall, but now she needed to know more about Alex.

The first search results gave her the same links and images she had seen in the Apple store at the mall. The beautiful home, her in a red dress smiling like a plastic doll for the camera. A photo of her and Alex at a charity event. She found articles about Alex's law firm and pictures of him with other men in suits, none of whom looked remotely familiar.

A new face popped up on the screen, and she stared at it.

Owen McCall, senior partner at McCall and Tobias.

As she clicked through the images of McCall, some memories filtered back. McCall in her home, at the law offices. And one fuzzy memory of sharing wine with him and Alex in a small café as Italian words floated around them. This man would have been a friend, at least to Alex, but the sight of him left a sourness in her stomach, and she sensed he had been no friend to her.

Then more new faces—two blonde women; one young, one older. The caption identified them as Joanna McCall and her daughter, Megan. She knew these people, too.

Her eyes locked on the younger woman, and she stiffened, a memory coming into focus. An argument somewhere, this woman yelling at her, something about Alex.

Amelia looked to the mother, Joanna.

The emotions this face brought were softer, warmer. A vivid memory full of noise and color—sitting with Joanna McCall in poolside chairs at a yacht club, drinking martinis and making jokes about the old geezers having man-boobs.

Joanna was a friend, Amelia knew. But she also sensed there had been some uncomfortable space between them, like something genuine had been missing from the friendship or something had been in the way.

She was filled with a sudden sadness. Her mother and brother were gone. The Bird couldn't remember her. Was there anyone left who cared about her?

Kiss a lover, dance a measure . . .

She blinked hard. Where had that come from? Who had said that to her?

Kiss a lover . . .

Had there been another man in her life?

This is for you, love, just a little thing to remember me by . . . kiss a lover, dance a measure.

Who had said that? And why couldn't she remember who he was? And suddenly, she was so very sure it was "he."

Amelia looked out the window, out at the flat white landscape beyond the parking lot. She felt so very alone. She needed to talk to someone.

Hannah . . .

Hannah was her friend, maybe her only friend. And Amelia had promised her she would check in.

Amelia spotted a pay phone on the wall and then looked down into the open duffel on the booth. She had Buchanan's phone tap receiver, and she doubted there was a second one anywhere. She would take the chance that it was safe to call.

Amelia went to the counter, asked for five dollars in quarters and dropped them all into the phone. It rang a long time before Hannah answered.

"Hi Hannah. It's me, Amelia."

"Oh my goodness, where are you? Are you okay?"

Amelia hesitated. She couldn't tell Hannah someone had tried to kill her and that she had shot him.

"I can't tell you where I am, but yes, I'm okay."

"Thank God, I thought he had found you."

Amelia stiffened. "Who?"

"Your husband. He came here the night you left. Someone was watching you, all right. And you were right to leave here."

"Are you sure it was my husband?" Amelia asked.

"He *said* he was your husband."

"What did he look like?"

"Dark hair, fancy clothes. He kept calling you Mel."

It couldn't have been Buchanan posing as Alex.

"And the other guy called him Alex," Hannah said.

"What other guy?"

"I don't know. I didn't hear his name."

"What did he look like?"

"Older guy, around sixty. Lots of white hair and reddish skin, like he drank too much. Like Ted Kennedy."

Owen McCall. Why had he gone to Georgia with Alex?

"Are you sure you're okay, hon?" Hannah asked. "Is there anything I can do?"

"No, Hannah," Amelia said softly. "There's nothing you can do. I still can't remember everything, and I can't go home until I do."

"Promise you'll stay in touch," Hannah said.

"I don't think I should risk calling again, Hannah. At least not for a while."

"Okay. Then you find another way. Maybe a postcard or a letter. And remember, you need to send me a real letter. I don't do that e-mail stuff."

"I have your address. I'll write you from my next stop."

"You take care of yourself, hon," Hannah said. "Be smart."

"I will."

Amelia hung up and returned to her booth. It had been good hearing Hannah's voice, but it had brought her no closer to knowing what she needed to do now or to finding someone who could help her.

A cell phone chirped from the booth next to hers, and she looked over, watching as a teenager punched at his iPhone while he ate his hamburger. Suddenly he looked up, and his eyes met hers. He was maybe seventeen, with a pale freckled face and a blond buzz cut.

"Why are you watching me?" he asked.

"I'm sorry," Amelia said. "I was wondering what you were doing."

"Answering e-mails. I got a situation going here. Why do you care?"

Amelia held up her iPad. "Can you help me with this? I need to get to my e-mails."

He gave her a look like she was crazy. "You don't know how?"

She hesitated. "I can't remember my e-mail address. Do you know if there's any way I can get it?"

The kid stared at her. "You like been locked up somewhere for the last ten years or something?"

Amelia forced a smile. "I was in an accident and lost part of my memory."

The kid's blue eyes warmed in sympathy, and he popped out of his booth and into hers.

"Sorry I was rude," he said. "I thought you were just another Aunt Tillie." When she gave him a blank stare, he smiled and added, "It's what we call old people who don't know how to use computers. Can I see your tab?"

She gave him her iPad. In a split second, he had a new screen up—EmailFinder.com.

"What's your name?" he asked.

"Amelia Tobias."

"Where do you live?" he asked.

"Florida."

"There's a listing in Fort Lauderdale for a female, age thirty-three. That sound like you?"

"Yes. Can I get my e-mail address from this?"

"Yeah, you can get a seven-day free trial but they're asking for your credit card number."

"I don't have one."

"Well, we can try to log into Gmail," he said. "That's what most people use nowadays. See if you can sign in using your name."

When he slid the iPad back to her she looked down at the two blank sign-in fields. The first asked for an e-mail address. She typed "AmeliaTobias" and the curser jumped to the password.

She stared at the second blank field.

"I guess you don't remember your password either," the kid said.

She shook her head. "How can I find it?"

"Not much I can do for you there. Most people use dumb stuff like their birthdays, nicknames, their cat's name, or where they were born. Like I used to use Mickeyhaha because my name is Mick and I was born in Minnehaha County. Get it? Mickey and Minnie? Ha-ha?"

Amelia gave him a smile.

"But ever since I got hacked I just use a bunch of numbers and letters and I change it every week. You don't want black hats finding wormholes to go phishing for your addy."

Amelia nodded. "No, you certainly don't."

The kid picked up his cell phone and rose. "Well, I gotta go, lady."

"One last thing," she said. "Can I get a cell phone without a credit card?"

He nodded. "Sure, you can buy a prepaid phone with cash. They sell them at the Walmart down by Storm Lake."

"Thank you, Mick," Amelia said.

"Watch out for the black hats," he said, and left.

Amelia looked back at the blank password field on her iPad and then typed in B-R-O-D-Y.

The password you entered is incorrect. Try Again.

A-M-E-L-I-A1981

The password you entered is incorrect. Try Again.

M-E-L-L-I-E

T-H-E-B-I-R-D

B-A-L-L-E-T

Amelia sat back in the booth. This was impossible. Her password could be anything, anyone, any place. There were millions of possible combinations.

She drew a breath and looked to the window. The Impala was covered in snow and the sky was a steely gray. She couldn't stay here forever, not in this diner, and not in Iowa. If Buchanan was alive, he would find her again.

And he wouldn't stop until he did. It was what he did. She remembered his book—*Nowhere to Hide*. And the descriptions of him from her Internet search yesterday—*hunter of humans. Relentless. He can find anyone with secrets to hide.*

Did she have secrets? Is that why Alex was looking for her? Is that why Owen McCall had been there at Hannah's house? Is that why Buchanan had tried to kill her? But what did she know?

She looked back at the iPad. Everything about her life before the accident might be locked up inside the thin little tablet—her past, her friends, her conversations, and maybe even her secrets.

Kiss a lover, dance a measure.

Maybe even the "he" who wanted her to remember him.

She stared at the blank password box. And at the cursor, blinking, blinking, blinking.

CHAPTER THIRTY-ONE

The walls felt like they were closing in on her. It was this place, she knew. She felt the same crushing claustrophobia she had felt as a child back in Morning Sun, caged in by the cornfields. That is why she had loved going to The Bird's lake house every August. Standing at the shore, looking out at the moving blur where the blue of the lake met the blue of the sky, she could imagine it was a curtain through which she could slip and escape.

Amelia let the drape fall and turned away from the window.

For two days now, she had been locked inside the motel room, paralyzed by fear that Clay Buchanan would find her again. He had followed her to Georgia. He had traced her to Iowa. He had even known she was at Arnolds Park that night.

Now he knew she was driving the Impala. He had the license plate.

She was trapped. Nowhere to hide. And no one to go to for help. Yet why did she *feel* there was someone out there? *He* was out there somewhere.

Her iPad was there on the bed where she had left it, but she couldn't bring herself to pick it up again. She was tired of trying to unlock the password to her e-mail.

She couldn't stand it. She had to get out.

Her sweater coat did nothing to keep out the wind as she walked across the crusty snow to the back of the motel where she had hidden the Impala. As she headed out on US 71, she glimpsed a smear of pale pink low in the western sky and guessed it was maybe four p.m.

There was a sign saying that Sioux Rapids was only three miles away, so she headed south. She needed hot food. She needed to be around people.

Sioux Rapids turned out to be a clone of Morning Sun, with old red brick storefronts, many of them vacant, lining a deserted Main Street. The only cars were parked in front of Max & Erma's Bar. She didn't linger after she finished her hamburger and a glass of red wine, intending to head down to the Walmart Mick had told her about to buy some warmer clothes and a prepaid cell phone.

As Amelia steered the Impala back out on US 71 into the dark night, her eyes kept flicking to the rearview mirror to make sure she wasn't being followed. About three miles out of town, headlights flashed in her rearview mirror. A car was coming up behind her, and as Amelia slowed the Impala, her heart started to race. The car was right on her tail now, but she couldn't see a house or even a light where she could turn in for help.

Then, suddenly, the other car accelerated and sped past her. She let out a hard breath of relief as she watched its tail lights grow fainter, then disappear as the car turned off the road.

She noticed the soft glow of lights ahead and realized the car that had been following her had pulled off into a parking lot. As she neared, she saw what looked like a factory set down in the middle of the dark fallow fields. A sign appeared in her high beams—SIOUX CENTRAL HIGH SCHOOL. And below that, all lit up, THE NUTCRACKER BALLET 7 PM TONIGHT!

She hit the brakes and stared at the sign. With a look at the dark empty highway ahead, she swung left into the parking lot.

♦ ♦ ♦

A sweet-faced old woman with hair the color of a Brillo pad was sitting at a card table in front of the trophy case. She took Amelia's five dollars and handed her a program. Amelia followed the murmur of voices to the gymnasium. A stage had been erected under a basketball hoop, forming a makeshift proscenium flanked with purple velvet drapes. Amelia sat in one of the folding chairs next to a big ruddy-faced man holding a video camera.

The front of the program showed a drawing of a ballerina and the words "Magda Purdy's School of Dance and Aerobics Presents The Nutcracker Ballet Starring Special Guest Star Jennifer Collins from Ballet Des Moines."

The gym lights dimmed. There were murmurs and giggles coming from behind the purple velvet.

The music began. It was a recording, of course, but as the first sweet notes of the overture echoed in the big gym, Amelia felt an expansion in her chest, as if breathing had suddenly become easier. When the drapes parted, little white lights went on all around her, the glow of iPhones held up by moms and dads.

It was a threadbare little production, with a gaudy painted backdrop of a Christmas tree and a few pieces of furniture that Amelia suspected had come from attics and basements. The dancers—all so very young!—wore costumes she was sure had been sewn on home Singers and makeup culled from some mother's cosmetics bag.

The steps were simplified and the dancers were awkward, but no one cared. As Tchaikovsky's music swirled through the drafty cold gymnasium, magic was being made.

Amelia sat motionless, hand to her mouth, tears in her eyes. All the Internet searches of herself had yielded nothing about her dancing, but now, here in the dark, things were rushing back to her, things about her dancing that she had thought were lost to her forever.

Sunlight streaming through the big windows of the ballet studio in Burlington, her teacher Dotty's voice urging her on, and how clear her mind was and how good her body felt when she danced.

The Bird was with her there in the dark.

You look like you're floating on air up there, baby.

That's what it feels like, Grandma, flying.

The memories were coming fast now. Falling asleep against The Bird's shoulder on a Trailways bus. Where were they going? Then she remembered—to the big audition in Indianapolis. A month later, the letter came that said she had a full scholarship to the School of American Ballet in New York City. Another long bus ride to a city so big and so bright that it reminded her of the Emerald City in the movie *The Wizard of Oz.*

Sixteen, Amelia thought as she watched the stage; she had been just sixteen, only a few years older than these girls. How had she done it? Where had she found the courage? But she knew. The Bird had been there with her. She had stayed with her that first month in New York and, after returning to Iowa, had called her every day.

It's hard, Grandma. All the other girls are so good.

So are you. Don't you quit.

I wish you were here with me.

I'm always with you, Mellie, even when I'm not there.

The second act was starting, the one set in the Kingdom of Sweets. There was a scraping sound as parents sat forward in their metal folding chairs. The tinkling music for the Sugar Plum Fairy's solo brought back another blizzard of memories. Getting accepted into the New York City Ballet, exhausting days and nights, living on coffee and wonton soup from Wok City near Lincoln Center, bloodied feet, and endlessly sewing ribbons on pointe shoes. And then, after two years in the corps, getting called into the office and told her contract was not going to be renewed, that she was too tall and her way of dancing too idiosyncratic.

That was the exact word they had used. She had to go look it up. It meant "personal, peculiar, distinctive, quirky, unique" and the last one . . . "all your own."

Wasn't that what dancing was supposed to be?

Familiar music brought her eyes back to the stage. It was the Arabian solo, the one that was called Coffee in the Miami City Ballet version.

Miami City Ballet . . . where she went after leaving New York. Where there was a man tall enough to partner her when she rose to almost six feet in her pointe shoes. Where no one thought her way of dancing was strange. Where she had bloomed in the spotlight.

The girls on stage were turning into blurs, and Amelia realized she was tearing up again. But they were tears of anger. Why couldn't she find this part of herself anywhere? What happened to her? Why did she stop? Why did she quit and marry Alex?

The urge to bolt from the gymnasium was powerful, but she stayed in her seat, not wanting to bother the others around her. It was almost over, just the grand pas de deux left.

The Sugar Plum Fairy came back on stage, the young woman named Jennifer who had come from Des Moines to this gym in the middle of nowhere.

Unable to watch any longer, Amelia looked down at the program in her lap. When she finally looked up, she focused for a moment on the young woman and then her attention went to the Cavalier. He was tall and licorice-stick thin, with wavy dark hair. His expression was earnest as he partnered the young woman.

Amelia stared at the boy, but she was remembering a man

There was an odd fluttering in her chest, like her heart suddenly wasn't beating right, and her vision was narrowing, tunneling down, the edges darkening, and everything was disappearing and all she could see was . . .

"Jimmy," she whispered.

He was the one who had been her partner in Miami. He was the one who had been her friend. He was the one who . . .

Her cheeks were burning, and the dancers on the stage were just ghost-blurs moving in the dark. It was flooding back now, Jimmy's deep bellow of a laugh, his wide easy smile that creased up his face like one of those drama masks, his hands tight around her waist as he lifted her, his hands soft on her breasts as he made love to her.

Kiss a lover, dance a measure . . .

He was the one, the person who had been there in the thick fog of her forgetfulness, the one she had *felt* was still there, the one who had loved her. The one who still loved her?

How had she forgotten him? How could she forget someone that important in her life? And where was he now?

The sound of applause brought her back. The dancers were lined up, taking their bows. Then the curtains closed, the gymnasium lights came on, and everyone started filing out. Amelia sat frozen in the metal chair, staring at the purple velvet curtains.

She shut her eyes tight, desperate to remember, trying to bring all her senses into play. Jimmy had left Miami, she was sure, because she had a sense of a tearful good-bye at an airport. But not Fort Lauderdale . . . at Miami International. Because she could see the strange airline signs for Transaero, Alitalia, Qantas. She could smell the strong Cuban coffee Jimmy drank in the café while they waited for his flight. And she could hear the babble of Spanish and the sound of the intercom announcing departures.

Last call for American Airlines flight sixty-five to San Francisco.

That's me, love, I have to go.

Amelia opened her eyes.

She remembered it all now. How Jimmy had been forced to stop dancing after his second tendon surgery, and how he tried to smile when he told her that there weren't many options for a thirty-one-year-old dancing king with bad knees. The offer to be ballet master and teach at the San Francisco Ballet came five months after his final performance in Miami.

They had been lovers. She was sure of that now. But had it been while she was married to Alex? And why had Jimmy ended it? Because something deep inside her was whispering that *he* had left her.

The hard slap of metal chairs being folded made Amelia look around. Two teenage boys were stacking the chairs against the bleachers. Two other boys were dismantling the makeshift stage. Amelia sat watching them as they stuffed the purple velvet curtains into Hefty bags.

Kiss a lover, dance a measure . . .

Jimmy's words, something to remember him by.

Then, suddenly, she could see it. Those same words, on a computer screen, but not a tiny screen like on a phone, but something bigger, like her iPad. A pink Kindle, *her* Kindle, stuffed full of books she told no one she read and e-mails she told no one she wrote.

I feel like I'm dying but I'm afraid to leave here, to leave him. —A.

Remember this? Kiss a lover, dance a measure, find your name and buried treasure. See you soon. —J.

It was a fragment from a book by Neil Gaiman that Jimmy had given her right before he left. She had hidden the book away somewhere. Maybe in her closet? The book was about a child called Nobody who was raised by ghosts in a graveyard and had to figure out how to find his way out to a real life.

The night she wrote that e-mail . . . she remembered that night now. That night she had been on her way to see Jimmy. Either he had come back or she had been planning to go to California. But what had happened that night to stop her?

Amelia stood up, gathered her sweater coat around her and left the gym. The lobby was filled with laughing girls, their hair still in ballerina buns, faces still painted. They were zipping their slender bodies into nylon-and-down chrysalises as parents ushered them out the doors.

Amelia spotted a pay phone near the trophy case. She dropped in some quarters and called directory assistance for the number of the San Francisco Ballet offices.

She dialed the number, her heart hammering as the phone rang and then went to a recording, saying the offices were closed for the night. She hung up.

No matter. Tomorrow morning she would try again.

A door banged open and Amelia looked over to see a tall thin boy emerge from the locker room. It was the boy who had danced the Cavalier. He shoved his arms into a red sweatshirt with SIOUX CENTRAL REBELS across the chest and gave her a shy smile as he passed.

Amelia followed him out into the cold night. She paused, looking up. The sky was huge and black and star-pricked. But for the first time that she could remember, Amelia didn't feel alone.

CHAPTER THIRTY-TWO

The Impala died in El Cerrito. Amelia managed to get the car off Interstate 80 and into a parking lot before it gave out.

She got out of the car, and for a moment, she just stood in the morning sunshine, looking around. Blue sky, green trees, and a cool wind that smelled of the sea and eucalyptus. She closed her eyes. After the emptiness and cold of Iowa, this place felt like a balm for her senses.

An acrid smell made her open her eyes. Smoke was pouring out from under the hood of the Impala. She was lucky the car had made it this far. It had taken her a day and a half to get to California and she knew she was somewhere in the East Bay, not far from San Francisco.

She looked around, considering her next move. People with briefcases and backpacks were streaming toward a blue sign that said Bart. With a final look at the old red Impala, Amelia grabbed her duffel and followed.

The map inside the subway station was easy to decipher. She knew where she was going—301 Van Ness Avenue, War Memorial Opera House. She just wished she knew what was going to happen when she got there.

Her search of the Internet revealed that Jimmy was still with the San Francisco Ballet. But she hadn't been able to reach him. When she had called the San Francisco Ballet offices, a woman told her the company was on break until rehearsals started for *The Nutcracker*. No amount of pleading on Amelia's part had softened the woman's heart enough to get Jimmy's phone number or address. She still couldn't remember her password to unlock her e-mails, so there had been no choice but to just show up at the theater. Today was the first day of rehearsals.

After a half-hour subway ride, the escalator deposited her back up in the sunshine on a busy boulevard—Market Street, just a short walk to the opera house.

Her heart was beating fast as she walked, with anticipation but also anxiety. Memories, she had come to believe, were such fragile things, so easily damaged, erased, or even distorted into whatever you needed them to be. She needed Jimmy to be here for her now. What if he wasn't? What if she was expecting too much from him after all this time?

The opera house loomed before her. She circled around until she found the stage door. It was locked. There was no point in knocking. She remembered how the stage doors at the Miami City Ballet's theater had always been locked, guarded inside by security guys. You either belonged or you didn't.

The door swung open. Two young women came out, swathed in sweats and wool scarves, tote bags over shoulders, hair pulled up in tight buns. Amelia grabbed the door before it closed.

There was no one inside, just a mug of coffee and a half-eaten sandwich on the sign-in desk. Amelia hurried up the stairs and into the dim backstage area. It was all so foreign yet familiar, a warren of hallways made even more narrow by rows of huge wardrobe crates. There was music coming from somewhere, faint but sweet, the snowflake waltz from the second act.

Two stout men were coming toward her, stagehands most likely, and she pressed against a drinking fountain to let them pass. Then she caught sight of herself in the mirror over the fountain.

Her gray sweater coat was dirty and shapeless. Her dark hair was spiked up around her face and the big purple plastic glasses . . .

God, she looked like a crazy street woman.

She tore off the sweater coat and stuffed it in the duffel. She wet her hands in the drinking fountain and slicked back her hair, then slipped the purple glasses into her jeans pocket.

When she squinted at the mirror, this time she saw a tall thin woman in a black T-shirt and jeans carrying something that looked like a dance tote—someone who might belong.

Slipping the duffel strap over her shoulder, she straightened her spine and headed toward the music.

She made her way through the shadows, past the stacks of scenery flats, scaffolds and ladders, the coils of ropes, and a curtain of cables. Past metal racks of jeweled costumes and an open wardrobe crate filled with flat yellow tutus arranged on shelves like pizzas in an oven.

The music stopped, and she heard voices and someone hammering. She was nearing the right wing and when she squinted, she could make out willowy bodies bending and stretching on the stage.

The pounding started again. Amelia looked down to see a young dancer sitting in the corner on the floor, whacking a pink satin shoe with a hammer. And suddenly she was seeing herself, going through her own ritual—bending rock-hard new pointe shoes until their spines cracked, coating the insides with Fabulon floor wax to make them strong, slamming them in doors so they would be beaten into submissive silence on wooden stages.

Amelia closed her eyes.

It was all there. Her past life as a dancer was all there in her memory and it was all coming back, just like Dr. Haskins had promised.

"Amelia?"

She opened her eyes.

He was just a blurry silhouette against the lights but she knew his voice.

"Jimmy," she said.

He came forward and folded her in his arms.

"My God, you're here!"

She wrapped her arms across his back and buried her face in his neck. His smell came back to her, sweet-sweat and smoky-clove. Djarum Blacks . . . that was the name of those things he smoked. She didn't want to break from his embrace but finally he pulled back, his hands on her shoulders.

"Why didn't you call me?" he asked. "I've been calling you and e-mailing you for more than a week. I've been worried sick. Where the hell have you been?"

How did she answer? How could she explain?

"Something came up," she said.

He was looking at her intently, scrutinizing her face. "Are you all right? You look—"

"I'm just tired. I had to drive."

"Drive? But the last time we talked, you said you were picking up your dog and getting a flight out here on Monday morning."

Amelia was quiet, thinking. It was coming back now. She was planning to leave Alex and fly out here. She and Jimmy had been talking about it for months, but it had taken her time to put aside some money, siphoning off cash from the allowance Alex gave her. Where was it? Had she hidden it somewhere? Yes, she could see herself tucking a wad of money in a cosmetics bag and locking it in a suitcase. She felt a small wave of sadness that her life had led her to such a low point. And her marriage—what had she and Alex been playing at for all those years?

That last Friday back in Fort Lauderdale was also re-forming in her mind now. How she had packed one suitcase and left it in its usual place in her closet so Alex wouldn't notice. How she had dropped Brody off at the spa that morning intending to pick him up the next day. How on Monday morning she had planned to wait for Alex to leave for the office, take a taxi to the airport, pay cash for her ticket and leave.

But then . . .

She had changed her mind. She had a sudden stab of memory, sitting on the edge of a bathtub, reading Jimmy's e-mails and crying because she had decided that she couldn't just run away like a coward, that she needed to tell Alex in person that it was over. She owed him that much. But what had happened after that? How had she ended up alone and hurt in the Everglades?

"Amelia?"

She looked up at Jimmy.

"What's wrong? It's like you weren't even here for a moment."

"I know," she said. "I'll explain everything later."

He hesitated and then smiled. "Okay, love, okay. It doesn't matter. You're here now and everything is going to be fine, just like I promised."

Promised? What did you promise me, Jimmy?

"Hey, Jimmy."

They both turned. A young man in practice clothes was coming toward them, wiping his face with the towel hanging around his neck.

"Do you have a moment to show me that lift?" the young man asked.

"Yeah, Victor," Jimmy said. "I'll be right there." Then he gave Amelia a gentle nudge forward. "I'd like you to meet someone special, Victor. This is Melia Worth of the Miami City Ballet."

Amelia blinked. *Melia Worth.* Her stage name. She had forgotten it. No wonder she couldn't find anything about her dancing on the Internet.

"I was her favorite partner in Miami," Jimmy said.

She looked up at him. He was smiling.

"Good to meet you, Miss Worth," the young man said. Then he left, rejoining the other dancers on stage.

"Miss Worth," Amelia said. "That made me feel old."

"You *are* old, love. We're both old in dance years." He gave her a hug. "Go have a seat. I'll be done in twenty minutes and then we'll go home."

Amelia made her way down to the front row and took a seat. She pulled out her glasses and slipped them on. All the dancers had retreated to the wings or were sprawled on the floor at the back of the stage. Jimmy was standing center stage with Victor and a blonde woman wearing a lilac leotard and tattered white practice tutu. Her thin pale face was sleek with sweat and she looked upset.

"He's pinching me, Jimmy," she said.

"I have to. You're sweaty," Victor said.

Jimmy held up a hand. "Okay, time out." He looked to the young man. "Victor, you can't just grab her like a football. Watch me."

Jimmy positioned himself behind the woman and put his hands firmly at her waist just below her rib cage. "Use your palms, not your fingers," he said. "Feel her weight before you push off to lift her."

Jimmy and the woman began to move in unison, his hands at her waist, but he stopped just before the lift, grimacing.

"See the difference?" he asked Victor.

The young man sighed. Jimmy pulled him away from the woman, toward the lip of the stage.

"Victor, this is the grand pas de deux," he said. "It's not a solo. It's not about you being a star. It's about a man and a woman, about trust and connection and telling their story."

Victor looked down at the stage, hands on his hips.

"To be a good partner, you have to sense her center of gravity," Jimmy went on. "You have to support her, make her feel secure, pull her back when she gets off balance, help her get through a difficult turn. And when you lift her, you must make her feel like she can fly."

"I feel invisible," Victor said.

Jimmy shook his head. "No, no. It's two of you appreciating what the other can do and trusting that everything will be all right. It's almost a spiritual thing. You feel each other. That's what creates beauty."

Victor glanced at the young woman and then back at Jimmy.

"Okay," he said.

"Good."

"She's still sweaty."

"Go rub some resin on your hands." Jimmy clapped his hands and retreated to the back of the stage. "Okay, Fred and Ginger, let's try it again."

Amelia watched as Jimmy coached the two dancers through the pas de deux, but she wasn't seeing the steps or hearing the music. She was seeing herself and Jimmy, years younger, dancing together, but someone was there with them, like a hovering shadow. It was a man, and slowly his face appeared, almost like he was stepping into the spotlight and she was . . .

His name was Neil. He was a writer, and Jimmy had loved him, too. Loved him more?

No, Amelia thought as she watched Jimmy on stage. Just *differently*. That was how Jimmy had explained it to her that night as they sat in an empty lifeguard stand on a moonlit Miami beach. That was how he explained that he was bisexual.

You own a piece of my heart forever, love. But I can't fill that empty spot in yours, not like you need me to. You want marriage. You want children someday. I can't be there for you in that way.

They decided to end their affair that night. The next day they went back to being partners on stage, and they had remained good friends. She felt that in her bones. But there was a gap in her memory, a huge black looming gap that kept bringing her back to the same questions: Why had she quit dancing? Why had she married Alex?

Amelia took off her glasses, turning Jimmy into a blur, overcome by a swell of emotion: an ache for what they had once had, but relief that she had not lost him completely. Jimmy's promise to her, in the end, was that he would still be there for her. As a friend. It was enough, she thought. It had to be.

"Amelia?"

She looked up at Jimmy. He was crouched at the edge of the stage, staring at her.

"Why are you crying, love?"

"Because I'm here," she said softly.

◆ ◆ ◆

Amelia was quiet on the short bus ride to Jimmy's apartment, thankful that there was no chance to talk. Fatigue from the long drive, her reconnection with Jimmy, and the tension of not knowing if Clay Buchanan was still on her trail. It was all weighing heavily on her. But as she unpacked her duffel in Jimmy's small guest room, there were other emotions at play.

And they centered around Alex.

He had been on her mind constantly during the last two days. With nothing to do but think as she drove from Iowa to California, things about their past began to come into clear focus. Some of the memories were good. How flattering and exciting it was in the beginning to be relentlessly pursued by a rich handsome man. How beautiful the wedding had been and how sensual their honeymoon had felt. How good it felt to create something of *beauty*—a house, a garden, her own image in a mirror or magazine—that made Alex so happy. But it hadn't been until this morning, listening to Jimmy coach the young dancer, that she realized what had always been missing.

It's almost a spiritual thing. You feel each other. That's what creates beauty.

She had loved Alex once. And he had loved her. But he was like Victor, trying so hard but never really understanding where her center of gravity was. And she had never really understood his.

"Hey in there, you okay?"

Jimmy was calling to her from the kitchen.

"Yeah, I'm fine," she yelled back. She changed her T-shirt for a sweater, ran a brush quickly through her hair, and went out into the living room.

"I have Earl Grey, Golden Monkey, and some strange stuff I found in Japantown," Jimmy said, craning his neck out the archway from the kitchen. "Name your poison."

"Earl Grey."

"Coward."

As she waited for Jimmy to make the tea, she looked around his apartment. It was small, on the second floor of an ugly fifties cubicle-like building. But its big window overlooked a park, and through the wind-tortured cypress trees, she could see the gray-green expanse of the Pacific Ocean. The furnishings were flea-market finds, the walls were filled with messy bookcases and theater posters, and the television in the corner was dusty and unused. It was so much like his studio back in Miami Beach, she remembered, but this apartment felt more settled, more secure.

There was a silver picture frame on the desk under the window. She picked it up and smiled. It was Jimmy and Neil, dressed in suits with white boutonnieres, standing on a balcony with marble columns in the background.

Jimmy came in with a tray and set it on the coffee table.

"Where was this taken?" she asked, holding up the frame.

"City hall. Very romantic, sort of like Mussolini's mausoleum."

Amelia looked back at the photo and then at Jimmy again. "You got married? When?"

He stared at her. "Last year. I called you right after the ceremony, remember?"

Amelia hesitated and then turned away, setting the frame back in its place. Of course she remembered now. That was one of the reasons Jimmy and Neil had moved out here, so they could marry.

"Where is Neil?" she asked softly.

"He's teaching a fiction workshop in Vancouver this week. We talked about this last month. I told you that with him away, this would be a great time for you to come because—"

She brought up a hand to cover her eyes.

"Amelia."

She turned to Jimmy.

"Talk to me," he said. "I need to know what happened to you."

What happened? She knew he was asking about what happened since the accident. But it wasn't just about that. What had happened to her had started long before that night in the Everglades. And it was a tangled yarn-ball, with strands that stretched all the way back to Morning Sun and the lake house, back to ballet classes in Burlington and lonely years in New York. The strands bound her up with her mother and father, Ben and The Bird—and Alex.

What happened was about feeling like she had walked out into a lake and the ground had given way, and she had been drifting down for years. That's why she had decided to leave Alex, leave her whole life in Florida behind. She needed to feel the bottom under her feet again.

Jimmy was still waiting for his answer.

"I had a car accident. When I woke up, I couldn't remember who I was," she began.

"An accident?"

Slowly, she told him what had happened, retrieving the pieces that she knew, about the amnesia, her fear that someone was trying to kill her, how she fled the hospital and tried to reconstruct her past. When she got to the part about Arnolds Park, she stopped.

"I shot a man," she said.

"What?"

"He was trying to kill me."

"Amelia," he said, "what the hell is going on?"

Amelia told him about Clay Buchanan, how his hands felt around his neck, how terrified and stunned she was when she saw him lying in the water. Jimmy's expression as he listened was unnerving, like he had no trouble at all believing she was capable of shooting someone.

"Is he dead?" he asked finally.

"I don't know. I've been searching for news about it for days but there has been nothing about it anywhere. But I feel like he's still out there, watching and waiting for the right moment to try again."

Jimmy had gone quiet, staring at the floor.

"I don't know what I did," she said. "I don't know what I did to make him want to kill me. It's the one thing I still need to remember, and I can't."

Jimmy rose from the sofa and came to her, wrapping his arms around her. He didn't say anything, just cupped the back of her head and pulled her down to his shoulder.

"The memory will come back, just like all the others have. You're here now. We'll figure this out. You're safe."

She closed her eyes. It was true. All the pieces were coming back, snapping into place like that jigsaw puzzle on the table at the lake house. Except another important piece was still missing—the thing that had once defined her and given her life shape, the thing that had been her center of gravity. There was still one other question, and she realized that Jimmy might have the answer.

"I need to know why," she said.

"Why what, love?"

"Why I quit dancing," she said.

Jimmy pushed gently away from her. "You don't remember?"

"I remember that I loved to dance, Jimmy," she said. "And I was good at it. I know I was."

"Yes, you were," he said softly.

"So why did I give it up?"

He let out a long hard breath and turned away.

Something was wrong here. Why was he hesitating? What could be so bad that he couldn't even look at her?

"Jimmy? I need to know," she said.

He turned to face her. "I let go," he said.

"What?"

"You jumped into my arms and I let go of you."

She shook her head, not understanding.

"We were on tour in Tampa," he said slowly. "It was the last night, the last ballet on the program, the *Tchaikovsky Pas de Deux*. We were almost at the end, and I was so tired, my legs were gone. But you were on fire that night and when we came to the fish dive, you jumped and I . . ."

Jimmy fell silent, unable to go on.

He didn't have to because it was coming back now. Just eight minutes, the whole ballet was only eight minutes, but it was one of the hardest in the repertoire. Its climax was the woman launching herself and diving head first toward the wings only to be snared by the man's arms at the last moment.

Amelia closed her eyes.

A crash to the stage. The gasp of the audience. Waves of pain. The heavy red curtain coming down. Voices yelling and the rattle of metal wheels. More pain as they lifted her onto a gurney and Jimmy's tearful face above her, his hand squeezing hers.

But he wasn't there when she woke up after surgery. Alex was.

It was Alex who had been there at her bedside in the hospital, holding her hand when that doctor told her she would never dance again. Six months later they were married. Soon after that, Jimmy left the company and moved away.

It was almost a year before Jimmy called her, a year of painful physical therapy and depression. He told her he felt guilty and that he was sorry, not just for the accident but for not being the man she needed him to be. *You had Alex*, he told her, *you didn't need me anymore.*

At first his apologies just added to the pain, but finally she accepted them, and their friendship re-formed and grew from afar. He was the only connection to the world she had lost, and in a way the only connection to anything *real* in a life that had become so false.

"I'm so sorry," he whispered.

She took his hand in hers. "Jimmy, it wasn't your fault. I told you that then and I need you to believe it now. You know what I was like. I wasn't afraid to push myself."

And she had, she knew. She would try for just one more revolution in a pirouette because she knew his hands were around her waist. She would go off balance in a turn because she knew he would pull her back. And she would risk a blind leap into the darkness because she knew he was there.

Jimmy . . . Alex. And even Ben.

They had all been there for her, and she had depended on all of them to help her find her footing when the bottom gave away. But it hadn't made her whole, it hadn't made her safe. And it hadn't made her strong, not the way The Bird said she once was. *Fearless . . . that girl wasn't afraid of anything.*

Was that girl still here?

Yes, Amelia thought. Yes, I am.

CHAPTER THIRTY-THREE

Amelia Tobias's life was spread out before him on the bed.

Buchanan's eyes swept over the contents of the Morning Sun cardboard box and then moved up over the room's stained walls and scarred furniture, settling finally on the limp orange curtains.

He had been holed up here for two days now, waiting for his strength to return. This morning was the first time he was able to walk around without his head spinning, the first day he could think clearly enough to consider what he was going to do next.

He rose with a grimace, went to the window, and jerked on the cord to open the drapes. He stared out at the empty highway and flat white landscape.

Eight days ago he had been looking out at the ocean from his suite at the W Hotel, getting prime rib from room service and Maker's Mark from the minibar. Now he was living on crap from the Kum & Go, watching TV until he fell into a black-hole sleep, and waking up in sweaty sheets with Amelia's terror-dark eyes staring up at him.

Buchanan flexed his fingers, as if that could somehow release the muscle memory of his hands around her neck. He pulled the drapes closed. Picking up the pint of Jim Beam he had retrieved from the floor of the Toyota, he finished it off and tossed the empty bottle in the trash. He glanced back at the bed, and forced his brain to shift away from Amelia and back to McCall.

Buchanan knew that if he went through with his new plan to help Amelia, McCall wouldn't stop at killing Amelia. McCall would have to kill him, too.

He rubbed his face. Somewhere in all of this, he needed to neutralize McCall, or both he and Amelia would be running for the rest of their lives.

He went to the table under the window where he had left his canvas bag, pulled out his Acer and fired it up, praying he could snag a signal in this godforsaken place.

Nothing. Dead air.

He got out his personal cell phone. He had no choice; he'd have to tether his laptop to his cell so he could go online. It would leave a trail if someone wanted to trace him, but he'd just have to take the chance. He turned on the iPhone and activated the Bluetooth setting. He did the same for the Acer, typed in his PIN and chose his PAN network. A minute later, he had Internet access.

He worked fast, not wanting to have his cell live any longer than he had to. The first Google page listed the articles and sites he had seen on his first search of McCall more than a week ago. But now he was doing a deep dive, looking for the debris and dark currents in McCall's life. And Buchanan knew they were there. Everyone had shit floating just below the surface. Especially lawyers.

He was four pages in, way past the glowing magazine profiles, business articles, and legal stuff when the word "death" came up:

SHERIFF INVESTIGATES DUI DROWNING
DEATH OF LAW FIRM SECRETARY

The article was dated almost eighteen months ago, and was from the *South Florida Sun-Sentinel*. It was a short piece about a woman named Mary Carpenter, an executive secretary for the McCall and Tobias firm, who had been reported missing by her sister. Two weeks later, her car was found submerged in a drainage canal in remote western Broward County. The autopsy revealed her blood alcohol content was .09, above the legally impaired limit, but not falling-down drunk, Buchanan knew.

There was a quote from a sheriff's department spokesman saying no foul play was suspected, that such accidents were "tragically common in South Florida." The reporter backed this up with a weather report about three days of torrential rain, and statistics from the National Highway Traffic Safety Administration that an average of fifty-seven Floridians drowned in cars each year in the canals that were used to regulate the Everglades and water supply.

There was a small picture of Mary Carpenter. She was around forty, plump with short brown hair and a broad smile.

Buchanan brought up another search screen and typed in "Mary Carpenter Fort Lauderdale." Only four hits: a brief obit, a link to the National Association for Legal Professionals, a basic profile on the background check site Intelius.com, and her Facebook page.

Buchanan clicked on Facebook. Mary Carpenter had been dead for eighteen months, but no one had taken down her Facebook page. The most recent posts were dated not long after her death, all notes of mourning and remembrance from friends. Buchanan scrolled down until he finally got to Mary Carpenter's own last posts. He read a month's worth but there was nothing out of the ordinary, just the normal posts about her friend's wedding, her dog Chico, and a trip with her sister Vivian to a Fort Lauderdale tourist place called Flamingo Gardens. Buchanan was about to close the page when he paused.

He stared at the large main photo at the top of the page. Most people chose a landscape, some place that held sentimental value. Mary Carpenter's was a vintage postcard of Hialeah Race Track in Miami with a flock of flamingos wading in the infield lagoon.

Something was itching at his brain. He clicked on the left column to bring up Mary Carpenter's photos. Just the usual shots of friends and family, but then he stopped, staring at a picture of Mary Carpenter behind a desk, probably at her office at McCall and Tobias. She was grinning, with a phone receiver at her ear, and all around her were . . .

Buchanan bolted from the chair and went to the bed. He rummaged through the papers and memorabilia from Amelia's cardboard box and pulled out the plastic flamingo.

It had to have been there, somewhere in the back of his brain when he first went through the box, that the plastic flamingo didn't belong there. The cardboard box held Amelia's best memories: of her dancing, her brother, favorite childhood books, and the T-shirt from Lake Okoboji. Nothing from Florida.

Buchanan examined the plastic flamingo. It was dirty, its pink feathers frayed, no writing on it, no clue where it had come from. It was just a cheap bobblehead. He turned it over. On the bottom was a piece of double-sided adhesive tape.

He looked up at the ceiling, but in his mind's eye he was seeing another piece of adhesive tape stuck to the dashboard of Mary Carpenter's car.

He held the toy under the light and turned it slowly. Under the dirt, he saw a spot of a different color, dark reddish-brown. Blood.

A dashboard trinket spotted with blood. Had it been in Mary Carpenter's car just before she went into the canal? And if it had, how did it end up in Amelia's box of mementos sent from Iowa?

The scenario began to play out in Buchanan's head. Mary Carpenter had learned something about the law firm she wasn't supposed to know, probably something to do with SEC violations or insider trading, maybe even a Ponzi scheme. The kind of thing that would have brought in the windfall of profits that rocketed Alex Tobias into Broward County's one percent.

Or maybe the Feds, conducting a secret investigation, came to Mary Carpenter and asked her to turn on her bosses. Either way, she ended up dead, a fatality in a one-car accident out in the middle of nowhere.

Alex Tobias, for whatever damn reason, took the flamingo and kept it. Until it turned up in Amelia's possession. She had to have known of Mary's accident, and undoubtedly had been to her husband's office often enough to see the flamingos on Mary's desk.

Had she put it all together? In recent months, had an already unhappy Amelia come to realize she was married to a murderer?

Buchanan went back to his canvas bag and pulled out the police report from Amelia's accident.

A second one-car accident, out in the middle of nowhere, during a rainstorm, meant to leave a woman dead. How had this one happened? Had someone tampered with the gullwing's brakes? No, that left too much to chance. McCall had to be certain the car crash would be fatal.

Buchanan sifted through the police photos of the smashed gullwing Mercedes. There were several flash-lit color photos of the interior, and Buchanan focused on a close-up of the area behind the bucket seats. There was a suitcase wedged in the small space and he realized it was a duplicate of the old tan one he'd seen in the garage of the Tobias home.

He let out a long breath. How had he missed this before? When he had researched gullwings, he'd read that they had no trunks, and they came outfitted with two matched pieces of luggage. That explained why Esperanza had seen Amelia bringing the old tan suitcase back into the house—she had removed the top suitcase to make room for something.

Her own suitcase? But nothing had been found at the accident site. What had she needed the extra room for in the car?

Buchanan moved on to the other photographs, sifting through the shots of the exterior. He stopped, staring at one that showed the entire car sitting on the side of the road after it had been towed out of the saw grass.

Damn.

Something about the car had bothered him the first time he had seen the it back in the Fort Lauderdale police compound lot, but now he knew what it was. Both the gullwing doors of the wrecked Mercedes were closed. The cops would not have shut them because they needed to record the car exactly as it had been found, for insurance purposes. Amelia had sustained a concussion and wandered away from the car, so she wouldn't have taken the time to close the doors. Which meant someone was in that car with her.

Someone who had caused the wreck.

Someone who had stuck around just long enough to make sure Amelia was dead.

But Amelia had survived, and the scheme had fallen apart.

McCall had caught a break—Amelia remembered nothing about the wreck. They had time to get her home and clean up their mess, maybe even try to kill her again.

But when she bolted from the hospital, the hunt was on. Why did she run? Was she spooked by her husband because she suspected he had something to do with Mary Carpenter's death? Had she remembered something about her own accident? But why hadn't she just gone to the cops? Why hadn't she told someone?

Buchanan knew she must have confided in someone because in his experience no one kept something like this buried inside them.

Joanna McCall said they were friends, but if Amelia suspected Alex was involved in Mary's death, there was no way Amelia would have confided in Joanna.

Who would Amelia have turned to?

He went back to the bed and sifted through the mementos. He picked up the children's book titled *The Graveyard Book*. It looked much newer than the other books in the box, he realized now. He opened to the title page. Someone had written an inscription there—*Kiss a lover, dance a measure, find your name and buried treasure. Love, J.*

There it was again—the mysterious "J" from her Day Runner. And this time Buchanan was damn sure it wasn't Joanna.

He set the book aside and picked up the packet of letters from her brother Ben. He had gone through them before, but maybe he had missed something, just like he had missed the inscription in the children's book. As he slowly read each one, he began to feel like an intruder into the intimacies shared between brother and sister. The letters began when Ben was in boot camp in the late 1990s and ended with his last letter from Afghanistan in summer 2011. Scribbled at the bottom of the last letter was a postscript: "I told you once to get out of Morning Sun, Mellie, don't stay in an empty place. Now I'm telling you don't stay in an empty marriage."

Buchanan set the letter down.

Ben had been her confidant, the trustee of the most private of her emotions, and he knew Amelia was unhappy with Alex. But there were no hints in his letters that Amelia was suspicious of something at the law firm. Who had she confided in? Was it "J"?

Buchanan pulled Amelia's Kindle from his bag. Whoever it was, he was still convinced the person was locked inside the pink tablet.

He turned the Kindle on. When the tiny padlock appeared, he swiped it and hit the "Give Me a Hint" button.

Hint: The Birds Nest

A week ago, it had made no sense to him, but now it did. He began to type in various new combinations with The Bird: Arnolds Park, Avis Martin, lake house, beach, amusement park, Edge of Heaven. He looked up in frustration, his eyes falling on the old souvenir T-shirt on the bed.

He typed "O-K-O-B-O-J-I." The padlock popped open and the desktop appeared, a rainbow of covers for books Amelia had downloaded.

The Secret Life of Bees by Sue Monk Kidd.

Lady Oracle by Margaret Atwood.

All the Pretty Horses by Cormac McCarthy.

Once a Dancer: An Autobiography by Allegra Kent.

The woman who read these was not the same woman who read the bland books shelved in that cold white bedroom. There were many other books, but what Amelia read in private wasn't what Buchanan was after now.

He clicked on the envelope icon, and her e-mails appeared. There were only five. Four of the fonts were bold, which told Buchanan Amelia had not yet read them. Once an e-mail had been read, even if the recipient saved it as "New," the font style reverted to its normal density.

It also meant she hadn't remembered her password or she likely would have walked into any Internet café and read her mail. What else had she still not remembered?

He shook his head slowly. The idea that she had survived this long without a good part of her memory and no one to help her took his admiration for her up a notch. The knowledge that he had actually wrapped his hands around her neck turned his stomach.

Move on, Bucky. Move on.

He switched over to the SENT e-mails, but there was nothing there, which probably meant that at some point she had deleted them all. He jumped back to her inbox. All five e-mails were from the same person—DancingKingSFB.

Buchanan clicked on the newest one, dated yesterday:

Where are you? Why aren't you answering your cell? I'm worried. Call me. –J

The next one was from three days ago:

Are you okay? You were supposed to be here by now. –J

Then from five days ago:

Are the plans still on? –J

Ten days ago, on the night of her accident:

Sorry I missed your call. Send me flight info. –J

The last one came twelve days ago, forty-eight hours before the accident in the Everglades. It was the only e-mail not in bold face, which meant it was the only one Amelia had opened and read—and then saved as "new."

Kiss a lover,
Dance a measure,
Find your name,
And buried treasure.

Love, –J

Buchanan leaned back against the headboard, remembering what Esperanza had said about finding Amelia crying in the bathroom, holding her Kindle. Was this what she had been reading? This had to be the "J" whose birthday Amelia had noted in her Day Runner. He had always felt in his gut that Amelia had a lover. And it was probably this man, this "Dancing King," who clearly had deep affection for her. But who was he? And where was he?

Buchanan went to his Acer, connecting again with his iPhone, and pulled up a browser window. But when he typed in "Dancing King," all he got were gyrating teenagers on YouTube and some lyrics to a song with the same name. He added the letters "SFB."

The first site that came up was for the San Francisco Ballet. He called it up and clicked on the link that listed the artistic director, dancers, administrative and artistic staffs, and board of directors. He scanned quickly through the dancers but there was no man with a first name that started with *J*. He bypassed the administrative staff and board and brought up the artistic staff.

Then, there he was. His name was Jimmy Reyes, and he was a ballet master. He was maybe forty, with a craggy thin face, wavy dark hair, kind eyes, and an easy smile. A man comfortable in his skin. A man the complete opposite of Alex Tobias.

Buchanan's gaze moved back to the mementos spread out on the bed. So now he had it.

Amelia's story, from her closed-fisted and closed-hearted childhood to the hypnotic spotlights of first New York and then Miami, where she crawled across the stage and into the arms of a man who cut up her soul and had the shards reconstructed into that ugly portrait hanging on his bedroom wall.

Buchanan picked up his burner phone and punched in McCall's number.

"Yeah?" McCall answered.

"I know where she's headed," Buchanan said. "It will be over in a couple days. The next time I call, all I want to hear from you is where the fucking locker is."

He hung up.

Maybe it was a stupid move, playing both sides at the same time and still expecting to get the two million. But he needed to buy some time. Flying was out of the question because he didn't want McCall to know where he was headed. He would have to drive, and San Francisco was eighteen hundred miles away.

CHAPTER THIRTY-FOUR

It was almost ten when Alex Tobias walked out of his office and punched the "Down" button for the garage elevator. He had spent the last hour on the phone with a Chinese investor and between his mind wandering to Amelia, watching the stock market drop two hundred points, and trying to understand the Chinese man's heavy accent, he was tired, disgusted, and discouraged.

Alex stepped from the elevator into a cool rush of air. Even though he was in the garage of his office's high-rise, he could hear the wind from Tropical Storm Bruno whistling through the concrete corridors. He shifted his briefcase and reached for his keys.

"Mr. Tobias, sir?"

Alex's head shot up. Huddled near a concrete pillar was a man. He was tall, big shouldered, wearing a dark jacket. But his face was lost in the shadows.

"Come out where I can see you," Alex said.

The man moved into the gray light, slowly withdrawing his hands from his pockets. His face was round with skin the color of oak, his black hair dripping rain onto his collar. He was Latino, maybe mid-thirties.

Alex stepped closer. "Who are you?"

"Jack Pineda."

Alex stared at him.

"Jack Pineda, Mrs. McCall's driver," the man said. "We met before, at the house."

"Right, sure," Alex said, still not remembering the man with any clarity. "What are you doing here?"

"I need to speak with you, sir."

"Look, Jack, it's late. Maybe you can come to the office tomorrow. I have to go."

Alex stepped around him and continued toward his car.

"It's about your wife, sir."

Alex stopped walking and turned back to Jack. The man's hands were stuffed back into his pockets and he looked ready to cry. Alex moved back slowly.

"Mel? What about her?"

Jack ran a sleeve across his face and shifted his weight. Somewhere above them, the squeal of tires echoed through the garage.

"Talk to me, Jack."

"Mrs. Tobias didn't just have a car accident, sir," Jack said. "I was out there that night."

"Out where? In the Everglades? Why?"

"Oh Jesus," Jack whispered. "I didn't want to do it. I swear to God I never wanted—"

"Stop it," Alex interrupted. "Start at the beginning. What happened that night?"

"I was washing the Crossover, you know, Mr. McCall's SUV, and

Mrs. McCall comes out to tell me she won't need me to drive her to Marco Island, that she is—"

"Marco Island?" Alex asked.

"Yes, sir. That's where you and Mr. McCall were supposed to be, celebrating that big business deal your firm had."

The Leggett merger, Alex recalled. The plan had been to celebrate with Leggett at his estate on Marco Island through the weekend. Amelia had told him she didn't want to go. He had used her absence to go to Palm Beach to get a fuck in with Megan before flying over to the West Coast on Saturday night to join the party.

Then something Jack had said finally registered. "Mrs. McCall? What did she have to do with this?"

Jack hesitated. "Mrs. McCall told me she didn't need me to drive her to Marco Island because your wife was going to pick her up."

Jack stopped again and wiped a hand over his sweating face.

"Go on," Alex said.

"Mrs. Tobias came by around six. I helped Mrs. McCall put her overnight bag and her leg crutches into the back of that little blue Mercedes car, and they drove away. About two hours later, I got a phone call."

"From who?"

"Mrs. McCall," Jack said. "She tells me she needs me and to come quick, that she had an accident and she's stranded out in the Everglades, on 29."

Alex was quiet, his neck growing warm with anger. Why hadn't McCall told him Joanna and Amelia had been together that night?

"So I go out there quick as I could," Jack said. "Mrs. McCall is sitting in the car, all banged up and wet, but okay. Mrs. Tobias is lying on the ground, and at first I think she's dead, but then she makes a sound and tries to get up but she can't."

"And you didn't help her?"

"Mrs. McCall told me . . . Oh, Jesus, oh, Jesus." Jack's eyes filled with tears and he started walking a small tight circle.

"Jack!" Alex snapped.

Jack faced Alex, drawing hard breaths. "Mrs. McCall told me to kill her," he said.

Alex stared at Jack, not sure he'd heard him correctly. Joanna—his partner's wife, Amelia's friend. And Owen—his partner, confidant. Alex couldn't count the number of times they had vacationed together, shared dozens of dinners, hundreds of bottles of wine, and millions of dollars in profits. It didn't make sense.

"You're lying," Alex said. "What are you trying to do? Shake me down? Shake Owen down?"

"I'm not lying, sir."

Alex spun around and blew Jack off with a wave of his hand. "Get lost!"

Jack yelled after him, his voice hollow in the empty garage. "I can prove it!"

Alex turned back. "How?"

"I have your wife's phone."

Alex walked back to him and threw out his hand. "Give it to me."

Jack reached into his jacket and withdrew an iPhone. He set it gently into Alex's hand.

Alex set his briefcase down and looked at the cell. It was encased in a pink cover, like Amelia's Kindle. The cracked screen was spattered with mud. It was hers, Alex was sure.

His eyes moved back to Jack's face. The man was standing very still, with slumped shoulders. Tears streaked his face.

"Tell me the rest," Alex demanded. "Tell me all of it."

Jack ran a sleeve under his nose and took a moment to pull himself together. "Mrs. McCall told me to take Mrs. Tobias far off the road into the saw grass weeds and kill her, to hit her with a rock or something and make it look like she stumbled out after driving into the ditch."

"Did she tell you why?" Alex asked.

"She said Mrs. Tobias was going to ruin our lives, that she was going to put you and Mr. McCall in jail and that if that happened, me and my wife might be sent to a detention camp—"

"Stop, back up," Alex said. "Joanna told you Amelia was going to put us in jail? Did she say how?"

"No, sir. She just said our lives depended on Mrs. Tobias dying out there and that it had to be done."

"So what did you do?"

"I told her that I couldn't kill anyone, especially a nice lady like Mrs. Tobias. But Mrs. McCall told me she would have my wife deported if I didn't do what she said. Pegha's carrying our first child, sir, and she doesn't have any papers and I—"

"*What* did you do to my wife?" Alex asked.

Jack wiped his face. "I dragged her to the swamp and I picked up a rock and lifted it up but then I saw her looking at me and I felt so bad I almost run off. But then I thought of Pegha and I knew I had nowhere to go, so I hit Mrs. Tobias."

Alex stood there, one hand gripping Amelia's phone, the other curled into a fist. He wanted to punch this piece of shit, to kick his ass all the way back to El Salvador or wherever the hell he came from. But he couldn't. He needed to hear more. He needed to hear it all.

"What happened then?" Alex asked.

"I was kneeling there in the mud, and I could hear Mrs. Tobias crying, and I couldn't hit her again so I went back to Mrs. McCall and told her Mrs. Tobias was dead. Mrs. McCall told me to take out her suitcase and crutches from behind the seats and to get Mrs. Tobias's purse and her overnight bag. Then I helped Mrs. McCall into my car and we drove home."

They drove *home*? They just left Amelia there. *They just fucking left her there.*

"Did Mrs. McCall say anything to you on the way home?"

"She said if I kept my mouth shut, she would make sure Pegha got legal and that our baby would be a US citizen and that we would never have to worry about being deported again, that we could stay here in America."

Jack started to cry, openly now, his sobs wracking his chest like he was suffocating. Alex stood there, watching him, thinking about Amelia left out in the Everglades in the rain but suddenly, he wasn't mad anymore. Not at Jack.

Amelia was in his head, a memory of a moment when she walked into his home office.

Esperanza needs some help, Alex.

Who?

Esperanza, our housekeeper. Her daughter's been picked up by Immigration and is probably going to be deported because there's something wrong with her work visa. She needs a new sponsor or something. Can we help her?

I don't know any immigration lawyers. Tell her to call legal aid.

You're a lawyer, Alex. You're important, you know people. Can't you call someone?

The look on Amelia's face had been so . . . so beseeching that he had made a couple of calls and ultimately, the girl was allowed to stay in the US. But he knew now he had felt no concern for the girl. In fact he couldn't even remember her name. He had done it for himself, hoping his actions might touch Amelia and melt the frost between them.

Alex put Amelia's phone in his pocket and looked back at Jack.

"Why are you telling me all this now?" Alex asked.

"Because I couldn't live with myself no more," Jack said. "I did a terrible thing. But this morning, I got Pegha a ticket back to Honduras so she'll be free of all this and now I'm willing to take whatever punishment you want to give me, Mr. Tobias."

Jack stared at him, waiting. Alex drew a breath and looked around the garage, watching as a Volvo rounded a corner and started down the ramp. When it was quiet, he reached into his slacks and pulled out his money clip. He slipped the folded bills free—almost nine hundred dollars—and held them out to Jack.

Jack's mouth dropped open.

"Take it," Alex said. "Buy yourself a ticket and get out of the country. Go take care of your family."

When Jack didn't take the money, Alex grabbed his hand and pressed the bills into Jack's palm.

"Thank you, sir," Jack whispered. "Thank you and God bless you."

Alex picked up his briefcase and walked away, taking long angry strides toward his car. He was having a hard time believing all this. He didn't want to believe it, didn't want to believe that Joanna McCall, despite her complete disregard for anyone not in her orbit, could have left her friend—*could have left anyone*—lying in the rain to die.

Alex yanked open the door of his car and climbed inside. McCall's home was a sprawling mansion set at the tip of Mercedes Drive overlooking the Intracoastal. It was normally a fifteen-minute drive from the office.

Alex made it in ten.

♦ ♦ ♦

McCall stood in front of him, one hand on the edge of the door, the other holding a glass of scotch.

"Alex," he said. "Jesus, I thought it was some madman beating on the door. What's wrong?"

"Where's Joanna?"

McCall stared at him, his eyes deepening in color, a slash of red rising in his cheeks. Alex had seen the reaction a hundred times before, whenever McCall was pushed or cornered.

"What is this about?" McCall asked.

"It's about Amelia."

McCall tensed but did not move. "You need to calm down."

"I don't need to do a damn thing," Alex said. "Where's Joanna?"

"It's late. We can—"

Alex pushed into the foyer and started toward the living room. McCall grabbed his sleeve and spun him back around. Alex was soaking wet from the rain and almost slipped on the slick marble when he jerked away.

"Don't touch me, you son of a bitch. I know what Joanna did. Now where the hell is she?"

"It was an accident," McCall said. "Joanna never intended to hurt her."

"But she did. I want to know why."

Joanna's voice came from behind him, terse and hollow in the marble hallway.

"She knew."

Alex faced her. Except for the crutches, Joanna looked like a shop mannequin, draped in a blue silk robe. But there were cracks in this woman now, like she was about to break apart right here in front of him.

"She knew what?" Alex asked.

"She suspected the firm was bilking clients," Joanna said.

Alex shook his head. "Mel has no head for finance. She never cared about the business."

"You always underestimated her intelligence, Alex," Joanna said softly.

"Joanna, that's enough," McCall cut in.

Alex moved closer. "No! Let her talk."

Joanna's eyes cut to her husband, and Alex followed her gaze. McCall's face was flushed and he had a death grip on the rock glass.

"What?" Alex demanded. "What else?"

"She knew about Mary," McCall said.

Alex's chest tightened. "That's not possible," he whispered.

"Tell him about the flamingo," McCall said.

Joanna shut her eyes.

"Tell him, damn it. He might as well know all of it now. Tell him what Amelia told you."

But when Joanna wouldn't speak, McCall stepped forward. "Your wife found that plastic flamingo in your office at home. She knew Mary collected them and she knew Mary didn't drink. She put it all together."

For a moment, Alex felt like he was going to black out. But it was just the rush of memory coming back, the memory of that night standing by that canal in the darkness.

It had been an afterthought. The flamingo had been knocked off the dashboard when McCall was beating Mary's head against the wheel. Alex had picked it up off the ground so the cops wouldn't find it. He had picked it up to protect himself and McCall. And he had kept it because . . .

Alex looked at Joanna. "I didn't kill Mary," he said softly.

Joanna just stared at him, tears in her eyes.

Alex shut his eyes. Plausible deniability . . . that was what had come to his mind that night standing by the canal. He knew the law. He knew that if he helped McCall push the car into the canal with Mary unconscious in the driver's seat he would be guilty of first-degree murder. So he had just stood there and watched as the car sank into the black water, because he knew that if this ever came to light, he could claim plausible deniability.

Such a lawyerly term. Such a clean term. It meant he was just in the wrong place at the wrong time.

Alex looked back at Joanna. "You are her friend. Why did you do it? How could you leave Mel out there to die?"

McCall stepped between them. "Enough."

"No!" Alex said. "I need to know."

"I need to sit down," Joanna said. "Let's—"

"No! Tell me here. And tell me everything, from the beginning."

"You don't want to hear this, Alex."

"Yes, I do."

Joanna shook her head slowly and took a long breath. "I knew something had been bothering Amelia for a few weeks. But she wouldn't tell me anything. The party on Marco Island . . . I thought maybe if we drove over there together alone, I could get her to open up to me. So I called her Friday, but she told me she wasn't going to go. I convinced her to change her mind, and she picked me up around six."

"You don't have to do this," McCall interrupted.

"Yes, I do, Owen," Joanna said sharply.

She looked back at Alex. "Amelia was very quiet on the drive, and I finally asked her if there was anything wrong between the two of you."

"Why would you ask that?" Alex demanded.

She shook her head again. "Oh, Alex. You only see what you want to see."

"But she loves me."

"She was getting ready to leave you," Joanna said.

"Bullshit," he said softly.

"She told me she didn't want to go to Marco Island, so she made up some story to tell you about visiting a friend who had a miscarriage."

"You said she changed her mind. Why?"

"She wanted to tell you in person that she was leaving," Joanna said. "She said she owed you that much."

"You're lying. I would've known if she was that unhappy. Why wouldn't she tell me?"

But then he stopped because he knew. Mel had been afraid of him. That was why she had bolted from the hospital. She thought he had already killed one woman, so why not his own wife as well?

He looked back at Joanna. "But why?"

"Why what?" Joanna asked wearily.

"I know what you made Jack do. Why did you try to kill Mel?"

McCall was there suddenly, his arm around his wife, guiding her down onto a bench in the foyer. Joanna slumped back against the wall and closed her eyes.

"It wasn't planned," McCall said. "Joanna didn't even tell me until Amelia showed up at the hospital. It wasn't planned, Alex. You have to believe that."

"I don't know what to believe anymore," Alex said.

"Look, things got out of control, that's all," McCall said. "Your wife got out of control and she started talking about shit she knew nothing about and—"

"Owen, stop," Joanna said.

McCall rose slowly and went to a window, his back to both of them.

Alex looked at Joanna. "You still didn't answer me."

"What?" Joanna whispered.

"Why you tried to kill Mel."

McCall turned around, his eyes locked on Alex. Then he went to Joanna and picked up her hand.

"She was going to ruin us," she said. "I couldn't let her do that." She looked up at her husband. "We still can't."

"We're in this together, Alex," McCall said.

Alex stared at Joanna and McCall. The law firm motto? That was all this came down to now? Some fucking perverted idea that if they closed ranks and stayed together they could survive this?

Alex moved toward the stairs, feeling like he needed to sit down. But then he stopped and looked back at McCall.

"I'm finished," he said.

McCall took a step toward him. "That's a little dramatic, Alex, we can still fix—"

"No," Alex said. "I'm finished. With the firm, with you, with all of it."

He started for the door, but McCall grabbed his arm. Alex pulled away hard.

"Where are you going?" McCall demanded.

"To find Mel. I'm going to make things right with her, and then we'll go away somewhere. You won't have to worry about either of us again."

"It's too late," McCall said.

"What do you mean it's too late?"

"She's probably dead by now," McCall said.

Alex's eyes swung to Joanna, then back to McCall, as he tried to make sense of what McCall had just said.

"Don't you get it?" McCall asked. "When she turned up with amnesia, it was a godsend. Even after she left the hospital, I figured we could bring her home and just get her back under control."

Alex's mind was spinning, trying to make sense of it, trying to get one step ahead of McCall. But he couldn't.

"But after she disappeared from Georgia, after she started thinking for herself, I had to adjust the plan," McCall said.

Alex suddenly knew what was coming.

"Buchanan," he said.

McCall didn't blink, didn't move a muscle.

"You turned him," Alex said. "You told him to kill her."

McCall looked down at his glass and then calmly raised it to his lips and finished it off.

"How much?"

"Two million."

Suddenly, everything started to dim, like the light was being sucked away by the closing of a lens that left only McCall's face in his view. Rage took over, and Alex charged across the foyer at McCall. The glass shattered to the floor and a spray of red spattered across the white wall as Alex slammed McCall's head into it.

Joanna screamed but Alex's fists kept flying, even as McCall sunk to the floor.

"Stop it!" Joanna shrieked. "Stop it!"

Finally, Alex stopped swinging and stepped back, drawing in hard breaths as he glared at McCall. McCall was crumpled near the stairs, gasping.

"Where?" Alex demanded. "Where is she?"

McCall wiped his mouth. "I don't know. I haven't heard from the bastard in days."

Alex ran a shaking hand across his face and shut his eyes tight. When he opened them, he looked up and saw Megan standing at the top of the staircase.

She was frozen, staring at him with her hand to her mouth. She took a step down the stairs.

Alex spun to the front door and jerked it open.

Megan shouted for him to stop, but Alex ignored her. The rain washed over him as he stumbled to his car. Once inside, he started the engine and jammed it into gear.

He roared out of the driveway and down the street, almost hitting another car as he swung wildly onto the main road leading back to the beach.

It was another mile, weaving through the traffic on A1A, before he eased off the gas. He swung into an empty parking lot bordering the ocean. For a long time, he just sat there, hands gripping the wheel, watching the dark beach appear and disappear in the slow sweep of the windshield wipers.

He pushed out of the car and started walking through the darkness, the rain pummeling his face, the ground beneath his feet turning from concrete to sand.

He could see nothing but he could feel everything.

He had been stupid, so damn fucking stupid. Not because he had picked up that damn plastic flamingo. But because he had believed that money could be spun from air. Because he believed he needed to partner up with a man like McCall. Because he believed a marriage could be kept alive on memories.

The pain was like a knife to the gut and he doubled over, sinking to his knees in the sand.

Oh God, Mel, what have I done?

He didn't believe McCall. He *couldn't* believe him. Couldn't believe Mel could be dead.

Where are you, Mel?

The phone . . .

He dug into his coat pocket and withdrew her iPhone. He pressed the power button. It took a few moments but finally the screen lit up, the only light in the pitch-black darkness. The battery was almost dead.

When he slid the lock open, the message came up: 9 MISSED CALLS FROM J.

Joanna. Fucking Joanna . . .

Alex was about to turn the phone off but then stopped. Why would Joanna call nine times?

He hit the phone icon and brought up RECENTS. All nine calls from J were listed, the newest one yesterday and the oldest call Friday, the night of Amelia's accident.

He hit the information icon for the most recent one.

The phone number was there, but Alex just stared at it in confusion. It was a 415 area code. It couldn't be Joanna. Where the hell was 415?

The phone went dead, and the darkness engulfed him. Alex struggled to his feet. He had to get home, get the phone recharged, and find out who "J" was.

CHAPTER THIRTY-FIVE

Alex looked down at the two open cases on the bed. One was his brief-case and held their passports, his iPad, and a second cell phone he had purchased at a 7-Eleven, a phone that revealed no caller ID and had no registered owner. McCall had told him Buchanan had bugged the old woman's house in Georgia. Alex had no doubt McCall could find a way to hack his phone, too.

Phones . . .

They could tell people a lot. Amelia's phone had told him things. Things that hurt. Things that made him mad.

His gaze drifted to Amelia's pink phone, lying on the dresser, still attached to the charger. Last night, he had brought it home and plugged it in, swiping the start screen like a maniac to get it to open again.

Then he had spent an hour scrolling through her calls, contacts, text messages, and websites. He was not surprised to find that Mel had made phone calls only off a limited contact list of friends, businesses, and this person "J."

This *man* called "J."

The 415 area code was in San Francisco, and a reverse directory had provided Alex with a name: Jimmy Reyes.

The name had been familiar, but it took a Google search to bring it all back. Reyes had been a dancer with the Miami City Ballet. Alex had seen him dance with Mel a couple of times, but he remembered him best from watching him offstage at galas and parties. Alex remembered how Reyes would circle the room as sleek as a panther, planting kisses on the cheeks of men and women alike.

Alex had seen the strange electricity between Reyes and Mel, something that went beyond what they did on stage. Reyes whispered things to her, smiled at her from across the room, always connected to her by something only the two of them understood.

Once, Alex had lost his temper when Reyes seemed especially attentive, and Mel had warned Alex to never do it again, that she was not a possession.

So he had stood there at that party like a putz, holding a watery drink and smiling like a fool.

Last night, he had started to call Reyes several times, but always stopped. He knew he should warn Mel that Buchanan was after her. That was the right thing to do, the best thing for Mel, but he couldn't bring himself to actually call Reyes's number.

It was selfish, but he didn't want to warn this man that he was coming to San Francisco to get his wife back. If she was already there, she might be safe from Buchanan, at least while she was with Reyes. And if she wasn't there yet, there was no way Alex could warn her of anything.

So he would just go and hope she made it, too.

He turned back to the two cases on the bed. He set the pink iPhone in his briefcase and snapped it shut. Then he finished packing his small suitcase. When the clothes were neatly in place, he added an old green and blue repp tie. He had bought the tie at Nordstrom's back when a fifty-dollar tie was a lot of money for him, and wore it to his first criminal trial, a case he should have lost but won on a bizarre turn of events during closing arguments. He had always considered the tie his talisman, with *juju* that somehow always turned the jury his way.

When he joined up with McCall, he had put the tie away in the closet. But now, as he made his plans for a new life, he wanted it with him.

He paused, trying to figure out what else he needed to pack. Shoes. Damn it, he forgot shoes.

Alex returned to the closet and grabbed brown loafers and running shoes. He was about to close the closet door when his eye caught a small wooden box sitting on the shelf. It was the box that he had found in his office days ago. He had brought it up to the bedroom but hadn't opened it.

He grabbed the box from the shelf, took it back to the bed, and sat down. He ran his fingers over the letters that had been burned into the varnished top.

ALEX

Nine . . . he had been only nine when he started collecting things in the box, his things, things he could hide away from the others. But eventually, he had put the box away and it collected only dust. He had found the box when he and Mel were packing up to move to the new house. He had almost thrown it away then, but in a moment of reflection on his new partnership with McCall, had decided to keep it to remind himself how high he had climbed. He had never opened it, never feeling the need to reminisce.

He opened the box now.

On top were two faded snapshots of himself—as a toddler sitting in the sand at a beach, and as a tanned boy in a T-shirt and shorts straddling a bike outside a yellow stucco motel. The memories came hard. The beach was somewhere up in the Panhandle, near Destin. The motel had been one of a dozen places they had lived in after his father left them. The bike was an old Huffy, a donation from the Boy's Club, and he was so ashamed of it that one night he had abandoned it behind a 7-Eleven and told his mother someone stole it.

He picked up a third picture. A tall thin man stared back at him, wearing a black gown with a garnet and gold Phi Beta Kappa sash. It was his graduation photo from Florida State, taken by one of his professors because his mother had moved away to Texas by then and hadn't been able to make it back to see her only kid start his new life.

He set the pictures aside and picked up the next item, a newspaper clipping folded in a square. It was dated 1993, when Alex was sixteen. The headline read:

RENOWNED ATTORNEYS ESTABLISH INNOCENCE PROJECT

He had forgotten he had this, but the memory of saving it was clear. He'd been busing a dirty table at Beachside Burgers in Panama City and picked up the discarded *New York Times*. As he read the article about Barry Scheck, it struck him as strange that someone would give up fame and money to fight the justice system. But he had ripped the article out and stuffed it in his apron. Had it been the reason he had become a defense attorney? It was too long ago, and he wasn't sure any more.

Alex refolded the article and looked back into the box. A red plastic slap bracelet. A couple Mercury Head dimes. A fake gold ankle bracelet, returned to him after a breakup with a girl in sixth grade whose name was lost to him. His first watch, a Timex with a frayed leather strap. And a pin.

Alex held the pin up to the light. It was an inch long, an octagon-shaped emblem with two embedded rubies. The embossed letters on the front said "NFL."

He had won it when he was seventeen, but it had nothing to do with football. The National Forensic League had awarded the pin to him for accumulating five hundred points in speech and debate tournaments.

You're just like your goddamn father. You can talk your way in or out of anything.

He shut his eyes. God, he had been good. He thrived on the tough mental preparation, staying cool as his opponents sweated and stammered under the hot white stage lights. And he loved the feeling that came after a win, the applause rolling over him like waves of warm water. He remembered suddenly what an opposing prosecutor had once said to him after Alex won his case.

You're a natural, Tobias. You can seduce a jury faster than a thousand-dollar-a-night hooker with a silk-lined hooch.

Alex put the photos back in the box and set it aside, trying to decide if there was anything in it he wanted. But maybe "wanted" wasn't the right word. Did he need it? Did a man need his past to have a future?

His eyes drifted up to a mirror. He needed a haircut. And a shave. And another drink.

How pathetic was that? How pathetic was he? Drinking himself into a coma last night. Drinking to kill the hours between his fight with McCall until this morning when the banks opened and he could get done what needed to be done.

Well, he would stop soon. He would get himself back under control when he found Mel. When things were right again, he would be right again. He placed the box inside the suitcase.

He closed the suitcase and carried it down to the foyer. He stood staring into the living room for another minute, looking around to see if there was anything he had forgotten. Just ornaments, he decided.

"Esperanza!" he called.

The housekeeper appeared in the doorway. He didn't know her well, never paid much attention to her moods, but it wasn't hard to see she was upset.

"I'll be leaving for a while," he said.

"For how long, sir?"

"I don't know. But I need you to keep coming here and maintaining the house, like you've been doing. I need you to make sure the gardener and the pool guy come as scheduled. Can you do that?"

"Yes, sir."

Why had he told her that? He had no intention of ever coming back here. But it seemed important somehow, seemed *right* to keep things clean.

He hesitated, and then walked to her and pulled out his money clip. He had been to the ATM the previous night and had taken out as much as his bank allowed on one visit—four thousand dollars.

"Here's some money to make that all happen, plus some for you," he said, handing her the bills. "I'll send more when I get where I'm going."

Esperanza accepted the cash with trembling hands. The woman's eyes were filled with tears.

Tentatively, he placed one hand over hers. "Everything is going to be okay. You're going to be fine. I'll take care of you, no matter what. Do you understand?

She nodded. "What do I tell people if they ask where you go?"

He hesitated. He couldn't avoid people forever, but he needed to buy enough time to get across the country and find Mel.

"Tell them you don't know," he said. "Don't tell anyone I left with suitcases. As far as you know, everything is completely normal."

"Excuse please for me saying," she said softly, "but things not normal in this house since I come here."

She didn't wait for him to reply, just turned and walked slowly back into the kitchen.

She was right, Alex thought. Nothing had been normal here in years. Nothing was normal now. He'd realized that days ago, when he was sitting in his study, going through Mel's scrapbook.

The Story of Us.

He turned toward his study, struck with an idea. It was stupid, a gesture triggered more by the haze of last night's vodka than any real sentiment, but he would do it anyway.

In the study, he pulled out the scrapbook and carefully peeled away the dry Scotch tape around the *fede* ring he had given Mel in France. He wrapped the ring in a Kleenex and put it in his pocket.

When he found Mel, he would offer it to her a second time, convince her to start another story with him, a better one this time.

As he started to put the scrapbook back in the desk drawer, he saw something that stopped him—the .45 automatic SIG Sauer handgun.

He had bought the thing when he was a public defender and had received a threat from a client who had accused him of "meet 'em and plead 'em McJustice."

Alex picked up the holster and pulled out the gun. The steel was cool against his palm, and it brought back the same discomfort he had felt when the dealer had first placed it in his hand. It was the only gun he had ever owned, the only one he had ever fired, and that was only a few times at the range with a cop friend where he rarely hit the X in the center of the target.

You own the gun, Alex. It doesn't own you.

His friend thought he was afraid of the gun, but he was wrong. It was just that Alex had never seen much use for them. They were the weapons of cretins and cowards. Civilized men worked out their problems using their brains, their ability to communicate. *That* was a skill he did have, one that had served him well in the courtroom.

But he was not walking into a courtroom now. He was going to face off against Clay Buchanan. A thug who wouldn't listen to reason.

Alex holstered the gun and returned to the foyer, where he tucked the gun into the suitcase. As he shut the suitcase, a strange thought crossed his mind, strange enough to give him pause.

Maybe the gun could be used to scare off Jimmy Reyes.

Had he really just thought that?

He pushed the latch into place and picked up his bags.

It was just the vodka talking. That's all it was. Just the booze.

♦ ♦ ♦

Alex made three stops on the way to the airport. His accountant was just coming back to the office from lunch when Alex showed up. He told the man to make arrangements to take care of all his financial obligations for three months. He didn't know why he'd chosen three months, it just seemed like enough time to find Mel and set up a life somewhere else. Then from wherever they were, he could sell the house, the cars, the yacht, and everything else.

His accountant asked a lot of questions, but Alex didn't answer them, just gave him the authority to see things through.

The second stop was at his broker's office. Alex instructed him to dump every fund and stock he owned. The broker asked a lot of questions, too, and advised him he was going to take a huge loss on a recent Japanese ETF, but Alex told him he didn't care. Two-thirds of the funds were to be sent to the Cayman Islands accounts and the rest to his bank in town.

The third stop was at the bank, where he picked up a hundred grand in cash. He was on his way to the door when it occurred to him that there was another way to kick McCall in the balls on his way out of town. It would be a small kick, but it would piss him off. He went back into the bank and wrote a company check for two hundred grand, the maximum he could withdraw without a second signature.

He arrived at Fort Lauderdale Executive Airport under a cobalt blue sky and cool bright sun. The smooth black tarmac was spotted with sleek white Learjets, Citations, and Hawkers, tended by tanned men in navy shorts and blue polo shirts.

The young brunette behind the counter looked up when he walked in the terminal. He had seen her many times before but couldn't recall her name.

"Mr. Tobias," she said. "You're right on time. Your aircraft is ready. We just need to complete the paperwork. Are we billing the firm, as usual?"

He reached into his pocket for the envelope he had filled at the bank. It was a shitload of money to hand over the counter, but he didn't want to leave a paper trail. McCall could find anyone he wanted with a few phone calls or computer clicks. And Alex didn't want anyone—especially Buchanan—knowing that he was going to San Francisco.

"No," he said. "I'm paying cash."

The woman blinked. "I'm sorry. Did you say cash?"

"Yes."

"I don't think we accept cash. I'd better check with—"

He laid the envelope on the counter. "Cash it is, or I'll find another charter service."

The young woman stared at him.

"Will thirty thousand cover it?" Alex asked.

"Yes, I suppose."

She drew the envelope to her, peeked inside, and then slowly slid it under the counter and into a drawer. "I'll need to write you up a receipt," she said.

"I don't need one. Where's my pilot?"

"That's him outside," she said, pointing. "Captain Bailey."

"Thank you."

"Have a nice flight to San Francisco, Mr. Tobias."

He turned and stopped short at the sight of the woman standing at the entrance. White dress, blonde hair flowing over her shoulders like yellow feathers.

Megan's eyes slid to the woman at the counter, then back to him, settling on his face like lasers.

"Who's in San Francisco, Alex?"

He moved closer to her. "Just business."

She propped a shoe on his suitcase. "I heard what you told my father last night. You quit the firm."

"I'm going out there for a job interview," he said. "How the hell did you know I was here?"

"I followed you. I was pulling up to your house this morning when I saw you drive away in the taxi. I wanted to know what you were going to do, if you were going to go to the police to report my father or some other stupid thing. So, I followed you."

Alex glanced back at the counter but the young woman had gone into an office. "So you heard everything I told your father?" he asked Megan.

"All of it."

He reached down to grab his suitcase, but Megan pressed her heel deeper into the leather. He straightened and looked at her, keeping his voice low. "Tell your father I'm not going to the police. He knows I have just as much to lose as he does. Now move your foot or I'll move it for you."

She stepped away slowly. He grabbed his bag and pushed the door open with his shoulder. She followed him outside. When he didn't stop, she yanked at his sleeve.

He spun around. "I'm warning you, Megan, leave me alone."

She stared at him for a moment and then she laughed. "What are you going to do, Alex, hit me?"

Alex glanced at Captain Bailey, who stood a few feet away, eyeing them uncomfortably. When Alex looked back at Megan, he was stunned to see tears in her eyes.

"You made promises to me, Alex," she said.

Alex hung his head. These were memories he didn't want, not right now.

She doesn't love you anymore, Alex.

She's my wife, Megan.

But she's not there for you. Not like I can be.

I wish . . .

What? What do you wish?

I wish I could go back and start over.

You can, Alex. With me.

And for a while, he had told himself that maybe he could. Mel had been drifting away, and now he knew it had been to this man Jimmy. Maybe they had both drifted too far and it was too late for them. Maybe this whole idea of finding Mel and running away was wrong. It was a huge risk. Wouldn't it be easier—*cleaner*—to stay here and let Owen make things right again? Wouldn't it be easier to stay here with a woman like Megan who knew what he had done, knew what kind of man he was, but who was willing to love him anyway?

But when he looked at Megan, he didn't see her. He could only see Mel.

The whine of the Learjet warming up filled the dead air.

"I have to go, Megan," he said.

"Stay with me," she whispered.

Alex shook his head.

"I don't care what you did, Alex. Don't you understand that? I know everything and it doesn't matter to me."

"I know," he said. "I have to go."

He started walking toward Captain Bailey.

"Get me out of here," he said.

"Yes, sir."

The captain fell into step with Alex as they headed to the jet.

"You're going to her, aren't you?" Megan yelled.

Alex quickened his steps.

Megan caught up and grabbed at his sleeve, but Alex shucked her off and tried to keep moving. Finally, Captain Bailey stepped in front of Megan.

"I'm sorry, miss," he said. "You're not allowed out by the jets. Stay back, please."

"Alex!" Megan yelled.

"Stop, miss, or I'll call security."

Megan's voice rose above the whine of the jet's engine. "My father is right! You're a loser, Alex! You can't do this to me, you son of a bitch!"

Alex climbed the steps to the jet, dropped into the first seat and turned toward the window. Megan was struggling with a security guard.

Captain Bailey appeared in the doorway. "Do you need anything, sir?" he asked.

"I need that door shut."

"Yes, sir."

With a thud and a gentle rock of the plane, Megan was muted. Alex closed his eyes and laid his head back.

"How long to San Francisco?" he asked softly.

"Just over six hours, sir."

Alex looked at his watch, then to the window. Megan was alone now, no longer yelling or fighting, just standing on the tarmac staring at his plane.

Then, just as the jet started to roll, she turned and went back inside the terminal.

Alex closed his eyes. Six hours. In six hours he would be on the other side of the country, on his way to a new life. He would find Mel and make things right.

If she was still alive.

CHAPTER THIRTY-SIX

The bullet wound was only the size of a dime. But it had cost Buchanan one more day and night in the orange-curtained hellhole motel before he was finally able to trust his strength enough to begin the long drive to California.

Interstate 80, he had learned, went straight through and dead-ended right in downtown San Francisco.

He just hoped his chances to find Amelia didn't. If Amelia was on her way to find Jimmy Reyes like he suspected, she had a two-day jump on him.

The first leg of Buchanan's journey was a numbing drive through the emptiness of Iowa and Nevada where for more than seventy miles, the road never deviated more than a couple yards from a perfect straight line. He reached Wyoming and crossed the Continental Divide. Then came the Great Salt Lake Desert, where the signs warning about driver fatigue were the only relief from the flat landscape.

It was past ten by the time he checked into the Motel 6, dragging in his duffel and a greasy takeout bag from Burger King. After a restless night's sleep, he was on the road by seven the next morning.

The second leg of the drive took another eleven hours, most of it through the lunar landscape of Nevada. The hours and miles crept by. There was too much desolation and too much silence, and his brain was filled with a white-noise buzz. He almost prayed to hear her voice, hear her call him Bucky, hear her call him by the name that only she said.

But she wasn't there.

The emptiness outside his window was echoed by the emptiness inside him. It was something he had not felt since the weeks after the disappearance of Rayna and his son. His years of working had disguised it, but it was back, the awful hollowness, the feeling that he was truly alone in the world. And that there might not be a good ending on this road he had chosen.

But there was no other choice. He had to see this through. He had to find Amelia Tobias.

And then what?

First he had to somehow convince her—a woman who had shot him after he had tried to kill her—that he was now on her side. And then he had to find a way to protect her from McCall. There were only two options on that front. He could persuade her to go to the cops and tell them about Mary Carpenter. But what did he really know about that? All he had was a theory and a plastic flamingo. And he couldn't count on Amelia remembering anything.

Which left him with only option two, the one he didn't really want to think about.

He would have to make sure Amelia Tobias disappeared forever.

It wouldn't be easy, but he knew it could be done. He had made a career out of tracking runners and renegades of all stripes, smart people with money and means who were desperate to disappear. Why couldn't he reverse the process and help Amelia start over?

A fake passport, a little money, a new name, a ticket to some country where McCall would never think to look.

A new life.

And what about you?

It wasn't Rayna's voice he was hearing now. It was just the hollow sound of his own.

What kind of life would he have when this was over?

In all the hundreds of miles he had driven, all the hours of thinking, he hadn't been able to answer that question because he couldn't see any easy outcome. McCall might let him live, but Buchanan knew he'd always be looking over his shoulder. The indictment might not result in new charges, but his daughter would always be lost to him. His work, the one thing that had sustained and distracted him, he now saw for what it was—an exile to a place where he didn't have to deal with the messiness of human emotions, a place as devoid of life as the desert now whizzing by his window.

And that little brass key in his wallet?

He'd never see a penny of McCall's blood money.

Buchanan was getting drowsy, and his body was one giant rod of pain from the bullet wound in his shoulder. He flexed his hands on the steering wheel and blinked hard, concentrating on the road ahead. He was about to pull over and grab a quick nap when suddenly the road curved to the left, the first break from the straight-line route in hundreds of miles.

And then he saw it—green. There were trees ahead and the gentle rise of the Sierra Nevada foothills. He was almost to the California state line.

He sat up straight in the seat and flexed his hands on the steering wheel.

◆ ◆ ◆

It was past five when he hit the sprawl of suburban Berkeley. The traffic was heavy, and so were his eyelids. He had to concentrate hard to make sense of the cacophony of signs directing him ever west. Then there was a spaghetti bowl of overpasses in Oakland, a pass through a tollbooth, and he was on the Bay Bridge.

Water . . . gray and white-capped. Suddenly it was there on his right. Was it San Francisco Bay? He didn't know. In all his travels for his skip tracing, he had never been to San Francisco. The Bay Bridge traversed a green island and then he was back out into the open again, on the top span of a grand suspension bridge. The setting sun was blinding, and he flipped down the visor, his head pounding with fatigue, his tired eyes hypersensitive to the light.

He had expected fog. Wasn't San Francisco shrouded in fog? But then he finally saw it—a city of pale buildings set down on undulating hills backdropped by an orange Creamsicle sky.

His thought at that moment hit him like a bullet in the shoulder.

What a beautiful place to die.

◆ ◆ ◆

Interstate 80 emptied onto a broad four-lane boulevard called Van Ness Avenue. As beautiful as the drive across the Bay Bridge had been, this was an ass-ugly stretch of highway, a row of muffler shops, car dealerships, and storage units. Once he crossed Market Street, the scenery changed to granite civic buildings. He leaned forward when he saw the Pantheon-like façade of the opera house. Buchanan's Google of the San Francisco Ballet's schedule had told him the company was getting ready to open *The Nutcracker*, but the opera house looked dark now.

No matter. He was heading to Jimmy Reyes's apartment.

Reyes lived in a neighborhood called the Tenderloin, just a fifteen-minute walk from the opera house. Yesterday, when Buchanan had found Reyes's address he had also booked a motel nearby. He didn't know the city and couldn't waste any time trying to figure out where things were.

He turned onto Eddy Street. The Mirage Motel was a puke-yellow relic from the sixties. Buchanan checked in, tossed his duffel on the stained bedspread, and was back outside in a few minutes. The pool in the courtyard was filmed with algae, and he had to step over a drunk near the motel entrance. But it was eighty bucks a night, the parking was free, there was a liquor store across the street, and he could walk anywhere he needed to go to get this job done.

He pulled up the collar of his jacket against the chill and headed back toward Van Ness on foot. His belly was sending up rumbles of hunger, he was tired and his shoulder ached like a sonofabitch. But he wanted to get to Reyes's apartment and start a stakeout. He walked slowly, in no big hurry. The burner phone in his pocket had been silent for hours, and as long as McCall believed he was still on the hunt, Amelia was in no danger.

Once he crossed Van Ness, the streets narrowed and the buildings shrank in scale. The walls were scarred with graffiti, the windows covered with metal grates. The writing on the tattered awnings and dirty windows was mostly Asian, and the smell was a fetid brew of urine and frying meat.

Reyes's apartment building was a four-story green Victorian on the corner of Geary and Larkin. The ground floor was occupied by a bar, but Buchanan spotted the apartment's metal grated door. He peered inside to the tiny vestibule. There were twelve mailboxes, but he couldn't read the names.

Buchanan stepped back, debating his next move. He noticed a red FOR RENT sign in the window of a second-floor unit. The printing on it said RING BELL FOR OWNER. NO APPTS AFTER 8.

He glanced at his watch. Five after eight. He rang the bell.

It echoed in the tiled vestibule. After the second ring, an interior door jerked open and an old guy with flowing gray hair and a beard, wearing a tie-dyed T-shirt, looked out.

"I'm here about the rental," Buchanan said.

"What, you can't tell time?" the guy shot back.

"Give me a break. It's only five after. I'd like to see the place, please."

The bearded guy came forward to peer at him through the grating. Buchanan stared back, knowing that even as ragged as he felt, he still looked better than ninety percent of the people who passed by this old hippie's doorstep.

"All right," the guy said, unlocking the grate. "It's on the top floor. You go up first. I don't go first up no stairs."

On the top floor, Buchanan waited while the old guy unlocked the door and slapped on the wall switch.

One room with bare white walls, scuffed dark wood floors, and bay windows covered by a fire escape. The kitchenette had scarred counters, a toy-sized stove, and a wheezing circa-1950 fridge.

"The bathroom's over there," the old guy said, pointing to a door.

"Where's the bedroom?" Buchanan asked.

"You're standing in it."

Buchanan decided to finish the ruse. "How much?"

"Fifteen hundred a month."

Buchanan choked back a laugh. He couldn't afford to offend the guy. "It's very nice."

The old guy was eyeing him. "Where you from, Mississippi?"

"How'd you guess?"

"My ex was from Natchez. You sound just like her."

Buchanan gave him a tight smile.

"You want it you better grab it tonight," the old guy said. "You won't find a place this good at this price."

"I know. That's what Jimmy told me."

"Jimmy Reyes? You know Jimmy?"

"Yeah. He told me you had a good studio for rent."

The old guy gave him a hard stare and then waved a hand at the room. "So, yes or no?"

"I need to sleep on it."

"Your loss, dude."

He turned off the light, locked the door and they headed back down the stairs. In the vestibule, Buchanan did a quick scan of the names on the mailboxes. No Jimmy Reyes.

"Which apartment is Jimmy's?" he asked.

"Reyes is gone. He moved out about a month ago."

Shit.

"Do you know where he went?" Buchanan asked.

"I think he's in Cole Valley. Look, I have to get—"

"Did he leave a forwarding address? I'd like to look him up. He's a really good friend."

The hippie arched his brow. "You don't look like his type."

Buchanan held out forty dollars. "It's worth a lot to me."

The hippie plucked the two twenties from Buchanan's hand. "I'll get it for you but it'll have to be tomorrow morning. Take it or leave it."

"I'll take it."

The hippie jerked open the metal grating, waiting impatiently. When Buchanan didn't move, he sighed again. "I'll be here," he said. "Eight in the morning. Now get out of here."

Buchanan nodded. "Thanks, man."

The metal door banged shut behind him. Buchanan stepped out into the street. The temperature had dropped a good twenty degrees since he had arrived and a cold fog was curling in, blurring the street-lights and neon. Or maybe he was just so damn tired his eyes were finally giving out on him.

The homeless men were starting to stake out their doorway beds. Buchanan headed toward Larkin Street, intent on getting back to the Mirage to crash.

But when he stopped at the corner to wait for the light to change, he heard a buzzing and turned. His eyes went up to the blur of flickering red neon above the entrance of the bar.

The Outsider.

Jimmy Reyes would have to wait until tomorrow. Sleep would wait a while longer. Right now, he needed a drink.

CHAPTER THIRTY-SEVEN

How could she be here, in a place like this?

It was dark, the fog blurring the red neon sign above the entrance of the bar. But no amount of fog could mask the ugliness of this place. Junkies shivering in doorways, homeless people pushing shopping carts around drunks passed out on the sidewalks. A woman in hot pants and halter top standing on the corner screaming obscenities at the night sky.

Alex shuddered and reached for the vodka bottle on the seat of the rental car.

Mel was so much better than this, so much better than this man Jimmy Reyes. How could she allow herself to step so far down?

It was her brain, he decided. It was still damaged, and he could only assume that at this point, she didn't know any better.

He took a drink, set the bottle between his knees, and focused on the doorway of the green Victorian building. It hadn't been hard to find out where Jimmy Reyes lived. The firm had excellent software for locating people, and he had his own account, which he'd used to get Reyes's address. The man lived above a bar on Geary Street, in an area of the city called the Tenderloin. From Alex's vantage point a half block away, it looked like the upper floors of the old building had been divided into six or eight small apartments. Behind the zigzag of the fire escape, he could see a FOR RENT sign in one of the windows.

He had been tempted to go barreling in, but he had learned something from his confrontation with the old woman in Georgia. If there was a way out through the back, Mel would run from him.

That night in Georgia had taught him something else, too, though he had not listened at the time.

She's a different woman. And you're going to have to be a different man to get her back.

As much as it gnawed at him to admit it, Buchanan had been right. He did need to be different, and he would be. He'd be smart and calculating and patient. He would wait until she was alone to confront her. That would give him the element of surprise and, even more to his advantage, allow him to isolate her from Reyes.

A siren wailed, and he glanced in the rearview mirror to watch a police car pass by in the intersection behind him. His eyes drifted back to Reyes's apartment building.

He shifted in his seat, uncomfortable with the lowlifes who roamed near his car and the smell hanging in the wet air. Uncomfortable, too, with the smell of his own body. It had been two and a half days now since he'd shaved or bathed. Maybe he should've taken the time to check into a hotel and clean up. But he had wanted to get here, to this place, as fast as he could.

Was Mel up there?

Was she still alive?

He took another drink of vodka and closed his eyes.

When he had been a defense attorney, he'd met people like himself—people hoping a missing loved one would suddenly walk through the front door alive and well. Parents were the worst, always so sure their baby was still alive. They talked of weird psychic vibrations, dreams, and even physical sensations that connected one body to another; feelings, they said, that would not be there if the child was dead. He'd always thought they were just in denial.

But now he had to wonder, because he felt the same thing for Mel. Like he was tied to her by an ethereal thread of energy that allowed him, inside his own body, to feel the soft beat of her heart. He had felt it all during the six hours it took to fly here, and he was still feeling it now.

She's here. She's here.

Alex opened his eyes, looking back at the apartment's door just as metal grating opened.

He straightened quickly and peered hard through the windshield. Standing in the white glow of the streetlight was a man. But it wasn't Jimmy Reyes. This man was light haired, too broad.

It was Buchanan.

Alex's eyes shot up to the windows of the apartments. All were lit by lamps except the one.

God, god. Mel is dead. The bastard had already been inside. He had already killed her.

And now he was just standing there, taking in the street like a tourist. He had nothing in his hands, and from what Alex could see, no blood or stains on his clothes.

Alex opened the car door and got out, his eyes bouncing from the apartment windows to Buchanan and then up and down the street. But he didn't even know what he was looking for. A police car?

No . . . no cops.

If Mel was dead and he got the cops involved, everything he had done—and everything McCall had done—would eventually come out. He'd never get out of the country.

Calm down and think.

Buchanan was moving now, walking slowly toward the corner, like he was out for a damn evening stroll. No one was that cool, Alex thought. Nobody could kill a woman and just walk away like nothing had happened.

Alex reached back inside the car, grabbed the gun from under the seat, and stuck it through his belt under his jacket. When he looked back at Buchanan, the man was standing on the corner, waiting to cross the street. Then Buchanan turned and disappeared into a bar.

Alex bolted across the street to the apartment's entrance. He had to know if Mel was in there. He had to know she was still alive. He had to get in.

He yanked at the handle on the metal grate, and when it didn't budge, he spun around looking for buzzers or intercoms. There was only one button outside the gate. RING BELL FOR OWNER. He jabbed at it and waited. When no one came, he punched it again and again. Still no one came.

Damn it.

He'd have to confront Buchanan.

No, that's stupid.

He would follow him. For now, he would just follow.

Alex walked to the bar, pushed open the door and slipped inside. The place was bathed in a smoky red light, but Alex could make out some people sitting in the booths that rimmed the empty dance floor—a young woman in a hoodie curled into fetal position, a skeletal man in a dirty Santa costume clutching a beer and staring into space, an Asian woman cooing into the hearing aid of an old white guy.

Where was Buchanan? Then Alex spotted him at the far end of the bar, silhouetted by the lights of the jukebox. Alex moved deep into the shadows and dropped into a booth.

So now what?

His hand moved inside his jacket and rested on the gun. Suddenly he felt very comfortable with the weapon. But he knew he couldn't use it now, not here with all these people. He slumped down into the darkness of the booth, tapping his foot nervously and stroking the butt of the gun.

Finally, Buchanan slipped off the barstool and pulled on his jacket. Alex waited until Buchanan left the bar and then hurried out after him.

He followed Buchanan as he made his way south on Larkin Street. He was easy to trail, his height and broad shoulders rising above the shorter Asians and hunched junkies. Again, Buchanan seemed to be in no hurry. He stopped to get a newspaper from a stand, ducked into a liquor store, and emerged with a small brown bag tucked into his jacket pocket.

Alex stayed against the buildings, breathing hard. His skin burned with adrenaline, and he was almost nauseous from the rush. How much farther? Where was he going?

Suddenly Buchanan stopped and started looking around.

Alex stepped quickly into a doorway, his feet brushing up against a man huddled under a blanket.

Now Buchanan was talking to someone, an Asian man who pointed at something down the street. Buchanan had gotten himself lost, Alex knew.

Buchanan headed across the street, cutting between the cars. Alex followed, creeping behind slow-moving cars as he hustled to catch up. For a second, he lost Buchanan in a crowd but Buchanan resurfaced, still heading south. Then the man vanished, like he'd been sucked up off the street.

Alex slowed his step and turned a full circle, afraid Buchanan had seen him and had doubled back to confront him. But Alex was alone. The fog had thickened, and Alex could hear the chest-thudding boom of a car stereo but couldn't see where it was coming from.

He cursed himself for losing the sonofabitch. He was about to turn around and head back when he saw the entrance to the alley. It was the only place Buchanan could have gone.

He edged up to it. It wasn't an alley. It was a narrow street—OLIVE the sign said—and it was just wide enough for one car to pass. But it was empty and dark, the only illumination coming from the streetlight on the far end.

Then, something halfway down the street moved in the dark.

A man . . . Buchanan moving away.

Alex started down the street, passing through a narrow canyon of buildings, his eyes locked on Buchanan, now about twenty yards ahead.

Alex pulled the gun from his waistband. This was the perfect place, dark and deserted, but he didn't have much time—Buchanan was almost to the corner.

Then Buchanan turned around.

Alex skidded to a stop and raised the gun.

"Who's back there?" Buchanan shouted.

Alex fired, blinking as the muzzle flash lit the street like the strike of a giant match.

Buchanan fell away from his view.

Alex heard the clatter of trash cans and the screech of rats.

He fired again.

Somewhere a woman screamed.

Alex turned and bolted from the street, clumsily trying to tuck the gun in his waistband as he ran. Back out on Larkin, he pushed through the crowd, knocking a woman to the ground, but he didn't stop.

He knew he hadn't followed Buchanan very far, but it seemed like a hundred miles back to the red neon of The Outsider bar. When he saw the sign, he stopped and spun, looking for his rental car.

Fuck! Motherfucker!

He couldn't even remember what it looked like. Then there it was, parked halfway down the block. A siren cried behind him, but he didn't even look back as he ran to the car. He climbed in, started it up, and with a screech of tires, got the hell out of the Tenderloin.

CHAPTER THIRTY-EIGHT

The cold felt good against his hot forehead.

Alex stood motionless, head against the window, eyes closed. How long had he been here, standing in the dark, head against the glass?

He slowly opened his eyes.

He was high up, on the thirtieth floor of the Parc 55 Hotel, and far below, the city lights glowed under the layer of fog. It was quiet, no sounds at all. His heart was pounding slow and hard but his body felt numb, as if the adrenaline he had felt after firing the gun had burned away the nerve endings just under his skin.

He took a step away from the window and wiped a hand over his face.

Buchanan wasn't dead. He had seen him get up and stagger out of that alley.

But everything after that was a blur, running back out to the street, driving crazily down dark streets. How had he gotten to this hotel? He couldn't remember checking in or riding up in the elevator. He looked across the shadowed room, spotting his briefcase on the desk and his suitcase on the floor by the bed where the bellboy had left it.

Where was it? What had he done with it?

He grabbed his jacket off the desk chair and fumbled through the pockets until he felt the hard metal. He pulled out the gun, releasing a breath of relief. The gun was cold and there was no smell, no evidence that it had been fired.

But he had fired it. He had tried to kill a man.

Back on Geary Street, when he had first seen Buchanan coming out of Jimmy Reyes's apartment building, he had asked himself how someone could kill a woman and be so cool afterward. But in his heart he had already known the answer, because six hours after he had watched McCall push Mary's car into the canal, he himself had sat in a meeting with two German investors. But later that night, alone in his study, with Mel sleeping upstairs, he drank an entire pint of vodka without moving from his chair. He realized now it had been the beginning of an almost nightly ritual, drowning Mary Carpenter over and over again in a bottle of booze.

Alex sat down on the edge of the bed.

Just a few days ago, in that same study, he had sat flipping through Mel's scrapbook, wondering what had happened to *her* that destroyed *them*.

But it wasn't her. It had never been her. It was *him*.

A voice he hadn't heard in years was suddenly in his head, raspy with the scorch of cigarette smoke and flat with the apathy of a woman who had given up on living.

It's your fault. Your father left because of you, Alex.

Then another voice—Buchanan's.

She's a different woman and you're going to have to be a different man to get her back.

He had been going about this all wrong. He didn't need to be different. He needed to be what he once was.

He turned back to his suitcase, pulled out the two suits he had brought, and laid them on the bed. The voice of his law professor was in his ear—brown is for used car salesmen, black is too severe, blue suggests "the truth."

He chose the blue. Next he pulled out a crisp, white button-down Oxford shirt, dark blue socks, and a pair of black wingtips. Nothing fancy or foreign looking.

Ties . . .

He had brought three. The solid burgundy or the blue stripe were the obvious choices, but maybe he needed the *juju* of the green and blue. He shut his eyes, feeling a rush of heat through his neck. This had to be perfect. He had to be perfect.

Green-blue *juju*. It was imperfectly perfect.

He turned back to his suitcase, pulled out his wooden box and took out the double-ruby debate pin in the bottom. He couldn't wear it on his lapel of course—that would be childish—but he could put it in his pocket.

When his clothes and shoes were laid out on the bed, he looked around to see if he had missed anything he would need tomorrow. The gun, lying on the other bed, caught his eye. He picked it up and set it down carefully next to the double-ruby pin.

Alex turned out the light, drew a chair close to the window and sat down. He looked at his watch—just after 3:00 a.m. Six more hours before he could see Mel. Six hours to get dressed and walk one mile to the opera house. That's where she would go, because he had checked and knew that's where Reyes would be for a rehearsal.

The watch's crystal face was smudged. Alex rubbed it on his sleeve.

Just like McCall had done the day he had given it to him. It was a Patek Philippe, the same one McCall's father had passed down to him.

Alex shut his eyes. What was that slogan, the one in the Patek ads. *You never actually own a Patek Philippe. You merely look after it for the next generation.*

I never had a son, Alex, McCall had said.

And I never had a father.

Alex took the watch off and set it on the table.

He turned back to the window. A reflection appeared on the glass, so distorted that at first he wasn't sure what it was. Then it sharpened into a face.

When he realized it was his own reflection, he closed his eyes, not wanting to look at it.

◆ ◆ ◆

Traffic was light on the Bay Bridge, but the fog was advancing fast across the bay, a slow white tsunami wiping out everything in sight.

Buchanan took his left hand off the wheel and flexed it. The damn thing was swollen, and his knuckles were burning from where he'd ripped the flesh off them diving into the trash cans on Olive Street.

He had sobered up fast, lying there in the stinking darkness, wondering if the shooter was going to come down the alley and finish him off. When he finally got up, he hurried back to his motel, planning to pack up and head back to Nashville to leave these crazy people to solve their own problems.

But he hadn't gotten very far when he started thinking about what had just happened to him.

No way was the shooter a robber or mugger; he would've confronted him face to face. And he wasn't some nut just firing at the sky because the shots had whizzed right by Buchanan's ear. And it wasn't

Amelia Tobias, either. If she had seen him hanging around the Tenderloin, she would have called the police, or run off again.

It was fucking McCall.

He had hired someone to take him out. How McCall had guessed he didn't intend to kill Amelia, Buchanan didn't know. Maybe the guy was just that good at reading people, hearing things in their voices that exposed their lies.

But it didn't matter how McCall knew. Buchanan was mad, and he wasn't running. Not from some chickenshit, silk-suited swindler who had built his business by snuffing out secretaries. But if he was going to stay in San Francisco and save Amelia, who was probably in greater danger now than ever, he needed more than just his wits and his anger. He needed a gun.

He had ducked into the first bar he'd seen, a place on O'Farrell with no name, just a buzzing neon cocktail glass above the metal-grated door. The bartender wore a T-shirt that said EVERYTHING DIES. Five minutes and fifty bucks later, Buchanan was out in the cold again with directions to Oakland.

Bay Bridge to the Nimitz Freeway South. Take Grand a few blocks into the city and look for any kid in a big jacket hanging out on a corner. Once you get the gun, get the hell out, fast.

The Toyota's headlights caught the blur of a green sign for Nimitz Freeway, and Buchanan eased off onto the exit ramp and around a curve that set him south. He hadn't gone far at all when he saw the sign for Grand Avenue and pulled off.

The smooth gray freeway lines and darkness gave way to a string of streetlights, their alien sodium vapor glow illuminating a landscape of vacant trash-strewn lots, brick warehouses, and sagging construction fences splashed with graffiti. The only open business Buchanan saw was a gated-up liquor store.

He drove deeper into the city, into a row of shack-like homes with weedy lawns and rusted cars in the driveways. Another turn led him down a darker street, with warehouses rising up on both sides, and only one streetlight to light the entire block. Music—hard, bass-heavy rap stuff—boomed from the darkness.

Buchanan put the car in reverse and swung around backward. His headlights caught the silhouette of a man standing against the building. No, it was a kid, his neon-striped sneakers lit up in the glare of the headlights.

Buchanan drove forward slowly and swung the Toyota up to the curb. The kid moved back into the heavy shadows, but he didn't run.

When Buchanan pressed the button to roll down the passenger window, the kid inched toward the car, hands in his pockets, head covered by a hood. He couldn't have been more than fourteen.

"You need directions, man?"

"No, something else."

The kid's eyes cut to the street and then back to Buchanan. "You a cop or just a stupid motherfucker? Nobody else come down here like this all alone."

"I'm not a cop."

The kid smiled. "You a funny guy."

"I need a gun."

"How much bank you got?"

"Three hundred."

"Lemme see it."

Christ, he was probably going to get ripped off and left for dead. He dug into his pocket and withdrew three one-hundred dollar bills. He held the money up but not too close to the open window.

The kid reached into his jacket and produced a small black gun. "Nine mil Nano."

"Good enough."

Buchanan slapped the money into the kid's hand and took the gun. He put the car in gear, but the kid was still at the window, his gloved hand on the door frame. Buchanan glanced in his rearview mirror, sure the kid had buddies coming.

"You got bullets, man?"

"What?"

"Bullets, you know, those little lead things you put in guns?"

"I can get ammo."

"Not here in California you can't, less you got a permit. New law, man."

Buchanan couldn't believe what he was hearing. Was the kid just trying to jack him for more money?

"How much?" Buchanan asked.

The kid held up a plastic baggie of bullets, swinging it gently. "One Ulysses, my man."

"What?"

"Man, where the fuck you from? Fifty bucks."

Buchanan rummaged through his pockets and came up with three twenties. The kid dropped the bullets on the passenger seat and disappeared into the night. Buchanan decided to do the same. He pulled away and drove slow but steady back to the freeway.

Back in San Francisco, he returned to the Mirage and packed up his stuff. It was past midnight by the time he checked into his new hotel. The Gateway Inn had a security guard in the lobby. He wasn't armed, but maybe his presence would deter an attempted hit. The Gateway was also closer to the apartment building where he was to meet the hippie landlord in the morning.

The room was cold, and the heater was on the fritz. Buchanan made sure the two deadbolts were secure, then stripped off his clothes, taking the gun with him into the bathroom. After fifteen minutes in a steaming hot shower, he toweled off, picked up the gun, and carried it with him back to the bedroom.

There was one change of clean clothes left in his duffel. It felt good to be dressed in something decent again, something that didn't stink of sweat and fast food. And it felt good to be alert, too. He figured that had come from the lingering adrenaline rush of being shot at and his trip to West Oakland.

He settled into a chair near the window, holding the gun in his lap. The view through the dirty, cracked window was of tarred rooftops and air conditioning units. Fog pressed against the glass, like the night was exhaling.

His adrenaline rush was subsiding. He rubbed his aching hand.

It had been his fury, his indignation at being shot at, that had put a gun in his hand. He had felt good about that, empowered even, and not simply because he had a weapon. He had taken action to defend himself, and he had taken it because he was sick of getting shit on.

How you doing, Bucky?

He thought she had deserted him, left him for good because he'd made such a mess of his life, especially with what he had agreed to do back in Georgia, sitting in the car with McCall. But he should have known she would come back. No matter what mistakes he'd made or what mood he was in, she always came back. Her being dead hadn't changed that.

"I'm okay," he said.

No, you're not.

No, he wasn't. Because he had no idea how this was all going to end, and no confidence even that he would come out of this alive. He looked down at the gun in his lap. The worst part was that even with this, he had no control.

But he had to see it through.

Tomorrow, he would go to Jimmy Reyes's apartment, and if he was lucky, Amelia Tobias would be there.

And if she wasn't?

She had to be there. Because he needed her to be.

There were no options anymore. He couldn't just help her disappear into a new life, because now she was the one who had control, she was the only one who could save him—and herself. If she couldn't remember what had happened to Mary Carpenter there was no way to stop McCall. And if McCall couldn't be stopped, he would kill them both.

She had to be there. She had to remember.

Buchanan stared out the dirty window, his hand resting on the gun on his lap. The chair was hard, and when he shifted to find a comfortable spot, he caught sight of an image in the cracked window—his face, sliced in half.

CHAPTER THIRTY-NINE

Alex stood at the bottom of the steps looking up at the opera house. Now that he was here, he wasn't sure what he was going to do. Had he expected to just walk in and confront Reyes? He wasn't even sure Mel was here. But where else would she go? She had to be here.

Two elderly women moved past him, heading up the steps. They wore dressy suits and heels, their perfume trailing strong behind them. He watched them enter one of the theater doors. Moments later, a quartet of women went in the same door. Alex climbed the steps and went inside.

There was a crowd of maybe thirty people, men and women, all well dressed, their laughter and talk echoing in the vast marble-columned lobby. Alex spotted the sign near the red-carpeted steps.

THE NUTCRACKER REHEARSAL

SPECIAL EVENT PATRONS ONLY

He had been here before. In Miami, of course, but he had been to one of these things in the past. You wrote a big check to the ballet and they gave you bad champagne in a plastic glass and let you watch a rehearsal.

Alex moved in among the others. He could feel his face sweating and he wondered if the gun made a noticeable bulge in his belt under his suit coat. But no one was looking at him. He fit right in.

The crowd was streaming into the theater. Alex straightened his tie and followed.

His eyes traveled up over the gilt walls and gold curtain as he made his way down the center aisle to where the others were gathered in the front center rows. The sounds of the orchestra warming up came from the pit. He took a seat in an empty row behind everyone else. His heart was kicking up, but he felt an odd calm, just like he used to feel when he would enter a courtroom.

A tall man came onstage, introduced himself as the artistic director, and made some comments. Alex heard almost none of it as his eyes swept the theater.

He was looking for Mel. He was looking for Jimmy Reyes.

The lights went down, the music began, the curtain opened.

There was nothing to do now but sit here, he knew. Sit and wait. Because he was sure, so very sure, she would be here.

And then, suddenly, there she was.

Appearing from behind a veil, dressed in a blue harem costume, moving like silk to the slow music. Alex sat forward in his seat.

No . . . it wasn't his Mel. It was just another girl posing as her, trying to confuse him.

He slumped back in the seat and shut his eyes.

When the lights finally came up again, he blinked and looked down at his watch. Two hours had passed, and he remembered none of it. The others were leaving, streaming back up the aisle. He sat still in the seat. The gold curtain rose slowly, but now the sets were gone, leaving just ugly concrete walls, exposed lighting, and a curtain of pulleys, chains, and winches. Big men in T-shirts and jeans were moving around on the stage, pushing flats of scenery, yanking on ropes. Noise . . . hammering, men yelling, a bell going off.

Teenagers in jeans and hoodies—the dancers, Alex realized—were scattering in all directions, flitting among the slow-moving men carrying violin cases. The theater was emptying fast.

Alex rose slowly and started up the aisle, but then he froze.

He was coming toward him. Jimmy Reyes, he was coming down the aisle right toward him.

Reyes didn't give him a glance as he passed. He bounded up the three steps to the left of the stage and began pointing upward toward the lights as he talked to a man with a clipboard.

The blood was pounding in Alex's ears, blocking out all the sounds, and for a second he could almost feel the gun radiating heat against his waist. He moved closer, standing at the rail of the orchestra pit, watching Reyes.

He wiped a hand over his sweating face.

No, forget Reyes. Buchanan is the one you want. He's the threat. Find the threat first and eliminate it.

Reyes finished with the other man and came forward toward the lip of the stage. For a moment, Alex thought he was coming to talk to him but then Reyes pulled out a cell phone.

"Hey, love," Reyes said.

Mel . . . is he talking to Mel?

"I'm almost finished. Did you get some rest?"

Smiling. The bastard was smiling.

"Good. Why don't you grab a cab and come down here? I'll take you to lunch at Indigo."

Reyes hung up and slipped the phone in his jeans pocket, and then he disappeared into the wings.

Alex looked up, feeling a rush of emotions. Anger and jealousy but mostly relief. Mel was still alive, just as he had felt she was. He could still save her from Buchanan. He could still convince her to come home. All he had to do was be patient.

The man with the clipboard was still standing on stage. Alex could hear him arguing with a stagehand, something about union rules and overtime and that everyone had to clear out in an hour.

Alex glanced around. The theater was empty. Most of the lights were off now. He spotted a door over by the steps near the stage. He went to it and opened it. It led into a long narrow hallway. Lots of doors, leading to other hallways. Backstage . . . it was a warren of rooms and hallways. He had been here before, waiting for Mel to come out of the dressing room—waiting, always waiting.

And that is what he would do now. Wait for her to come.

◆ ◆ ◆

Buchanan had been waiting, watching, for two hours now.

Then, suddenly, she was there. Amelia was standing in the large picture window of Jimmy Reyes's second-floor apartment. She stayed there for maybe a minute, looking out as she drank from a coffee mug. Then she was gone.

Buchanan leaned back in the booth and let out a long tired breath. He felt a small surge of satisfaction that he had been right in assuming she would come here to Reyes. The doubts had been there these last couple days but he had been right after all. At least he still had that—he still knew how to do his job.

Reyes had left hours ago. Buchanan had watched him head up the hill toward Geary Street. It had taken one call to the San Francisco Ballet offices to find out there was a dress rehearsal today. But why hadn't Amelia gone with Reyes?

"Another refill?"

Buchanan looked up at the waitress. She was perturbed that he had taken up her prime table this long for a lousy fifteen-dollar burger and coffee.

"Yeah, another refill," he said. Then he slid a twenty-dollar bill across the table. "If you leave me alone there's another twenty for you when I leave, okay?"

She refilled his coffee, pocketed the twenty and left. Buchanan went back to watching the apartment.

The corner booth at the Seal Rock Inn restaurant offered him a clear view. He had checked out the neighborhood and the building's exterior already. It overlooked a park that sloped down to the ocean and two popular tourist places, the Sutro Baths and the Cliff House. There was a steady flow of MUNI buses, sightseeing coaches, and tourists on foot. Reyes's building had no other way in or out except for the main entrance on El Camino del Mar.

He again considered going up to the apartment and trying to talk to Amelia. But his best bet was to wait until she was out in public. She might feel safer, and so would he. And she was unlikely to try to shoot him again.

Buchanan took a drink of coffee, his eyes scanning the street. Whoever had taken a shot at him last night might be lurking around, watching him, hoping he'd lead them to Amelia. No, he'd be patient and wait for the right moment. As long as she was up there in that apartment, no one could get to her.

Buchanan shifted in the booth, trying to find a more comfortable angle to ease the ache in his shoulder. He picked up the coffee mug but set it down again.

His gut was churning too much right now. And it sure as hell wasn't from the coffee.

He looked back at the apartment just in time to see Amelia come out the door. She looked around and started across the street toward the park.

Buchanan jumped up, grabbed his canvas tote, tossed two twenties on the table and hurried to the exit.

She was getting into a cab. He had parked the Toyota a block away on the chance Amelia might recognize the car. He ran to it and cranked it up, but by the time he got the car turned around toward the apartment, the cab had disappeared.

Fuck!

He sat back in the seat, pissed at himself. But then it hit him that she was probably going to meet Reyes at the rehearsal. He steered the Toyota up the hill toward Geary Street.

He left the car in a public lot near the rear of the opera house. He ditched his jacket, slipped the nine-millimeter Nano in the waistband of his jeans and pulled his sweatshirt down over it. He circled the building until he found the stage door. Someone had left an old Velcro-tabbed back-support belt in the trash. He pulled it out and slipped it on. When a guy came out, Buchanan grabbed the stage door and ducked in.

The old man at the security desk barely gave him a glance as he went by. As Buchanan made his way through the dim hallway, he saw no one else and heard nothing. He had to go slowly, the only light coming from red exit signs. But he could feel a soft rush of air and see a white light ahead, so he followed it up a short flight of steps, past an electrical panel and crates.

He slipped between two black curtains and stopped. He was in the left wing of the stage. In the middle was a plain metal floor lamp topped by a bare bulb, its light glowing stark in the middle of the vast empty stage.

Voices . . .

Buchanan drew back between the two curtains.

A tall thin man came out of the opposite wing—Reyes? And then, there she was—Amelia. They stood close, talking, Reyes's hand on her arm. Buchanan heard him say something about having to go check something at the box office and Amelia replied she would wait here.

Reyes went down the stairs and up the aisle, disappearing into the shadows of the theater. Buchanan waited until he heard the echo of a door closing and then stepped out so he could see Amelia better.

She was just standing there, the Vuitton duffel over her shoulder. She turned in a slow circle, looking up, and her face, caught in the glow of the bare-bulb light, looked like that of someone visiting an old cathedral.

She stopped and set the duffel on the stage. She walked away from it, heading toward the back of the stage. Then she turned around and stood there, perfectly still, her head bowed.

Buchanan heard someone humming. It took him a second to realize it was Amelia. She was singing to herself, something very slow and soft.

She began to move. Just one arm swept slowly across her face first, like she was hiding behind a veil, but then she began to glide across the stage with small quick steps. Two delicate little leaps and then . . .

She slowly raised one leg, unfolding it upward as she spread her arms behind her.

Buchanan eased back into the shadows, not wanting to watch because the moment felt so private. But he couldn't look away. So he watched, transfixed and motionless.

This one's special, Bucky.

It was what Rayna had said to him that first night in the hotel back in Fort Lauderdale. He hadn't understood what she meant then but now he did.

There she was, dressed in black jeans, a black T-shirt, blue Converse sneakers, and purple plastic glasses. But Amelia was as exotic and ancient and as beautiful as the pyramids.

Buchanan bowed his head. He got it.

For the first time, he got it. It was the unicorn effect.

That's what birders called it—those rare birds that lived only in your imagination. You heard of them or maybe saw a drawing in a book, but you never ever got to see one. Then, one day, there it was in front of you, as if some mythical creature had stepped out of a storybook and come to life.

A thing of beauty where before you only saw the mundane.

He felt a jab in his back and then the voice came from behind him. "Don't move."

CHAPTER FORTY

"Walk out onto the stage, in the light."

Amelia spun around at the sound of his voice. Before he even came out of the shadows, she knew it was Alex.

Oh my God . . .

That man Buchanan was with him, moving slowly into the light. He was a few steps in front of Alex, his hands raised.

"Alex, what are you doing here?" she demanded.

Alex poked at Buchanan to get him to walk. Did he have a gun at his back? Her eyes cut to her Vuitton bag at the edge of the stage where she had left it. Should she make a move for her own gun?

"Get on your knees," Alex said.

Buchanan lowered himself to one knee, then the other. When Alex stepped around him, Amelia could see him clearly. He had a gun, and she remembered seeing it before, in his desk back in Fort Lauderdale.

"Alex, look at me," she said.

Alex's eyes came up to her slowly, and caught in the harsh light, she could see a storm of emotions in them—anger, confusion, need, and . . . Love?

"What are you doing here?" she asked, more softly this time.

"I came to stop him." Alex gestured toward Buchanan with the gun. "He wants to kill you."

Buchanan shook his head. "That's not true."

Amelia's eyes shot to Buchanan's. She didn't say it out loud, she didn't want to antagonize Alex, but she knew Buchanan could read her look. *You already tried once.*

"Tell her, Buchanan," Alex said. "Tell her you were hired to kill her."

Amelia started taking small steps toward her duffel, her eyes darting between the two men. Alex was looking at Buchanan, but Buchanan was watching her. He knew why she wanted to get to her duffel, but would he let her?

"Tell her!" Alex yelled.

Alex kicked at Buchanan, catching him in the shoulder. Buchanan let out a yelp and fell forward to one hand.

"Tell her, God damn it."

Buchanan pulled in a hard breath and looked up at Amelia. "Owen McCall offered me two million to find you and kill you. But after . . . after the lake, I knew I couldn't do it. I kept following you so I could warn you. Maybe save you from the next man McCall would send."

Amelia was at her duffel now, but she forced herself not to look down at it. The name Owen McCall registered as Alex's partner, the man she had seen on her computer screen when she was looking up Alex's law firm.

She looked at Alex. "Did you know about this?"

"God, no, Mel."

"He knew all about it," Buchanan said.

Alex came at him. "You're a goddamn liar! It was all McCall's idea. Tell her that, Buchanan. Tell her!"

"I only know what McCall told me!" Buchanan shot back. "And he said you knew!"

Alex swung the .45 at Buchanan's head. Buchanan tried to grab it but he missed, and Alex smacked him behind the ear with the butt.

Amelia reached down and grabbed her gun from her bag, whipping it up so fast she nearly lost her grip on it.

"Alex, stop it!"

The faces of the two men registered in her consciousness like snapshots.

Alex—pale and damp, his eyes dark and jumpy.

And Buchanan—no fear or even surprise in his eyes, just . . . relief? Why? Did he think they were on the same side now?

"Mel . . ."

Just a whisper, but it made her swing the gun back to Alex.

"Mel, you don't need that. I have this all under control. Give me the gun."

Amelia shook her head, glancing quickly toward the seats. Where was Jimmy? Why wasn't he here? Was he watching this from the control room? Had he called the police?

"Mel, come on," Alex said. "Let's talk this out."

"No! I want to hear him talk," she said, swinging the gun toward Buchanan. "Tell me why Owen McCall wanted me dead."

Her hands were trembling and she locked her elbows to try to make them stop. Buchanan was looking at her, his face cut with white light, black shadows, and a streak of red blood.

"Tell me," she said. "Tell me the truth."

"You remember Mary Carpenter?" Buchanan asked.

The name sounded familiar but the woman's face was out of focus. "I . . . I'm not sure," Amelia said.

"She was your husband's secretary," Buchanan said. "She knew something illegal was going on in the firm and she was probably going to turn them in. Or they thought she was."

Alex jabbed his gun at Buchanan's temple. "Shut up or I'll shoot you," he said.

"Alex, be quiet." Amelia looked back to Buchanan. "Go on."

"First you tell your husband to take that gun away from my head and let me stand up. I don't talk to anyone on my knees."

"Alex, back away and lower your gun," she said.

"Mel, none of this matters!"

"It matters to me!"

Alex moved away slowly, but he kept a white-knuckled grip on the .45. He was sweating and his eyes were still jumpy. She had no idea how far she could push him.

Buchanan stood up slowly. Amelia wasn't sure who to aim at, so she kept her gun moving slowly back and forth between the two men.

"Talk," Amelia said.

"McCall and your husband killed Mary Carpenter by faking her car accident," Buchanan said.

"How do you know this?" Amelia asked.

"Your husband kept a souvenir from that night that I found in—"

Buchanan stopped talking and just looked at her. At first she didn't understand why, but then she knew. He wanted *her* to remember. He needed her to remember this by herself so she would believe him. But she couldn't remember.

"What do you mean?" she asked. "What kind of souvenir?"

"You tell me," Buchanan said.

"Leave her alone!" Alex took a step toward her.

"You found it in your husband's study," Buchanan prodded. "You hid it with your mementoes in that box from Iowa. The box your mother sent you."

Amelia stared at Buchanan. And then it came. First the memory of the cardboard box, with all the photographs, books, jewelry, ballet shoes. Her mother had sent the box to her before she died. It was where she had hidden the book Jimmy gave her. And Ben's letters . . . she remembered those, too, now.

"Mel, listen to me, please."

Her eyes shot to Alex but she was seeing herself in his study, going through his drawers looking for his hidden bottle of vodka so she could throw it away. But she had found something else.

"It was a flamingo," she whispered.

It took a moment, but Alex managed a nervous smile. "He's lying to you, baby. There's nothing illegal going on at the firm. There was no murder and there was no souvenir or anything else. He's just trying to plant fake memories in your head and confuse you."

Amelia started to back away, more memories coming that didn't make much sense. "No, it's true. It was a little plastic flamingo, just like the ones on Mary's desk."

Alex shook his head. "Mel, you need to trust me. You're still confused."

"Yes, yes, I am," she said. "I'm not sure what it meant, but I know it bothered me. I know he's telling me the truth."

She spun back to Buchanan. "That night in the Everglades. Was that McCall, too? Did he try to kill me?"

"I don't know. I can tell you someone was with you that night because you took the tan suitcase out of the Mercedes to make room for something. And someone closed the doors of the car after you were hurt." Buchanan looked at Alex. "Ask your husband what happened out there."

Amelia turned to Alex. "Tell me."

Alex just stared at her, and in that long silent moment, she could see something in his eyes that made her feel uneasy. She had seen this look before. Had she confronted him before about this? Was that why things had gone so wrong?

"Damn it, Alex, tell me!"

"It was Joanna," Alex said.

"Joanna? Why would she . . . ?" Amelia stopped, desperate to bring up something from her memory of that night. The gun suddenly felt too heavy in her hands.

"You and Joanna were going to a party on Marco Island," Alex said, his voice a monotone. "On the way, you told her about these . . . concerns you had about the firm and Mary Carpenter. It was dark and raining hard. Joanna said you argued and that you lost control of the car."

"But why?" Amelia whispered.

"Why what, baby?"

"Why did she leave me out there?"

Alex was quiet, lips pressed tight.

"Finish the story or I'll shoot you right here and now!" Amelia said.

Buchanan raised his head. "She'll do it, man. You better tell her," he whispered.

"All right, all right," Alex said. "Joanna called her driver and he dragged you off into the weeds but he couldn't finish the job. Then they drove home and left you out there to die."

The dark-haired man in her visions. Not her husband, but that chauffeur who drove Joanna's car, the man whose name she didn't even know, who probably didn't even know hers.

Amelia's knees started to give, and all she wanted to do was sit down and try to process all of this, try to figure what was true and what was not.

"Mel."

Alex's voice brought her back, and with it came a vision of oranges on a windowsill and the blue sea beyond. And herself in a wedding dress and then a harem costume. A pink cell phone and a little black dog. Sighing Vivaldi violins and tinkling *Nutcracker* celestas. Burnt cookies and Tabu perfume. The hotness of her sick mother's brow and the roughness of her father's hands as he pushed her away. And that cold white mansion and that cool blue-green bubble, the two places where she had almost died.

Little things will bring it back.

That's what the doctor had told her back at the hospital. But it was all too much and it was all too fast, a sensory avalanche from the past that was threatening to bury her now.

"Enough," Amelia said.

Alex was staring at her. And then he nodded slowly. "Yes, enough. Now we can move on."

"Move on?" she asked. "To where, Alex?"

"Anywhere we want," he said. He reached into his jacket, pulled out two small dark blue things, and held them out to her.

"Look, I have our passports," he said. "We can go, right now. We can leave here and go anywhere we want. We can start over."

Amelia was stunned. "No. I can't go anywhere with you."

Alex moved closer to her. "I promise you it will be different this time, Mel," he said. "No more scams. No more drinking. I'm different now."

She shook her head slowly. "It's too late."

Alex tossed the passports to the stage and was at her in three steps. He grabbed her wrist, wrenched the gun from her hand and tossed it to the back of the stage. She tried to pull away, but he caught her and yanked her back to him and locked an arm around her neck. He started to drag her toward the wings.

"Stop it!" she cried. "Let me go!"

"You're coming with me," Alex said.

"No, she's not," Buchanan said.

Alex spun her around, pinning her back against his chest, so she was a shield between himself and Buchanan.

Oh God.

Buchanan had a gun, pointed at Alex—not her. But she knew Buchanan didn't have a clear shot at him.

"Let her go," Buchanan said.

Alex tightened his arm around Amelia's neck and wedged his gun under her chin. "Stay out of this."

"You have nowhere to run," Buchanan said. "McCall won't give up. He will hunt you down—both of you—and kill you."

Alex clumsily shifted her to the side. "I have money, lots of money," he said. "Millions, I have millions. We can go anywhere in the world."

"And there will always be a man like me one step behind you."

Alex thrust his gun toward Buchanan. "I said stay out of this! Let us go or I'll shoot her. I swear I will."

"No you won't," Buchanan said. "You came all this way to get her back and now you're going to leave her dead on this stage? Is that how you want this to end?"

"No!" Alex yelled.

"Then what do you want?" Buchanan asked.

"I want it to be like it was." Alex lowered his head so he was speaking into Amelia's ear. "You understand that, don't you, Mel? Don't you want us to be like we were?"

Amelia stayed silent. She was afraid to say anything because Alex had a choke hold around her neck and she didn't know what he would do, didn't know who he was anymore. She locked eyes with Buchanan.

"I thought you were a different man now," Buchanan said.

Amelia felt Alex's arm tighten around her neck.

"I am," he whispered.

Buchanan slowly lowered his gun down to his side. Then he took several steps back and nodded toward the wings. "Go ahead," he said. "I won't try to stop you. Go ahead and drag your wife off to Timbuktu."

For several long moments, no one moved.

"Alex," Amelia said.

His breath was hot against her neck and he was making strange little mewing sounds.

"Alex, let me go," she said.

And then he did. His arm dropped slowly from her neck and she eased away from him. She knew she should run, but she didn't. She turned to face him.

His hair was damp with sweat, his cheeks cut with tears. When he brought his hands up to cover his face, the gun gleamed in the light. For one awful second, Amelia was afraid he was going to shoot himself.

"Alex," she said softly.

His hands came down and he stared at her, but his eyes were unfocused and flat, like she wasn't there. Like he wasn't there. Alex drew in a hard breath, stuffed the gun in his waistband and reached for something in his breast pocket. When he uncurled his palm, Amelia saw a silver ring.

"You remember this, baby?" Alex whispered.

She looked down at the ring and then up into his eyes.

"I bought it for you in Menton," Alex said, his voice growing more earnest. "Don't you remember how much you loved it there?"

"Alex . . ."

"Don't you remember how much you loved *me*?" Alex asked.

Amelia stared at the ring. She didn't remember it, though she did remember that she had loved him once. But she didn't love him now, and that truth was not what he needed to hear. Amelia took a step back, away from him.

Alex closed his fist over the ring.

"I'm sorry, Alex."

He bent and picked up the passports. He opened one, looked inside, and then held the other out to her. She took it. He turned and started away.

"Where are you going?" Amelia asked.

He stopped. "I don't know."

"But—"

Alex hesitated and then came back. He leaned into her, and when he kissed her gently on the lips, she closed her eyes because it hurt. It hurt because they had been so good together, but for so brief a time. It hurt because they had both lost themselves somewhere in *us*.

"Good-bye, Mel," he said softly.

He backed away a few steps, took a long look at Buchanan, and then disappeared into the wings.

Amelia stared into the darkness. She didn't move until she heard the faint echo of a door slamming shut. She looked back at Buchanan. His gun was stuck in his belt. Her revolver was a few feet away and she went to it and picked it up.

"You won't need that for me," Buchanan said.

"How can I be sure?" she asked.

"I told you. Because I'm not a murderer."

Amelia lowered her gun. "Then what are you?"

He held her eyes, as if he were unsure how to answer. "I could've answered that a few weeks ago. But now I can't."

She looked toward the wings, then down at the revolver in her hands.

"You should keep that handy," Buchanan said.

"I don't want it."

"Owen McCall still needs you dead."

"I'm no threat to him."

"He doesn't know that."

Amelia hesitated and then went to her duffel. She slipped the gun inside and stood up, looking Buchanan straight in the eye. She was tired and still confused about Alex, what had happened to her, and the motives of this strange man Clay Buchanan. But there was one thing now she knew for sure.

"I'll take my chances," she said. "I'm not running anymore."

CHAPTER FORTY-ONE

Traffic was light as Buchanan steered the Toyota south on Interstate 280. He had the window down, breathing in the cool night air, which smelled of the bay and something vaguely medicinal. He could hear the whine of jets heading to San Francisco Airport. There was no need to hurry. In fact, he was looking for the right place to stop.

Finally, he saw it off in the distance to his left, a gleam of dark water. He took the Islais Creek exit and headed down a dark empty road past warehouses and trash-heaped lots until he stopped at the dead end of Indiana and Tulare Streets.

To his left was a massive corrugated steel building, locked and abandoned. To his right was a lot filled with ruined and rusted MUNI buses.

He killed the engine, got out and walked toward the water. There was a park of some sort—or at least the start of one—with concrete benches and saplings braced with wires. But the trees were dead and the benches were slashed with skateboard scars. One bench bore a neon-yellow graffiti tag—*You thought you knew and now you do.*

The only sound was the whir of tires from the nearby freeway.

Buchanan went to the edge of the walk and looked down. The water was dark and swirling, moving fast out to the bay. He pulled the nine-millimeter Nano from his pocket. He looked at it for a second and then flung it into the water.

He went back to the Toyota, started it up, and drove it into the bus lot, parking it between two dead streetcars. He got a screwdriver from the trunk, took off the license plates and heaved them into the trash. Then he flung his canvas tote and duffel over his good right shoulder and started walking back up Indiana Street.

◆ ◆ ◆

It was near nine by the time the cab dropped him off at the airport. Inside the terminal, he paused in front of the departure board. There was a Delta flight leaving at eleven for Nashville. A quick layover in Atlanta and he would be home by eight tomorrow morning.

But then his eyes drifted right.

Auckland.

Beijing.

London Heathrow.

Hong Kong.

Manila.

Sydney.

He had about three thousand dollars in his wallet, all that was left of the last advance money McCall had given him. He couldn't risk using his credit card—for the same reason he had taken the trouble to remove the plates from the Toyota. McCall was probably still going to come after him, so he had to make himself as hard to find as possible. That meant he was about to become a runner for the rest of his life.

His eyes lingered on the international departure board. Then he went to the Delta desk. As he waited his turn, he pulled out his wallet to count his money. Wedged between the hundred-dollar bills was the photograph.

He pulled it out and stared at Gillian's face.

"Sir?"

He looked up at the clerk and stepped forward.

"Where are you headed, sir?"

"Nashville, please, your eleven o'clock flight."

"Yes, sir. Will that be economy?"

"Yup. One way."

The young woman punched at her computer keyboard. "You're in luck. One seat left. Row thirty-five, seat F."

Fuck. Right in the middle of the Airbus.

"I'll take it," Buchanan said.

He started to put Gillian's photograph away, pushing it down as far as it would go in the wallet. It caught on something, and he pulled out the little brass key.

Buchanan stared at it. He stared hard at the key in his big hands, but he was suddenly seeing it instead hanging around the slender wrist of someone else, a young blonde woman who was snapping the key's plastic band impatiently because no one was paying attention to her.

His eyes shot up to the departure board.

"Wait," he said.

The clerk looked up.

"You got any seats left on the eleven-fifteen flight to Fort Lauderdale?" he asked.

The clerk tapped some computer buttons and then nodded. "Yes, we do. I can give you seat G in row twenty-one."

Buchanan started to hand over the money and then paused. "How much for business class?" he asked.

"Two thousand seven hundred and fifty-five cents," she said.

Buchanan pulled out the wad of money and counted out twenty-eight hundred-dollar bills. A few minutes later, the clerk handed him his ticket and pointed her pen to the left. "Gate eight, sir. Boarding is at ten thirty, but you're welcome to wait in our Sky Club lounge."

"I think I'll do that," Buchanan said. And he started away.

"Sir!"

He turned back.

"You forgot your change."

He looked down at the money on the counter. Ninety-nine dollars and forty-five cents. He scooped it up, thanked the clerk, and walked away.

Do you like to gamble, Mr. Buchanan?

I don't like giving my money away.

I love to gamble. It's not about the money, it's about winning.

Megan McCall was right. It wasn't about the money and this was probably a stupid thing he was about to do. But he had a hunch about this, and he was putting all of what was left from McCall's last bundle of advance money on double zero.

♦ ♦ ♦

The red-eye flight got him into Fort Lauderdale at nine. He grabbed a coffee and bagel from the Dunkin' Donuts kiosk at the airport, snarfed them down, and then headed outside. He got a cab and asked the guy to take him to the nearest mall.

In Target, he bought a pair of white shorts, a white Mossimo polo shirt, white sneakers and crew socks, and a seventeen-dollar tennis racket. He changed clothes in the store's restroom, stuffed his other clothes into his duffel and caught another taxi. The cabbie didn't ask any questions when Buchanan asked the driver to leave him two blocks away from his destination and wait.

The guy manning the parking lot booth at the Lauderdale Yacht Club didn't ask any questions either as Buchanan walked right past the gate with a smile and salute of his tennis racket.

Buchanan paused just inside the entrance, bouncing the racket lightly on his palm. The place was almost deserted; it was too early for the lunch crowd. But the same guy who had stopped him that day he had come to meet Joanna McCall was at his station outside the restaurant.

Squaring his shoulders, Buchanan headed straight toward him.

"Can you direct me to the locker rooms, please?"

"Yes, sir. Just down that hall there," the young man said with a smile.

"Thanks."

"Enjoy your game, sir," he said.

"I intend to."

Jizz. All you had to do was have the right jizz.

There were two old guys in the locker room, sitting in towels on benches, and neither looked up as Buchanan made his way through the rows of beige metal lockers. There weren't that many and for a moment Buchanan was beginning to doubt his hunch. And then, there it was.

Locker 328.

Buchanan stared at the number for a long time and then pulled his wallet from the pocket of his shorts. The locker was small, one of those half-length ones. He inserted the little brass key into the small padlock and turned.

The lock clicked open. Buchanan swung the door wide.

The blue vinyl Adidas gym bag was wedged in sideways. Buchanan eased it out, testing its weight. Heavy, maybe forty pounds.

He sat down on the bench, the gym bag on his knees. He took a deep breath and unzipped the bag.

Neat white-gray bundles of paper. Lots of them.

Buchanan glanced around, saw no one, and pulled out one of the bundles. There was a crisp hundred-dollar bill on top, with a gold band over it that said $10,000.

How many bundles? His brain was buzzing too loud to do the math. He didn't want to. He just wanted to get out of here as fast as he could. He slipped the bundle back in the Adidas bag and zipped it shut.

Back in the lobby, the young man in the blue blazer gave Buchanan an odd look as he headed to the entrance.

"Quick game," Buchanan said. "I won."

♦ ♦ ♦

The cabbie who had waited for him got a hundred-dollar tip. The kid who carried his bag up to the suite at the W Hotel got a fifty, the last of McCall's dirty advance money.

Buchanan put the Adidas bag in the room safe, flung the sliding glass doors wide open, poured a Maker's Mark from the minibar and laid down on the king-sized bed.

But he didn't take a drink. He just lay there, eyes closed, feeling the warm ocean breeze wash over him. He was thinking about what he was going to do with the money, about how he could buy a good lawyer to help him with the indictment and getting Gillian back, how he could go back to Nashville and get back to his life. He was thinking about . . .

Turtles.

Those poor damn baby turtles down there on the beach who lost their way and followed the wrong lights to their death. He was thinking about turtles and birds and unicorns and his head was getting really fucked up, and he hadn't even had one drink. He was thinking that what he had been doing since he had lost her was not really what he wanted to do anymore.

Then what are you?

It took him a moment to realize it wasn't her. It wasn't Rayna talking to him. It was Amelia.

And it took him another moment to realize he didn't know the answer.

He sat up slowly in the bed. He didn't know the answer, but he knew where he had to go to find it.

But first, he had to go find one last runner.

CHAPTER FORTY-TWO

Alex had to wait until the fishing boat made its way through the inlet. It didn't matter. He wasn't in any hurry now. The low drawbridge eased back down into place, and Alex put the car in gear and drove on, past the old lighthouse and down a narrow road.

The car window was down, and the air flowed over him sweet with the smell of the sea and something in bloom. The sky was starting to turn pink and gold as the car entered a thick tunnel of trees, the twisting banyans and sea grapes swaying in the stiff breeze. The road was lined by huge lush ferns, magenta bougainvillea, and scarlet hibiscus bushes.

Alex slowed, looking for the sign, and finally spotted it almost hidden in the row of date palms—BHG BUILDERS. The chain-link fence was open. He swung his car down the rutted dirt road, parked behind a yellow Caterpillar backhoe and got out.

It rose up before him, huge and gray, a concrete shell of a building. Three floors, the windows covered in protective blue film, the balconies rimmed with scaffolding, the unfinished staircases leading nowhere.

He spotted a black Bentley half-hidden behind a bunker of cement bags and started toward it.

"Alex!"

He looked up. McCall was standing on a second-floor balcony, leaning over a makeshift wood railing.

"Come on up," McCall said. He disappeared into the concrete shell.

Alex picked his way across the construction debris and through a yawning gap in the front of the house into a cave of rebar and dangling conduit. He spotted a bare concrete staircase and went up to the second floor.

The breeze was brisker here, snaking in through open archways that led to a trio of balconies overlooking the ocean. Alex glanced around as he walked, at the cathedral ceilings and the rainbow marble slabs that framed a hole in the wall for a future giant aquarium.

"You're late," McCall said.

He was a large silhouette in an archway, the sky behind him a gradient splash of orange and blue.

"I got caught in traffic."

"How was your trip to California?" McCall asked.

Alex was quiet, not surprised McCall knew where he had been. Megan had probably told him.

"It was a failure," Alex said. "As you would say, I couldn't close the deal."

McCall nodded. "You used to be the best closer I ever met."

"I can be again."

McCall's brow lifted. "Is that why you wanted to meet me? You wanted to ask if you could come back?" he asked.

"Yes."

McCall walked out to the balcony and stood at the railing. Alex followed him, hands in his pockets. Out in the fading light, Alex could see the lingering bruises on McCall's cheek, where he had hit him the night they argued.

"I'm ready to move on, get things back to normal," Alex said. He tried a smile. "Get to work on the next million."

McCall was silent, just staring at him. "What made you change your mind?"

Alex hesitated. "Mel. It's over between us. I see that now."

McCall shook his head. "You know it's not that simple. We've still got a problem out there. Both of us."

"What do you mean?" Alex asked.

McCall took a step back, his gaze moving slowly over Alex's body and back up to his face.

"You wearing a wire, Alex?"

"What?"

"Did the Feds get to you? What did they offer you?"

"Fuck, Owen . . ."

"Take off your jacket," McCall demanded.

Alex slowly removed his coat and spread his arms. McCall stepped close and patted Alex down, from his shoulders to his ankles.

"Empty your pockets," McCall said.

"I would never turn on you, Owen. I have as much—"

"Prove it to me. Empty your pockets."

Alex stepped back inside the shell of the house and set his keys, cell phone, change, money clip, and his jacket on a worktable, leaving his pants pockets turned inside out. McCall motioned him back to the balcony, where he led him a good twenty feet away.

"Want me to strip naked too?" Alex asked.

McCall stared at him, his eyes dark with suspicion. "Trust is like a mirror, Alex. You can fix it, but you can always see the crack."

"Trust goes both ways," Alex said. "You hired someone to kill my wife."

McCall reached into his pocket and withdrew a cigar. Alex watched him as he bit off the end and turned his back to the breeze to light it. The smoke disappeared quickly into the dusky light.

"I only want one thing," Alex said.

"And what's that?"

"I want you to call off Buchanan."

McCall just stood there, sucking on the cigar.

"Mel doesn't remember anything," Alex said. "She doesn't remember finding the flamingo. She doesn't even remember why she was going to Marco Island or who was in the car with her."

"But she might."

"The doctor told me she'd probably never remember what happened. I'm telling you, that night is lost to her."

"But you still love her. And that makes you a liability to me."

Alex nodded slowly. "But I love something else more."

McCall glanced at him, as if he were bored. "What?"

Alex gestured toward the view. "This. I want this. I want what you want. I want to be able to buy four houses on the beach, tear them down and build something better." He paused. "You were right about me, Owen. You always were."

McCall laughed softly and blew out a stream of smoke.

Alex drew a shallow breath, shivering in the cooling breeze.

"All right," McCall said. "I'll call Buchanan off, but only temporarily. I'm going to be watching her."

"I can live with that."

"And I want you to give me that damn bird from Mary's car."

"I'd like to hang on to it," Alex said. "I need some insurance of my own. Like you said, our trust level is a little low right now."

McCall stepped closer to him. "Understand one thing, Alex. Nobody extorts me. Not you, not your crazy wife, not anyone."

"You killed an innocent woman."

"It had to be done. And I will not be held ransom with a damn plastic toy you picked up out of the mud. Are we clear?"

Yes. Yes.

"I said, are we clear?"

"Yes."

"Bring it to me tomorrow at the office," McCall said. "Once I have it, you can come back to work."

Alex nodded. McCall walked to a trash can, stubbed his cigar out on the side and tossed the butt inside.

"We're finished here," he said. "Let's go."

Alex looked out at the horizon. The orange-blue had faded to a thin red line that hung over it like a streak of blood.

"You coming?" McCall asked.

"I think I'll stay a few minutes and watch the sun go down. Do you mind?"

McCall hesitated. "Suit yourself."

Alex stayed on the balcony until he heard McCall's footsteps fade, and then slowly walked to the table and picked up his jacket. As he gathered up his things, he paused, staring down at the money clip.

It was platinum, yet another gift from McCall when they had closed some big deal. He couldn't remember which one now, but it didn't matter. He pulled the bills from the clip, put them in his pocket, and set the clip on the worktable.

Downstairs, he walked to the center of the sandy yard, but instead of heading toward his car, he followed a path up through the trees, into an adjacent empty lot. He could hear the rush of the ocean, taste salt in the air, feel the beat of his own heart.

A man in a navy-blue windbreaker stepped out from behind a bush. The yellow letters stamped across the right side of his jacket said FBI. Behind him was another man, in a dark suit and white shirt.

The FBI agent held out a hand. Alex took off his Patek Philippe watch and handed it to him. The agent turned it over, peeled off the small electronic bug, and looked back at Alex.

"Well done, Mr. Tobias."

Alex didn't say anything, couldn't say anything. The man in the suit stepped forward. "You got him to confess to the murder of your secretary but you didn't get him to talk about the securities fraud."

Alex looked away, toward the dark ocean. "Just do a forensic audit of the books," he said. "You'll find everything you need."

The man in the suit walked away. The FBI agent held out a pair of cuffs.

"It's time, Mr. Tobias."

Alex turned around and put his hands in front of him. He closed his eyes as the agent snapped the steel cuffs around his wrists. He had managed to broker himself immunity from any SEC or fraud charges in exchange for getting a confession from McCall on Mary's murder.

The first charge was just about stealing money from people, the agent had explained, something banks did legally every day. But Mary Carpenter's murder, that was something different. Because Mary was a potential witness, killed to prevent her from testifying about a crime, her murder was considered a federal offense. The lowest charge the Feds would offer him was Accessory to Murder. Five to fifteen years in a federal prison.

"Let's go, Mr. Tobias," the agent said, taking his arm.

Alex walked with the agent, across the sand, toward a dark sedan sitting near the road. His breath started to quicken and his heart rate kicked into high.

He was scared. Scared of what was going to happen to him in prison. Scared of what his life would be like for the next decade. Scared he would not survive it.

But, Mel . . .

She would be safe.

And that thought, that one single thought trickling through the wash of almost paralyzing fear, gave him the strength to keep walking.

CHAPTER FORTY-THREE

Jimmy insisted on getting a tree. He had dragged it into the apartment the night before, a scrawny four-foot blue spruce that he had found in a lot somewhere in the Mission District. Amelia chided him about being sentimental but secretly she was pleased.

Her memories of past Christmases were still re-forming, the ones from Morning Sun and Fort Lauderdale, and they were all cold and white.

She was sweeping up needles from the carpet when the doorbell rang.

The intercom was broken, so she looked out the window. The man at the door below was big with blond hair, wearing a leather jacket.

"Who is it?" Jimmy asked, coming in from the bedroom.

The man looked up, and Amelia drew in a sharp breath.

"Buchanan," she said.

Jimmy came to the window and looked down. "Don't answer."

But Amelia pushed the buzzer.

Buchanan was coming up the stairs when she opened the door. He was carrying a Vuitton tote. He stopped, midstair.

"Permission to come aboard, Captain Kirk," he said.

She moved aside, and he came into the living room. She shut the door and leaned against it, watching him. He was looking around the room, his eyes lingering for a while on Jimmy and then focusing finally on the tree.

"What are you doing here?" Amelia asked.

He turned to her. "I brought you a Christmas present." He unzipped the Vuitton tote.

A small black head popped out.

Amelia gasped. "Brody!"

She came forward, grabbed the dog from the bag and spun away, holding Brody so tightly he gave a small yelp.

Buchanan was a blur when she turned back, and she took off her purple glasses to wipe her eyes. "I called the spa and they said someone had picked him up, but they couldn't tell me who it was. I thought the police had taken him to the pound or something. I called everywhere, but no one knew where he was."

"Your maid had him," Buchanan said.

Amelia looked up at him. "Esperanza?"

Buchanan nodded. "She went and got him after the Feds came in."

Amelia stared at him for a moment and then nodded in understanding. After Alex had turned state's witness against McCall, things had happened fast. FBI agents had shown up at Jimmy's apartment to question her about Mary Carpenter's murder. The SEC agents had followed, grilling her about the law firm's finances. But with her faulty memory, neither agency had any use for her testimony.

The story had made the West Coast papers briefly and then dropped off the main pages. But Amelia had followed it online and knew that

McCall was facing capital murder charges and federal securities fraud charges. All of McCall's assets—and Alex's, too—had been seized. It was all gone. The big pink house, the yacht, the cars, her jewelry.

Alex had been sentenced to fifteen years in prison. He hadn't tried to contact her. She wanted to call him, but everything was still too raw, and what he had done for her was almost too much to fathom. She finally decided she would write to him after the new year. It would be an opening, at least.

And Jimmy? Amelia looked to him. He was, she had come to realize in the past week, what she needed more than anything—someone who shared her history, someone who was there for her, someone who would always be a very good old friend.

Buchanan was still standing by the door. There was an oddly expectant look on his face. His eyes were blue, she realized in that moment, a soft gray-blue.

Black . . . she had been positive his eyes were black. Weren't his eyes black that day at the lake when he had put his hands around her throat?

"I guess I'll be going," Buchanan said.

Amelia stepped forward. "Where?"

"I don't know yet," he said after a moment.

There was a long awkward silence. Jimmy broke it. "Would anyone like some coffee? Or maybe some tea?"

"You got any beer?" Buchanan asked.

◆ ◆ ◆

When Amelia looked up at the window, Jimmy was watching them as they started away down the street. Buchanan looked up, too, then down at Amelia.

"He doesn't trust me," He said.

"Neither do I," Amelia said.

"Well, I don't trust a man who doesn't keep beer in his house."

Amelia said nothing; she just kept walking. The day was cold and a heavy fog was rolling in from the ocean, softening the harsh edges of the Sutro Baths ruins and obscuring the outcroppings of Seal Rocks just off shore. The barks of unseen seals followed them as they made their way toward Louis' Restaurant at the end of Point Lobos Avenue.

Inside, the restaurant was deserted so they claimed the prime corner booth. The windows were wrapped in gray flannel fog.

Buchanan ordered two Anchor Steams. Amelia was quiet, reaching into the Vuitton tote at her side to scratch Brody's head.

"You didn't come all this way just to bring my dog back to me," she said finally.

"No, I didn't."

"Then why are you here?"

"I wanted to make sure you were all right," he said.

Amelia sat back in the booth, considering him carefully. She had thought about Clay Buchanan often in the last two weeks, but she couldn't figure out why. And sitting here across from him now, being this close to him, she felt a strange connection. She had heard or read somewhere that if you saved another person's life you were responsible for that person forever. Maybe it worked in the reverse, too. Maybe that one moment at the lake, when he had let go of her, had bound them forever to each other.

But was she fine? Not completely.

"I have something to show you," she said, reaching into her pocket and pulling out an ivory-colored envelope. She took a paper from the envelope, unfolded it, and handed it to Buchanan.

"This came in the mail yesterday," she said. "I haven't shown it to Jimmy. I didn't want to worry him."

Buchanan read it out loud, quietly. "You took my life, my family, and the man I loved. Now I have nothing and you have everything. I will make you pay for what you did."

He lowered the letter and looked at the postmark on the envelope. "Who do you know in Tampa?"

"No one," she said.

Buchanan reread the letter.

"Do you think it's from Joanna?" Amelia asked. "She's broke and her husband is facing the death penalty."

Buchanan shook his head. "I think there was a part of Joanna McCall that sincerely liked you." He paused. "Plus this isn't her style."

"Then who sent it?"

"Someone younger. Someone very selfish. She uses the word 'my' or 'I' five times. It's all about her."

Amelia frowned, but before the name came into focus, Buchanan said it.

"Megan McCall."

Amelia stared at him.

Buchanan nodded. "She came to see me, and she told me lots of interesting stuff. She said that Alex abused you."

"What? Alex never touched me."

"She told me she had been raped in college and that she confided in you about it."

Amelia just shook her head. "We barely talked. God, I'd remember something like that."

Buchanan hesitated. "And she told me that it would be better for you if I just let you disappear for good."

Amelia was quiet, letting the pieces click into place in her head. "It was Megan," she said finally. "I knew Alex was having an affair with someone, and that is who it was."

Buchanan said nothing, and she realized he had been waiting for her to give voice to what he already suspected. She looked down at the letter, folded it, and slipped it back in her pocket.

"You still got that revolver?" Buchanan asked.

"Yes."

"Keep it handy."

They both looked to the windows, and the silence grew, stretching into discomfort.

"So, are you going to stay here?" Buchanan asked finally.

She nodded. "Jimmy says I could teach dance." She paused. "I can't teach."

"Why not?"

"I don't know. I think it would be too . . . safe."

She was surprised to see him smile slightly and nod. She took a drink of beer.

"You'd make a good investigator," Buchanan said.

"What makes you say that?"

"You have the right kind of mind. You stayed one step ahead of me for a long time."

She slowly set her glass down. It had been there in the back of her mind all week, this question of what she was going to do with herself now. But she hadn't realized until this moment that the answer had been inside her since that first day she walked out of the hospital back in Fort Lauderdale.

It was there in the faces of the people she had met. The redheaded woman in the pawnshop warning her to run from any man who would hit a woman. The old man on the bus trying to spirit his great-grandson away from a bad home. And Hannah, having to pick up a gun to defend herself from her own husband.

"I want to help people start over," she said. "Maybe even disappear if they need to."

Buchanan had picked up his beer, but he didn't take a drink. He set the glass back down on the table and just stared at her.

"You think that's crazy, right?" she asked.

"No," he said.

Again, they fell quiet. Amelia sensed Buchanan wanted to say something, but he just sat there, his fingers tapping lightly on the beer glass, his eyes looking out at the blanket of gray outside the windows.

"What about you?" she asked.

"What about me?"

"What are you going to do?"

Buchanan shook his head slowly. "I'm not sure. I can't go back."

"Back where?"

"Where I was."

"Nashville."

"No, where I was in my life."

"Why not?"

He looked away again, and when his eyes came back to her the color had changed, less blue, almost the color of the fog.

"Can I tell you something?" he asked.

She nodded.

"My wife and son are gone," he said.

He started slowly, but then it poured out of him, what had happened to his wife and baby son and what had happened to him after that. It was hard to hear, but Amelia listened, not saying a word, until finally Buchanan sat back in the booth. He seemed spent and couldn't look at her.

"What about the grand jury?" Amelia asked.

"They didn't indict me," he said. "They didn't believe my daughter's memories were . . . reliable."

Amelia nodded. "Someone told me once that memories are like diamonds. The fake ones can seem the most real."

"But if Gillian believes them, she still thinks I'm a killer. How am I supposed to live with that?"

The waitress appeared. "Two more?" she asked.

"No, just the check, please," Buchanan said.

She set it on the table and left. Buchanan picked up his glass and finished his beer.

"Come on," Buchanan said. "I'll walk you back."

They went to the cash register where Buchanan paid for the beers, and they stepped out into the cool fog. The ocean was lost from view, and the only thing visible was a soft glow of lights coming from the Cliff House at the far end of the street.

"The air here smells like medicine," Buchanan said. "Like if you breathed it long enough, it could heal you."

"It's the eucalyptus trees," Amelia said. She hesitated, shifting the bag holding Brody. "How's your shoulder?"

"Almost like new."

"I'm sorry," she said.

Buchanan didn't look at her.

"For shooting you, I'm sorry."

Still he wouldn't look at her. So she stepped closer, moving around in front of him so she could see his face. She was astonished to see tears in his eyes.

"Can you ever forgive me?" he asked.

Amelia touched his sleeve and nodded. Anything else would have made her break down.

They started walking back up the street. Amelia took Brody out of the tote, and he walked along on his leash for a while but then stopped cold and looked up at her, waiting. She scooped him up and carried him the rest of the way.

At the door to the apartment building, she turned to face Buchanan.

"Your daughter . . . you asked me how you live with her thinking you killed her mother," she said. "You do it by proving her wrong."

Buchanan was quiet, staring at her.

"You said the police never found your wife and son. You need to do it. You need to find them."

She knew he understood what she was trying to say, that even though they were dead, he'd have to find them or he'd never be at peace. It was what she had learned about her mother and Ben. Especially Ben.

Buchanan looked away and for a moment she thought she had offended him. But then he turned back and held out a hand.

"Good-bye, Amelia Brody," he said.

She hesitated. Then she leaned in and wrapped her arms around him. When he pulled back, he couldn't meet her eyes. He gave her a brisk nod, turned and walked away.

CHAPTER FORTY-FOUR

Rayna Buchanan's life was spread out before him on the bed.

It had been a long time since he'd looked at this stuff. And even longer since he had looked at her. At least in the way a man should look at a wife.

He was back in Nashville, back in his apartment. It was near two in the morning, a February sleet storm was pinging against the window, and sleep was still far away. Two months had passed since he had returned home. In that time, he had thought often about Amelia Tobias, and the fact that he had managed to keep her alive gave him a small piece of comfort.

But it was not Amelia who had come to him in the dark on nights like this when he had trouble sleeping. It had been her husband, Alex. The man was as shallow and selfish as they came. But he had walked away from his job, his home, and his easy life, and with a gun in hand

and against all odds that she would take him back, he had gone in search of the woman he loved.

Tobias had been crazy, of course, made crazier by the constant swill of vodka. But still, Buchanan couldn't help but admire that part of Alex Tobias that reacted with passion when hit with the hard reality of what he had done to his marriage.

Had it been too late for Tobias?

Of course it had.

Buchanan picked up a photo of Rayna taken at the Loveless Café, a countrified hot spot for biscuits and gravy just off the Natchez Trace, south of Nashville. Buchanan had taken the picture at the start of their driving vacation, five great days that had taken them down to the Gulf Breeze Motel in Dauphin Island, Alabama, where Gillian had been conceived. Or that's what Rayna had always wanted to believe.

In the photo, Rayna was standing under the café's vintage neon sign, wearing a white sleeveless blouse, dark Capri pants, and a ponytail. It looked like a snapshot from the fifties.

Buchanan stared at the photo and then he looked up, into the shadows of his bedroom.

"Are you here, Rayna?"

He heard nothing.

"I need to know something," he said. "I need to know if it's too late."

Still, silence.

He started to set the photo back in the box and then paused. It was just an old shoe box, but it had been Rayna's depository of memories, something she had kept from her early twenties, long before she met him. She had stored all their newer photos on the computer, but she had always said that when she got lonely she liked the idea of being able to hold in her hand the people who were gone.

He propped the photo up against the lamp on his nightstand, put the top back on the shoe box and set it aside. He turned his attention to three manila folders bound with a rubber band.

In the early days of the investigation into Rayna and Corey's disappearance, he had made one friend at the Tennessee Bureau of Investigation, a sergeant who was a few weeks from retirement and, as it turned out, six months from a heart attack. The cop had always believed that Buchanan was innocent and had slipped him copies of some investigation reports.

Buchanan had looked at them once or twice in the past five years, but he'd been so lost in his grief—and the bottle—that nothing in them made any sense.

But now he was ready to take another look.

There wasn't much there.

A few statements from his neighbors in Berry Hill. A couple of reports on sex offenders who lived nearby. And, stuffed by themselves in the third folder, four color photographs of Rayna's abandoned car.

He had seen the photos before but the memory of where and when was fuzzy. Now, as he looked at them, something caught in his chest, sharp as a knife.

The driver's door standing open. A close-up of the headrest, stained with blood. Rayna's brown loafer, left in a puddle near the rear wheel.

And the last photo . . .

A shot of an empty blue and white Hug-Me-Tite car seat.

Buchanan touched the last image with his finger and began to cry. He probably could have cried himself to sleep—there was so much still inside that needed to get out—but then he realized his tears were dripping onto the photo. He quickly pulled himself together, wiping his face with his sleeve, and carefully tucked the photos back in their folder.

He would need to keep the photos pristine. He would need all of this, little as it was, if he was going to find Rayna and Corey.

And he would find them.

He was never more sure of anything in his life.

CHAPTER FORTY-FIVE

The sky was the color of a spring iris, but there was still some scattered snow, like a clothesline had broken and left white sheets strewn on the ground.

It was cold, and Amelia reached down and kicked the car's heater up a notch.

"Are you warm enough?" she asked.

The Bird, sitting in the passenger seat, gave a grunt but didn't look at her. She was too intent on looking out the window. Amelia wondered what she was thinking. The Bird hadn't been out of the nursing home in a long time, Jill had told her, and her view of the world had narrowed to what she could see from the window of her room.

That's why Amelia had wanted to take her out today. Jill said The Bird's mood hadn't been good lately. Maybe this would cheer her up.

So far, the trip hadn't gone well. When Amelia had arrived at The Edge of Heaven that morning, it had been a repeat of her last visit in December. The Bird seemed happy to get the Teaberry gum that Amelia brought, but she still didn't recognize her.

It was never going to change, Amelia thought as she turned the rental car off US 71 and down a side street. This was how things were now for her and her grandmother. But she was coming to accept that. It was similar to what she felt for Clay Buchanan. He had e-mailed to tell her that he had begun investigating the disappearance of his wife and son. She had written back saying she was still staying with Jimmy and had started work at a women's shelter. They had exchanged other e-mails since, which left Amelia with a sense that while they would always be in each other's lives, there would still be a space between them.

Amelia glanced over at The Bird.

She was swathed in a red down parka that Amelia had brought for her. But there was a peacock brooch pinned on the front, one of the pieces of jewelry Amelia had found in the box of mementoes Buchanan had returned to her.

"What day is it?" The Bird asked.

"Wednesday," Amelia said.

"What month is it?"

"February."

The Bird nodded, looking out the window. "February is Mother Nature's way of giving us the finger."

Amelia laughed.

They turned onto Fairfield Street, and Amelia slowed the rental car and then stopped in front of the faded gray house. She turned off the engine and looked over at The Bird.

"Is this where you live?" The Bird asked.

"Well, I'm thinking about maybe coming back here in the summers," Amelia said. "What do you think?"

"I think it needs to be painted."

"Let's go inside," Amelia said.

The realtor who had been caring for the house had given Amelia the key. Amelia helped The Bird make her way slowly down the sloping yard and they went inside. The air was musty and cold, and when Amelia tried to turn on a light, nothing happened. The Bird was standing in the middle of the living room, her eyes flitting over the old furniture, the fringed lamps, and flowered wallpaper. Then she walked slowly to the back windows.

Amelia came up behind her and they stood side by side, looking out at the lake.

"It's really cold in here," The Bird said finally.

"Yes, it is. Maybe we should go."

The Bird nodded and started back toward the door. Then she stopped. She was staring at something. At first Amelia thought it was the aluminum walker in the corner, but then The Bird went to the old player piano. She looked at Amelia then back at the piano.

"Do you play?" Amelia asked.

The Bird nodded. "Yeah, with my feet."

She eased down onto the piano bench, putting her feet on the pedals, but she didn't try to pump them. She just sat there, staring straight ahead.

Then she began to sing, so softly that Amelia could barely hear her.

"Life is long since you went away, I think about you all through the day, my buddy. No buddy quite so true . . ."

Amelia went to the piano and sat down next to her grandmother. The Bird had stopped singing. But Amelia knew the words.

"Miss your voice, the touch of your hand, just long to know that you understand, my buddy," she sang. "Your buddy misses you."

The Bird looked at her with cloudy green eyes. Then she smiled.

"You're my Mellie," she said.

Amelia took her grandmother's hand in hers. "Yes, I am," she said.

ACKNOWLEDGMENTS

It takes two of us to write a book. But it takes many others to make it fly. So stand up and take a bow . . .

SJ Rozan, dear friend, fellow writer, and avid birder whose expertise gave our character Clay Buchanan wings.

Tom Clark of Motorcar Gallery Collectible Exotics in Fort Lauderdale, who knows his gull wings.

Peter Lent, esq., an odd bird who is nonetheless okay for a lawyer and Patriots fan.

Sharon Potts, Neil Plakcy, Christine Jackson, and Miriam Potocky, who helped push this story out of the nest.

Daniel . . . for being there.

And to our amazing flock at T&M: Ahn Schluep, Alison Dasho, cover designer David Drummond, and the eagle-eyed Faith, Scott, Nicole, and Sharon.

ABOUT THE AUTHOR

P.J. Parrish is the *New York Times* best-selling author of ten Louis Kincaid and Joe Frye thrillers. The author is actually two sisters, Kristy Montee and Kelly Nichols. Their books have appeared on both the *New York Times* and *USA Today* bestseller lists. The series has garnered eleven major crime-fiction awards, and an Edgar® nomination. Parrish has won two Shamus awards, one Anthony, and one International Thriller competition. Her books have been published throughout Europe and Asia.

Parrish's short stories have also appeared in many anthologies, including two published by Mystery Writers of America, edited by Harlan Coben and the late Stuart Kaminsky. Their stories have also appeared in Akashic Books' acclaimed *Detroit Noir*, and in *Ellery Queen Mystery Magazine*. Most recently, they contributed an essay to a special edition of Edgar Allan Poe's works edited by Michael Connelly.

Before turning to writing full time, Kristy Montee was a newspaper editor and dance critic for the *Sun-Sentinel* in Fort Lauderdale. Kelly

Nichols previously was a blackjack dealer and then a human resources specialist in the casino industry. Montee lives in Fort Lauderdale and Nichols resides in Traverse City, Michigan.

The sisters were writers as kids, albeit with different styles: Kelly's first attempt at fiction at age eleven was titled "The Kill." Kristy's at thirteen was "The Cat Who Understood." Not much has changed: Kelly now tends to handle the gory stuff and Kristy the character development. But the collaboration is a smooth one, thanks to lots of ego suppression, good wine, and marathon phone calls via Skype.

The first eleven books in the series, in order, are: *Dark of the Moon*, *Dead of Winter*, *Paint It Black*, *Thicker Than Water*, *Island of Bones*, *A Killing Rain*, *An Unquiet Grave*, *A Thousand Bones*, *South of Hell*, *The Little Death*, and *Heart of Ice*.